"CARRIES THE READER THROUGH BY HIS EMOTIONS, LEAVING NONE UNTOUCHED...."*

"Filled with the passion of Irish love, it carries the reader through by his emotions, leaving none untouched, and then at the finish, as all great books do, has him wanting much more."   —*Buffalo Courier-Express*

"Remarkably colorful and sensitive.... The characters are very well drawn, sympathetic and, above all, honest. The reader must respect their dignity and their courage."
      —Frank G. Slaughter

"A hauntingly sensitive love story ... a *must* read."   —Dennis Smith, author of
      Report from Engine Co. 82

GONE THE RAINBOW, GONE THE DOVE
was originally published by Trident Press.

Gone the Rainbow, Gone the Dove

⬥ by ⬥
Joan Bagnel

PUBLISHED BY POCKET BOOKS NEW YORK

GONE THE RAINBOW, GONE THE DOVE

Trident Press edition published 1974

POCKET BOOK edition published April, 1975

L

Standard Book Number: 671-78793-4.
Library of Congress Catalog Card Number: 73-8286.
This POCKET BOOK edition is published by arrangement with Simon & Schuster, Inc. Copyright, ©, 1973, by Joan Bagnel. All rights reserved. This book, or portions thereof, may not be reproduced by any means without permission of the original publisher: Simon & Schuster, Inc., 630 Fifth Ave., New York, N.Y. 10020.
Front cover illustration by Bob Schulz.

Printed in the U.S.A.

To the Irish people, past and present, to my father and my husband, and to all men and women everywhere who fight the good fight, this book is dedicated with love, gratitude, and deep respect.

Gone the Rainbow, Gone the Dove

Chapter I

Jamie Daley heard voices, low and murmuring, from somewhere. He tried to open his eyes, but he couldn't. He tried to move his arms and his hands, but they felt strangely weak and he stopped trying after a few seconds. He was surprised that he could not move at all. He thought he might be dead, except for the voices. He strained to hear who was talking, what was being said. Oh, of course. It was Jerry. Whom was he talking to?

Doctor. He heard Jerry say "Doctor," and the day's events came pushing into his mind. At once, because he had always been a man to grasp things clearly and immediately, he knew he was not dead but dying. He had had a heart attack. And close upon that realization came another. He didn't feel pain anymore. He thought he must have awakened between the pains. He waited for the agony to begin. But it did not. He waited again, cautious, not trusting it. They must have given him something.

So, it was here, then, at last. Strange, he didn't mind so much. He had known, maybe he had even hoped, it would happen like this, even when he was back in New York City planning the trip home to Ireland. He wished Jerry would come over and talk to him. Maybe he would, later, if there was any later.

Meanwhile, he thought, he would just lie there and listen and enjoy not having any pain. Maybe that was the way things would be afterwards. He hoped so. Life was full of pain. He tried vaguely to recall if there was a time when he had not known about pain. He sensed there had been, but other feelings and memories soon crowded it out.

Jerry's voice was becoming clearer, so Jamie Daley lay very still inside his mind, listening to it all, listening to Jerry talking about him.

And who is Jamie Daley? I'll tell you who. He's an Irishman—an Irishman out of the past, untouched by the follies of the last couple of thousand years. He's pagan, heart, mind, and soul.

And more than that: He was the greatest fighting man we ever had in Waterford and half of Ireland. Jamie was always the boyo you needed at your back in any fight, him with his great tall hulk and the head of black curls and the cool gray eyes that could stab you in two and then describe both halves to your face! He had two great fists, and once he'd an idea in his head there was no arguing with him at all.

But if bravery and fighting were all there was to Jamie, there'd be little special about him. Those things come fairly natural to us, as you may have heard. But Jamie had a mind in him, not just a brain, a *mind*. He thought straight and he saw far and he knew what it would take to make Ireland her own land again. Ah, if he had only been in charge of the thing, we'd have had a chance at something better than what we've got now.

Jamie and I and all our friends were raised by the fireside of rebellion. There were mighty few of us who thought, as other lads in other places might think, of what they would be when they grew up. To us, Ireland and her freedom and her return to sovereignty were always the thing that must be taken care of first, and we felt it as we felt no other feeling, that Ireland was waiting for us, for each of us, and that we had no other life and no right to any other life until our task was accomplished.

But we're old men now, Jamie and I, and Ireland's not free yet, for all we dreamed and fought and hoped. Not free up in the north that's still separated from us and tortured this way and that because of religions and politics and things that haven't anything to do with what is really Irish business. No, and not free in the south either, but strangling on churches and priests and foreign investors and a class system as frozen fast as when the English were here in full force.

Jamie knew all this was going to happen. I tell you, he knew it somehow. He said one time that we Irish were one of the best-educated, most ignorant races in the world—ignorant of what was right for ourselves. Oh, Christ's sweet sake, but I'd give the rest of my years for another hour's talk with Jamie Daley!

We had so little time for talking, Jamie and I, since he came back. It's odd, I saw him young and now I've seen him old, and I look straight at his face now, wrinkled and pale as my own, and I can only really see him as he used to be.

I don't pay any attention to that old Jamie Daley lying there so quiet and so close to death as he is now. No, sure that's not Jamie at all. *My* Jamie Daley is as young as the new snows in the meadow. And all here melts like those same snows whilst I remember back to the big voice and the glad laugh of him, and all *that* is the only thing that is real.

We're cousins, Jamie and I, blood kin on our mothers' side. Jamie's mother, Ellen, was my mother's older sister. We lived in Dunknealy, just down the Blackwater River from the Daleys, back to back by way of the fields.

My uncle, Martin Daley, was Jamie's father, a tall, proud, straight figure of a man with trim mustache and a beard going gray in the middle. He was no true farmer like the rest of us. Martin was a Dublin man and raised to be a scholar. I heard once they'd hoped to make a priest of him, but nothing came of it and he had to find a job of work instead. Whatever his heart's hopes might have been, no one ever heard of it, for my uncle was not the man to complain of his life.

He joined the Royal Irish Constabulary when he was only twenty. But, in due time, my Aunt Ellen married that great, tall, blue-eyed stalk of a policeman and Martin gave up the Force and came home with her to Dunknealy and the farm.

But, God save us, Martin Daley was a greener farmer than ever Ireland was a land! For a couple of years it was

a wonder at all they met the payments on the farm. My
father had no money to help out, but he tried to teach
Uncle Martin what he needed to know to run the place,
which was just about everything.

And he learned, he learned well. He never really became a farmer in his heart, you understand, but he did
gain supreme control of it all. I can remember him out
plowing in the fields wearing a stiff white collar in the
heat of the day, and a tie too, though you couldn't see it
under his grand, flowing beard. The collar and the tie
were Uncle Martin's way of asserting himself over unco-
operative cows, sheep with the mange, wild rutting pigs,
broken harnesses, mealy potatoes and whatever other
devious devices nature was likely to throw against him.

My father and Martin Daley and every other man they
knew belonged to the Sinn Fein party, which was the
political arm of the Fenian Brotherhood. They spoke for
and fought for Home Rule for Ireland and an end to divi-
sion and foreign domination forever.

There were meetings in Dunknealy. Everyone knew of
them; no one spoke of them. Our fathers went and spoke
there, and in public too, against the insane demands England was making for Irish volunteers to fight in her army
against the Germans. One war at a time, said my father
and Martin Daley and many, many others. And our old,
old war with England seemed to us to have a definite
priority.

Mind you, though England was preoccupied with the
war in France, she was not unaware of what went on here,
for she began to feel the chill nip biting at her flanks even
then. The Fenian meetings were secret meetings, the
doings of revolutionaries, and the British War Office tried
its best to keep them quiet. Oh, they knew it would come
to a fight someday before it was all finished, but, as
politicians always have, the more they knew the truth of a
thing, the less they wished to believe it.

Well, and there we were in our small heap of the world,
lost, I suppose, under the cannon smoke from all directions, but the Fenians were active everywhere. And, in the
north, Ulster Union Conservatives fought every step of the

way toward Irish independence, determined then as now
to remain part of Britain at all costs. And English reinforcements were pouring in every month, threatening to
mutiny if Home Rule was ever enforced.

Chapter II

Amidst all this, we boys were expected to be educated somehow, and to tend to our own business, which was school.
Five miles on foot it was, there and back, five long hard
miles, winter and summer, and not seeming much worth
it, I thought on many a cold day. But Jamie would come
by the house for me, down the *boreen** through half a mile
of slush and mud, with a book under his arm and always
a new tale to tell me or an old one to finish up. I think
he sort of mesmerized me to school every day with his
everlasting stories and his blather.

"What's it to be today, then?" he'd greet me.

I'd shiver gruffly, coming out the door to meet him. My
hands would still be red and stiff from the milking of sixteen fat cows and not warmed up by half for having been
clasped around a steaming mug of tea at the breakfast
table.

And Jamie would smile. Then out would come the
book and off through the snowy fields we would trudge,
knee deep in freezing, with only Jamie's enthusiasm to
warm us on our way.

We paid scant attention to the Greeks and Romans and
ignored old British Arthur and his trumpery knights altogether. Tales of Irish heroes were what we liked best, from
the dim, far past. Jamie told them all to me, as Martin

---

* A short side road or driveway off a main road.

had read them to him, in the Gaelic. I heard the sorrowful story of the death of King Conaire Mor as if he were a
close, loved relative of my own, and I shivered with relish
thinking about those wild pagan war goddesses, the Mor-
righan, who taught the youths of Erin all the fine arts of
battle, then roamed over the battlefields spreading terror
and despair among the ranks of their enemies.

But, of them all, I best liked the tales about the Fianna
warriors, the roving, wildhearted fellows who came from
all the five old kingdoms when Ireland was truly herself
and knelt at the High Table of Tara and swore their
loyalty to the High King who sat there, and to glorious
Finn MacCool, their Fian leader.

Jamie had coaxed me along to school through a very
drear spring with dribs and drabs of the Fianna adventures,
just to give me the strength to get there at all. But, one
April, I recall, I had made up my mind that nothing was
worth those damned five miles through the cold mud. Oh,
the snow had stopped, of course, and there was only the
usual drizzle, just to keep up the green, you know, but I
sat at my breakfast sullenly thinking up a good reason to
stay home by the fire.

But Himself came bounding up earlier than ever, and
me not half through my meal and not even so far into the
perjuries I was having to invent as the price of my day.
And, by God, he dragged me out of my own house! There
was no appealing to my mother at all. She standing there
laughing and stuffing our pockets with apples and raisins
as we went and giving me a great push and a "Get along
with you, you great lazy *omadhaun!*"

"A shield and a hazel stick, that's all they let them
have," muttered Jamie all dreamy-eyed, not even bothering to look at me there sniffling and rubbing off the
crumbs from my mouth as we went along. He was balanc-
ing himself on top of the stone fence three feet high beside
me, and I didn't know if I'd heard him right and I didn't
much care at the time.

"Who gave who a shield and a stick?" I mumbled.

Jamie leaped down like an ape in front of me, waving
his open book in my face.

"Them. The Fianna," he said impatiently. "If a man wanted to join them, he had to prove himself worthy of it. They didn't let just anyone in. You had to go through terrible tests of courage and endurance—"

"Then I'm ready right now," I growled at him, feeling my nose and cheeks raw-cold and miserable. "I thought we'd got through the Fianna yesterday."

"Don't you wish they were still around now?" he cried. "Maybe we could join them. But first we'd have to stand in a hole in the ground up to our waists. With our shields and our hazel sticks, you know. And then nine warriors would cast their spears at us in turn—"

"Well, and that settles us, doesn't it?" I yawned.

"No, no! Only if we got hurt. But that isn't all. Then we'd have to run through the woods with all of them after us. We'd leap over a tree limb as high as our heads and stoop under one as low as our knees and draw out a thorn from our foot without slowing down. And if we could do all that, they'd let us in!"

That sounded so unreasonable to me that I began a hot argument with him and, with me asking questions and disagreeing with the answers, the schoolhouse appeared suddenly up ahead of us, and me left in the middle of things and not knowing how anything turned out till we would go home that afternoon.

Jamie had me just where he wanted me; he always did. But I suppose that's all that ever took me to school at all. Because of Jamie and his books, I learned to look a bit carefully and see those armies on the hilltops, the heroes at every crossroad, and giants in the clouds. But mainly, because of Jamie and his tales, I grew up more Irish than anything else, and that was a feat worthy of the Fianna of all five kingdoms in those days!

We had a very small school, one room was all of it, and all grades in it together. Whilst one group of us would be reciting, another would be working in their copybooks and still another would be reading. Well, and none of that is of any interest, neither to you nor, believe me, to us either!

But, what *was* of passing concern was our schoolmaster.

English he was; tall and thinnish in places, he was; a bastard he was, to one and to all, and the name of him was Master Drum. As to whether any one of his relations or acquaintances ever thought enough of him to christen him properly with another, I cannot say, but I doubt there's a name in the whole catalogue of saints that would fit the man.

Master Drum had been sent over to Ireland by the thoughtful Ministers of Education in England, at great trouble and even some expense, I've no doubt. He was sent to inculcate us Irish brats with a bit of culture, and just enough learning of practical use to render us somewhat productive when we grew to man's estate, if we made it. Reading, writing and English history, that was about all they figured we could manage, and it was up to Master Drum to see that we did manage it.

I remember him well, Master Drum, indeed I do. He was a hunched-up, pinched-in *squelcheen* of a man with a face like an overripe turnip. He wore pince-nez glasses clipped to his beaky nose and he used to stare at us over the glasses, never quite focusing on anyone in particular, but taking in the whole of what stood before him with equal malevolence.

I hated him on sight. Jamie always thought he was a joke; sure, even God must like a little joke once in a while, he used to point out, and Master Drum was the best one in Ireland!

Master Drum had the teaching of children from the age of six through fourteen, if they could last it out. Few enough did. Many fell by the wayside for one reason or another long before they reached the maximum age.

Master Drum used to get to school ahead of any of us, and thus, automatically, everyone was always considered to be late. He had a house, rent-free, on the edge of town, a nice, snug little shelter, and there he lived quite alone and quite content, with his curtains always drawn closed and his lights never lit, and we used to say he practiced black magic as a pastime, but it was never proved. It was only a quick walk for him to get to school, and, no matter the weather, no matter how often or how early anyone

tried to beat him to it, whenever we came in the door,
there was Master Drum, squinched up all pinch-nosed and
yellow-faced, with that sideways smile he always wore, the
smile that looked as if it were just about to slide slipperly
off his face onto the floor. It was with great effort that he
held it balanced precariously at the angle he did, anyway.
It never widened, never narrowed, never deviated in the
slightest. I believe he was born slightly smiling, or froze
that way one time. At any rate, there he'd be, waiting and
smiling, smiling and waiting.

Well, but you'll get used to anything after long enough
of it goes by, won't you? And we'd been looking up at his
ugly mug so long we almost didn't notice Drum anymore.
He spoke in a loud, braying donkey voice, opening his
mouth very wide top and bottom and carefully enunciating
every word he said with deliberate British exaggeration.
His entire weight was in the stomach. It rolled and strutted
out before him roundly, like a pregnant woman, and he
often rested his hands and his arms upon it as he padded
softly about the classroom, looking at what you were
doing, creeping up behind you and tapping you over and
over with the sharpened end of his pencil on one place on
your head, whilst you were trying desperately to think of
some answer that would satisfy him. For, make no mistake, no matter the subject, no matter the question, legiti-
mate or otherwise, we were there to supply answers that
would satisfy Master Drum, or we'd be caned.

Now, caning, I don't suppose you're all that familiar
with the procedure. It's pretty much vanished these days,
as an art form, I mean. But Master Drum caned with the
lustiness and energy and skill of a man born to caning, as
if he'd never had any other thought nor ambition in life
but caning, as if God had purposely set him on earth to
seek out his fellow men for caning. And he'd developed
many small tricks of his trade, as anyone will who devotes
himself zealously to a subject.

Master Drum caned boys and he caned girls, up in the
front of the classroom, in plain sight, and all other work
had to stop whilst the caning was carried out. It was something like piping all hands on deck to witness punishment

as they used to do on board the old British warships. The
culprit, furthermore, was forced to have a hand in his own
punishment. For first he had to go outside, across the
schoolyard to where a good thick clump of black thorn-
bushes grew, and there he had to cut however many canes
he was told. Master Drum used each branch or cane three
or four times, no more. So we knew pretty well how many
strokes we were going to get according to how many canes
he told us to cut, multiplied by three or four. He caned the
girls on their hands and arms, though I remember once he
caned Lizzie Flaherty seventeen times across her back and
tore her dress to shreds doing it. But Lizzie sassed him to
his face and whispered unmanly things about him, so that
was an exceptional case.

It was really the boys he hated. To him, I guess we were
all damned Irish rebels, just waiting to do him in, and he
knew we laughed at him, especially when we found out
that he'd tried to join up when England went to war and
the army wouldn't take him, and someone wrote on the
blackboard the same words Lizzie had used against him.

From that time on, Master Drum was in a perfect fit
with us at all times, and his special victim was Jamie.
Drum had heard Martin speak out against Irishmen sup-
porting England in the World War. To him, Martin spoke
treason, and I suppose he thought he'd carry on the fight,
even though they wouldn't have him on a bet, by getting
back at Martin's son.

But Jamie, come 1915, was fourteen and a man grown,
six foot three with shoulders like a horse, and Drum
couldn't stare him down as he once had long ago. But he
delivered himself of an epic address to the whole class,
going on and on about treason and rebellion, and worked
his way, God alone knows how, around to ingratitude and
disloyalty! Well, now, I'd caught the cut of his remarks
from the outset and had myself the grandest nap that day,
so I wasn't a good witness to what else was said, but Ed
Shean and a few of the lads told me later that Jamie had
been muttering while Drum talked on, and there was a bit
of sneering too, back and forth, so I knew there would be
trouble soon enough.

And soon enough, which was the next day, there was trouble aplenty.

"Daley," says Drum, his nose, compass-true, pointing straight at Jamie, though he was staring bug-eyed at nothing.

"Daley!" says Drum again, and Jamie stood up lazily, staring straight back at him.

"Yes, sir!" snapped Jamie smartly, and a little snicker went around the room.

"Ah—um—ah," continued Drum, breathing hard now, his small fingers pecking away at the buttons on his coat. "Daley, give us a comparison of English government under the monarchy of Queen Elizabeth and under the Protectorate of Oliver Cromwell."

Well, and he couldn't have picked two historical names more repugnant to us if he'd spent a lifetime researching them!

Jamie looked quite thoughtful and the room became quiet. It was a routine enough question, just weighted enough to give Drum a jumping-off place for another tirade on his pet subject.

"Well, Daley, we're waiting!" snorted Drum, and his smile pinned itself in its usual position.

"Well, sir," offered Jamie sweetly, "Elizabeth sent Essex to Ireland and he massacred the people for politics, and Cromwell came to Ireland himself and massacred the people for fun!"

An awful silence filled the small room then, though there were one or two smothered giggles. Master Drum's eyes almost focused for a moment, out of sheer astonishment, no doubt. But he was cool, was Master Drum, he was a miracle of self-containment! No Irish lout of fourteen was going to get the best of *him!*

"Sit down, Daley!" says Drum, turning himself and his stomach away. But I could see his mind was not on his work after that. He was brooding and I noticed his nose was often turned in Jamie's direction.

The blow fell immediately after noon recess. Drum had a very queer look on his face when he ordered us to take out our Shakespeare plays and open them up to *Richard II*.

"We shall now read aloud as called upon," says Drum, gaping at us like a frog.

The younger pupils began to mumble and buzz as soon as they heard this, for most of them couldn't read much, and they loved it when we older ones were busy reading aloud, sure they got away with murder for the time it took. But Drum was having none of it that day. He rapped on his desk for attention, and in one second's time there was absolute silence in the little room. He started to explain the play to us, but I was too busy leafing it, trying to find out what gloomy message it contained that made him choose it for us. If only I'd had more time, if I'd been able to get to the second act, I would have seen it at once and maybe been able to prevent what happened. But Drum's introduction was unusually short that day, and he called upon several of the best readers to deliver some short passages out of the first act, then he hurried on to the second. Of course no one had the least idea of the story we were supposed to be learning and no one cared, more's the pity, and then Drum, breathing a bit fast for himself, called upon Jamie.

"Daley," he called loudly. Jamie stood up, lounging against the wall next to him, gazing out the window.

"I insist upon your attention, Daley, if you will do us the honor . . ." Drum let it trail off, biting his livery lips.

Jamie blinked and straightened up at once. "Oh, yes sir, I'm *that* sorry, sir, Mr. Drum, sir," he said smartly.

"Read, Daley," commanded Drum. "Act Two, Scene One, the lines spoken by John of Gaunt, beginning with, ah, yes, uh, 'Methinks I am a prophet new inspir'd.' Got it there? Very well, proceed."

Well, now, in the meantime, you recall, I was already flitting my way like a bee in rut through the scenes, and I was only opposite the page Jamie had to find. I soon had the speech Drum ordered up under my forefinger, and I ran down the lines quickly, absent-mindedly admiring the poetry of them, until I came, as I must come, and as *Jamie* must come, to the last line of all. One look and I gulped;

another fast one to make sure; a dart of a glance up Drum-way and I was sure of it all. Drum's eye met my own and he nodded ever so slightly, to himself, not to me, but he knew that I knew what he was about. I was desperately trying to think of some way to warn Jamie, but there was no chance. He had located the proper page and the proper speech. Glancing with a gay smile at the girls, so that they all giggled, he launched forth into the speech, speaking loudly and mock-dramatically, whilst Drum sat back in his chair, hands resting on his stomach, his two bony elbows sticking out either side of him like the wing stubs of an ostrich.

Jamie was giving it everything he had, and he hit his stride as he came into the home stretch:

> . . . This royal throne of kings, this sceptered isle,
> This earth of majesty, this seat of Mars,
> This other Eden, demi-Paradise,
> This fortress built by Nature for herself
> Against infection and the hand of war,
> This happy breed of men, this little world,
> This precious stone set in the silver sea—

"Sure, I didn't know Shakespeare ever got over to Ireland!" yelled out Dermot Tiernan from the back of the room, and at once everyone laughed and applauded. Jamie stopped reading, of course, and laughed with the rest of us, but the few seconds it took, his eye roamed down to the bottom of the page. I saw it happen. I saw him read the last line of the speech, I saw his eyes leap up to Drum and Drum's smile. Then he turned and looked at me, his face growing very red and the two black eyebrows of him arched beyond innocence. Drum pounded for order, which was soon restored. But Jamie slowly closed his book and placed it upon his desk, then folded his arms and stared at Drum.

"Go on, Daley," said Drum. "It's not finished. There are four more lines."

Jamie shook his head, and Drum jumped up, waving his hands wildly at him.

"Finish the speech, Daley, that's an order!" cried Master Drum.

"I will not," said Jamie quietly. By now, every head in that room was bent busily over the speech, trying to discover, as I had, what was the root of the argument. And the boys were on their feet, shouting and throwing their books about.

"Don't do it, Jamie!" they were calling.

"Shame, Drum, don't open your mouth, Jamie Daley!" yelled Ed Shean.

"The next one of you who makes a sound will be expelled today," thundered Drum, but he never took his eyes off of Jamie. Then he came around from behind his desk, down to Jamie's seat, and, without looking at it, he reached out and picked up the book. He opened it to the same page and thrust it against Jamie's chest, saying at the same time, "Read the last four lines, Daley, or I'll cane you till you bleed!"

"Mr. Drum, sir," called out Nancy Kiernan in a very small, shaky voice. "Mr. Drum, I'll read it." She sounded on the edge of tears.

Drum turned on her almost snarling, and told her to be still. It was not the words he wanted to hear, it was that he wanted to hear them from Jamie's lips. Only then would he have won, and he was determined that day that he would win.

Jamie threw a grateful smile Nancy's way, then his face became once more grave and set.

"Well, Daley, what's it to be?" queried Drum, growing impatient.

"I will not read those lines—Mr. Drum, sir," repeated Jamie.

Drum once again thrust the book against his chest, hard, into the ribs, and Jamie suddenly grabbed it from his hands. He began tearing pages from it and throwing them into Drum's astonished face. Drum quickly backed off, and at last Jamie pitched the book through the window, which was closed at the time. It made a most emphatic sound, I recall.

Once more safe behind his high desk, Drum considered

his situation. His eyebrows met in the middle of a most awful frown, and he said icily, "Cut cane, Daley. Cut ten good, stout canes at once."

Ten! He couldn't mean ten! Jamie never blinked an eye, but walked slowly up to the desk and took the knife from Drum's hands.

"At once, sir," said Jamie. He strode to the door, winking at us, and went out.

For a while we sat silently, listening to the sounds of the canes being cut. Jamie was whistling as he did it. The class stirred uncomfortably, a rustling of talk and whispering passing uncertainly through it. Then, tapping his fingers steadily on the desk before him, Drum looked at us fiercely through his glasses and, speaking in a tone usually reserved for funerals, he said, without warning or explanation:

> . . . this precious stone set in the silver sea,
> Which serves it in the office of a wall
> Or as a moat defensive to a house
> Against the envy of less happier lands,
> This blessed plot, this earth, this realm,
>   this ENGLAND!

He said the last word as one might say God or Mother or Kiss me again! And he looked at us, at all our silent, angry, helpless faces, and there was triumph written on his own.

Then Jamie was standing in the doorway, a good armload of fresh-cut blackthorn sticks in his arms. He handed Master Drum back the knife and laid the canes neatly across his desk, within convenient reach. Drum got up, removed his coat and folded it carefully across his stool.

"Insolence, Daley," said he with relish, "will not be tolerated in my classroom, nor in any British classroom in the world."

"Oh, no, sir!" murmured Jamie, nodding his head cheerfully.

He, too, removed his jacket and placed it very carefully across the nearest desk, muttering to the boy sitting there,

"Be careful of that, now, mind!" Then he obligingly laid himself stomach down across Drum's desk and waited.

Drum was snorting to himself. He reached out blindly and took a cane from the pile, raised his arm and brought it down with all his might. The girls gasped and flinched as they watched it descend, but then the strangest thing happened.

The cane hit Jamie all right, but with the same force as a blade of wet grass might have had! And Jamie let out the most frightful scream, you could hear the sound of it for a mile, I'm sure, and writhed as if he'd been ripped to the bone. Drum glared at the cane in disgust, slapping it experimentally against the wall a few times, at which point it proceeded to splinter soggily into long, thin green strands. Everyone howled with derisive laughter. Green rods! That's what Jamie had cut, green rods, soft on the inside, not woody yet, with no more strength to them than a leaf in a gale!

Drum threw the cane down and picked another. The same thing happened. And, once again, Jamie quivered with imaginary pain and shrieked out, "Ah, oh, uh, Master Drum, you're killin' me altogether!"

Drum strode past Jamie, around to the other side of the desk, his eyes positively yellow with fury. He gasped like a man dying of the asthma, his belly inflating and deflating alarmingly. One by one he picked up the canes and lashed against his desk. And one by one in turn they splintered instantly into soft, limp ribbons running sap down their lengths.

Drum seized the last four of them wildly and smashed them down with every bit of energy he could muster, on Jamie's naked back. The one blow they made together was quite enough to break the skin, and it did, I saw the canes cutting deep and the blood start, quick and scarlet. The girls screamed and the lads all jumped up, yelling and throwing things. But the last canes were now as useless as all of the others and, with an oath, Drum threw them from him. He grabbed Jamie by the collar and dragged him up across the desk till they were face to face.

"You bloody Irish bugger!" cried Drum. "They'll hang

you, Daley, someday they'll hang you and your damned traitorous father and your whole filthy clan with you!" Now he flung his right arm far to the left and brought it straight backhand, bareknuckled, across Jamie's ear.

I was out of my seat and half up the aisle. Jamie saw me and waved me back, but I just stopped where I was.

"Go on, Jerry," hissed Ed angrily behind me.

At that moment, Jamie twisted about and got loose from Drum's grasp. Now he picked the teacher up like a puppet, loosely shaking in all joints, and shook him like a dog shakes a rat, till the teeth fairly rattled in his head. Then he set the man down steady and punched him one grand smashing blow in the mouth, and landed him sprawling on the floor amidst a jumble of soft green mushy canes.

"Good day to you now, Master Drum," pronounced Jamie, looking down at him, then he strode to the door, threw it open, and walked away out of the school.

"Daley, I'll get you for this!" sputtered Master Drum, trying to pull himself up. I guess he thought I was coming to help him, for, as I walked quickly past, he reached his hand out to me, but I ignored him entirely and ran after Jamie. It was the end for both of us, I knew that, but whenever the end came, I wanted to be with Jamie.

He was halfway up the hill on the road ahead of me. I called and called after him, but he walked straight on, paying me no mind at all. I had to run like the devil to catch up with him, and still he said not a word. He walked along, hands thrust in his pockets, staring blackly at the dirt beneath his feet.

"At least wipe yourself off, you're all over blood," I shouted to him, but he never looked at me. I dug out my own pocket handkerchief and dabbed a bit at his back.

"You're a sight, that's what you are. You look like you've been in a fight, all right. What did you do that for, anyway? You'll be expelled. You'll be arrested, that's what, and, my God, me along with you! Why do I have you for a cousin? Why can't you be a priest or a girl or something quiet? What will you do when your father hears of it, and your mother? She'll roast you alive! Drum'll get you, he said it himself—Jamie, will you slow down for the love of Jesus?"

It was my last breath that said it. He did slow down some, but would not answer. We walked on and on in gloomy silence, I looking back every once in a while to see the police coming for us.

"Well, we can't go home again, that's one thing," I said, trying to think of a plan that would make sense. "We'll have to keep off the main road, they'll have their patrols out, God, maybe dogs too! We could go up to Wexford and hide out there. My father has cousins somewhere in Wexford. But how will we get there? I've no money, have you?"

I went on and on in this same way, making myself more and more wretched with my own blather. But Jamie still said nothing. And, at last, I too lapsed into sullen silence, cursing him and his black Daley temper in my heart, and we went on together.

It began to rain. Late afternoon found us hiding in a ditch. It always rains in Ireland, suddenly, like the bad moods of her sons, black clouds low in the sky and sodden, chilling rain down the backs of our necks. I shivered, my shirt collar pulled up high around my neck, trying to make my head disappear into it as much as I could, the cold droplets dribbling off the end of my nose and blowing into my cold ears. I had thrown my jacket over Jamie's bare back and now I sat there in stiff mud, my eyes set in the direction we'd come in, for the first sight of the troops. I wondered dismally if they would shoot us as we sat there or if they'd allow us to come out with our hands over our heads.

"You know, the Irish are the most ignorant, educated people on earth!" Jamie suddenly broke his long silence. His voice had the effect of a gunshot on me and I jumped in terror. I felt miserable and I wondered what he was talking about now. Jamie was only fourteen and sometimes he said the damnedest things you ever heard.

"That's the only way to handle them," he mused, talking to himself. "There's Drum, now, knocked sprawling and they've all seen it done and seen that it can be done and none of those kids will ever take him seriously again. And that's how it's got to be done. Why does it have to take so long to get done?"

"Jamie," I croaked hoarsely, and it was his turn to be startled.

He grinned. "Och, Jerry, I'd forgotten you were there."

"Jamie, what'll we do?" I'm sure I was whining by now.

He smiled placidly and shrugged. "Wait till the rain stops, I expect," was his answer. "And then we could head up into the hills. We'll find some of the Volunteers up there, I know they have camps somewhere, and we'll join up and become soldiers." His voice sounded very warm and excited, but I was only chilled and afraid. I just wanted to go away and never be found again.

"Think of it, Jerry," he went on. "A thousand years of Celtic kings and where's it all gone to now? Divided, that's us, every man's a king with an opinion and no one rules at all—except them. That's their strength. When are we going to remember first we're Irishmen and after that anything else we like, but Irishmen first!"

He spoke so bitterly I felt the warmth of his anger and dismay spread through me. But then he fell silent again. After a while the rain stopped. It was getting on to dusk, and the sun, all lemony in the west, was sinking behind the hills.

"We'd best be getting on," he murmured.

"No, we can't get back on the road yet, they'll see us!" I cried, struggling stiffly to jump out after him. He stood brushing himself off at the side of the road. We heard a sound and I was preparing to jump right back into the ditch, but there was a great milling about of sheep, and a lone boy, no older than the two of us, came along sprightly enough behind them.

"Hey," called Jamie, and the boy jumped, for it was shadowy and all he could see was a muddy apparition coming at him.

"Which way have you been this afternoon?" asked Jamie.

The boy squinted at him curiously. "Over to Cappogh with the sheep and back now, what's it to you?"

Jamie looked nonchalant. "Have you heard anything of
. . . any excitement, maybe, over Dunknealy way?"

The boy frowned and shook his head. "You mean the
old sow getting loose from the cart and being shot for a
boar?"

"That's all?"

"And what else would there be?" The boy sauntered on
with his sheep, leaving Jamie behind on the road's edge,
looking after him with a strange expression on his face.

I climbed up out of the mud again. "What's up?"

Jamie put his hands into his pockets and began walking
slowly back toward Dunknealy. "We might as well go
home, I guess," he said, and I swear he sounded disappointed!

"They're not out looking for us?" I fell in beside him
with new energy, feeling as if I'd been suddenly yanked
from the shadow of the gallows, so to speak.

"I wonder if old Drum's got up off the floor yet," remarked Jamie, a small smile playing about the corners
of his mouth.

"We'll catch it," said I glumly. Sure, the whole thing
had taken on a sort of glamour when we thought the police
and the army were being called out against us for laying
hands on an Englishman. We would have cheerfully
walked up the gallows' steps, confident we had won our
right to die as patriots, for the cause. But now it all sank
back into proportion and we were not patriots, only two
schoolboys in trouble, each of us due for a very nice beating at home and who knew what fiendish torments reserved for us by Drum. Our steps became slower and
slower as we came into town and circled about toward
home. It was quite dark when we reached the *boreen* and
I left Jamie to go on alone.

Of course everyone had already heard the whole disgrace of it and I got a beating from my father as I knew I
would. Later I heard tell of what had happened at Jamie's
house:

"You missed tea," said his mother, eyeing his muddy
condition without the crack of a smile. Jamie apologized
very formally and went upstairs to wash up. He came back

down whistling and received a great clout on the head as
his foot hit the bottom step.

"You've heard, then?" was all he said to his mother, as
she sat down to keep him company at his tea. "What did
Da say?"

She smiled, pouring him a mug. "Not much. Drum was
here. The poor creature'll never be the same. Sure that
was a fearful blow you dealt the man, son; it's knocked his
nose clean to one side, and I do believe there'll be some
kind of scar over his eyebrow." She began to butter the
toast.

"He won't let you back into the school, he swore that,
and your father did not oppose him," she said, looking at
Jamie to see what effect her words were having.

He pursed his lips, raised his eyebrow and helped himself to the toast.

"Aye, I thought it would break your heart," said she,
angry now.

"It wasn't done for that purpose, if that's what you
mean," said Jamie calmly.

She sighed, resting her head against the back of the
chair, gazing off into the fire.

"Your father wants you to go on with your education,
before all else," she said.

"There's a few things to be done before that," answered
Jamie bleakly, and she nodded.

"There always are," she said.

"Where is Da tonight?"

"At a meeting. He'll be in late, I expect. There was
some message came in from Roscommon, I don't know
what."

They sat in silence for a while more; then she said, "I
promised Drum I'd take a stick to you."

But Jamie only smiled at that, and, after a moment, her
eyes began to twinkle and she laughed.

Well, and of course, Jamie never got the strap as *I* did.
But at least Drum let me back into school after a week of
my mother and father pleading with him. Jamie didn't
even make an appeal. In fact, he seemed awfully pleased
with himself.

I missed him a lot, walking to school and back alone each day. Drum saw to it that my life was made even more miserable than usual. He kept me late every afternoon and caned me soundly ten days in a row, to pay for the fateful day I'd gone off after Jamie. That day, insisted Master Drum coldly, was the day I had sided with the devil, and I couldn't help but think what a remarkably intimate acquaintance with old Satan all these people in authority seemed to have.

When Jamie heard this state of affairs, he said nothing. But the next morning, as Master Drum trod his dainty way along the path of his house, he got an awful shock.

Jamie had stolen over into town and spent a good part of the night digging a very large hole in Drum's pathway. He filed the hole carefully with a load of fresh manure, then covered it from sight with a light blanket of dirt, leaves, and twigs.

Drum didn't show up for class till close to eleven o'clock, and he was in a wonderful murderous mood, but he never caned me again. Jamie shook his head sadly when I spoke to him about it. Oh, for one blessed moment's sight of it, he wished. It wasn't fair to think of such a perfect way to fix a man and then not be around to enjoy the sight of the man being fixed—in this case, Master Drum up to his bony knees in hot horse manure!

Chapter III

So it was that Jamie Daley left school and began his education, which is often the case anyway. Now he spent his days with Martin, and Martin was a scholar who knew the Latin and the Greek and the Gaelic as well, and more of the world than lay cupped in the Atlantic Sea's hand like a green nestled bird.

It had been almost summer when Jamie faced Drum down, and soon I was free of school myself. I saw Jamie a dozen times a day, for our two farms were well-nigh one, and the families were always back and forth. Often I used to watch Jamie and his father together in the fields, silent at work with scythe or hoe, or cutting the rich, dark, dank peat for the fires. And I watched them sometimes on top of the hay wagon coming home up the *boreen* to the house, sundown coming on and the sheep moving white in the road about them, the trees already dark and the mist moving in cool and shining over the fields down below. And they'd be laughing and talking, the two of them, and there was a world of listening and understanding there you'd look far to find.

Yet peace was slipping away as the months passed by. We heard many stories from the cities, strange exciting stories about a new wind blowing, coming our way for a change. Our fathers were part of it and we longed to become part of it, too.

We had always known, of course, that someday we would grow up and be Irish soldiers. We did not expect there to be peace before our time, and hardly thought of peace *in* our time. No, we would fight, like the others had before us, in our turn.

Once the thought of Irish soldiers fighting for Ireland had been a thing of prayers in the dark night's despairing and wishes in little boys' dogged hearts, not reality for grown men. But it had grown in Jamie's heart and in my own, and it must have been growing all over the country, for an army was born at last, a real army. No more bands of struggling rebels armed with pitchforks and rocks, no more victims forever abegging of the world's pity, never again! Word was flitting around that Irishmen were a queer breed indeed, for they would not go down and stay down as had the Scots and the Welsh, but they *would* keep popping up again and again, to England's eternal annoyance and expense. And why did they not let us go,

for we were a thorn in their Atlantic side all those long
years?

Well, and to hell with letting us go, we were going
under our own steam. Ireland had raised herself an army
at last, in November of 1913, only a whisper it was, but
it grew into a great voice, and the hills of Ireland began
to resound as they hadn't, I hazard to guess, since the
monsters and reptiles of old once pounded the earth as
they walked along. The new Army was to be trained
properly, to have uniforms and arms, to receive pay (at
a later date, of course), but none of them cared about
the money. They were to have officers and ranks proper
in all respects and equal to any army in the world. There
was only one small tick in the muscle, and that was, as I
told you, our grand new Army was illegal, underground
and not respected, as yet, by the English. They tried to
call it just another pack of rebels, of Fenian trouble-
makers, even of Communists, but soon enough they discovered what they were dealing with.

Every man in Dunknealy who could fire a gun volunteered for the Army. I daresay every man who could *walk*
volunteered, my father and Uncle Martin among the first.
How Jamie and I had begged them to let us go, too, but
they'd have none of it. We were still only boys. We insisted there must be things that even boys could do, and
there were, but that was not until later. No was the answer and no we had to take and shut our mouths, however
fired up we might be.

We stomped about in low spirits a good deal of the
time. Jamie worked hard on the farm, as I did at home,
but it never filled us and it never tired us. In the evening,
sometimes, he used to come riding up for me and the two
of us would take our horses over half the county, riding
them hard, for no matter what our fathers said or thought,
we were becoming men by then, and life was rising up
in us.

We rode the horses so hard that often we'd have to sit
a few hours under the night sky, along the Blackwater
River Road letting the animals rest and graze, whilst we

sat and talked and talked and made a thousand plans that came to naught.

I had a strange feeling during all those months that I was really sleeping most of the time, dreaming that I was riding just above the earth on a soft cloud and trying like hell to climb down off it and walk with solid ground under my feet.

Rumors were racing about the countryside, and Jamie and I were like life prisoners in solitary confinement, grabbing hold of scraps of information eagerly, like grabbing at crusts of bread. The Army was blowing up police vans, throwing bombs into barracks, ambushing British convoys on the roads! It was grand, and it was tantalizing, for we lived only to be in it, and we were as far from it as two boys who lived there could be.

One night, we rode the horses far up into the hills along the coast, where it was hard to see and we would have done better with mountain goats or donkeys, for the poor creatures stumbled more than once on the dark, rocky trails. The cliffs were all just to one side of us; we could hear the crashing of the surf far, far below and the gurgling gasp of the water as it eddied in between the rocks along the shore.

We had long since stopped talking, concentrating hard on not slipping down to our deaths, and the horses were clammy with sweat, their heads low and tired. Jamie finally said, "It's no use. We'd best get down and wait for the moon."

We had another hour or two to wait for the moon to rise, then we could walk the horses down again, seeing at least a foot ahead of us. I picked my way along, finding a small path that turned inland among the rocks, and we moved quietly through some thick brambles. But suddenly I stopped, for far ahead I saw the flickering light of a small brushfire, and I heard the low, guarded voices of several men.

"Jamie, hush!" I hissed at him. At once he stopped and crept up to my side.

"What is it?"

But then he heard them, too, and listened carefully for

a few seconds, a grin spreading over his face. "That's little Johnny O'Donnell talking," he whispered. "You can hear him plain as day. Listen."

Sure enough, it was Johnny, though I could not make out his words.

"It's a meeting!" exclaimed Jamie with great delight. "Let's get closer."

I didn't think that was a good idea; already the moon was trailing along the horizon, and the clouds overhead were lighting up more each minute. "They'll see us," I objected.

"Well, and if they do?" he asked. *"We're* not the enemy. Come on."

Taking the horses' reins in our hands, we led them farther toward the campfire. I could see many men sitting there in a big circle. The fire was very small, illuminating only the faces of a few who sat nearest it with a weird reddish glow that distorted their features and made them seem something far different than the neighbors I'd known all my life. It was eerie there. My heart beat faster. I knew we shouldn't have come so far; we shouldn't be there at all, and we certainly shouldn't be sneaking up on them as we were. We tried to be absolutely still, but the horses were nervous and edgy from having had to pick their way along the rocks with such tiny steps. As we lay hidden among the bracken, listening, Jamie's horse tossed its head high and whinnied loudly.

At once there was a great commotion. I saw someone quickly kick out the fire with his feet, so the men seemed to disappear, but I heard them running about, looking, and they called to one another. We had not gotten quite close enough to encounter the sentries they had left on guard; the four of them came running toward us immediately when they heard the horse.

"Jamie, we've done it again!" I groaned ruefully, trying vainly to hug the ground flat. Jamie raised his head, just as the big gorgeous full moon broke through the clouds. He jumped to his feet and stood, patting the horse on its damp nose, comforting it and talking in a good, loud, everyday voice.

"Jamie! Are you daft? They'll hear you for sure," I croaked from the ground, but Jamie tossed his head just as his horse had done, no wonder they suited each other so well!

The horse nickered softly and, only a few feet away, someone called out sharply, "There they are!" Instantly we were surrounded on all sides. As they came up to us, pistols aimed straight at us, I saw who they were. Sean Culhane was there, and O'Rourke, and Willy Devlin, and Uncle Martin, with my own father beside him, and one other man, tall and good-looking. I did not know him.

"Jamie! And Jerry Noonan!" cried Willy Devlin, laughing and lowering his weapon. Culhane raised his eyes to heaven.

"You two came pretty close to early graves just now," he said sternly. "What are you doing up here?"

Jamie stood very tall and met his eyes levelly. "We weren't trying to find you, if that's what you're thinking," he said as cool as ice. Then he caught Martin's eye on him and added quickly, "Honest, Da. We were just out riding and we saw your fire. But you ought to be more careful, next time it could be a patrol."

Culhane nodded his head in agreement. "He's right, Martin. This was a bad choice. Well, now that they're here, what are we going to do with them?"

"Go home right now," said my father, giving me the eye.

Jamie cried out, "Oh, let us stay, won't you? Let us join up. There must be something we could do. Maybe we could carry messages. We're still young, like you keep saying, but isn't that a good thing? We can move about fast, they'd never think of us, they could look straight at us and never see us at all!"

Culhane was laughing at him, but Martin spoke up then.

"You cannot join up now, but if you can keep your mouths shut, I'd like the two of you to stay this night—if it's all right with you, Desmond." He turned to my father, who sighed and gave in. "There's someone here we've not seen before. He's come to us from far away, and he's got something to say to us all. I want you to hear him, boys. So bring the horses along and sit down quietly, now will you do that?"

Eagerly we nodded, and followed behind them, and in a moment the small fire was rekindled. There was little need of it; with the moonlight pouring down over us like rain, every man's face stood out clearly. The others murmured as they saw us being brought in.

Little Johnny O'Donnell looked very grave when he took the reins from us and led the horses away. "Ah, sure can you not remain lads a while longer? Must you be men so soon, then?"

Martin showed us where to sit down and warned us again to be still. Culhane was still shaking his head, he didn't approve, but Jamie and I were in a regular daze at the turn of events. We crowded in among the men and waited to see what would happen next.

Culhane lifted his hand for silence, then he began to speak.

"Gentlemen, to the purpose which brought us here this night: You all know the name of the man who is with us, after many long years of sorrow and exile. The Army has sent him here into Waterford, to train us and make us into fit soldiers for Ireland. So, gentlemen, without more delay, I present to you Captain Ian Riordan of the Army of Ireland!"

There was a shout and much applause despite the danger and all the men stood up to see a real Irish soldier at last! It was the tall man we had seen on the cliffs. He smiled at us all and waited patiently until we were still again.

"Men of Ireland," he began, and an aching thrill went through my stomach such as I'd never known before. Men of Ireland! Sure, God must have known sometime, somewhere, the world would know us as men again, and we'd be servants and lackeys and jokers no more!

"Men of Ireland, I greet you in the name of the Irish republic that is to be, and in the name of our Army!" Once again he had to wait, for we were cheering wildly.

"And Army it is, make no mistake," he went on, looking at each of us with suddenly hard eyes. "I have been away from Ireland these eight years past. Some of you may know the place where I have been waiting for this moment. I come here from Dartmoor Prison, on the wild moors of England, where it once seemed to me that half my countrymen have been at one time or another. There are still Irishmen in Dartmoor, gentlemen: the unmarked graves behind that wall hold Irish armies by the score. If we only had, by God's grace, the heroic spirits of those patriots who have died in that hell, then our task would be a simple one, only to follow them to victory.

"But we have only our poor selves, with all the weaknesses of living men, and our country has been waiting six hundreds years for us to rise up together. You come here tonight, in your turn, to join the thousands who have risen up before you. You stand before the banked graves of your fathers and their fathers and all of them fell in defeat, yet you keep coming.

"But this time there is no defeat for Ireland! This is the last Army we shall ever raise, and this is the Army that will drive the conqueror from our land, from all of our land, forever! We have help and sympathy at last from that powerful young neighbor across the sea, America, and our sons and brothers there have not forgotten us, though far from home. Money is coming in, gentlemen, money and arms, and you may be sure we shall soon have the Army that knows how to make use of both.

"This time Ireland will not be put off. This time we rise for the last time, and we shall not stop until our freedom has been won back with honor, and the black stains of six hundred years of shame have been wiped away with blood—English blood, gentlemen. If we must, we'll dye the seas with it. Let these boys here be the last of Ireland's sons dragged too early from their classrooms and fields and homes!"

He was a glorious man, Ian Riordan, standing there with his silver hair haloed in the moon's full light, and his face lit up and his eyes shining, whilst tears streamed unheeded down his sunken cheeks, as he stood with his arms stretched out to us. I tell you, if God ever once took small notice of the doings of men down here, then God did pause an instant that night to listen, for the echoes of centuries seemed to cry about Riordan's head, and for the first time in my life I believed that Ireland really might be freed. It was a heady thought, for we had just taken it for granted that we would grow and fight and die someday and nothing would change at all—and here was Ian Riordan and our fathers and men we had known always, challenging the very schemes of Heaven. I glanced over to Jamie, who sat leaning forward intently, and I knew he felt the same way.

"I would like to turn your thoughts back," Riordan went on, "back through all these years that we have endured the bitter gall of slavery. Once, Ireland was ruled well and was a nation among the nations of the world. Those were old times, I know, and remind us of beliefs long lost in the mists and whispered in the night's darkest hours. We have been taught a gentler faith, but much of that faith has not sat well with Irishmen. That faith has taught us to submit, it has taught us to bow our heads and accept the inevitable, to trust in God's justice in the end. I do not turn my back on the God of my boyhood days, gentlemen, but I have had six hundred years of the 'inevitable,' six hundred bitter, useless years of waiting for justice. And, in that time, the numbers of my people have fallen away, and the broad and hotblooded lust for living that was so much a part of them has shriveled up and turned to ashes and whiskey in their mouths, and meekness has turned their bowels from pride and glory to drunkenness and unending despair.

"I cling with all my heart to the gentle precepts of Him who gave his life upon that hard cross long ago, but I cannot help remember that Ireland once had a god, very like Him in name, a god we called Esus, who was also a woodcutter and a carpenter—and whose enemies were pinned in bloody torment upon the once wild-wooded hills of Ireland!

"We cannot go back, for the world keeps on spinning its way through the dark womb of time. The world has known many gods in its day, and I say this to you: If

Jesus of Nazareth will bring Ireland freedom and dignity once more, then I shall carry the banners of Jesus of Nazareth to hell itself! But if I meet the sovereignty of Ireland wandering lonely, and waiting on a lonely road, then it is she, Erihu, the old goddess, whose pennant I will bear until those who wait and watch in the Under Kingdom can lift their heads in pride once more.

"Ireland has in it room for Jesus and His kind, but for what we must now accomplish I call upon that Christ of wrath and anger, who strode with mighty steps, a lash in His hand, into the temple of His father and drove the unworthy men out of that holy place. I call upon all the gods of Ireland to join together in our hearts, lend us your united strength for this one last mighty cause!"

After the first hard shock of it hit me, listening to words the priests might have called witchcraft, remembering ruined towers and odd stones and strange mounds above openings into the earth, I thought the men around me seemed suddenly unknown. They lost their identities, their bodies, clothing, all familiar things about them vanished away altogether, and at last I saw only their glowing faces and bright cool eyes and flushed cheeks bathed with a radiance that whiskey nor suppressed lust nor forced wit nor vain brawling ever put there—I saw Viking eyes and Iberian dark brows, tall Celtic bodies, broad Firbolg shoulders, but Irishmen all, loving a king that lived within a magic circle in the middle of the land called Meath, upon a sacred and lovely hill named Tara. I saw men of temperament and steel, not a sign of that sly, elfin charm that the rest of the world likes to make believe is an Irishman.

And I thought of what we had become, little by little. Would we ever become again what we once had been, or better? Or would we go on dwindling away heartless, despised, despising ourselves, nursing private grievances, weeping for kings that came no more, and the spirit of Ireland moaning in agony forever along the byways of her land? Oh, Riordan was right. Better let us all die at one time, have an end to it, rather than go on and on with this minute dribbling away of time in a never-never land where we could not even recognize ourselves anymore!

I had no idea how long Riordan held us with the magic of his words and visions, or how long I had been swallowed up in my own strange dreams. A chill dawn wind was blowing up from the sea and I shivered and suddenly was once more back upon a hilltop with friends around me, a small fire dying out, and Riordan still speaking, much more quietly now, but with great bitterness in his voice, and the great heart and soul of him that had been so open and visible to us a moment before was now quite gone. Now he spoke with harsh contempt and anger about Ireland's chief curse, the informers in her midst. I saw the whole uplifted spirit of the group there change abruptly.

"They must learn that there is a new, united, and unflagging determination to deal with them in kind," Riordan was telling us. "No organization can exist weighed down with spies and traitors. We propose to deal with these people harshly, without mercy and without exception. Any man or woman who gives information to help the enemy or to hurt his fellows will be taken from their homes, no matter the time, no matter who they are. Charges must be brought against them and they must be judged. And, if guilty, they must be silenced forever.

"Above all other loyalties, to husband, wife, mother, father, brother or sister, above all must come loyalty to Ireland. For I tell you, we shall come to nothing and that quite quickly, we shall continue to be ridiculous and scorned in the eyes of the world, if we cannot act in a united way. The time has come when Irish men and women must stand by their country and serve her, even if only with their silence. We will root out the traitors and the informers and make an end of them."

An hour later, after many questions had been asked and answered and some business taken care of, the moon sank and the first early shaving of sunlight speckled the hills with gold. And Jamie and I stood with many others and gave our solemn oath as soldiers of Ireland's new Army—and neither my father nor Martin Daley forbade it anymore. As we stood there, feeling the warmth of day-

light on us, I glanced up at the sky to watch the darkness
flee away, and a battalion of red clouds advanced before
the sun, splendidly lighting up a new dawn for my country. Like a goddess the dawn came on and enveloped us
in light, and our voices rose together in those words which
would bind each of us till we died to our nation's destiny
and honor. Below, the light swept a broad path through
the churning sea, where the old god Manannon MacLyr's
bride's hair rippled on the breast of the waves. The sea
birds whirled and dipped and spread their wings gladly,
freed from the constraint of the dark night, and suddenly
I remembered a few of the lines from the old poem—

> *Th'anam au Dhia!* but there it is,
> The dawn on the hills of Ireland,
> Oh, Ireland, isn't it grand you are
> Like a bride in her rich adorning—
> Oh, Ireland, up from my heart of hearts
> I bid you the top of the morning!

Chapter IV

It was long after dawn before the last of the men were
gone out of the hills. They left in twos and threes. Ian
Riordan, who was going to stay with O'Rourke and his
wife for the time being, stayed till most were away. Jamie
and myself decided we'd wait a bit and have a rest. Our
horses were tired and still skittish, so we stretched out on
the warm grass and slept for a couple of hours.

It was a nightmare coming down with them afterwards.
We couldn't mount, for the creatures were kicking and
snorting with each slow, careful step and would easily have

pitched the two of us into the sea if we'd so much as set a foot near the stirrups.

But at last the rocky, steep cliffs fell behind us, and we entered the rolling green hills above the river road. Now the horses moved along impatiently, so we let them go free, grazing here and there where they wished, slowly making their way home behind us. They had no wish to run away. I suppose their uppermost thoughts centered about warm barns and breakfast, a good rubdown and a sleep.

Jamie and I hadn't had enough sleep to be wide awake, but we were in a wonderful dither of excitement that made us just as skittish as the animals. We felt that we had become men that night, and we were still boys enough to enjoy the feeling. Ahead of us, at a steep incline, was the hill just above the river road. That hill flowed down upon itself, dotted with bushes and brambles, tall grasses and wildflowers and a few scraggly trees, and it broke off abruptly at the road's edge. It was not a leisurely kind of a hill, if you get my meaning. Jamie and I used to love to run down this particular hill, at mad breakneck speeds, risking our lives and limbs on the absolute assurance that we could stop ourselves each time from being flung straight into the river.

That day we saw the hill, hiding the road from view. A breeze pushed us roguishly from behind. Jamie looked back, shading his eyes from the strong sun overhead.

"Oh, there they are." He pointed to the horses. "Way back there. It'll be noon and more before they get home. Let's *run!*" he shouted suddenly, turning and leaping ahead of me toward the brow of the hill. With a shout, I followed him.

Ah, but it was a glorious feeling, the wind pushing at our backs, hurling us headlong and breathless down the length of that wild hill! Faster and faster we flew, till our feet forgot the feeling of the earth, and seemed to tread on air so strong it could easily bear us upward. Down and down we plummeted, our arms flung out at our sides, feeling the push of the air give way before our bodies, shouting like fools, sending our voices into the wind in long halloos, our faces red, stumbling and tripping on brambles, darting about bushes if we could, like skiers, our heads thrown back exultantly, threatening to snap off at the neck but never quite doing it, shouting, passing each other, gaining speed, more and more and more, feeling nothing, hearing nothing but the rush of ourselves in motion, dizzy, the green ground now up, now down, the sky turned tipsy-turvy, all broken images: bits of green and gold, white cloud and brown bush, everything whirling, blurring, speeding away on all sides, till it seemed 'twas we two who stood still and the earth ripped by around us, and Jamie's long legs just in front of me, his great laugh as he turned a bit to see where I was, his arm stretched out, my-self almost up to him, then the two of us flinging ourselves at the last moment, face forward, down into the black dirt and green grass. And there we lay, panting, exhausted, rolling about in the hot grass, hitting and slapping at each other, wrestling and rolling about like two great babies for the very real joy in our hearts.

Then, with only a bit of breath back into us, up we sprang once more and on again to the bottom. Jamie was ahead of me, his great legs taking leaps like an antelope, his hands flapping to the back of him. Then it was that we heard a sound, or what might have been a sound, for it was hard to hear anything but the roaring in our own eardrums. But Jamie half turned his head and lifted his hand toward me, motioning me to catch up to him. I tried to shout, but he turned again and headed on, and sud-denly I saw clearly that he wasn't going to stop at the bottom of the hill as we always had to do, by pitching ourselves down bodily and rolling to a gentle halt just a few feet from the road, just a nudge this side the river. No, Jamie was racing onward, scrambling and sliding, the scrub brush far behind him.

"Jamie, look out!" I tried to call to him loudly, but my wind was gone, my throat dry, and the breath long since knocked out of me altogether.

It was then that I heard the new sound again, closer this time, and coming even closer in the space I take to tell of it. It was screaming, a girl's high-pitched voice screaming without words, a most frightening sound. Along with the screams, there came the creaking rumble of wheels and a wild, frantic beating of hoofs on the hard-packed dirt road. It was then I fell, catching my toes in a shallow root, and I tumbled over and over, clutching at the meager bushes as I went, till at last, scratched and half blinded with dirt, I rolled to a stop and lay quite stunned.

But Jamie had gone on, and leaped like a mad devil down the six-foot cutoff, across the ditch and into the midst of the road, when I heard him utter a furious roar of pain and saw him rolling over clutching his left foot—ah, that left one, 'twas ever and always your weakness, was it not, Jamie, lad?

"Goddamnit forever!" screeched my brave Jamie in a most undignified way, getting back to his feet and scrambling to the edge of the road by hopping and holding the left foot in his hands. He only made it in time to avoid the high, two-wheeled cart and the donkey red-eyed and hell-bent for catastrophe which was coming straight for him. And, sure enough, there was a girl in the cart, standing on her feet, her long black hair streaming out behind her, her broad-brimmed straw hat knocked to her shoulders, holding on to the reins with all her strength, never letting up on the screaming.

The cart and its enraged donkey brushed Jamie in passing, knocking him into the road again, and I saw the girl's head turn back briefly, just before she came to the bend in the road. I staggered to my feet and began running down as best I could, but Jamie had jumped up again and gone chasing after the cart, hobbling along as best *he* could on the hurt foot, swearing every step of the way.

I wouldn't have believed it possible, but he caught up with them and grasped at the cart from behind. Just at that instant, the fool donkey decided to pitch himself and the cart, girl and all, into the river. He turned sharply and looked over his shoulder, braying furiously to find the same damned appendage still very much part of his problem. He kicked his hind legs and reared—which in a horse is a brave sight indeed, but in a small, long-eared, recalcitrant donkey is nothing short of ridiculous, as long as you're not the poor creature inside the cart he's bent on destroying entirely!

"Help, help!" screams the girl most unnecessarily, looking back at Jamie, who clung like gum to the rear of the cart. As it pitched up and down, he was flung up and down with it, like a doll, but Jamie would not let go, and he and that bastard donkey exchanged many black glances, for the donkey now seemed to blame Jamie for the whole situation, and was determined to shake him loose any way he could.

The girl cried out sharply, "His head, his head, you fool, try to get his head!" And she added to the misery of the day by laying on with the whip, thinking she was helping. Well, and didn't the sting of *that* surprise his gray little highness, I'll tell you. He let out one mighty snort, cut out his rearing and kicking, and took off once more down the road, the cart lurching far over to one side and then the other, with the young lady almost thrown first into the ditch and then into the river.

But Jamie had had just enough time to scramble up into the open-backed cart, which he barely did before they took off, and landed head first with his two long legs sticking straight up in the air. However, he managed to crawl the small distance to the board where the girl sat, pushing her aside without so much as a by-your-leave. He dumped her into the back, grasped the reins from her two hands, and began pulling. I report all this faithfully, and I was in a most excellent position to witness it, because I had not fared so well as my athletic cousin, Jamie, and had fallen miserably down the six feet of dirt into the muddy ditch, which also contained several sharp stones and a mixed assortment of various manures left, no doubt, in the passing. I was now running behind the cart, too far behind to do more than watch.

Well, now, and what do you suppose that long-eared, cursed idiot did when he felt suddenly an altogether new touch to the reins? He looked back again, and great was his indignation when he beheld Jamie. And straightforth, doesn't he just stop dead in his tracks.

"Jesus Christ!" were Jamie's own words into the soft river breeze, even as he himself, with a great, shocking bounce, went flying ass over tip out of the cart altogether and, upon slamming into the donkey's backside, ricocheted onto the road between the beast's wicked sharp hind feet and the cart!

The girl, meanwhile, had pulled herself up to the seat again, but now she could do nothing, for the situation was quite delicate. The reins trailed down the donkey's side and she could not reach them. She was afraid to move an inch, for the beast stood snorting nervously, picking up first one foot and then the other, putting them down lightly, and tossing its fool head. Jamie was afraid to move, too, for fear of arousing the creature's fury once more, and, for a few seconds, the three of them seemed frozen where they were.

Then, of course, myself, panting and purple in the face, smelling, I'm sure, like several old friends to the donkey came straggling alongside.

"Get the reins, Jerry," gasped Jamie. But even that the donkey would not tolerate. He picked up his hind legs and aimed a good kick right at Jamie, who instinctively covered his head with his arms, and thus just barely missed being stove in.

I approached the beast quietly, picked up the reins, and began talking to him slowly, in a calm voice, as I walked to his head, scratched him behind the ears and took firm hold of the bridle. Jamie gingerly extracted himself and took the reins from me. The girl had not said a word, but when Jamie came back to her, she stared at him wide-eyed, then her glance roved over to me, then back to Jamie again, and suddenly she opened her mouth and began to laugh softly, though with the strength of a good, lusty lung on either side of her rather spare figure.

"Ah, God, but you're a sight, the two of you!" she cried, not neglecting to fish about for her hat and plunk it down with a firm hand more or less in the center of her head. But we were staring at her, too, for she seemed somehow familiar.

'Twas Jamie who spotted it first and exploded. "Margaret Culhane! It's you, isn't it?"

She stopped laughing, although a smile kept working its way from one corner of her wide red mouth to the other, but her voice grew a good deal warmer. "It's me," says she pertly. "And I'd know you and your cousin anywhere, Jamie Daley!"

Considering the looks of the two of us at that moment, I do think she could have chosen a more suitable compliment. I stood by the donkey's head, who now had caught his breath and nuzzled my neck and face with great, inexplicable affection.

Jamie stood lounging his long length against the cart, grinning at her like a fool Cheshire cat, whilst Margaret told how the donkey had been scared by a motorcar as she was heading back from town after doing a bit of marketing. As she spoke, her two quick hands were busy pinning the long, wild black hair into a neat bun at the back of her neck.

"When did you come home?" Jamie was asking. And then I remembered, why, it was true of course, when *was* the last time we had seen Margaret? Not since just after her mother had died. Why, it was over two years since the funeral, two years since Margaret had gone back to boarding school in Dublin, only we'd not taken enough notice to remark on it. We were not interested in the comings and goings of girls, you know, and, with that in mind, I thought fleetingly that Jamie looked like something of a great ass himself standing there all muddy and bruised, smiling his dark head off up at the wench!

"I've been back a week or two," says Miss Culhane quite coolly now, recovering faster than any of us from the events. And I saw with some disgust that she had that way girls sooner or later seem to discover, of not quite looking at you when they talk to you, but seeming to look at something fascinating just over your shoulder. But where the devil was all Jamie's *mishna,* sure he didn't seem to notice anything at all, but only nodded with keen interest written all over him, the damned liar, as if he had done nothing else but think about where she'd been the past two years!

"I was at school, you know," added Margaret. "And I shall probably be leaving again, one of these days. Maybe to London, or Paris even. But now I'm wanted at home."

I stared. Was this the wild Margaret I remembered so well from school, never her hair plaited but scraggly and hanging down her back, a rose flush always coming and going on her dark-ivory skin? She looked down at us primly, and now had got her wayward mouth under tight control once more, for the little peeping smile that teased about her lips was gone. And suddenly I was aware that I was very tired, very dirty, very hungry, and very sick of holding on to that brazen beast's head whilst Jamie and Margaret Culhane smiled back and forth at each other.

"If nobody minds, I'll be going on home now," I put in, and both of them looked at me in some surprise. Jamie handed her the reins and moved off from the cart, but suddenly his leg bent double under him and he moaned.

"Och, he's hurt!" cried Margaret, suddenly all concern, bending over to look at him. "Jerry, will you leave off holding the donkey! Come round and help Jamie into the cart at once."

"No, no, we've two horses to take home." Jamie shook his head weakly, whilst I looked around for the two blasted animals.

"They're long gone," I said. "Don't you think they'd have a sight more sense than to wait around for us? Sure the two of them are both home and rubbed down and warm, with their stomachs full and sleeping, where we should be."

Margaret jumped down from the cart and took Jamie's arm.

"Then that settles it," she declared, pulling him toward the step up. "And it's only right Ned should carry you home, and him almost killing the three of us. Come on, Jerry, help me get him in here."

Ah, but Margaret had the true voice and style of a real Irishwoman, born to command either through charm or through her wits; you can tell it in them, in all of them that are true to themselves and their birthright. A flash from her great brown eyes and I was obeying her every word. To Jamie's great discomfort, she and I dragged and hauled and mauled him up into the back of the cart. And I myself jumped lithely up next to Margaret, who sat looking back at Jamie, giving over the reins to myself.

"We saw your father just this last night!" said Jamie, then he stopped and coughed to cover his embarrassment, for he wasn't supposed to mention where or how or under what circumstances he had seen Culhane or any of the men. Margaret's face froze. She stared ahead of her then, a flush of some emotion I did not understand covering her cheeks and throat.

"Did you, now?" she said shortly. And for a while, as we trotted peacefully along, there was a strained silence among the three of us.

Then I tried another topic of conversation. "How do you find Kevin these days? Much changed? I saw him myself at Mass Sunday week; sure he's quite a man now, isn't he?"

Margaret's smile returned at once when I mentioned her brother and her whole face lit up. "Yes, isn't he? God bless him! Oh, I missed him so when I was away, though we used to write three times a week and he came up to spend Christmas with me last year."

"How old is Kevin now?" ventured Jamie, and he was rewarded at once with another bright smile.

"Twenty-one come September," she answered with much pride in her voice. "He's going for a priest, did you know that?"

"A priest, is he? No, no one in town has said anything. That's strange," mused Jamie, "wouldn't you think news like that would have gotten around? And, you know, Kevin would make a perfect priest. He was always a religious kid, I remember. No wonder none of us has seen him at the dances or up at—"

I knew he was going to say "at the meeting," but once more he stopped in confusion. Margaret's eyes flashed.

"That's it, you see," she said, very cool again. "Why, had you thought something different?"

Jamie's eyebrow arched and he matched her tone. "I thought whatever Kevin did was his own affair," he said.

At once Margaret found her smile again. "I'm sorry. I didn't mean to be talking of good news and spoiling it in the same breath. Kevin's wild to be a priest, he always wanted it, since we were children. He's one of those fellows you don't see much. I mean, he's not going into it because he thinks it's a great opportunity for himself, or he's sacrificing his life or anything like that. He's always been full of—well, a sort of love, I guess, that's too big and too much for just a few people. Oh, listen to me, I couldn't explain it if I tried." And now it was her turn to be embarrassed. She dropped her eyes and gave a little apologetic laugh, which was more charming and more Margaret than anything she'd been saying or doing since we'd met her that day.

"I remember Kevin, Margaret," Jamie said gently. "He was always yearning toward heaven, even as a boy, and he was always the kind we all liked. I hope he'll do well. You and your Da will be mighty proud of him."

Well, and it just wasn't Jamie's day, for, the moment he mentioned Culhane again, Margaret turned pale and bit her lip quite hard, and I thought I saw a tear in her eye.

"*I'll* be proud of him, as I always have," she said vehemently. "But my father is against it. As he always has been. Why else do you think Kevin isn't gone yet, but must wait till his twenty-first birthday? My father can hold him till then, and he is. He's got strong feelings about the estate, you know, and Kevin is his only son. He wants him to carry on the family name when all the wrongs are righted at last and the Culhanes can hold up their heads in Ireland again!"

Oh, but there was a lifetime of bitterness and anger in those words and the greatest contempt in her voice, and she would not look at either of us. Jamie nodded. We both knew Sean Culhane and his dreams well. And his son and heir lost to the priesthood just didn't fit those dreams at all.

"Well," blustered Jamie, trying to sound cheerful, "it's only a few more months and then he's his own man.

Don't fret about it, Margaret. Your father can't hold him then. And, maybe, when he sees Kevin in all his fine robes with the collar at his throat, sure he's bound to be proud, too. You'll see."

Margaret reached back and patted Jamie's shoulder softly, without saying a word. Then, abruptly, she smiled, threw back her head in the old familiar way she had as a child, and cried exultantly, "Oh, but anyway, it's good to be home again. I'm glad I met the two of you, though I wish it hadn't been so painful for you!"

And then the three of us laughed together, so loudly that the persistent donkey tweaked a warning ear and flicked his tail in disapproval, which made us laugh all the more, for we were wary of his little quirks by then.

And from that moment, all the stiffness and awkwardness left us. We talked and laughed and even sang as we drove along slowly, turning off the river road and up the *boreen* toward Jamie's house and my own.

"Tell us, now, Margaret," teased Jamie, his gray eyes all of a twinkle, "do you still have that little wooden doll —you know, the one you used to carry to school every day, and Drum told you to get rid of it or he'd throw it into the stove for kindling wood?"

Margaret nodded merrily, her mouth twisted into scorn at the mention of Drum. "Aye, Ellen Anne, that was her, and I kept her all these years. Drum scared me so, I used to put her to bed, wrapped up in my handkerchief, inside one of those old cracked stones in the fence, every morning before school started. I love that doll. My mother took me to a fair once and bought it from a stall, and made the clothes for it herself. Funny, Jamie Daley, you remembering such a thing, you big lout!"

Jamie flushed purple, but I saw he was smiling to himself. So, with this and that, we soon found ourselves near home. Culhane House was first, but we were close by, and, though Margaret argued hotly to drive us each home, we thought she should be getting in herself and letting poor Ned be attended to, for the little fellow was all of a sweat now, and his short little legs were trembling.

Soon enough we were outside the tall iron gates of

Culhane House. It looked deserted, but for a smart-faced gray cat with a flat head and wicked eyes, who sat drinking daintily on the fountain inside, his tail lashing as he beheld the donkey. Margaret insisted on helping me get Jamie out of the cart. I noticed her glance toward the house, and I thought she seemed somewhat relieved.

"Now that I'm back, will I ever see the two of you? And Kevin will be so glad I've found friends—" She looked anxiously and rather strangely from one to the other of us, one of her small hands resting on mine, and one on Jamie's, and her cool, long fingers pressed firmly against us. "We are friends, are we not, the three of us?"

"Sure we are that, Margaret Culhane," said Jamie as heartily as ever he could with the pain from his sore foot shooting up and making him quiver as he leaned against me. "Who else but friends like us could have pulled off such an elegant rescue, now I ask you?"

But Margaret did not smile. "And I haven't even thanked you," she murmured ruefully, and once again I saw her glance nervously toward the house. "I can't ask you to come in," she added, very low. "My father doesn't like me to have company." Then her face brightened. "But I have my own horse now, and I'm going to ride every day and get to know my home again. Will you ride with me sometimes? I think Kevin might come, too. He'd be glad enough for the change," she said eagerly.

As she spoke, an elderly, white-haired old *maneen* came shuffling stiff-legged around from the back of the house and waved at her.

"Oh, there's Patrick now," she said. "I'll have to go in and help him with Ned. Goodbye, and thank you both," she said with a warm smile and a pat for each of us, then she led the donkey off toward the gates, which the old man was slowly opening. Jamie and I stood there in the dust of the road, watching her slim figure coaxing the beast ahead as she held up her skirts with the other hand. Patrick, she had said his name was, looked over at us disapprovingly, and frowned.

So we were off then, slowly limping along up the dirt road, and Jamie looked back once or twice.

"She's quite a lady, isn't she?" he mused.

"Well, that's what the father's always wanted," I replied.

Jamie shook his head thoughtfully. "It's not right, about Kevin," he said gravely. "There's a damn good fellow, you know, Jerry? No matter what Sean's plans are, surely he could see years ago that Kevin had his own ideas."

"He's crazy," I tossed lightly. "Think how many sure would be glad to have a little priesteen in the family, it would be the saving of them!"

Jamie threw back his head and laughed, I don't exactly know why. But, with the strange night we'd put in and the morning after it, we'd both become tired and silly, and we wobbled along the rest of the way home singing at the tops of our voices—and did I mention to you that the top of Jamie's voice was like the death cry of a banshee? Well, but Margaret was right, and it was nice to see her again.

We went straight to Jamie's house, for I would not let him go alone on that leg, and we startled poor Aunt Ellen dreadfully, as we two great clods, muddy and ·tinking, came crashing into her neat kitchen, hopping ridiculously on three legs, singing lustily,

> Yer currant cakes and tea was nice,
> Before he left, he kissed her twice—
> she laned acrosst the half-door!

Chapter V

Uncle Martin had been home long before ourselves, had taken a couple of hours' sleep, and was out hard at work in the fields. Aunt Ellen was sitting shelling peas from a bushel basket in the kitchen whilst Jamie and I filled our shriveled stomachs with rashers of bacon and eggs, for neither of us had eaten a bite since the night before. We told her all about the runaway donkey and about meeting Margaret, each of us talking in turn depending on whose mouth was empty at the moment. She kept shaking her head and muttering, "Oh, dear, blessed God in heaven!" as we elaborated on every harrowing detail and I rather thought both of us came off looking like heroes of old by the time we got through embellishing the story.

She smiled when we told her what Margaret had said as we left her. "Yes, yes, I always wanted you children to be friends. I know it isn't the easiest thing—because of himself, you know. They're like their mother, both of them. Warmhearted she was, poor little creature, how she worried and fretted about those two at the end!"

She put a soft hand on Jamie's arm and looked at him intently. "James, I would like you to be very kind to Margaret and Kevin. They are lonely children, up there in that big house with only the father for company. And Sean Culhane has never been the best company known. It will do them good to have playmates like you and Jerry."

Jamie's eyes met mine across the table and the two of us nearly choked on our tea. Playmates! Well, and that's mothers for you, and both of us towering over the slight five feet of her like beanstalks!

Then Jamie, frowning a bit, said, "I don't know that

Culhane's all that bad, Ma. I guess not everybody can be all full of charm like yourself, but Da says he's a good man to have on your side. You sound like Margaret— every time we mentioned Sean, she didn't like it a bit. I suppose all they say about him and her mother i: true."

Aunt Ellen continued her shelling very deliberately. "I'm not one to repeat idle gossip," she said.

Jamie snorted. "It's not gossip," he protested. "You and Aunt Annie were with her the whole time she was sick. You know it's true. They say he never loved her at all, but only wanted the money."

"Oh, I suppose she knew what she was doing well enough," said Aunt Ellen evenly. "She wanted a man with ambition and something besides money to leave his children. Culhane has always been a fine, honorable name in Ireland, when there was money to go with it and even when there wasn't. But Mary wasn't the type to live with coldness. And that's himself. He can't help it. I suppose every drop of warmth or caring in the man went into all his fine plans and hopes—"

"And his work, don't forget that, Ma," put in Jamie very warmly, remembering the passionate face of Sean Culhane at the meeting the night before.

Aunt Ellen glanced at him and sniffed. "Aye, and his work, of course. That's important to him. It furthers his personal schemes. I don't know, it must be an awful weary strain on a man always to be worrying about living up to himself. Well, anyway, he's got a son to come after. And Kevin is a fine lad."

Jamie smiled, wolfing down another piece of bread. "Well, he won't have him long, from what Margaret says. Did you know Kevin's going to be a priest?"

Aunt Ellen threw her head back with a great sigh, and smiled broadly. "Ah, then he didn't put it aside. I thought he had. It was his mother's dearest wish for him. But the father never agreed. Oh, how they used to quarrel about that boy, for hours and hours, and her coughing and weaker every minute with it all! But Mary never gave up praying that Kevin would have his way. Margaret told you this for a true fact?"

Jamie nodded. "Aye, but he's having to wait till he's of age. Culhane hasn't changed his mind. I guess they're still arguing about it. I can understand, maybe, how he feels. Look at Da, now. He hopes one of us will stay here and keep the place up after him. And, no matter what he says, I know he felt proud to have us up there at the meeting with them all last night!"

In a flash, she turned on him. "Shut your mouth," she snapped angrily, her eyes filling with tears. "Did you think I didn't know where you were, and me waiting all the night long and wondering if they'd catch you all! I gave your father a good thought of it this morning, I'll tell you, and him sitting here when the two poor creatures of horses came wandering back, worn out and nervous as kittens! How could he let you stay, and Desmond, too, both of them, and you only boys!"

"We're men now, Ma," argued Jamie, and she slapped him across the face, then burst into tears and hugged him hard against her.

"Ma, Ma, don't take on so," begged Jamie, but she couldn't seem to stop.

"I've seen it all before," she sobbed. "My own father and my two brothers, before you lads were born. It's no use, Jamie, lad, it's not going to change the way things are. I've tried to tell that to Martin, but sure he's always with his nose in the books, and he'll never listen! Don't get mixed up with it, Jamie, Jerry, oh, don't, please. You'll all get yourselves killed or in prison!"

Jamie kissed her and dried her tears and teased her gently till at last she gave him a wan smile and pushed him away.

"Go on with you, you *spalpeen!*" she sniffed, and I noticed her hand lingering for a long second on his broad shoulder. "Well, I've nothing more to say about it. I don't want to know about it. But, mind what I told you both, try to be good to those poor children. They need friends, and, now that Mary's gone, I have no more reason to be going over there."

It was not a hard promise to keep, for we had always

liked them years ago. We had seen little of Kevin for a long time.

No one I knew ever thought less of him because he did not become mixed up in politics or join the Army. Kevin felt that Ireland should be free to work out her own destiny and, in light of that, that each man should do what he could in his own way. And, God knows, prayer has always had power in it, any true prayer, anywhere ever in the world. Prayer is the speech of adrenalin, that stuff that pumps through you and fires you up for what you have to do. More power to you, Kevin Culhane, dead these forty years, I recall, a good man, a good priest, one of the few men I've ever known who truly believed that men were brothers, spent his few years in the slums of Dublin working with the young people dying of despair there.

Well, oddly enough, when things start to happen they keep right on, and it wasn't but three or four days later when who should Jamie and I run into down on the edge of town but Kevin himself, trudging along the road home on foot, his head stuck in a book as he walked briskly along. We had been sent in on errands and, since we'd the wagon with us, we hailed Kevin and offered him a ride with us.

He hopped up by Jamie's side, a broad smile of pleasure on his mild face. "Margaret told me she'd seen the two of you," he said. "I wanted to thank you for helping her out. I've known her to be thrown from a horse half a dozen times straight and end up riding it home meek as a lamb, but I never thought a donkey would be too much for her!" The three of us laughed about it.

I looked at Kevin curiously as we rode along. He was talking to Jamie about some hurling match Jamie had seen him play in one time, and I had the chance to take a good look at him.

He was a nice-looking fellow with good shoulders on him, not too tall. He had the wavy black hair and dark eyes of the mother, as Margaret did, and Culhane's fine, straight nose and strong chin. I noticed his hands, small, with long straight fingers, and I was surprised to see them calloused and cut, like the hands of any farmer or laborer, certainly not what I'd expected from someone heading toward the seminary.

"What have you been up to these days, Kevin?" I asked.

He shrugged. "Not much. I've put in a vegetable garden behind the house, and I'm trying to keep Mother's flowers from withering away. But I don't have her touch with growing things, I'm afraid. Neither does Margaret. She's pulled up more young shoots than weeds, and I'm not much better. Still, it's something to do." To hear him talk, you'd think he was seventy and waiting to die, but I knew he meant the waiting to go was weary. I didn't know whether to say anything or not about his plans, but, as usual, Jamie had no polite scruples.

"I think it's great news, you finally getting ready to go off to the seminary," he launched into it heartily.

Kevin didn't seem surprised, but smiled a bit shyly. "I've waited a long time, but it's these last few months that are so hard to get through. And then," he added, the bright smile fading quickly, "there are always a few problems to be worked out before you're free to go." There was a small, awkward silence then, for it was obvious he didn't know we were aware of the trouble between him and his father, and he wasn't going to bring it up.

"Well, we'll have to give you a grand send-off," Jamie threw in hastily. "Meantime, there's the whole spring and summer ahead of us, and the four of us can have some great times. Do you ride still?" he asked, remembering, as I did, that Kevin had always been a fine rider; he'd even entered the races in Clonmel a few times as a boy and not done too badly for himself.

"Oh, indeed, whenever I get the chance," he answered. "My poor old Sailor is slowing down now. He's going on fourteen, but he can still put in a pretty good day for himself."

"Then it's settled," cried Jamie enthusiastically. "You tell your sister to find herself a mount easier to handle than that blackhearted donkey and we'll all meet together at the end of the *boreen* tomorrow morning, after chores."

Kevin laughed. "Wait till you see the horse she's gone and picked out for herself! I think they were made for each other."

We let Kevin off outside those iron gates. Jamie craned his neck trying to peek inside to get a glimpse of Margaret, but she was not about, and when I accused him of doing it he clouted me across the shoulders, shouting a loud goodbye to Kevin, and we went on about our business. I turned around myself, before the bend in the road, and Kevin was still standing there by the gates, his hand resting on one of them, looking after us, and it made me uneasy, for he seemed so very lonely.

As if echoing my own thoughts, Jamie sighed. "For his sake, I wish the summer would pass quickly. He looks like someone on the edge of two dark pits. It's queer, I don't think I've spoken so much to Kevin Culhane in all my life before today, but somehow I feel very fond of him."

I nodded. "Aye, some people are that way. It'll be handy for when he's a priest."

Jamie said, "Wouldn't you think Culhane would be glad about it? Oh, I don't mean because having a priest for a son is the next best thing to a free ticket to heaven. But I mean proud that at least he's got ambition to be something. There's plenty, and not just in Ireland, I'll bet, who never find out what they are or what they might be."

I turned the horses toward my father's barn. "Well, the Culhanes have never been shy on ambition," I said.

Jamie pursed his lips. "There's a lot worse failings a man might have." And he pointed across the road to his brother Will, disheveled and staggering drunk, just coming up behind us. Jamie's lip curled and he jumped down quickly.

"Well, this time he's only been gone four days," he called back lightly, running after Will. "I'd best make sure he gets where he's going. See you tomorrow!"

I got down to unload the wagon, which I had been assured was a job Jamie was going to share with me. But I could see he had his hands full, for Will tried to shake him off and stumbled about, heading back to town again. Jamie grabbed him, and Will clipped him on the chin.

Jamie could have laid him out in a ditch with one hand tied behind him, but he only laughed and jollied Will along till he turned about again, and I saw the two of them arm in arm going toward the farm. Problems to solve, Kevin had said? Well, now, and who hasn't a few of them himself?

After the early rain, next morning turned out bright and warmer than any so far that spring. Jamie and I rode a few minutes late down the road, and there were Margaret and Kevin standing beside their horses, looking for us. Margaret rode a horse full as wild as herself, black tossing mane and wild, rolling eyes; sure I thought the creature was mad, for he had a habit of nervously kicking and rearing at any sound, and you could not touch his ears or he'd kill you with stomping. But Margaret loved him, for all his faults—and, as far as I could see, he had nothing but faults!

The four of us raced across the fields full speed, the black devil in the lead all the way, and I could see Margaret didn't have to give him his head, for when she sat that horse she was in complete control, and it was her choice to ride him wild and tossing, her slim body going with him all the way. Sure I don't think he could have thrown her if he'd stood on his head.

Kevin's horse was a gentle creature, a chestnut stallion past his weaknesses. You could see he was old, but very game and in good condition, and obviously used to the shenanigans of the other one, for he paid it no mind at all and would not be goaded into winding himself for the pride or the folly of it, although the black horse, which Margaret called Byron (for, as she explained it merrily, he had a charming way with the fillies) often whinnied back at him challenging. But then, Byron challenged all horses. My own, a pretty little bay mare, was at once captivated and thrust herself ahead in a burst of speed I didn't know she had in her. Jamie rode Martin's favorite horse, a big gray dapple named Dan, and Dan at once struck up a friendly acquaintance with Kevin's Sailor, paying no heed whatever to the cavorting and showing off of Byron and my lass. They were too wise for Byron, gay

blade that he fancied himself, and if you don't believe a
horse can fancy himself, then, boyo, you don't know the
half of horses!

We rode down to Bearsey's Bridge, galloped across the
wooden planks of it at a frightful din, and finally came to
a halt on the other side beneath a clump of trees. There
we dismounted and settled ourselves on the riverbank to
talk and eat the lunch Margaret had surprised us by packing. There was plenty for an army of us, and Kevin proudly picked over the contents of the basket until he pulled
out three scraggly-looking carrots and held them up
dangling by their pale-green stems.

"Now, there's carrots for you," he smiled, and Margaret rocked with laughter. "That's my entire carrot crop,
after my sister got through weeding it."

Margaret laughed till tears filled her eyes. "There's
more fine healthy weeds in Kevin's little garden than anything fit for people to eat. And, oh, how I worked to do
it." She shook her head. "I hurried, you see, for Kevin
was off to church and I wanted to make him proud of me,
so I pulled as fast as my fingers would fly. And when he
came home, there they all were, my 'weeds,' lying in the
compost heap!"

Jamie took a small bite of one of the carrots and pronounced it a blessing to the world, and Margaret had done
a good deed, for they were the bitterest, tartest carrots
he'd ever eaten, with which Kevin heartily agreed. In the
end, to keep ourselves honest, we all tasted them, and,
with one accord, we fed what was left to the horses, who
enjoyed them immensely, being creatures with highly un-
civilized tastes.

Kevin strolled over to the water and looked about with
a smile of great satisfaction. "You know, I haven't felt
this good since I was small," he said slowly.

Margaret watched him from under her tree bower, as
she packed up the picnic things, and her face was somber,
her eyes very soft.

"It'll fly, you'll see," she said to him. And he smiled
and nodded, his brown eyes that were so much of a match
for hers bright and without that touch of pain I'd seen in

them before. He picked up a handful of pebbles and began skittering them across the water. In no time, the four of us were lined up abreast, tossing and judging and claiming impossible distances with the stones, till I think every respectable fish a mile either way was disturbed out of his muddy nest.

Margaret threw from the shoulder, like a boy, and outdid us all. She had a sly way of curving her wrist inward and then flinging outward with a twist that sent her stones pell-mell six feet beyond even what Jamie, a redoubtable skimmer of rocks, could manage. She and himself began a long, wrangling tirade about methods, which Kevin listened to with much amusement until he finally broke it up by reminding his sister that she'd never catch herself a husband by besting a man at his own tricks.

Margaret's long black hair tossed and her eyes flashed. "Who wants a husband?" she said pertly. "There's worlds of things to do without having one of them!"

"Oh, maybe you're thinking of following Kevin's example, is that it?" teased Jamie. "Sister Margaret—it has a nice ring to it, don't you think, Jerry? Or maybe, since you're a bit of a pushy witch and bad-tempered, too, I hear—maybe you've the makings of a mother superior!"

Margaret looked at him in disgust and threw a leftover sandwich in his face.

"Margaret!" cried Kevin, quite shocked, but Jamie never blinked. He calmly picked it up and began to chew on it, nodding away to himself as he carried on his conversation.

"Oh, that shows I was right. Definitely a mother superior, or mother general, isn't that what they call the real high-up ones? Oh, God help the poor little novices with Mother Margaret stamping around the convent halls, laying in wait for the creatures, armed with stale sandwiches and too much mustard, to fling into their wan faces—"

But he got no further, for, with a furious screech, Margaret threw herself at him bodily, scratching and spitting like a cat. Jamie collapsed under her weight, laughing and choking on the sandwich, trying to push her off as she beat him with both fists. Kevin and I had to haul her off.

"I should have warned you," panted Kevin, neatly ducking a fist aimed in his direction, as he tried to grab her two hands. "My sister is a very direct person, and given to a great lack of discipline—ow!" She had snaked out a booted foot and landed a kick at him that sent him sprawling alongside of Jamie.

"Och, the two of you make me sick," cried Margaret. "I hate to be teased and you know that, Kevin Culhane!"

But we were all laughing at her now, and, seeing her brother and Jamie still lying in the grass and weeds on their backs, she soon began to laugh at herself. And there we sat through the long, lazy afternoon, alternately talking, singing, eating, fighting, and making plans for the rest of the summer. Not once did anyone mention Sean Culhane, no, and, to be fair, no one mentioned any other grown man or trouble at all, and the whole world might just as well not have existed save for us four there at Bearsey's Bridge.

As early evening came on, we recalled hastily that there were cows waiting to be milked at home, and we packed up quickly. Jamie and I left the Culhanes going up the *boreen* together, their horses tired enough to trot along peacefully side by side, while Margaret turned about in the saddle to wave and Kevin was still singing the remains of High Mass in Latin, which we had dared him to do and didn't believe he could do. But he remembered most of it, and said it wasn't fair because he really didn't have to know it for a few more years, and we reminded him that a man ready is a man to win, and so he had stumbled good-naturedly through it, with Jamie only too ready to throw in a missing phrase or two at the top of his dreadful voice.

That was only the first of many such days, and long hours spent roaming together over the countryside every free minute we could find. Of course, Jamie and I had work that had to be done, but the Culhanes were always there, at our meeting place, waiting patiently for the two of us, and we would wheel the horses' heads about together and go off in a new direction.

Sometimes Kevin would be busy and it was just Margaret and Jamie and me. On those days, she used to come over to our houses, tethering Byron out of harm's way and near a drink of water, and she'd pitch in and help us with our work, just to get us out faster. Oh, but Margaret was no hand for a farm, not herself! Whatever she helped us do must be done yet again, and then she would get very annoyed and sit perched up on the fence, slapping her gloved hands with her riding crop, which she never used on the damned horse, though God knows he could have done with a touch of it! And she would bicker endlessly with the two of us till Jamie came marching over to her, glowering and sweaty, having spent an hour longer at work than he would have had to had she not helped him milk the cows and gotten the bucket kicked over, and threatened to throw her to the bull if she did not immediately become silent.

She gave him a well-aimed kick in the shins, then turned and jumped up on Byron, to that creature's undying surprise, pulling his head about sharply and riding off furiously. Jamie, his hands on his hips, stood staring off after her in disgust and amusement.

"Well, she was always wild and crazy," I told him. "What do you expect?"

He then passed along the bad temper and also the swift kick to me, but an hour later we were free and rode out to find her highness meek as a rabbit, sitting on the bridge with an armful of wildflowers she'd picked as a peace offering. That was Margaret; you either loved her and didn't hold it against her, or you could not be friends with her.

She always seemed to be in a terrible hurry through life. I hardly remember her still, but always on the move, restless and high-spirited, yet she had a very gentle side, which I noticed she tried hard to show whenever we were with Kevin. But Kevin understood her and never minded her moods, being a kind of moody lad himself. But his moods came on in quietness; he simply pulled back into himself for a while and, though he was as good-natured and pleasant as ever, you could see he wasn't really thinking of

what he was doing at those times. Jamie and I were fascinated with the Culhanes, both of them. They were so very
different from all our other friends. They had few friends,
indeed, and never seemed to want any but ourselves, and
that had all fallen out only by accident, after all.

There were days, usually Sundays, when we had to do
without both of them. And, so used to one another had we
become, that although Jamie and I had been together all
our lives, yet now, when we rode alone, we seemed incom-
plete and were lonely. Usually we came home early on
those days and hung around talking about when there
would be another meeting and when we would begin to
train with the Army, fretting because nothing seemed to be
happening where we were.

Those were the afternoons when Sean Culhane enter-
tained certain of his British friends at tea. Margaret was
expected to attend and be the hostess, dressed up in a
white gown, neat and combed and a lady. Kevin too had
to be there, though what he might have added to the witty
conversation I cannot imagine. Margaret and he always
hated those days. She amused us with imitations of the
English ladies and officers, mincing up and down on the
grass, holding the train of her black riding dress out like a
ball gown, taking tiny steps, her head held stiffly, whilst
she spoke in broad nasal tones. Jamie pointed out to her
quite seriously that she ought to be careful, for her own
sake and for her father's, for Sean Culhane walked a very
narrow line, keeping in with the English to curry favor
whilst he got information out of them.

I couldn't understand it at all when Margaret fairly spat
at us both then, cutting Jamie off in the middle of a word
and riding away without warning. That day she did not
come back, nor did we find her waiting for us anywhere.
Kevin apologized, for he saw that Jamie was really angry.

"You know Margaret, Jamie," Kevin said, but Jamie
was having none of it.

"Margaret can't go through the rest of her life with
somebody trailing after her saying to everyone she scorns
and insults, 'Oh, well, you know Margaret!' " he declared.

Kevin sighed. "We Culhanes are a hard lot, I suppose,"

he said slowly. "There is not much love lost between our father and us, that's no secret. And Margaret is ashamed of his playing up to the English—"

"He takes terrible chances to help our cause. Everybody understands that, it's just his work, and no one else around here could do the same job. Why doesn't *she* understand?" insisted Jamie.

Kevin seemed about to say something and then changed his mind and murmured instead, "She will not have him defended."

Jamie was stubborn. "I only know your father as a soldier in our Army—no, now, Kevin, don't stop me. I'm not saying I like your father. He's—he's not easy to get to know, but what's that? He's an Irishman serving his country, and whether he beats his wife or hates his kids is no business of mine!" He said this in great heat, but still was surprised and upset to see a flush of anger on Kevin's pale face, and Kevin stood up abruptly.

"Margaret and I happen to be those 'kids' he hates, and that makes a difference to *us*," he said coldly.

I could see Jamie was ashamed of his hasty words. "Kevin," he said, "I'm sorry, I really am. I don't know, your sister—your sister has a way of making me lose my temper. I don't know how she does it, or why I always let her, but I'm sorry you're the one who's had to pay for it today." He held out his hand to Kevin, whose face relaxed at once, and he grasped Jamie's hand with both of his own.

"Let's forget the whole thing now and not speak of it again, do you agree?"

Of course we agreed. It was the only bone of contention between us ever, and therefore it was good that we never used it against each other.

Chapter VI

Then—Easter. The Sunday of it came quietly enough, but the only rising up that was done in that year of 1916 was on the Monday. Two thousand desperate men, led by Padraic Pearse, came out into the streets of Dublin and, for six days, almost made Ireland a free country. They seized the Post Office, and it was from the steps of that building that Pearse read aloud his proclamation of liberty. He knew, as did the other leaders, that they would not succeed, not that day, not yet. But Ireland needed an awakening to the struggle that was going on afresh; her people needed to learn that the time had come, the Army was preparing, the battle was just beginning.

Pearse said, "Irishmen and Irishwomen, in the name of God and dead generations from which she receives her old tradition of nationhood, Ireland, through us, summons her children to her flag and strikes for her freedom. We declare the right of the people of Ireland to the ownership of Ireland and to the unfettered control of Irish destiny. . . ."

Within a month, Pearse and his friends were shot to death inside Kilmainham Prison. But what they started sprang into life all over our land.

We in Dunknealy did not know what was planned for Eastertime. Rumors had reached us from the north that something was to happen. But we were not involved in it. We had been waiting and hoping for a long time for that one great blow that would catch England off guard. Men I knew had argued bitterly, urging that more be done than we were doing. Dozens of schemes and plans were sent up to the leadership in Dublin. Now many of the leaders were

dead, and others in hiding. De Valera, thank God, escaped
the firing squad and eventually got to America, where he
raised money and support for our cause.

For six days, Jamie and I and our friends prayed and
prepared for our own rising, grabbing at every stray rumor
we could get as the business in Dublin went on. And when
it failed, we were bitter and said we should have taken our
guns and gone to help them. With horror we read in the
newspapers of the reprisals all over Ireland. Eight hundred
wounded. Nearly four hundred killed, including twenty
children. Many, fleeing from burning houses, were shot in
the streets. Thousands were rounded up and held prisoner
in theaters, churches, schools, whatever would hold them.
The Lord Mayor of Cork was thrown into jail for his
support of the rebellion and starved to death on hunger
strike. The prisons in England were soon overflowing with
yet another generation of Irish prisoners—but those very
prisons proved to be the training ground of men and
officers who, in a few short years, would return and take
command of the new Army, and prove at last to England
that Ireland must and would be satisfied.

Some of the leaders in Dublin were not found, but were
able to get away clean. One such was Brian Cavenaugh,
shot the third day of the rising, and spirited off to the west
by some friends. Posters went up and a price to match his
handsome head, with the flaming red hair and deep-set
dark eyes, but no one heard of him. Weeks passed. Every
town and village was searched, and searched again. Many
believed Cavenaugh was dead.

Yet he was not. When the wound was fairly well
healed, about the beginning of June, it was decided that he
should be smuggled out of Ireland, into France. Arrangements had to be made. Meanwhile, Cavenaugh was a
danger to those who sheltered him. He was moved, many
times, always working farther south, farther east. And
even with the roads blocked and the patrols out round the
clock, what was necessary was done.

And so it was that, late one stormy night, a band of
tinkers wound their bedraggled way up the *boreen* to
Martin Daley's farm. No light was lit in the house, yet a

door opened and a voice spoke to them, and it past eleven, with the lightning clawing brightly across the black sky.

There were only five wagons of them, and they pulled up about the barn. Inside 'twas warm and dry, and for once the horses had a good feed and a sleep under a roof, whilst the people dried off and helped themselves, as was their custom, to a few chickens and whatever else might be waiting for them to throw an eye to.

Next morning, late and leisurely, around ten, they left again, their pack of dogs barking down the road ahead, and anyone who happened to see them thought only it might be a good idea to stop back home and lock things up securely. For the tinkers were a merry lot who took the words of Christ quite seriously: they did not sow, neither did they reap, but they lived damned well all the same, taking a bit here and a bit there from those that did! They made a fairly good living by way of agricultural blackmail: that is, any farmer who did not want the ground under his feet and the sky over his head stolen in front of his eyes was wise enough to turn his back on the pilfering of a stray pig or chicken, a bag of potatoes or what have you, and be thankful when the tinkers had passed on their way.

But that night, one of them did not pass along with the others. One of them was taken into the darkened house and remained behind.

Later that afternoon, when Jamie went in from the plowing and stood in the barn mending a piece of harness, Martin came to him quietly and touched his arm. And there was a look on Martin Daley's face that Jamie had never seen before.

"When you're finished with that job of work, come to my study, lad," said Martin, oddly low and urgent. Jamie nodded, surprised, for that was where he usually went after finishing up, and Martin knew it. But now, suddenly, Martin gripped his arm tightly and added, "There's that to show you inside which does not bear speaking of."

A few moments later, Jamie went up to the house and into the parlor, where the entrance to his father's study was. I haven't told you of that study before, with its secret door that looked like a tall bookcase. All the long years that Martin had used it, the door had stood wide open, and the bookcase had been used for storing odd pieces of china and glassware.

But that June day, as Jamie headed for the little room, he stopped abruptly and stared. The door was shut, and the bookcase filled from ceiling to floor with his father's books from the study. No one who did not know about the secret room would ever have thought it existed. No ray of light, no sound, no tiniest crack in the frame betrayed the fact of its existence. And, behind him, almost soundless herself, Aunt Ellen, with an awful look of womanly forced calm masking great fear and dread, tiptoed about her own cheerful house as if the dead were lying in state in the kitchen.

"Go on, Jamie," was all she said, and Jamie was dismayed to see her own gray eyes dart quickly to the windows, then back to his once more. Without a word, he pulled the bookcase aside carefully, and stooping down under low lintel arch, he entered that room he knew so well.

Inside, all was different. One wall of the books was gone, doing sentry duty on the outside. A small oil lamp, trimmed low, burned on the little desk, which was now pushed over against the wall. There was a low cot with bedclothes on it, and there sat a man, talking animatedly to Martin Daley. At the sound of Jamie entering, softly as he trod, the man on the cot sprang wildly to his feet, a pistol Jamie hadn't noticed pointing straight at his heart. But Martin reached over and pushed the man's arm down quickly.

"It's only my son, Jamie," he said softly. "Nothing to fear here, I told you that."

Jamie was wide-eyed, you may imagine, and hesitated to come any farther, till his father impatiently told him to close the bookcase door again quickly, and be quiet.

"He's a great, clumping clod of fifteen, to be sure, but will you do him the honor of shaking his hand?" asked Martin, whilst Jamie stared and stared. The strange man pulled himself together, gave a short, embarrassed little laugh, and stood again, reaching out his hand toward Jamie, who just managed to remember his manners and shake it. It was a good warm, hard hand, a man's hand, Jamie recalled many years later; he never forgot a look or a line of that man's face, nor the strong, firm clasp of his hand.

"Jamie, this man is Red Rory," said Martin, smiling faintly. "That's what we'll call him, although it's not his name. He'll be our guest for a short time—"

"What have you done?" asked Jamie quickly, eyeing the fellow coolly, and yet, at the same time, thrilled to be thrust into the thing at last.

"Red Rory" shot an approving look over at Martin. "He's no fool, Daley," he said, and then he turned back to Jamie.

"I've been to Dublin recently," he said quietly. "And they hated to see me go so soon, for many of my friends cannot get away, it seems."

"The tinkers brought him in last night, bless their black Irish hearts," sighed Martin. "Seven weeks in the bringing, hiding him in their wagons, handing him over from one band to the other all the way from Galway. It's a miracle he's here at all. We're to keep him safe with us, till they bring word of a ship from France. We'll get him from here to the sea, and a boat will be waiting by Helvick Head."

Jamie whistled between his teeth, but only nodded. Then the three of them sat down together in the cramped little room. Jamie soon got used to the shadows, and saw that their guest with the bright head of red hair was terribly thin and pale, that his hands shook and he controlled them only with great effort, an effort that brought beads of sweat to his white forehead.

Martin had just brought him in a bite of supper, which he picked at with little enough appetite, his eyes, large and darkly shadowed, ranging about the small space and back again, always coming to rest on Jamie. Then he would smile, a small ghosteen of a smile fleeting about his thin, trembling mouth, then disappearing again.

"It's small," he murmured several times, with a shiver,

and Martin would clasp him on the shoulder and beg him to be patient only a while more and the world would resume its normal size. Finally the pretense of eating could not be continued any longer, and Red Rory settled back, exhausted, on the low cot. Martin covered him like a baby, speaking softly, and several times stopped to wipe the sweat from his face with a cloth. Through all of this, Jamie sat and wondered and said nothing.

Then his father motioned him to come away. The stranger lay sleeping at last, uneasily starting and tossing about. They took the supper tray with them and left the lamp burning, for, it seemed, he could not bear the dark, for reasons which Martin would soon enough explain.

They sat down to their own meal in the kitchen and Martin said, "Do you see that man in there, Jamie, lad? He's our responsibility. If anything should ever happen to me—" he ignored the great gasp from Aunt Ellen—"I repeat, my son, if aught should harm me or keep me from preserving him, then I charge you now to do the job for me. See that he is saved and tell no one in all this world that you have heard of him or know where he is."

Jamie gave his word, of course, and kept it truly, for it was not until many weeks afterwards that I heard about it.

Days went by. The work on the farm went on as usual. Kathleen and little Janet played about the door of an evening before supper was ready. And, children being so ready to accept any new order of things pretty readily, the little girls had long since stopped watching their mother knock on the parlor bookcase and hand in a tray of food three times a day.

Martin tried to stay close to the house when he could, but he had the spring planting to get done. In the evenings, the usual tasks of mending harnesses and sharpening tools and such were carried on as always, with Martin and Jamie and sometimes even Will sitting on a bench outside the house in the cool shade, mending and smoking an occasional pipe and chatting with whoever might happen by.

I wondered why Jamie wanted to stay so close to home those days. I came by for him more than once, but he made much of the spring work, and when I would have stayed to talk about our training in the hills and when we would be getting some guns from America, he put me off a bit, and then he apologized and asked me to do him a favor and tell Margaret and Kevin he was busy and would not be out riding for a while.

This upset Margaret terribly—she knew he was still put out with her about that quarrel he'd almost had with Kevin. With all the turmoil about Easter and after it, they had never really gotten around to smoothing it over. Now, Margaret felt, Jamie was deliberately avoiding her, so of course she got angry at him and told me to tell him she was too busy to go out riding, anyway. I conveyed this new message faithfully, and wondered why Jamie neither laughed nor got annoyed, but hardly seemed to hear me as I spoke, and forgot to say goodbye when I rode home again.

Well, and the weeks went by that Cavenaugh was kept hidden in Martin's study, and still there was no word of his going. He had been traced as far as Waterford; no more than that was yet known by the English. But if he could be traced this far, it was only a question of time till they had him pinned like a bug on a board.

Finally, a meeting was held and the matter was discussed, and that was the first I heard of it all. Jamie was much relieved that night, for at last he could talk about it to someone. My father begged Martin to contact the tinkers again and send the man on elsewhere. There were others, in other towns, who might have taken the risk. But Martin would not listen, no matter how they all argued with him. He had pledged Cavenaugh his word, and was operating under orders from Dublin, anyway. Besides, as he pointed out, whoever was to come for him would come to Daley's; the boat would anchor just outside the harbor. It was too late to go changing everything about.

But the thing of it was, none of us could stand much of a search if it came to the house-by-house. There wasn't a house, nay, not so much as a wee cot in all Dunknealy that didn't have its guns, and guns were not allowed the Irish. The local leaders went about growing grimmer every day. Taking no chances, they called off all further meetings till the thing was done.

The town was quieter than a wake. In fact, the very quietness of it was alarming. We had a large police barracks in our midst, and the police were growing nervous at all the unaccustomed peace they were suddenly getting.

In view of this, to keep up appearances, you might say, Jamie and I and a few of the other lads tried to organize a respectable-looking raid on the barracks; there must have been fifteen or twenty of us, but all we did was break some windows with our rock-throwing. The boyos came running, cursing and waving their sticks at us, and most of the lads fled away. I hit one of them with a grand mudball right in the nose, but when they saw us scrambling away up the hillside, didn't the bastards stop in their tracks and stand there laughing at us! They didn't even do us the courtesy of a chase, and then there wasn't one of us, even Jamie, who didn't get a good tongue-lashing at home when it was heard.

"Christ in heaven," were my own father's words, "aren't things bad enough that you have to go and stir up the pot to a froth?"

Our little raid did accomplish one thing, however: it gave everyone something to talk about and it did relieve the growing suspicions of the police. Luckily enough, the very next day a man passing through selling brooms brought a message to Martin Daley and his guest, and the gist of the message was that they were to be ready a week Thursday, about midnight, and have themselves down by Helvick Head Cove, with a lantern lit. There a boat would row in, a signal be exchanged, and Cavenaugh would be on his way to France at last.

It had been four weeks since he came to Dunknealy, but that last week seemed like all four put together again and then some. The waiting was incredible slow, and everyone's nerves were wound up tight.

At last the day of it came. Jamie had promised me I could go with them and see the ship as it lay at anchor. I rushed through my jobs all that Thursday, my heart in a high state of excitement. But when I came in from the fields for supper, my father forbade me to leave the house again that night.

"But Jamie said I might go with them!" I stammered.

My father shook his head. "Not a step out of this house tonight, Gerald," he insisted. "There's enough in it now. The smaller the party, the less chance of discovery."

I was unconvinced.

"Don't you see, it's not yourself I'm thinking of at all," he explained patiently. "It's them."

When he put it that way, what could I do but promise, and it was done sulkily enough, to be sure. I moped about after supper, wishing I could be with them, wishing it was our house and my own father that had the honor. Then I would be the one to see it all and do something grand for Ireland. Oh, I was worked up into a great fit of woe by the time we'd got the cows bedded down for the night. I went upstairs without a word to a soul, and tried to read a book. I must have fallen asleep there, lying across my bed, with my chin on the book and a very warm fire blazing up in the hearth.

I don't know what woke me. It was dark, and the moon was up high overhead when I rubbed my eyes and looked out the window, very confused. The house was still. I figured my parents were long asleep, and there was I, crumpled and musty-feeling, still dressed, with a hole in the pit of my stomach a roasted Leviathan could hardly fill. I decided to sneak downstairs and find what I could to eat. I had no idea of the time, save that it was past midnight, from the moon's position in the heavens. Midnight! Suddenly I remembered it all, and the bitterness swept through me again. Sure and it would be all over by now.

When I got downstairs, I was surprised to find the kitchen fire still bright and full, with fresh peat laid on. There were tea mugs still on the table, and the door was not latched, but open, and swinging a little in the night breeze, creaking a bit back and forth. That was not like my mother, to leave a fresh fire burning in the middle of the night and the door open and dishes not washed and put away. Something was wrong, or not *wrong* maybe, but different.

I stared stupidly about me for a moment, latched up the door myself, and then, on an impulse, crept quietly up the stairs again to my parents' bedroom. I knocked softly on their door. There was no answer. I knocked louder and still no answer. Finally, feeling like a silly kid again, with the nightmare or the toothache, I opened the door a bit and looked inside, calling.

"Ma? Ma, wake up, it's me." But she did not answer me.

I opened the door wide. They were not there! And the clock on the wall said close to one o'clock! Where could they be? I thought to myself, with some resentment, that they had gone out to help the Daleys, leaving me home asleep and safe in my bed. God love parents, but a boy'll never thank them for keeping him safe, not till he's lived a few more years to enjoy it! I slammed their door shut, and took myself back downstairs once more, puzzled, and now a small claw of fear began working industriously on my stomach, for no reason, really, save that it was all strange, and hadn't happened before, and it fell in together with that night and what I knew was to happen.

I looked longingly at the door. Three or four times I got up and opened it and almost went out. But then I'd remember what my father had said, and I'd sit down again at the table, wondering what to do. My appetite was long since gone, the very thing that had brought me downstairs in the first place, but I thought a drop of tea would be just the thing. I went to wash out the teapot, which was also on the table, with the mugs, and it was hot, burning hot! They'd been here, up and awake, not more than half an hour before, if that much.

Well, and that did it. Thrashing be damned, a man's got so many thrashings he must get in his life anyway! I opened the door and went out, uncertainly, but determined to find them and learn what had happened. Half of me was set on making a beeline for the beach, but I thought of English patrols and searchlights and what would I say if they picked me up? That my parents were missing in the middle of the night and I out for a stroll to locate them? No, it was much too risky.

Of course, my feet knew where I was going long before the message reached my head, and I found myself running over the back fields to Jamie's house. Oh, I don't know, maybe it had all come out well, and they were all together, sitting around celebrating. That was the idea I now fixed firmly in my mind, and it eased me, by fits and starts, as I traveled quickly through the familiar fields in the moonlight. That was it, of course, sure, maybe the whole Fenian brotherhood was over at Jamie's this very minute, telling of the boat and the men who came for Cavenaugh and the great ship outside Dungarvan Bay, and I left home like a baby, safe and snug in its bed!

But it was not that way. As I approached the house, I heard loud noise and the sounds of a crowd of people shouting and jeering, harsh, angry voices they were, and I saw many lights around the house. I ran in earnest now, turning in a long swath which brought me up around the front of the house, just across the road from it.

I almost cried out at what I saw then, but stopped myself just in time, for rearing up with a sharp whinny right before me in the dark was a big, tall horse. I'd startled him, and several others nearby, tied up together, horses with saddles on them. And, as I lay there with my face now pressed chin-down in the dirt, I saw a score, nay, two score people, my mother and my father in among them, neighbors from nearby, milling about, and pushing in together, only to be pushed out again by English soldiers with rifles. There was a large lorry backed up in the roadway, and a great searchlight trained on the Daley house.

I crept up as close as I dared, my heart in my mouth, watching closely. I saw Jamie's mother, with the two little girls, leaning against the fence in front of the house, and my mother with her arms about them, and both sisters weeping. Next to them stood Jamie, pale-faced, his eyes staring about him like a trapped animal. He seemed to be in an odd position, but then I saw him pull his arms in a strange way and I realized sickly that he was tied to the fence and struggling hard to get free. I looked about for Will, but he was not to be seen, off somewhere drinking or abed with some girl, I thought, how like him not to be there now!

There was an English sergeant standing in the yard, with his holster unbuttoned. He had the weapon in his hand, pointed at the people, and they calling him vile names. But the man was cool, aye, the kind who wouldn't speak a word when a bullet might utter the same message faster and harder. He motioned to his men to push the crowd back away from Aunt Ellen, and I saw a soldier pull my mother back, though she clung to Aunt Ellen and slapped at him in fury. But my aunt said something to her, and she, shaking her head, walked away backward, never taking her eyes from her sister and the little girls, who stood hugging their mother's skirts and hiding their faces from the soldiers.

As the people reluctantly moved back, I was at last able to see the front door clearly. There stood my Uncle Martin and—oh God help us but he had never made it to Helvick Head at all, poor hunted creature—next to him, tall and white-faced but straight-backed and proud, stood Brian Cavenaugh, "Red Rory" no more. The two men's hands were tied behind them, and two soldiers pointed rifles straight at their hearts all the while. Well, and it was all up now. I lay there, whilst the sergeant spoke. I could not hear his words, and my mind fluttered from one desperate plan of action to another, and all to no avail. What could I do? What help could I fetch? Five miles into Dunknealy on foot I could go—and even if I was able to muster our small troop, without proper arms, heavily outnumbered, how could they stop what was going on? No, there was nothing to do but stay hidden and watch it all.

Suddenly the sergeant gave a wave of his hand, and the soldiers guarding my uncle and Cavenaugh poked them hard with the rifles. They started to walk. I thought they were taking them to the lorry and then to the barracks in town, and I watched in anger as the crowd readily made a path for them to pass through. Then my Aunt Ellen began to scream and she reached out her arms toward Martin. Jamie was pulling desperately on the ropes that held him fast, until a soldier knocked him in the side of the head with his gun butt and I saw him fall, not six feet from where his father passed. He fell awkwardly, sideways slipping to the ground, a great bleeding gash on his head. But he struggled to stand again, and this time no one stopped him.

Where were they going, I wondered, as the group, instead of coming to the front path where the lorry stood, walked to the side of the yard, to the big oak tree, the one that shaded the parlor in summertime. And still my Aunt Ellen's voice rang out with shrieking and calling upon God.

"Jesus, Jesus, Jesus, don't let them do it! Don't let them do it!" she called, her voice so loud and so awful it seemed to come from the moon, down straight out of the heavens in a terrible, straining, broken, rough roar. She pushed the girls from her and ran the few feet to Martin, throwing herself upon him, her hands beating on his chest, and Martin didn't move at all, but tried to smile at her. They pulled her away from him roughly, though she fought against them with all her strength, but at her heaviest Aunt Ellen never weighed more than ninety pounds, and they soon had dragged her back to the fence and stood there between her and her husband. My mother broke away from the crowd again and came to her. This time no one tried to push her back.

And then, even as I was puzzling over just what was going to happen next, they hanged them. Even as I saw them stand just under the oak tree, even as I saw the ropes go up, even as I watched them knot the nooses and slip them over the two men's head, I didn't really believe what was happening. Aunt Ellen never stopped screaming for one second. Now all she cried, over and over, was "Martin, Martin, Martin!" and little Kathleen and Janet were crying, staring over at the tree and at their Da with frightened, unknowing eyes, staring curiously at the ropes. Jamie, never moving now, stood like a stone, and he stared, too.

I saw the ropes go on their necks, I say, and I saw the long ends dangling down behind the tree, a soldier holding each of them. I saw the sergeant glare about, warning the people to stay where they were. Then, in an instant, he gave a signal, and the ropes were pulled hard over the branches.

The crowd uttered one great cry of horror, then fell deathly silent as they saw Martin Daley and Brian Cavenaugh hang, their feet thrashing and whirling about as if trying to find footing in the very air itself . . . I knew no more.

For the world whirled around me; with a roaring rush all that I had eaten that day came up into my throat and I vomited it out there in the darkness, sobbing, not caring anymore who heard me, my throat on fire, my eyes and nose running. I heard many noises then, but I would not look up. Not for all the world would I look at that awful tree again. I heard the lorry's motor start up and I heard it move off. I heard the soldiers riding out, the steady, quick clopping of their horses' hoofs gradually disappearing down the road, and still I wept and choked and beat my two fists against the earth beneath me.

The night was full of sounds, all sound to me, for I would see nothing. I had seen too much for me already. But, though my eyes were tightly closed, burning and scalding with hot tears from the world I knew suddenly abandoning me, though I could not and would not see any of this anymore, yet I could hear it, oh, Christ yes, I could hear it all!

It was like one of those terrible modern symphonies, not one sound in it made to blend or harmonize with another, but all sounds separately grinding themselves out against one another. My aunt screaming, rising and falling screams with her breath, as if screaming had replaced breathing at last, being the more natural condition of human life. There she stood and screamed, and beneath that, the smaller sobbing of the two girls. Old women and, aye, many a man too, keening in the background. Prayers here and there, the name of Jesus, like a magic talisman, punctuating the drone of the rest. And, underneath it all, for rhythm, the ceaseless, endless creaking, creaking, creaking of the oak tree branches, as the bodies swung to and fro in slowly smaller circles. Above it, sharply, a shrill wind from the sea swept round and about, scolding, as it tore itself ragged upon the trees and the housetops. And death sat looking on, watching this celebration of himself, this grim Mass of defeat.

I lay there sick in my own vomit, wretched, cold and terrified, a small child once more and left out of all of it, with no place to comfort him in all that violent ritual of death, alone out there with the manure of the English horses still steaming and stinking about him. My mind was tired, exhausted of horror; I could no longer consciously sort out the sounds and their brutal meanings. I allowed the whole thing to flood at once through me. The flood was too much. I was swept away by it, and I fainted.

The moon was down, the sky sullen black, and no star shone when I at last awoke. The silence about me was even more terrifying than the sounds had been, but somehow I realized that I had not died myself. There was a second of quick-fading anger at the thought that I had, for none of this seemed like heaven to me, and I was only sixteen and had not yet been bad enough for hell.

I stood up. No, I was not dead. I was in the field across from Jamie's house. All was the same as I remembered it. But all the people were gone, the lights gone, the soldiers, horses, lorry, neighbors, ah, how very long I waited before I finally forced myself to direct my eyes toward the great oak tree by the house! How slowly my eyes focused, the last image they had seen still burned on the retina, the image of those two quivering bodies, no longer human, not yet divine, hovering between life and eternity exactly as they hovered between air and ground.

They had been cut down. The rope ends hung there still, limp, their business accomplished, no more to anticipate, the end of them had come as they had brought off the end of the two men, for I could not imagine any Monday wash ever hung upon those two gray deadly things.

I could make out no light inside the house, but still I made my way stiffly and slowly across the fence, the road, the yard, now unable to keep my eyes away from the tree. Though they saw what there was to see, yet my mind persisted in presenting me another picture, like a puzzle piece, an overlay, and my Uncle Martin and Cavenaugh hung there still, aye, and they do to this day, when I think of that poor innocent tree, another of God's lovely things used for man's wicked purposes.

"Jamie," I called in a shaky voice. "Jamie?"

No answer. I grew afraid. "Jamie, it's me, Jerry. Where are you?" a bit louder; still nothing.

I was weaker than I had thought. My legs could barely hold me up as I came to the door and found it slightly ajar. No smallest beam of light shone through it. Inside all seemed as full of death's dark spell as the land outside. I pushed the door timidly. It opened. I slipped inside the dark hallway.

"Jamie!" I called to him once more, and then I ran the length of that shadowy hall, crying forlornly, "Jamie, Jamie, are you dead, too?"

But I stopped, hearing a sound ahead of me, low voices evenly together in prayer. I tiptoed into the room, the parlor it was, and looked about me.

There were the two men of my nightmare, laid side by side, Martin on the dining table, his guest nearby on the low cot from the study. The bookcase door was smashed apart, the books lying all over the room. White sheets had been placed over the two bodies, but the faces were still not covered.

Around them, by the light of one small lamp, were arrayed the wan, stunned faces of the family and some friends, like a circle of white moons hung in the darkness of the sky. Their lips barely moved as they murmured the prayers for the dead. I don't know how long I stood there, but suddenly my mother glanced up. Her eyes widened as she looked at me, taking in my filthy, crumpled condition, and I saw new tears spring into them. Without a word to anyone, she came gliding silently toward me, drawing me gently out into the hall again.

"You saw it, lad?" she asked me, her hand resting very heavily on my head, whether to comfort me or gather strength for herself I cannot say. I wanted to go to her arms, to hide my face against her as Kathleen and Janet had against Aunt Ellen, but something made me stand quiet still and upright.

"Yes, I was over the road," I answered her.

She sighed and kissed me on the forehead. "Your father's gone for the priest," she explained. "Will you come in and pray with us?"

I didn't want to, but of course I said yes. We were about to go in together, when suddenly she shook her head.

"No," she said. "There's something else you can do."

"Jamie!" I whispered. She nodded.

"The poor boy is in a dreadful condition," she said sorrowfully. But I felt like shouting. He was alive, then! To hell with however dreadful his condition was, a condition of any kind in life was better than the one awful, final condition of death!

"Where is he?"

"Where do you think? In the study, in there all these two hours past, and will not come out, nor say one small prayer, and Martin's poor murdered body not ten feet away in the next room. Go to him, Jerry, and bring him out to his mother. Bring him out of there before the priest gets here."

I agreed at once, and yet I looked at my mother oddly at that moment, for, in spite of all the horrors of that dark night, I wondered that she could still worry about the impression any of us made on the priest. But on such triviality is civilization built, and I was not there to argue the point.

I stopped to kneel by the side of the dead and whisper a short prayer, my eyes fixed not on them at all, but on Aunt Ellen's face. She had aged in those short hours. She was old. She was an old woman, like a tree branch chopped off from its trunk and roots. She was dried up; her face that had so many, many lively expressions was drained numb and blank of them all.

I said "Amen" rather too loudly, and then went quietly to the bookcase door in front of the little secret room. I pulled away what was left of the chopped-in shelves, but it was soul-dark inside. I could see nothing. There was no window, if you recall. I pulled the wrecked door closed behind me as best I could, and stood there uncertainly, wondering where Jamie was and what I would say to him.

Then I heard weeping, harsh sobs, such as you hear from a man crying in pain and sorrow and rage altogether, and I knew I had found Jamie. There seemed nothing else to do but wait and be there with him, so I slid down next to him on the floor, leaning my head back against the doorway.

The crying soon stopped. "Jerry, is it you, then?"

"It's me," I answered. "Are you all right?"

I heard him laugh, a short, jagged, bitter sound it was. It was his answer. And so we sat in the dark, the two of us, not talking. And then I remembered what my mother had sent me there to do. I honestly did not think he'd come out and, knowing Jamie, I really did not think the priest's coming would do it.

"Are they still praying over them in there?" He did not whisper but spoke aloud, and the sound of his voice made me jump.

"Yes. They're waiting for the priest now," I answered, wishing he'd keep his voice down. But once again I heard him laugh that awful laugh and I shuddered.

"Where's my brother?" he asked suddenly.

"What?" For a moment I didn't understand. "Oh, Will. I don't know. He hasn't been back?"

A long pause. "No. Not since morning. He took a pound from the box in the kitchen and we haven't seen him since."

It was taking me ages to grasp his meaning. His voice was so awfully flat and hard.

"Well, you know Will," I answered rather lamely. Usually that was all anyone had to say. Everyone did indeed know Will, and anything else went without saying.

"I wonder," breathed Jamie. "Were you there?"

"Yes."

"You saw?"

"Yes."

He said nothing for a little while. Then I heard sounds

where he was. He got up and moved about. Then he lit a match and turned on the little lamp on the desk.

The sight of him shocked me. I went cold all over. He was blood from head to stomach. His clothes were crusted with it, dried and half-dried together, red and brownish. There was a great open cut on the side of his head, and his hair was flattened down on that side with it. His face was filthy and streaked, with dried tears and blood mixed. His eyes were shadows and stared fixedly, yet he didn't seem to be looking at anything.

"Jamie—!"

"Don't say it!" he cried, holding up his hand as if to keep off a blow. "Don't say anything about it!"

I could not even go to him as I wanted. I think the smallest touch of a loving or a friendly hand would have disintegrated him on the spot. What held him together I cannot say, but it wasn't much. So I simply sat there on the floor, hearing the low murmuring of the endless praying outside, and footsteps back and forth, new people coming in quietly, and I wished something would happen. Jamie stood unmoving, his eyes fixed on the books. He paid not the slightest heed to the prayers going on.

And myself, now, I was beginning to wonder about things. The first horror was wearing off, and one or two very cold questions began to creep into my mind. I longed to put voice to them but didn't dare. Yet Jamie must know what had happened.

As if he read my mind he said to me, "Someone informed, you know."

"Oh, God." I said it without surprise, only surprised at myself for the knowing weariness of my own voice. And yet, what else could it have been? The secret had been stretched out too long. The time for successful action had passed weeks earlier, we had all sensed that.

And then, in a flash, I saw what was in his mind. He thought Will had done it! No, not Will, I knew it for several good reasons having nothing to do with decency or nobility. Just, not Will because he wasn't the type. He wasn't bad enough, he wasn't evil, no, not even for money, for Will had enough for his drinks and his girls, always enough on hand to keep him going.

"It wasn't Will, whoever it was," I said.

He raised his doubting eyebrow.

"He likes to talk big, brag. When he's in a pub and had enough to make him important, he can say anything," said Jamie, a terrible ache in his voice.

I thought about it. I'd seen Will drunk many a time, and him always boasting how the girls loved him and what a big man he was. No, I was still convinced.

"No, it was not Will. You'll find the man and it won't be him, Jamie."

He nodded, but I couldn't tell whether he believed me or not. "We'll see," he said. "Well, then, but it was *someone,* wasn't it?"

"Who?"

"I don't know," he sighed, absent-mindedly picking out an odd book, riffling the pages, replacing it, taking another. "But I will know," he added, his voice growing hard again. I felt a huge knot tightening in the pit of my stomach.

The voices droned on in the parlor.

"Listen to them," said Jamie. "Praying after the deed's been done. Isn't that a fine piece of Irish irony for you, now?"

"Jamie, your mother needs you," I said. "Ma asked me to bring you out, before the priest gets here."

His head whipped around, his gray eyes dark as storm clouds.

"And what would I be wanting out there?" he snapped.

"Jamie," I began, "your father's—"

"My father's in here, right in here, with you and me, and his books, like he always is!" He shouted it so loudly there was a pause in the parlor.

"This is the place he loved to be," said Jamie, at last allowing the feeling of it to come in. "Here with his books and all that knowledge, all that goodness and wisdom. He was a good man, Jerry. He was a damned good, good man!" And he broke down completely, sinking on his long knees to the floor slowly, his hand clutching at one of the books, I know not which, as he went. And then he cried, in a way I had never heard him before, no, not even when I had first come in there. He was wracked and torn and crushed with crying; he moaned and clutched the book to his heart with both hands, as he would have clutched his father. And I, his cousin and his friend, more than a brother but so much less, alas, than a father, I could only sit by his side, the two of us together, patting his shoulder and saying, "Ah, no, no, Jamie, no, no. It's all right, Jamie, it's all right, don't cry, now, don't."

"It's not all right. It'll never be all right!" he groaned, rocking back and forth in agony. At that moment I heard horses pull up outside, new voices, the hall door opening and footsteps coming quickly into the parlor.

"It must be the priest," I whispered to him. "Jamie, come on outside with me and let's say a prayer together."

With a look of contempt, he flung the book as far as he could against the wall, so all inside could hear it.

"Prayer!" he cried. "There's blood on this house and two dead men betrayed, and all they can think to do is pray! I'll not pray again, no, never, till I find the man who informed. I swear before Heaven, Jerry, I swear it, I'll find him someday and I'll kill him. Then I can pray again, if anyone at all is listening. And maybe I'll pray for forgiveness and maybe I'll pray for my father's soul and my own, but, by God, before I do that, I'll kill him!"

"Jamie!" I tried to stop him, but he brushed me aside and pushed open the bookcase door.

I had a glimpse of all the shocked white faces, turned to look at him, the priest in the midst of his appointed work, looking up, too, at the bloody apparition emerging from the wall of the room. I noticed that Sean Culhane had come in, too, and there were Margaret and Kevin behind him, both staring grief-stricken at Jamie. But he seemed not to see anyone.

"Oh, my God, we are heartily sorry for having offended thee!" cried Jamie with mockery in his voice, and he pushed his way past all the people and gathered his father's poor body up in his arms. "What offense? What offense has he done? Stop praying for my father! Pray for the man who betrayed him. He needs your prayers, he's going to die. My father is in heaven this night—" He glared about wildly, and kissed Martin's cold brow, while Aunt Ellen moaned, shaking her head as he spoke. "And that poor man there along with him. Why are you wasting your time praying for the dead? They don't need it; they don't want it. Pray for the living, pray for all the poor goddamned ones of us still with a piece yet to go!"

With one last, fond, savage kiss, Jamie gently put Martin's head back on the table and flung himself from the room, lurching drunkenly down the hall, with me after him and Margaret beside me.

"Go after him, he's half crazy! No telling what he'll do," cried out Sean.

Jamie flung open the door and ran out down the front steps. I couldn't see which way he was going. I stood there trying to hear him, but there was no sound. Then, a moment later, from behind the house, I heard a horse's hoofbeats and, a second after, I saw Jamie galloping wildly toward the roadway.

"Jamie, come back!" I yelled after him, but he didn't even hear me. He jumped the horse clear over the fence, and disappeared along the moon's own low path toward the Blackwater River Road.

Margaret turned and went back inside, sobbing, but I had no comfort to give her. I stood alone, thinking that it was God's plan for me that night to be a spectator and little else, and my father came out and stood with me, his arm on my shoulder, the two of us looking up the empty road together.

"He'll ride till he drops," my father observed gently. "It's the best thing he could do. Then he'll sleep."

"And then he'll wake up and remember," I answered, my mind no longer on Jamie, for the instant, but on my father, and remembering how I'd wished so hard it was us that had Cavenaugh hiding in our house and my father in charge of it all. Then, I thought, it would be *my* father lying dead in our own back parlor at home, and *my* mother waiting for a touch of comfort from me.

"Oh, Da!" I cried brokenly, and I turned my face to his warm chest, where he held me as he had when I was very young, and I wept my heart out in an all-encompassing sorrow that took in each and all of us, then and in everything that was yet to come.

Chapter VII

Jamie rode that poor horse into a sweat that awful night, and himself into a worse one, before morning light found the two of them exhausted, down by Bearsey's Bridge and far from home. Then he let poor Dan rest and graze as he would, and himself lay down to sleep on the riverbank. 'Twas there I found him, late in the afternoon. I'd waited for him to return till noon was high in the sky and I could wait no more.

He wasn't the least bit surprised to see me riding up. I was wondering if he could be spoken to at all yet, but he put my mind at ease at once. He stood up, and I could see he had washed himself clean, and he called out to me, "Did you bring something to eat!"

I slid off the horse, shaking my head. I'd never even thought of food, 'tis always so when your own belly's full, isn't it?

"I'm glad to see you're hungry."

He was looking about for Dan, finally spotting him twenty yards away, staring off into the sky as horses do. Mine trotted over to have a word, and I sat down by Jamie's side, fiddling about in my pockets to see if there might be a bite of something to eat. I came up with a very old apple I'd been meaning to feed the horse and forgotten about for two or three weeks, but Jamie fell upon the shrively thing with good appetite.

I suppose I must have been staring pretty steadily at him without realizing it, for he caught my eye and smiled a little.

"Well, I'm still here," he commented wryly. Then I didn't know what to say.

"I'm all right now," he added. "I'll ride back home with you."

I was very relieved, for if he had been in the same spirits as the night before I wouldn't have been sure how to get him to come home.

"How's my mother?"

"Like you, she's a wonder. Very calm now. Lots to do."

He nodded. "Aye, there's enough."

"Will turned up around nine. Still drunk."

"Who told him?"

I shook my head. "No one. He was too drunk to understand. I put him to bed. Let him sleep it off, then we'll tell him in time for the wake."

Jamie's face became quite grave. "You know, Jerry," he said hesitantly, "I'm pretty sure, last night, somewhere in there, I said something—about him—"

"Whisht, now." I spoke quickly. "You said a lot of fool things last night, didn't you? And who's to blame you? I never took you seriously about Will. Poor Will." I felt very much ashamed, remembering what both of us had wondered about him. But now Jamie looked at me very coldly.

"The only fool thing I said last night was *that*," he said, his fighting eyebrow raised up high. "The rest of it, there was nothing foolish at all."

Well, the last thing I wanted to do was quarrel with him! "Jamie, Jamie, I know how you feel," I answered him. "About the—you know—the informer, but, well, you were pretty *spare* with the priest, you know, and I'm sure you shocked hell out of them there in the parlor."

"The hell with the priest and the rest of them too!" retorted Jamie, his eyes flashing. "It's not going to be a priest nor a bunch of people on their knees are going to find my father's murderer, is it, now? And from the looks of things, it isn't going to be the same will free this poor damned country from such things, is it? Is it, Jerry?"

I looked away for relief from those icy eyes of his. "No, I guess not," I said slowly.

Well, but then a small ghost of a smile crossed his face, and he leaned over and slapped me on the back.

"Then we'll have to do it ourselves, won't we?"

I sighed. It all sounded like an echo, and too familiar.

"That's what they've been saying these six hundred years, isn't it?" I suddenly felt bitter and utterly hopeless. "I guess it's about time we joined the long line of them."

Jamie got up stiffly and whistled for the horses. "This time it'll be different," he said. "They've never had you and me in it before, have they?"

Riordan and Culhane and the others did not wait for the funeral to begin asking their questions. An informer was amongst us, that was certain. Regardless of Jamie's own personal vows of vengeance, it was an Army matter and the Army intended to deal with it. But how? Who was the man? No stranger, and no known enemy. They never were. No, they were always our own, ours, neighbors you'd lived near all your life, friends, even relatives. They were all over, sprinkled in amongst us like grains of salt in a sugar bowl: you had to taste of them once before you knew to spit them out. Kill them as we might, and we killed many a one, the treachery went on. They did it for many reasons: for money, for power, for the easing of an English law upon themselves. Many informed out of hatreds that went back a thousand years, family hatred, clan hatred. Blood feuds that had never been settled. Most of these disputes had long since been put aside in the face of the common enemy, but some had not forgotten and could not forget.

"Root them out," Riordan had told us, "find them and kill them wherever they are, whoever they are!"

The informers dealt in terror and thus we dealt with them. Yet one for one, an eye for an eye, it never was, and that was a black pity indeed. For this crime, and for this crime alone, the death of the criminal did not suffice. It was as if a terrible inherited disease passed into a family, and down and down through the family and all its branches, from one generation to the next and the next. No one forgot the name of an informer, and it has been known that for five and six generations after the original deed people spat upon his descendants as they walked down a street. Indeed, there is a law now which protects the living descendants of such criminals by keeping all existing records secret documents which cannot be got at under any circumstances.

But, of course, in those days there was no such protection, and woe to the family of the betrayer!

Much was done by all of us, in those terrible days just after the hanging. Every man had to give account of himself and proof of his account. Every family within ten miles was visited and questioned. Every stray beggar and every tinker band was stopped. Pub owners were called out and made to remember what they might have heard said. Will Daley was questioned and questioned again, and every word he said was checked out. He didn't remember most of that night and with good reason, for, we discovered, he had passed out cold in the upstairs bedroom of a certain house, and three young ladies, with much scorn, swore that his snoring disturbed them the entire remainder of the night. He had not been talking with any English soldiers or anyone who had talked to English soldiers, and all he had mentioned at the bar itself was that he was planning to have his chest tattooed when the traveling Chinaman appeared in town again. So much for poor old Will.

Jamie asked no questions. Sean Culhane and my father spent a long evening with him, after Martin was buried, and they told him they had been able to find nothing, no clue whatsoever.

But Jamie said merely that he had not expected they would have any success, that he appreciated their efforts, but that he would see to "the matter" himself.

"Now, look here, James," bristled Sean Culhane, evidently not caring for Jamie's tone or his attitude, "we'll have none of this private revenge business. You're in the Army, and you'll act under orders and no other way."

Jamie's eyes narrowed, but, though he seemed about to speak, he said nothing.

Culhane softened his tone. "I knew Martin as well as any man of us, Jamie," he went on. "And I know he would not rest easy with you wasting your life trying to settle such a score. You've got your mother and sisters to take care of now, you know, and that big farm of yours."

Jamie nodded, then he said, "Oh, I won't be wasting my life, Mr. Culhane. If you and the others haven't been able to come up with anything, then I won't by myself. Not now. But he'll show himself, sooner or later. He'll talk again, and maybe again after that, and we'll find him out. That's all I want now."

And they had to be satisfied with that, for he would not say another word on the subject.

It was true, a hundred acres is a lot of farm without the man of the house around. Aunt Ellen tried to get Will to do his share, and Jamie, not wanting to hurt her, said nothing. But if the farm was to depend upon Will for its future, then there was no future to it. So, quietly, Jamie arranged to take on an extra man from town; there were enough, God knows, glad for the opportunity. The important thing was that the rents be paid every quarter, without fail.

So it was, with such practical matters to occupy our minds, we moved slowly through that strange year of 1916. Our lives were changed forever, but we didn't know that yet. We began to live as in a dream, knowing it was a dream yet surrendering ourselves to it, half out of lethargy, half out of curiosity. The countryside continued to be ripped apart like a miser's featherbed, and an untidy job of it they made, too, as the British lion still roared in fury over Easter Week, and kept on demanding that new conspirators be turned up. I don't know how many thousands were taken prisoner, or how many were sent over to England, but I do know that if all the men they sent to prison had indeed been involved in the uprising, it would have succeeded in the first place.

But, for Jamie and me, Easter had been a long time gone; Martin's death seemed as if it had happened years and years ago. We were part of what was coming, and the past was only a springboard from which we leaped into the fires ahead.

Ian Riordan knew his business and his business was killing, whatever kind of man he might be otherwise—and I knew him, for a fact, to be a very gentle man, a good and compassionate man, and a good friend. But God help any world when such a gentle, compassionate man becomes aroused to injustices, for *his* anger exceeds the anger of all others, and there is a kind of immovable, iron zeal in his obsession to restore balance and harmony. So it was with Ian Riordan. Not one of us who learned from him but came to respect and love him. He taught us coolly and objectively all the various methods of killing, whether it be one man quietly garroted from behind at a sentry outpost, or the mass attack on heavily defended barricades.

He taught us to use grenades, dynamite, gelignite, various kinds of hand weapons and rifles, and even machine guns, though there was little enough chance of us ever having the luck of finding one to use. He taught us discipline and self-control, more by placing those qualities always before us in himself than by anything he said or did on purpose. He was an excellent man in all ways, and the highest compliment I can pay him is that I never came to his training group but that I was yet again surprised such a man knew of such bloody things, and I never knew a man less anxious to use his deadly knowledge. In another life, another, more settled time, he would not have been a soldier, and *that* I hold against this mad-dog world of ours forever.

There was little activity in those months in Waterford, for the county was creeping with soldiers. It was not a good time for isolated raids and bombings and the trappings of revolution. We were too weak, too vulnerable, and most of us were too new and green to the life. And our Army could not take to the field of honor face to face with soldiers of the enemy, though that was what we longed above all else to do.

But our war was the worst and deadliest kind, a war of

time and patience, unnatural in every way. Outrages must be forced to lie quiet in our breasts until the air was clear again. So by day we worked the land and waited impatiently to be called to serve it another way. We listened eagerly to any rumor in the air; we longed for the war in Europe to be over and England beaten, yet we heard dreadful tales of the Germans and began to have doubts about them too.

Still our hearts thumped, in nervous fits and starts, for we knew we were to be a part of something truly different—and if you don't think that has the same bright, hard, wild appeal to the soul as any religion steeped in martyr's blood and flaming with heavenly outrage, then you've not been young and a man.

Yet, boys we were still, part asleep in the arms of our families, familiar work, old personal dreams and ignorance of what lay ahead, part awake to the new wind blowing. We waited with an impatience that felt like hot coals in our chests, and yet, paradoxically, we waited with a patience found only in nature, the patience of the wolf stalking his quarry, the bear silently watching the trout in a stream, patient as any creature that knows it cannot lose what it stalks—cannot lose it and survive.

And, tangled through all these raw new feelings, there spread through our beings, for a few short months, a strange, soft unreality that seemed more akin to the Other-World times than our own times, and maybe it was so. For, although the Danaan people never mix in mortal affairs, they do not like Ireland stirred and groaning, nor filled with strangers nor forever at war, and who was there to say they did not brood most morosely under the fairy mounds that led to their home? Who was there to say their very presence did not have a power of its own, and did not breathe a mist into the air that the true sea never owned, no matter its legends?

For us, this misty time had most to do with Kevin and Margaret Culhane. In the midst of our preparing for our all-out battle with fate, a kind of peace descended upon us and enveloped us in itself. Though our blood raced as others' did, though passions learned in books and from the lips of remembering old men, and at last with our own hearts' tearing, now presented themselves to us in real and irresistible form, yet whole days and weeks of our lives were spent in childish pleasures, in doing things we had done all our lives now, as if for the first time; we keenly felt new pleasure in doing them, perhaps because we felt we were doing them for the last time.

Ah, well, now I see Jamie leaping his horse over stone fences in fields of green and gold and red; I feel the rush of the wind, myself beside him or just behind him always, doing the same thing, at the same time. Into all this came Kevin and his sister, and, although we four were very much different from one another, yet we felt one another very keenly and inside of us a wild and beautiful voice was calling out, Come with me, I am like you, I am your brother, sister, lover, father, mother, god or goddess— and then the voice had always to lapse into pure song, for we poor humans do not have any words for the glory of those other multitudes of relationships between the souls of us, and only music can speak dumbly of it.

I see Margaret, a face so alive with life, changing every moment so that you might spend a sleepless life on watch and never see all her expressions and never tire of any. Long, oval, cameo face of Margaret's, soft, small lips with dimples at the corners and stubbornness under the chin, dark-brown eyes with sunlight in them, always some kind of light in them: sunlight, moonlight, rainbow light, and, when she was angry, the darkened, menacing light of lightning in the summer afternoon's lowering sky.

I see Kevin too, a friend you were glad to see from afar and glad to be near. I remember how often I used to catch a glimpse of his face when we were riding or talking or walking through the fields or on the streets in town, and there seemed always to be another voice attending him, one whose sound he did not like to hear, from the pained look of him, and it was often an effort for him to recall himself to where he was. At times he seemed like a man in a bad dream.

First, I thought some stupid romantic thoughts that he was only going to St. Michael's Seminary to keep some kind of deathbed promise to his mother, and that he didn't really wish for the cloistered life. Many times I even started to speak to him about it, but one glance from his troubled, distant eyes and I thought better of it and let it go. And glad I was, too, later on, that I had not insulted him with saying it, for I was very wrong. The only part of his life that was untroubled was the religious part of it; that was as a calm and placid lake in the midst of a mountain torrent.

I was at a loss to explain Kevin to myself. I knew that the waiting was long and that things at home were difficult. Jamie noticed it, of course, and once or twice he asked Kevin, as they walked along together or sat fishing side by side. But, you know, Jamie had a way of putting something that I never caught on to, and even to him, with his gentle, piercing eyes that understood so much, even with him—nay, I thought, *especially* with him—Kevin could not speak of it. Often he would press Jamie's shoulder mutely, with such a sad, regretful eye, then look quickly away as if he were about to speak, that it was past understanding. People may look for darker motives in this day of introspective misunderstandings, but those motives did not exist.

Margaret stormed her away through most of those days. Only with Kevin was she gentle-spoken, and that in a sort of jesting, playful way. Yet she was puzzled, too, for his sorrow now was unlike that we had seen in him before. Many a time I saw her look at him with wonder and pain, then she would spur her horse to leap a fence, or challenge the three of us to a race, or force herself to do some utterly reckless thing, throwing back her dark head, laughing wildly, as if her will alone could dispel whatever was haunting them both.

Fear and strangeness, loss and melancholy sat amidst us four everywhere we went that autumn, so, of course, we were gayer than human beings know how to be. Jamie stayed away from town and old friends, and seemed to want no other company than my own and Kevin's and Margaret's. Only with ourselves, who shared many secret sorrows and understood that there were many others as well, was Jamie now himself. Cool to lads, standoffish with other girls, he set himself apart since Martin's death. Some understood, missed his company, and trusted to time to bring him back to them. But, you see, Jamie was thought to be something of a *catch,* as they used to say. There wasn't a fellow we knew who hadn't a sister or a cousin who hadn't set her heart on him at one time or another. And I suppose I had set one or two feminine hearts to beating a bit faster, if the truth be told, but neither one of us cared very much about girls at the time.

And anyway, no matter how pretty they were, and many of them were prettier than Margaret, somehow there didn't seem much to them. They talked of little but themselves; they giggled all the time and didn't seem to know how to look at a fellow straight, but their eyes were constantly darting about, their lashes fluttering like butterflies' wings, and they all seemed so much *younger* than we were.

But Margaret, Margaret who was too thin, too tall for a girl, bad-tempered, undependable and wild, she seemed exactly right to us. After her silly carrying-on the day we'd met her with the donkey cart, she'd never tried to impress either of us again. She was herself at all times and it was herself we wanted with us. She had a level, straightforward look when she spoke to you. She listened to what you said and thought about it before she'd give you an answer. She had no wiles, no guile at all, such as women insist they need. I suppose, in a way, they are right, for our friendship with Margaret Culhane continued a long time as that with a sister, which women will not have, which, in fact, women despair of and write long columns of advice as to how to avoid in newspapers, my own included, God help me! No, a friend is not a woman. A woman can be a relative, sweetheart, lover, wife, mother, but she cannot be to a man what another man is!

Since that is so, it would seem obvious that our friendship with Margaret was doomed, yet it did not die, but only grew deeper and more involving as the days passed. Though it took little to annoy her, her tempers were soon over like summer squalls, and she would have been distressed beyond belief if you remembered them, or conducted yourself in light of them. Margaret in a happy temper was not full of air and spirits, but rather of a belligerent and aggressive jollity, which took for granted that what she said fell on friendly ears, and what she did was appreciated for its own sake—and also because it was she who did it. Margaret in a bad temper was sometimes amusing, and sometimes awful to behold, for she became wracked by a kind of passion I had never before seen in anyone. It simply took her over, body and soul, and she knew herself this well: that when it became too much for her, and you could see it rise up like a blindness in her eyes, then she took off with the horse and rode like a madwoman till the mood was gone. What might have been the results if she did not have that way of throwing off her evil spirit I would hate to think—Margaret in a houseful of screaming children, Margaret in a convent, let's say, or a boarding school, Margaret anywhere and under any circumstances where there was not room to walk or ride in, fresh air and motion within and without, I fear she would have become dangerous in some way, or her wild and glorious spirit might have simply become broken altogether.

Yet, with all her passion, Margaret wanted no untethered life, with an independence of action and responsibility such as any man might need or wish. In that, at least, she was every bit a woman. Far might be her roaming, but she wanted to be called back at the end of it. She might ride away in a temper a hundred times, but, in the end, she rode back again, her spirits calm. And if those she loved were not there waiting, trusting that this one more time she would come back again, Margaret was the sort who would have died of it, of the sorrow and loneliness of it.

It seemed that each of the four of us stood on the edge of something else, being pushed toward it, by time alone, if not by our own desires, and by the forces of change and revolution that were gathering strength and making strategies whilst we were trying to hold on to one another and what we knew.

Margaret knew a hundred ways to build bridges over

our loneliness, treating us all as children, grandly planning out schemes to advance our future careers. And Jamie watched her with fond eyes; I don't believe he took his gaze from her while she was within sight. The two of them bickered constantly, but it always ended in laughter, for, no matter what she said, nothing would do but that he top her, and for Jamie that was easy enough. Yet he was amazingly patient, and all it required was patience, for sooner or later Margaret's temper betrayed her and she could not answer.

We sat on Bearsey's Bridge one afternoon, fishing without luck for three hours and just thinking of giving it up and going home. But Margaret served us out tea from a flask and said, "I shall have three children, I've decided. All boys, and I shall name each of them for the three of you—Kevin, James, and Gerald."

"I thought you didn't want to get married," I said, but she only sniffed at me.

"Wouldn't the father of those luckless lads have a word to say about the naming of them?" drawled Jamie lazily, lying back and staring up at the clouds. Kevin chuckled.

"I'll be the mother, and I'll have all the saying," said Margaret, tossing her head.

"Ho ho," cried Jamie, looking at me, "God help the man who has to share his life with you, miss. The poor creature won't have any peace till he's laid to rest, and you'll probably follow him there out of spite."

"Huh!" snorted Margaret inelegantly, throwing a handful of wilted dandelions at him. "I'll just train him up with the three boys and, at the end, you'll find four of the best men in the county!"

"But what will you train them up to, Margaret?" asked Kevin mildly, but he exchanged a droll smile with Jamie, and Margaret knew they were having her on.

"Well, I won't have any old straitlaced priests, for one thing"—this for Kevin, who made a face at her. "And no soldiers, either. They're all a bad lot and can't get used to living peacefully with decent folks."

"That's true enough, Margaret darling," said Jamie,

"but tell me, do you really think you're just the right one for the rearing of decent, peace-loving, quiet people?"

It was a light, teasing question, the answer obvious. He meant nothing by it, yet what an effect it had on Margaret! Her eyes blazed; she leaped to her feet, her breast heaving, her voice choked.

"What did you mean by that, Jamie?" she demanded, as we looked at her wide-eyed. "Answer me!" she insisted as he said nothing. "Tell me, you don't think I'm good enough to raise children, is that it? The Culhanes aren't good enough—"

"Margaret, let it be!" said Kevin in a low voice, and then Jamie stared incredulously at him.

"Are you as crazy as she is, then?" cried Jamie, and Kevin flushed and turned his head away.

"Leave Kevin out of it," warned Margaret. "It's me you were speaking of, and it's me you'll answer right now."

"I was speaking of your famous temper, your great dislike of discipline—I was joking with you!" shouted Jamie in no joking tone of voice, and he too stood up, towering over her.

"Will the two of you sit down and shut up, for Christ's sakes?" was my sole contribution, but I was really disgusted and puzzled, too, for I could not understand the issue between them.

"Jerry, don't get into this," Margaret said to me, without taking her eyes from Jamie's stormy face. I shrugged, got up and inspected my fishing line, which had nary a nibble all day.

"I just want you to know one thing, Jamie Daley," she went on. "If anyone in this world knows what peace and quiet and joy would be like, it's me. I've never had them, so I can see what they are. You and Jerry, you grew up with them, and with love and trusting and understanding in your families . . ."

She was crying now, which made her furious. Jamie's face had grown quite grave as he listened to her outburst. He stood quietly till she'd finished talking, and when she put her hands up to wipe her eyes impatiently, he took both her small hands in one of his big ones and gently pulled them down again. With his other hand he wiped her tears away himself, and there was a sweet smile on his face.

"Hush, hush, Margaret," he said softly.

She seemed about to speak again, but something in his expression stopped her. She looked up at him with such a wan look as you'd see on a rabbit in a trap, and her dark eyes welled with tears again.

"I'm sorry, Jamie," she whispered, but he just shook his head and smiled at her and patted her head with his free hand, never once letting go of her hands. He succeeded in calming her where no one else ever had, and I was glad. Kevin, who had come over by me when the argument began, was watching the two of them with great interest; and I might have been mistaken, but, for the first time since before Martin's death, I saw a small, leaping look of happiness on his face—but it could have been just the moving reflected light from the river.

Margaret finally swung away from Jamie, who let her go as gently as he had held her. She stood staring off across the fields, her arms folded tightly against her small body.

"I don't know why I do it," she said quietly. "A great hot feeling comes over me, I can feel it like waves in the sea, pounding in my head and my ears, and I feel as if I must strike out at something or die. Then I strike out, and who is it there to take it? Someone I would never hurt, someone who is a close friend to me and mine—" Then, as she said the last word, she fell again to weeping wildly, and when Jamie would have stopped her once more, she shook her head and ran off from us, sobbing as though her heart would break.

Jamie stood there looking after her and then, irresolutely, began to follow, but Kevin called to him, "Jamie, leave her be now."

Jamie turned and came back to us. "What did I say to upset her like that?" he asked Kevin.

Kevin gave him a long steady look, but then dropped his eyes and mumbled. "Margaret has things that . . .

trouble her . . ." he said uncomfortably, knowing we knew he wasn't explaining anything at all. "She needs friends."

"Well, she's *got* friends," retorted Jamie shortly. And then he took up his own fishing pole and, without another word, sat down and cast his line again.

Margaret reappeared a while later, dry-eyed and contrite, and, to smooth over the awkwardness, I asked her for a drop more tea all around. There was only a bit left, so we got mostly the leaves, and she promptly decided to read them for us.

"We shall meet one another right here, at the bridge," she said dreamily, staring into her cup. "We'll all be quite important then, of course. I'll be a great lady with servants and diamonds and kangaroo leather riding boots from Australia. Jerry will be— Oh, let me see your cup there. Ah, yes, Jerry will be the richest farmer in six counties, with stables full of horses and never the same boots twice without polish."

"What about me? What do you see for me, then?" asked Jamie, reeling in his line and clucking in disgust, for the worm was long gone and nothing in its place. Margaret took his cup, turned it over into the saucer and wiggled the tea around so the leaves moved into shapes.

"Not fair," called Jamie, "you're changing me fortune, darlin', and I want to know it without any fooling around."

"Oh, shut your gab!" snapped Margaret absently, her eyes fixed on the soggy tea leaves, her pink tongue caught at the edge of her teeth as she concentrated. "Here you are, Jamie. A general, that's what it says, General James Patrick Daley, with thousands of troops under him and a lackey to blacken his boots."

"God, you're a rare one for boots today," remarked Jamie. "What about Kevin, now?"

"Oh, there's no need to do me," protested Kevin. "Besides, I'm not supposed to sanction this kind of thing, strictly speaking, you know!" Whereupon Jamie pushed him down and wrestled him unmercifully for a couple of minutes, Kevin emerging laughing and muddy, but Jamie had succeeded in pulling up the collar of his shirt and knotting it sloppily.

"There, now you look like a priest," said Jamie with a satisfied smirk.

"Kevin is to be Pope at least," announced Margaret proudly, and when we all roared at that, she defiantly held up the saucer with the tea leaves in it so we could see a mitre-shaped figure in the middle of it. "There, you see?" she said smugly.

Jamie made a great business of looking hard at the leaves, inspecting them from one angle and another.

"No," he said finally. "It has more the shape of a pound note, do you see that, Kevin, there?" he held his finger on the leaves and pushed them under Kevin's nose.

Kevin paid it great mind and said he had to agree with Jamie, which was peculiar, because what did a priest have to do with worldly goods such as money?

"Oh, God bless us all," chortled Jamie, tossing the cup aside, "I hope they'll wise you up in the seminary. What has a priest to do with money? Listen to him. And what would you say to a fine, rich parish, somewhere up near Dublin, say, with batty old ladies pouring money into the poor box by the thousands and thousands? Oh, I'm afraid your future's cut out for you, Father Culhane: you'll wear the cassock of poverty—with black silk drawers under it!"

But Margaret stubbornly stuck to her point. "Pope, I've said it and I'll not change it. It's in the leaves—"

"And the leaves do not lie," croaked Jamie, squinting his eyes.

She glanced at him sideways mischievously. "Well, sometimes they do," she admitted, and grinned.

And then she made us all join our hands together and swear a solemn oath that on a certain day, at a certain hour, ten years in the future, we would each come from wherever we were, and meet together once more in the middle of Bearsey's Bridge. And we clasped hands together so tightly and trusting and promised it, and each of us knew we could not keep that poor promise, ever.

Chapter VIII

Well, mind, now, I'd best bring along someone else we knew in those days, God help us, who was not the most perfect of men, and his name—don't forget it—was Charlie Norwood. Ah, fat Charlie Norwood, the darling of the county, Charlie—didn't dare to set his foot beyond his own gates, Charlie didn't, unless he had his private bodyguard with him.

Charlie had the right to police protection and Charlie needed that protection, and, though I'll venture to say any policeman worth his brass buttons would have cheerfully done him in in a day's work and whistled himself home happily afterwards, still, as the representative of a prominent landowner, he was entitled to all the protection he could get. Now, I've often wondered how that worked out, seeing as how those who had business with Charlie Norwood usually had a deal more need of protection than he did, but somehow they never got any at all, Charlie was so busy hogging it to himself. Ah, well, and that was Charlie.

But who was Charlie, you ask? Charlie was the son of Lord John Norwood, himself a fine, upright English landlord, who only set foot in Ireland twice that I heard of. Now, Lord Norwood owned the Daley farm, and it was one of the best farms in the county, of about a hundred prime acres, and he owned much, much more in Waterford. All of it, except the big Norwood estate, was rented out, and Charlie stayed in Ireland to keep it all in order for his father, and to collect the rents for him as well.

"I'll see you in hell, Norwood!" was the usual greeting Charlie heard from most of his ungrateful tenants, and them living off his good nature—that was the Irish for you, now, wasn't it? Old Norwood, Lord John, he was a game one, fought Davitt and the Land League to the bitter end, till he was forced to accept the idea that tenants had some rights, too, though not many, to be sure. Old Lord Norwood and many others who owned huge parcels, God, miles and visions of land they owned, or at least the English government *said* they owned them—well, they tried to stick together and stare down the Land League. But when Land Reform in Ireland was finally squeaked and pushed and dragged bodily through Commons and Lords and what have you back in '95, Norwood bore up under it bravely. He was a gentleman, was Lord Norwood, which is to say, when his back was pinned up against the wall he gave in. According to Land Reform—now pay close attention or you'll be lost forever—it was admitted grudgingly enough that after a tenant had been on a piece of property and cared for it, and his father and grandfather before him and far back to the original owners, why, then the landlord had to let him stay on that piece of property, as long as he kept up his rent payments. Oh, don't cluck in your teeth, now—that was a leap and a stride forward for Ireland, you may believe it. Before that blessed bill was made into law, any landlord could put any tenant off of any piece of property just by taking the notion to do it. Says the lord's wife, riding by a neat little cot and farm, "My, my, what a charming place for a rose garden!" and, next day, off go the farmer and his family, and in goes the rose garden!

It was that simple, but now, according to the new law, a tenant had *tenure*—isn't *that* a grand word to fill your empty belly with, and you with the potato blight two years in a row and nothing in the stocking behind the tea chest to hand over to himself next quarter! Still, it was better than nothing. After that, you were still stuck with the same old problem which was where the hell to get the rent money, but you can't expect Parliament to solve all those little, personal dilemmas for you, now, could you? No, you could not. Anyway, old Norwood gave in to the thing, and was unable to throw anyone off his land as long as they kept up the place decently and kept on paying their rents over to Charlie darling.

However, when Parliament fell so far from empirical wisdom as to take one more step to aid the poor tenants, Norwood refused to budge—because he didn't have to. Another grand law, passed not long afterwards, suggested —mind you, merely suggested—that any landlord might, if he wished, sell over the land to the tenant, so that someday, very far away it's true, after making every payment on time, and so forth and so on, the tenant might actually own his own piece of a place in his own name. The English Parliament encouraged the landlords to go along with this piece of liberality; some of them did (which is how my father came to own our small place eventually) and most of them didn't (which is how come the Daleys were stuck with the likes of Charlie Norwood).

Old Norwood had liked Martin Daley well enough. He seemed to think Martin was a cut or two above the rest of us. Martin had written a parcel of letters through the years to Lord Norwood, petitioning him to let the land go, and for a very fair price, too. But Norwood would not hear of it, and Charlie would not hear of it, so that was that. Charlie used to ride by that hundred acres with a hungry look in his ratty, close-set little eyes. Four times a year Charlie bestirred himself to collect his rents; what he did the rest of the time was pure conjecture, and sure the Irish would spin dizzy with conjecturing, from holding Black Masses in his basement to contributing to the white-slave traffic south of Dublin. Four times a year, Charlie left Norwood House and rode up the *boreen* with six picked men about him, like an honor guard. A surly, dirty lot they were. Two were our own, though God knows from where. Two Scots he had, they were the only sober ones, I'll give them that, and no more in the way of virtue. And there were a couple old cronies Charlie had brought over from the back alleys of London or Liverpool. They never said a word, but sneered all the time. They were filthy, unshaven; compared to them, a tinker's dog was a gent. But they suited Charlie. Once or twice I heard they'd beaten up a few tenants who were slow in paying, but, of course,

Charlie knew nothing of that. He was a gentleman, and, oh, how he wanted to get his flabby hands on the Daley place. Why let it stay with one family, a whole hundred acres like that, when you could move in a score or more and get rents from them all? Unfortunately for Charlie, Martin paid his rent smartly on time, whether things went well or badly, so Charlie could only fume and fuss and bide his time.

Sean Culhane's house was the only Irish home in Waterford where Charlie Norwood was welcome, along with any other permanently attached or stray Englishman who might be about. I used to love to see Margaret's imitation of Charlie, who was a regular dinner guest every Sunday, and whom Margaret despised more than all the others put together. It's true enough, Charlie didn't have much in the way of looks. He was tall enough, I guess, but sloppy-fat and half-boiled-, half-crusted-looking. He had one of those fat biscuit faces, nothing but dough, with odd bumps of features here and there that must've popped up in the oven. Pudgy and sallow, green-eyed and something-colored hair all of a cowlick was Charlie, and his orange boots forever dirty besides. But when Margaret got through walking his way and talking his way—did I tell you Charlie was the only man I ever knew who could talk and lick his lips at the same time?—when Margaret did him for us, sure you could almost end up feeling sorry for the creatureen!

Anyway, now it was that Charlie Norwood reared his ugly head again; it was his time to rear it, anyway, for the quarter rent on the Daley place was due. Things were hard for Jamie's family then. The man they'd hired from town did not stay, for a hundred acres is a lot and only Jamie to work with him. Oh, Will had tried to stick it out and do his best, but Will's best was a muddle and he was soon wandering off again for days and weeks at a time, so, as always, it was Jamie who ended up doing his work.

One day before Norwood showed up, Jamie and I sat out by the barn, he mending harnesses and I helping him, for my father sent me over as often as he could spare me. "Will you look at that, now?" said Jamie, annoyed, holding up a leather strap so I could see it. It had been poorly mended and was about ready to pull apart again.

"The next time we use it, one good tug and someone will be off the horse and into a ditch," he stormed, ripping apart the strap and preparing to fix it properly. "That's Will's doing," he muttered angrily. "I wish he'd not try to do these things at all. He does them so badly—"

"Ah, whisht, Jamie," I said, knowing him too well. "If it wasn't for Will, you wouldn't be half the farmer you are today!"

He looked at me suspiciously, then laughed, for it was true: young as he was, he did the work of a man, of two men, and did it well.

"Will is all right," he said slowly then, a huge needle between his teeth. "He's no farmer. He doesn't know what he wants to do yet, but he'll come round."

I happened to glance up the road and I said, "Speaking of coming round, look who's here and guess what for?"

It was Charlie darling, of course, and his noble band, him with his hand already extended to greet Aunt Ellen, who was out front weeding her flowers. Well, and you could see that Charlie was gathering himself to pounce. He knew Will Daley as well as anyone did, and he knew damn well that Will would let the farm fall into disastrous decay within the year if it were all left in his hands.

He rode in, a look of frustration lighting on his face like a leech on a boil, as he noticed the crops ready for harvesting, the creatures in fine fettle and fat as himself, the house well mended, the flowers late-blooming and cheerful.

"Morning to you, Mrs. Daley," says Charlie, licking his lips.

Aunt Ellen stood like a statue, arms folded, a contemptuous look on her face, and would not answer him.

Charlie looked around very carefully. "Hm, it's nothing to mention, you know," he said, "but I do seem to notice a loose board over there on the barn roof, do you see it, now? Oh, I see young James is still here," he added, greatly disappointed, and Jamie and I waved energetically over at him.

"Where would he be?" sneered Aunt Ellen. "As for the

board, we're waiting delivery on the lumber," she went on, in a voice like thick strawberry jam. "If you'd be good enough to give Hanrahan back his lumber that you took for rent, we might get it finished that much faster."

"Oh, yes, Hanrahan," Charlie stuttered absent-mindedly, gazing longingly at the meadow nearby. "So, everything is doing well since Mr. Daley's unfortunate—"

"Will you take the rent now, Mr. Norwood?" snapped Aunt Ellen, staring him deadly narrow in the eyes. "I've work to do."

Poor old Charlie, thwarted once more, grabbed the money and rode off away with his cohorts behind him, whilst my aunt stood nailed to the spot till the last of them was out on the road again. As we came up to her, she was shaking her head.

"I hate that man," she said. Then a worried little frown gathered between her eyes. "Lads, we'll have to work like a miracle to meet the next payment. And—I'm going to sell some of the horses at Clonmel next week."

Jamie's eyes darkened. "How many?"

"Four, I think, four at least. We need the money, son."

"Will you go, then?" he asked, and she nodded.

"Culhane's sending a dozen two-year-olds and he said his men would gladly take mine with them. I'll go by train and take care of the business myself."

"Why don't you let me go?"

Aunt Ellen shook her head. "No, you've never bargained with horse dealers. I used to go up with Martin every year, you remember, and I learned a lot from listening. I hope I remember how it goes." She sighed. "But you stay home and look after everything. I'll not stay overnight, but I'll come in on the late train, and I'll take Kathleen with me for company."

Jamie watched her walk slowly back to the house, his lips clenched together tightly, and then he glared down the empty road after Norwood and ripped the new-mended harness strap clean in two again, throwing both halves into the bushes in a fit of rage.

So it was that the following Monday my Aunt and little Kathleen drove off to catch the train in Dungarvan, leaving

Jamie alone at the house, with Janet to look after. But Janet was no problem, 'twas the turkeys were the problem. Aunt Ellen had a flock of about fifty of them, nasty, stupid, vicious, egotistical, silly birds; compared to a turkey, a goose is a Rhodes scholar in good standing! And tending those blazing birds was a sacred task my aunt only trusted a few special people with doing, for the turkeys were her pin-money crop, you might say. The money they fetched around Christmastime paid for many a small necessity, many a Christmas present or doctor bill. But, God, what prompted our American cousins to choose the turkey to offer thanks to Heaven for their prosperity I cannot imagine, unless it was a crafty revenge on the part of the ousted Indians to suggest it to them. None of us would eat a turkey, were we to die of starvation in the face of it roasted and stuffed.

Now here it was late August and the creatures had to be taken out of their pen in the morning, marched off like so many sheep to pasture, and watched and tended and protected all day from one another's vicious tempers and the usual assortment of natural enemies. It would be more like tending a herd of domestic wildcats, actually, than sheep, and poor Jamie that day had the doing of it, although it was usually Kathleen's job. And, furthermore, in the evening he would have to take them all back to their pen, feed and water them, and shut them up safely inside for the night, like so many noisy babies. Janet swore she would do it all herself, but of course she could not begin to handle them alone.

I had promised Jamie I would come over as soon as I could to help him, but I had a great deal of work to do myself at home. Along about noon, Margaret appeared, without Kevin. Byron was in one of his wilder moods and snorted, tossing his handsome head impetuously toward the barn, where my little bay mare was calling to him, but Margaret was patient with him that day. As I came out quickly from the potato field, wiping my hands on my pants, I was surprised to see her there, leaning over from the saddle, patting his head and calling him silly, pug-dog names in her sweetest voice.

"Let's go get Jamie," she greeted me. "I've the whole day free, but Kevin had to go to Cork, so it's just the three of us. What shall we do?"

My eyes swept around the place and I shook my head. I had several more hours of work ahead of me. "No, I can't come now," I told her, shading the sun from my face as I looked up at her.

"Oh," she said pouting, "I *knew* you'd have work to do! Can't you get out of it?"

"No, I can't get out of it. And there's no use your going over to Jamie's, either. His mother's off to the horse fair in Clonmel, and he's stuck with the turkeys, *and* he's in a foul temper over it. Why don't you go shopping in town or whatever young ladies do to pass the time?"

She wrinkled her nose. "Turkeys? What's Jamie to do with the bloody things? Do they need wet-nursing?"

"Oh, go along, then, I'm busy!" I laughed at her and turned away in no great enthusiasm to get back to the potatoes, a hot, dirty, back-breaking job. As I walked to the field, I heard Byron leap the low fence, and I wasn't positive, but I thought I heard Margaret call back to me something about "going to help Jamie." Oh, no, I thought to myself, but then I shrugged it off. I must have been mistaken.

Now, as it turned out, Kevin came home earlier than he'd expected and, late in the afternoon, came by my place asking after his sister. I was worked around to the near end of the flaming field, half bent over double permanently and ready to grab at any excuse to be out of it. I told him to go into the house till I'd washed up and changed my clothes, and I made short work of that. Then we rode over to Jamie's.

But when we got there we couldn't see a soul anywhere about. It was close to five-thirty and I would have expected him to be bringing the creatures back, for the cows were home already with the boy, who had come and gone. They were beginning to set up a stir to be milked. I looked through the house. Kevin searched the barn and the out-buildings, but no one was about. The shadows of evening were fast falling and the cows a disgrace to the county, so

I sent Kevin traipsing off on foot to the pasture where they usually took the silly birds. I, still bent in half and aching all over, cursing myself, pulled up the milking stool and prepared to relieve all fourteen of those distressed animals.

Of course, the faster I milked, and the happier the cow I was milking became, the louder the mooings of complaint and anguish from the others grew, and I wished I had kept Kevin with me to help with the job. Although, to tell you the truth, I didn't know whether he could milk or not. I just took it for granted he could. Now, as I sat there working as fast as I could, I heard a great uproar of yelling and shouting and feet running outside, then someone burst open the barn door and ran in, calling me breathlessly, obviously knowing I was in there. It was Margaret. She stopped short at the stall when she saw me. Her riding dress was torn and muddy, there were hay and straws and grass stains all over it; her long hair was streaking down her back, and her face was sunburned and sweaty.

"Oh, thanks be to God, Kevin said you were here!" she gasped.

"What's the matter? What's wrong?"

She sank down on a heap of straw, pushing stray wisps of hair from her flushed face, and sighed with weariness.

"Jamie's just coming, he was right behind me," she said. "You haven't seen any of them, have you?" she asked hopefully.

"Seen any of what?" I couldn't let go what I was doing; sure the blasted cow was already looking moodily at Margaret and slapping her long strong tail about dangerously. "What's happened?"

"The turkeys, Jerry, the damned devil turkeys!" she sobbed, and I watched her amazed, for, sure enough, there were tears streaking her dirty face and for once she wasn't trying to hide them.

All that for a few turkeys? At that moment, Jamie burst into the barn, looking as raggedy-edged as Margaret, wrath all over his face, his eyes dark and snapping with anger.

"There you are!" he said to her. "Oh, you're here, are you, Jerry?" he threw at me without even a look to match.

He strode over to Margaret and pulled her to her feet roughly, all the while she was sobbing louder and louder. Oh, damn the udders of that overflowing Mother Hathor cow of the world, but would she ever be milked out so I could leave off squeezing?

"Are you mad?" I yelled at Jamie, stuck where I was as he pushed Margaret about and looked as if he might punch her one any minute.

He sneered at me. "Little it is *you* know about it, where the hell were you all day?" he demanded.

"Out in the goddamned bastard potato field, that's where, and you bloody well knew it!" I yelled right back at him. "Let her go. What's gotten into the two of you, for Christ's sake?"

"Tell the man what you did, Miss Culhane, Your Majesty!" he ordered.

Margaret kicked him viciously with the sharp heel of her boot and he promptly kicked her right back.

"Ooh!" yelped she, trying to slap him but missing. Then she began crying again. By now the damn cow was milked dry, so I jumped up, and in came Kevin, now a dirty, mucky mess himself though only on the premises a half hour. He also wore a look of terrible wrath, and stood staring at his beloved sister with a look of mingled anger and dismay.

Then he looked past her, to Jamie, and said, "Not a sign. Not a feather. I can't fathom it!"

"Will someone tell me what the hell is going on?" I shouted at the top of my voice. The three of them turned as if on one neck and gawked at me.

"The turkeys, man, she's lost them, every last one, that's what it's all about. And when Ma gets home, she'll have the hide of us—"

"Now, how can you go and lose fifty fat turkeys, will you tell me that?" I still spoke in the explosive tense.

Kevin nodded his head up and down several times. "Margaret can," he assured me quietly. "Margaret can, if anyone can."

"Oh, shut up, Kevin," screamed Margaret. "What do I

know about turkeys? I just came over here to help. I volunteered to take those blasted birds off his hands—"

"She had a regular temper tantrum till I gave in and let her lead them out," put in Jamie, scowling at her darkly. "I told her to bring them back to the pen at four o'clock."

"I thought you'd be coming with me," she said indignantly. "Who ever heard of trusting me with fifty turkeys all by myself? What a damned fool thing that was to do!"

"I sent Janet along to look after you," said Jamie icily, and then he turned to Kevin and me. "I told her I had other jobs to be done around here. I told her she was on her own, but Janet would know what to do if there was any problem. And she said that was fine!"

"Say, where *is* Janet?" I asked, for I hadn't seen her since I'd got there.

"Poor little thing is still out searching for the birds," muttered Jamie.

Margaret winced. "I brought them back at four, I brought them back at four!" she insisted. "I marched those idiotic creatures right back here and into the pen. I even fed them and filled their pans with water—and then I went to look for you."

Jamie closed his eyes and sighed. "And you forgot to lock up the pens. And an hour later every damn last one of them was gone. Missing. Disappeared."

Kevin was still agreeing with him. "Not a trace, not a feather," he repeated.

Margaret fairly spat at him. "Ooh, will you stop *saying* that?"

I glanced outside. It was almost sunset. "Well, what are we going to do about them?"

Jamie curled his lip scornfully. "We have been crawling under every bush and rock in the county trying to find them. Do you have anything better in mind?"

"Oh." I hadn't.

He nodded, satisfied, and, without any further conversation, set to work on one of the cows. Kevin, who turned out to have a very deft hand for the job, settled down by another, and the three of us finished it up in silence, while Margaret sat dejectedly on her pile of straw, twisting a long strand of hair around and around her fingers, deep in thought. Aunt Ellen would have a fit, I knew that. Presently Janet came running in, very sad to say she hadn't found the turkeys and could she please have something to eat. Jamie sent her into the house to wash up and eat, then rest herself.

Soon the cows began to quiet down and there were only two more to go. 'Twas then we heard Margaret murmuring to herself, almost as if she was having some kind of an argument.

". . . It might have been him, or half a dozen like him," she was saying, and we paid scant attention at first. "There he sat on the edge of the well, cool as you please, and I walked up, yes, it was him, a handsome red devil, too, didn't move a hair when I lowered the bucket. . . . Not afraid of anything. . . . I wonder . . ."

"Margaret," said Kevin, "what are you mumbling about?"

"Oh, the fox. Just the fox. I saw him this afternoon at the well, and I wondered if—"

Jamie jumped up, almost knocking over a bucket of fresh milk. "Fox? Did you say fox?"

"Yes, I said fox," answered Margaret. "What of it?"

Jamie let out a great puff of air. "Well, and that's the answer. He was after the turkeys. And he got them, too, from the looks of it."

Margaret sneered. "One fox? Fifty turkeys? He'd have burst himself in two after the fifth one. He was a very small fox, mind you, not some giant of a fox. A very bold fox, but small, for all that."

"No, no, he didn't wait to eat them—and if he had eaten a few, we'd have found the traces, blood, feathers, bones, something. No, he's carried them off somewhere, to his den probably."

"How could one small fox carry off so many big mean turkeys?"

"I don't know!" roared Jamie. "But, by God, I'm going to find out."

"I'm with you," said Kevin with alacrity, and I echoed it, so the three of us headed to the turkey pen. We crawled about on all fours in the fast-fading light, examining every inch of the earth around the pen, whilst Margaret, trailing behind us, stood with her arms folded, apparently aloof and disinterested, staring away at the sky.

After a little while, Jamie cried, "Ah-hah!" and triumphantly jumped up, holding the tiniest bit of a dark pin feather you can imagine. "The dirt is marked here, like something was dragged along. Whatever it was has wiped out the pawprints, but I think we can follow it. Let's go."

The gray dusk was settling in as we set off through the fields, the four of us, for of course Margaret insisted she go along. In no time each of us claimed to have come across the very and only imprint of the right trail, and, since there were now four trails instead of one, we separated with a few terse words, and each went off following little more than our own noses, for you could not have seen the trail of an elephant in the clustering darkness about us. Every once in a while, one or the other would shout, but it always turned out to be nothing at all. I fell into a rabbit hole and wrenched my knee, but I was in it all the way and would not use that for an excuse to quit, so I crawled out painfully and went on.

Jamie headed across the stream, and it was when he reached the other side that I saw him jump up and wave his arms frantically.

"Over here, over here!" he motioned. We came on, crashing along from our various positions. His eyes were fixed on something near the water's edge. He pointed silently.

It was the fox, red and bushy-tailed, bright of face and sleek as ever, a truly handsome and intelligent-looking creature. But he had worn himself out in one grand, mad theft to end them all; in all the annals of foxdom in all the world there couldn't have been recorded one such magnificent feat! He had stopped to eat his well-earned dinner, after dragging the fifty turkeys away in his mouth, one at a time. Now he had killed three, eaten two, then sat down, rinsed his dinner off neatly in the cold water of the stream, and begun to gorge himself on the third. Now he was sleeping the sleep of the just and unguilty, his little red furry belly bulging like an egg. All around him were feathers and claws and heads and half-picked bones.

We were careful to whisper, not wanting to awaken him just yet. Two of us stationed ourselves on one side and two on the other side of the stream. Once we were in position, Jamie gently jabbed him with his foot. The bold creature merely stirred about, clawed the ground a bit and curled right up again! Again Jamie poked him, and this time the fox jumped up, staring about him sleepily and angrily, to see who had dared bother him after such a day and such a feast. Then he caught sight of Jamie and darted off wildly into the field behind him.

"After him, quick!" shouted Jamie, and we all ran blindly along in the darkness. "He'll head for his den," cried Jamie. "I'll bet he's got the rest of the turkeys there!"

Fortunately the moon began to rise and cast a small bit of light to help us out.

"There he is!" cried Jamie, and, with one final great leap, he landed beside a small cave, before which the exhausted fox had turned to defend his home and hearth, and stood poised for springing, snarling and snapping, with great verve and courage. And, sure enough, from inside I could hear the turkeys set up a wild squawking and flapping. Jamie reached in and pulled out one of the blasted birds, which promptly nipped a good bite from his hand.

Well, they were all there, all forty-seven of them, leaving out the three he'd eaten. We didn't dare try to lead them back to the pen in the darkness and risk losing them all over again. And we could only carry one of them at a time, for it took two strong hands to manage one of them. God knows how the foxeen accomplished it! So, wearily and grimly, we left Margaret to guard the entrance to the den and keep the fox off, and the three of us each picked up a bird and began the long walk back to the farm.

Back and forth we trudged for hours with those birds screeching and flapping and nipping at us, till every single one of them was accounted for and locked in securely. We were on our way back for the last one when we met up with Margaret, looking utterly dejected, carrying the struggling creature upside down, although that was not her intention, and Jamie took it from her with a short, curt "Thanks."

Nine o'clock at night it was when we all sank into the chairs in Aunt Ellen's kitchen, waiting for a bit of water to boil up for tea. None of us had had supper. But the turkeys were saved. Somehow, the accomplishment of it didn't seem so enormous, now that it was done. That fox must have had more stamina than we did, for we were dead out.

Poor little Janet lay fast asleep by the fire, her blond head tucked on her arm, curled up in my aunt's big rocking chair. Margaret carried her off to her bed, and I began cutting up the remains of a cold ham whilst Kevin sliced the bread and Jamie set out the tea things. Mind you, now, not a solitary word was spoken amongst the four of us all that time. It was getting late. Soon Aunt Ellen would be coming back with Kathleen, and someone would have to tell her.

Kevin sliced six or seven crumbly, uneven pieces of the bread, a thoughtful expression on his face. Then slowly he said, "If it will be of any help at all, I'll explain it to your mother, Jamie. And of course I'll pay for the three birds that are missing."

Jamie had been crouching on his heel, a big grin on his tired face, the flames leaping red devilish shadows into his eyes. He shook his head.

"No. Thanks for the handsome offer, Kevin, but they were my responsibility and I'll tell her, and I'll pay her for them, too."

Now, I didn't open my mouth, but I thought Jamie was out of his head for passing up such a golden opportunity. Who could get mad at Kevin Culhane, and him just a spit from the priesthood? Aunt Ellen would be sweet and forgiving of him if he did the telling. But then Jamie never was a practical man like myself, and had to do things the hard way every time!

Soon, tired as we were, we had a big, cheerful fire going, a pot of tea nestled into a cozy, brewing away as nice as you please, and a good spread of food ready for one and all. We washed up the best we could, but our clothing was rags. Margaret borrowed one of Kathleen's shawls from back of the door. But the thing of it was, when it came time to pour the tea and eat a bite, we none of us had much appetite. Jamie was glaring at Margaret. She had two angry red spots in the middle of her cheeks and wouldn't look at him or Kevin either. For some reason, she wasn't including me in her wrath, and I was in the very uncomfortable position of having to relay everything to the others, like "Jamie, Margaret would like you to pass the salt down her way. Kevin, Margaret is finished with the cream, it's your turn next," and so on.

And then we heard off in the distance the sound we'd all been listening for, and dreading. It seemed louder because the night was so still, the sound of the cart wheels and the tired horse clopping slowly up the *boreen*. We looked at each other dejectedly. And then Margaret glanced from Jamie to Kevin to me, pushed away from the table, and ran out into the hallway.

Jamie pursed his lips. "That's a woman for you," he said, and there was none to argue the issue. "See, now that the moment is at hand, off she goes for a good cry, leaving ourselves to do the dirty work and straighten out the mess she made!"

Kevin agreed soberly, although there was a twinkle in his eye. "Aye, Jamie," he said. "For man that is born of woman . . ."

And the three of us sat there nodding away, listening with faint breath for Aunt Ellen's steps. And we listened and listened and listened, but they did not come. Now we were even more apprehensive. Was she so bloody fond of those damned birds that she was going to count them and check up on them before she came in?

The front door opened. We three jumped and shuddered. I'm *not* exaggerating, man dear, you've no idea of the flailing tongue of an Irishwoman aroused in her heart! They're all passion to the marrow, God love them, but there's passion and passion, now!

Well, and down the hall she comes briskly, for all her

long hard day, and I heard Kathleen's pretty laugh and a small yawn, and my aunt murmuring, and Margaret's laughter! Then the kitchen door was swung open and there they stood framed in the doorway, the firelight dancing in their eyes.

Aunt Ellen glanced back at Margaret and chuckled. "Well, now, and I hear you poor lads have had that busy a time!"

Jamie flushed. "Now, Ma," he began, as she walked over to him, putting her gloves and hat on the table. But she gave him a rough, playful push back into his chair.

"Hush, now, it's all told and over," she said as she peeked into the teapot and sniffed. "Phew, now, the smell of that mess in there would poison a wart! James, some fresh hot water at once. Evening to yourself, Kevin dear, and how are you? Gerald, boy, fetch my special India tea. You know, what your mother's got the other half pound of—there, under the sugar sack. Ah, there's a lad. Margaret darling, just be good enough to clear away these moldy old cups and spread fresh, there's a lass. Kathleen, sweetheart, tiptoe into Janet's room and lay the little doll on the bed by her, will you, so she'll find it in the morning?"

We were all so delighted to have something useful to do, we whirled around the small cozy room, bending and craning our necks, exchanging puzzled glances and shrugs, and all of us staring at Margaret, who went around like a queen, her head very high, a great smile on her face.

"Will's not home, Ma," Jamie reported, speaking quietly.

But Aunt Ellen only nodded. "No fear, I know where he is tonight. He met us at the train. He—he needed a pound or two," she said very steadily. "And I dropped him off at Bill Crotty's. They're having a bit of a do, his sister's to be married, you know."

"And—uh—and how was Clonmel?" I asked quickly, hoping we might stay away from the subject of birds indefinitely.

"Very nice." She sighed a bit. "It's the first time I've ever been there without your Uncle Martin. But Kathleen was my good company today, and we sold the horses without any trouble. James, we'll put that bit of cash away, and with what I get from the turkeys, there'll be enough to buy off Norwood next time and maybe a bit left over, too!"

"Ah, that's grand, that's grand," whispered Jamie, but I could hear him gulping all the way across the room.

Aunt Ellen smiled. "Oh, yes, Margaret told me you had a deal of trouble with the turkeys today," she said lightly, not looking at any of us, but seating herself in her rocking chair and putting her foot up to unbutton her tight boots. Instantly Kevin knelt by her side and helped her off with them. She patted him fondly on the head.

"Ah, but it's glad I am to be home again and find all of you here. It's good to have loved ones waiting and a fire made against your coming." She looked long at Margaret, who stood near the hearth, one hand on the mantel, staring down into the fire. "Margaret *ashthore,* you're a brave girl."

Margaret shook her head. "No, it was all my fault. And they had to work so hard, just because of me. I always make trouble."

"Oh, bless you, darling," scoffed Aunt Ellen. "Thank God there's only the three of them gone to that fat-bellied liar!"

"Liar? You mean the fox?" puzzled Margaret, as Jamie almost sloshed the tea to the floor in surprise.

Aunt Ellen nodded. "Aye, the fox indeed." She took her cup from Jamie and swallowed half of it down with great enjoyment. "I know that blackhearted rip—big and red he was, with a crooked bushy tail, wasn't he? Sure I've known him a year at least. And I've been feeding the creature, and him with a den and a wife and babes to support, too. I made a sort of a bargain with him. 'Fox,' says I, and I looked him square into those honest-looking, lying little beady eyes of his, 'fox, let's be decent with one another.' That's what I said to him, and he listened, for foxes are no fools, you know. And I says, 'I've no wish in the world to evict you from your home—there's been enough evictions in Ireland,' I says; 'so I'll keep to my place and you keep to yours. Leave me and me turkeys in peace and I'll leave you your support by the well every day at noontime.' And I've kept my part of the bargain. Every day since, I've put out his wee plate with scraps on it— Oh, Jesus, Mary and Joseph!" She let out an awful screech and set the cup down on the table with a bang. Instantly we all ran to her, but she was rocking back and forth with her shawl over her face as if she'd gone mad, and she was laughing as I had not heard her laugh since Uncle Martin was killed.

"Mrs. Daley?" asked Margaret timidly.

"No, no, child, I'm fine," panted my aunt, pulling her shawl down again. "Don't you see? The fox, the poor honest maligned fool of a fox—I forgot to leave him his dinner today! And when he came to the well to get it, what was he to think but that I'd broken my word—"

"That's where I saw him, at the well!" cried Margaret. "He was sitting there, not a bit afraid of me, and he kept looking at me as though he were waiting for something."

"Aye, aye." Aunt Ellen nodded. "And he *was*—for his dinner. No wonder he plundered the birds. The truce was broken and they were fair game. Poor creature, I'll have to make it up to him."

"Don't forget the three he did get," said Kevin.

"Oh, God help him, but won't he have the bellyache tomorrow?"

Now we all laughed, and suddenly found we had great appetites. Margaret and Kathleen already set out the cheese and soda bread, and the ham disappeared in a minute.

"Ah, if only Martin was here to see this tonight," said Aunt Ellen, simply, not sadly. "How pleased he would be to have you two children under his roof and sharing our food with us!"

Kevin flushed and turned away, the most peculiar look on his face. My aunt saw it, and went over to him, putting her arm about him. "Why, Kevin, love, what an old fool woman I am. I'd forgotten you were here that dreadful night. Why, yes, you and Margaret and your Da stayed to say the Rosary with the priest—I'm that sorry. But hush, now, Martin's never very far from us in this house, you know." Kevin did not turn to look at her, and I could see his two hands clenching and unclenching at his sides. But, before I could ask what was the matter, little Janet, still in her bedraggled dress, appeared in the doorway, rubbing her sleepy eyes and demanding to know if Ma was going to take a stick to the fox.

Aunt Ellen smiled and held out her hands for the baby to run to her, then wrapped her against the chill in her shawl and rocked her in her lap in the rocking chair. We all settled down again and began talking. My aunt told several little stories of times she had spent with Mary Culhane, funny little things that had happened, and gradually Kevin brightened again and sat down with the rest of us. Margaret sat before the fire, her dark head resting against Aunt Ellen's knees. In a little while, Kevin dozed off. Our talking did not disturb him.

Margaret seemed almost like another person. Her voice was soft and gentle, her mood very sweet, and her eyes wandered from my aunt's face, as she spoke, to little Janet asleep in her lap, to Kevin as he lay stretched out asleep. The lines in his face had nearly disappeared, and there was a little smile on his mouth. Margaret stared at him. "That's the way he used to sleep," she whispered. "When we were young. How young he looks now!"

Aunt Ellen smiled down at her. "He *is* young," she said. "He was always a good boy. I remember him as a baby, looking not much different than he does now. And you, you minx—" she poked Margaret teasingly—"you were always a little witch!"

Margaret acknowledged this with chagrin. Then my aunt leaned over and kissed her soundly. "Ah, you've just as good and kind a heart as your brother, Margaret *ashthore*," she said softly. "Don't ever be letting the world change you."

Margaret sighed a little and murmured, "I wish we could stay here forever."

And then, because wishes always attract too much attention in all the wrong places, there came a loud knocking at the front door, so loud it awakened both Kevin and little Janet, who began crying.

"Gerald, just go and see who it is, will you?" said Aunt Ellen as she lifted Janet to take her back to bed. "At such a time of the night, too. I hope no one's dead!"

The knocking continued, growing louder and more insistent although I called out that I was coming. I opened the door, and there stood himself Sean Culhane, his fist raised just about to knock again, nearly hitting me in the face.

"Mr. Culhane."

He entered quickly, after a look about outside before closing the door himself. "I'm glad to find you here, Jerry. Your father said you probably were—"

"You were looking for me?"

"Aye, lad, you and Jamie. Is he here, then?"

"Oh, yes, sir, he's inside. Will you come with me?"

"No, I don't think—" But Aunt Ellen's voice, calling from Janet's room, interrupted him.

"Gerald, who was calling?"

"Mr. Culhane, Aunt Ellen," I answered her.

At once Jamie's face appeared in the doorway at the end of the hall, looking that surprised.

"Jerry, I won't be a minute," Culhane said in a very low voice, and he sounded quite rushed. "Just get Jamie out here and tell him there's some news he might want to hear."

But Jamie was already coming down the hall, and I heard Kevin's voice, and then Margaret's, and Culhane heard them, too. He glanced from Jamie to me, apparently puzzled. And then my aunt came from the kitchen, her hand out, smiling.

"Sean Culhane, welcome to this house," she said very warmly.

"God bless all here," said Culhane hurriedly. "I'm sorry to disturb you so late at night, Ellen. I just wanted a word with the boys—"

"Army business, Sean?" said Aunt Ellen, dropping her hand abruptly.

"Looking for us, Father?" It was Kevin, standing in the

doorway, his two arms up, leaning on the frame, and he spoke in a voice I had never heard before.

Sean Culhane straightened up, his face tightening. "I didn't know you were here," he said coldly. "It has nothing to do with you. Margaret is with you?"

"We were just leaving," came Margaret's voice behind Kevin.

"Oh, no, children," protested Aunt Ellen, trying to warm the suddenly chilling air with her smile, but it was no use.

"It's late you're out," said Culhane, ignoring Aunt Ellen and the rest of us. Kevin smiled oddly. "Well, get on home, then. We'll speak of it later."

Kevin sauntered slowly down the hall, never taking his eyes from his father's face. "Did you bless the house and all in it, Father, when you came in?" he asked.

Culhane started, his face a study in anger and the struggle to control it.

"I did that," he answered quietly. Kevin laughed very loudly.

"Kevin!" exclaimed my aunt, and quickly he regained his composure.

"I'm sorry, Mrs. Daley," he murmured, then kissed her very tenderly on the cheek, and, without a look or a word more for anyone, he walked swiftly to the door and let himself out.

Sean turned to look after him, and the pure, open malignity of his expression was enough to shock you.

"Margaret," he called, after a second, "come along, then, your brother's gone."

Margaret took her time leaving, and lightly went round kissing us all in turn, and grandly apologized to Jamie for the whole situation with the turkeys.

"Good night, darling," said Aunt Ellen. "And please come again, come often, will you? You're always welcome, will you remember that, Margaret?"

Margaret caught Sean's eye on her and shook her head very slightly. "I don't think so," she whispered so low you almost couldn't hear her. "Goodbye." Then, with her head high, she sailed past her father and went after Kevin.

"Sean Culhane, God keep me from offending a guest in my house," began Aunt Ellen, her blue eyes blazing up as she watched Margaret go, "but I cannot abide the cold way you treat those two children! Have you learned nothing, then?"

Culhane waited till she paused for breath, then very quickly jumped in. "Ellen, I've neither time nor inclination for that subject. Let it rest between us as it has these years past. You must excuse me, but I've come to talk with Jamie and Jerry."

Aunt Ellen opened her lips as if to say something more, then thought better of it, glared at Culhane and the two of us, turned on her heel and went back into the kitchen, slamming the door very hard behind her.

Jamie and I were staring hard at the floor, both of us embarrassed by what we'd just seen and heard. But Culhane drew us into the parlor and closed the doors carefully. From his manner now, it seemed as if nothing whatever had happened.

"What's up?" asked Jamie eagerly. "It is something to do with the Army, isn't it?"

Culhane nodded briskly. "Now, listen, Jamie, I don't want you to get your hopes up for nothing, but I'm here to tell you to be at Johnny O'Donnell's house tomorrow night, early, and you may meet the man who betrayed your father."

Jamie jumped. "Who is he? What's his name? Do we know him? Tell me, Mr. Culhane. And who found him out?"

Sean waved his hand at him. "Keep your voice down, boy. Your mother'll have no liking for this bit of business, but, if it proves true, you know what must be done."

Jamie nodded impatiently. "Yes, yes, but just tell me who he is!"

Culhane shook his head. "I cannot," he said. "There's to be a hearing tomorrow night. Riordan's kept quiet about it all this time, but we've been on to him almost from the first. Now, strictly speaking"—he looked intently at Jamie—"you don't have to be there. But I thought that you, both of you, had a right to face the man down and witness whatever happens to him, if he's guilty."

"*If?*" cried Jamie. "Aren't you sure?"

"Sure enough," answered Culhane tersely. "We'll hear what he has to say, of course—"

"Kill him!" whispered Jamie.

A fleeting smile touched Culhane's thin mouth, and was gone. "We know what to do, just be there," he said, and, with a cautionary finger to his lips, he opened the door to the parlor once again. "I must get home. There are arrangements to be made. We've been rather busy on your account, James Daley," he said. "Let's hope it was worth it."

"If, as you say, he's the one, it was worth it, never fear," answered Jamie.

We went to the door with Culhane, changing what we talked of to nothing more important than the weather and the crops, and then, just as he was leaving, Culhane shot Jamie another of his strange, cold looks and said, "James, your father and myself shared many a thing in this fight of ours, and I like to think he was my friend."

"That he was indeed, Mr. Culhane," said Jamie heartily, but I could tell he was puzzled by Culhane's manner.

"And, as my friend," Culhane went on as if he had not heard Jamie at all, "Martin Daley understood many things about me, about my life, my plans, my family—"

"I think most of us understand those things, sir," said Jamie respectfully, but now Culhane raised his hand imperiously, and Jamie's words faded fast.

"Let me go on, if you will, Jamie. It's come to my attention recently that you and my children, and Gerald here, of course, have been together very often. I welcome your good intentions toward them. But I should like for us to understand each other clearly. My daughter—"

In the instant, Jamie's nostrils flared and his eyes grew dark. "What about her?" he asked in a dangerous quiet tone.

Culhane paused, then said, in much the same tone, "I would regret it very much if any unrealistic notions that might arise between yourself and her would change the good feelings between our two families. Margaret's life has been carefully planned for her. Whatever foolish, romantic dreams she might have, they are just that. She is hardly more than a child and easily influenced. But soon she will be on her way to London, to school. I should like her to go with a clear mind and no—regrets. Do you understand what I'm telling you, Jamie?"

"Yes!" answered Jamie harshly, his face very red.

"I mean nothing against yourself," added Culhane, but Jamie's mouth twisted scornfully. Seeing this, Culhane shrugged and opened the door.

"Has she nothing to say, then, about her own life?" called Jamie after him.

Culhane turned about. "She will say much, no doubt," he answered. "But it will come to naught. Good night, then." And we watched him stride quickly to the front gate, untie his horse, leap into the saddle, and ride off down the road.

Jamie slammed the door. His face was contorted with anger and hurt pride and humiliation.

"Why didn't I say anything?" he raged. "Why couldn't I open my mouth and tell him to go straight to hell! *That's* what he thinks has been going on? Why, damn him, anyway!"

"No, Jamie," I put in, hoping to calm him down a bit. "That's what he wants to *keep* from going on! Ah, sure, he's her father, and you know how fathers are about their daughters. And him especially. He does have big plans for her, she told you herself. Don't let it get you so. Didn't he bring great news for you, and isn't that worth more than a bit of a scolding?"

He landed a punch on the door that I swore nearly splintered it. "Scolding?" he thundered. "Did you see the look of him, then? He thinks I'm not good enough to live alongside of, not to say have anything to do with his damned high-class daughter!"

"Hey, hey, it's not Margaret you're sore at," I reminded him.

It took a bit of effort, but he did manage a short nod and a smile. "Ah, never mind, it's all nonsense anyway," he said, as we went back into the kitchen. "It's tomorrow night that's important."

If Aunt Ellen had heard anything we'd said, she never let on. We found her rocking by the fire, staring off into the flames, and there was a sorrowful look on her tired face. She'd combed out the neat bun she always wore pinned at the back of her head, and was absently brushing the long gray hair that hung down over her shawl.

"Is he gone?" she asked, not looking up.

"He is," I said. "And I'd best be off, too, before they send after me. It's near midnight."

"Ah, go along with you, then, child." She smiled at me. "Tell Anne I'll come over tomorrow night."

"I'll do that, then," said I, but Jamie was watching her curiously.

"Why tomorrow night, Ma?" he asked. She looked at him levelly and said, "Because I'll be wanting company, I expect, and you'll be away, won't you?"

She wanted no answer, there was none to give. She closed her eyes and sighed, and I left them there by the dying fire, sitting together in silence.

Chapter IX

Little Johnny O'Donnell and his wife, Rose, had a home three miles from town, out along the road to Kilmac-thomas. It was a snug place, set well back from sight, with a low stone fence running round it to the front. It had belonged to Rose's family; her mother used to grow geraniums planted in rows along the top of the fence. It was a very pretty sight, and Rose was always taking prizes at the fairs for her flowers. But, devil take the flowers, the best thing about them was that they served as a good cover between the house and the road. And, in those days, like these, when you were having a dozen or twenty men over of an evening, anything that offered a bit of cover was cheering.

Well, but Jamie had worked himself up into a rare fit of nervousness and temper by the time we got there the next night. We'd stopped by to pick up Willie Cassidy and his brother, Frankie, along the way. But still we were a bit early when we arrived.

O'Rourke, him with his eyes always upturned to heaven, nary a word out of his mouth he didn't weigh three times, he was the only other man there yet, besides Johnny himself. Johnny was bolting down a bite of supper in the kitchen, having only just come in from the milking.

"Will you take tea?" inquired Rose of the five of us, propped up very formal in her parlor, staring down at our shoes whilst her mother and father's pictures over the mantel stared down at *us*. Rose was a pretty, plump little woman, but I could see right off she was very nervous and all of a tremble that evening. Somehow she'd got it into her head that everything had to be done just right, as if there were some particular kind of etiquette for holding meetings of an illegal and revolutionary nature in the front parlor. She'd gotten all dressed up for it, and all the best china was spread out on the table, too. I couldn't believe that Johnny had told her exactly why we were meeting that night, and I really wondered why it was at his house, him with the little girls already asleep in their beds upstairs.

"No tea, thank you kindly, Rose." O'Rourke was near to whispering, for the parlor had a dire effect upon his usual raw manner, and I could tell from the uneasy shifting of his eyeballs here and there that he wished they could have had the damn gathering down at the pub and be done with it. Rose looked disappointed, so Jamie and I gallantly accepted some tea, and Johnny finally called her away so we were able to talk freely.

"Why did Riordan pick here?" I asked O'Rourke.

"Cautious," he drawled laconically. "More patrols, dogs. We'll be moving about more from now on."

"But Rose and the kids," said Jamie, frowning. "This is a bad bit of business."

"It won't be done here," replied O'Rourke, his voice remote.

In bounded little Johnny, shaking hands with all of us as if he hadn't seen us in a year. A moment later Riordan arrived, and soon my father and Sean Culhane came in, and the rest, in twos and threes, came a few minutes apart from one another. All eyes seemed to focus on Jamie and, to a lesser extent, on myself, but he was too keyed up to notice, and, of course, not a word was said.

Rose greeted everyone, offering them tea, but they all declined. She looked about at us all hesitantly, then said good night very quietly. Willie's brother, Frankie, was the lookout, just out by the door, but I knew that Rose would go upstairs and sit by the window and do her sewing in the falling darkness with one eye on the Kilmacthomas Road.

Riordan made his way over to Jamie and me. "I take it your brother's not a convert to our cause yet, Jamie?" He smiled, trying to put us at ease. "He'll come in, never fear. Every day new recruits are joining up. We're just beginning here."

Jamie smiled cynically. "Will is going to show up the day we start issuing whiskey along with the rifles," he said.

Riordan clapped him on the back, a gesture which began in a rough, hearty way but ended more as a soft patting, and he dropped his light manner as he said, "Sean's told you about tonight?"

Jamie nodded.

"Whatever happens, remember, you'll not be the one to do it," said Riordan sternly. "This is no question of personal revenge. A crime may have been committed. A trial will be held. If someone is found guilty of the crime or crimes, the Army will exact justice. Do you understand that well, Daley?"

"Yes, sir," snapped Jamie.

Then Riordan nodded and walked back to the doorway, where poor Johnny was quickly removing all of Rose's good china, piling it precariously on shelves and chair arms, for they needed the dining-room table for the hearing. I swallowed very hard, suddenly, realizing what Riordan had called it, a *trial,* and it began to sift in to me, unpleasantly, that in a little while some man, perhaps even someone we all knew, was going to be fighting for his life at that table.

Riordan and Culhane, my father, O'Rourke, Liam Mc-Loughlin, the mayor, and two other men from town sat down around the table, leaving one empty chair for us all to gape at. Riordan took some papers from a leather case and put them in a neat, precise pile in front of him on the table, then looked up and gazed around very gravely as he began to speak.

"Gentlemen, you all know why we are here tonight. For some time now we have been plagued by betrayal from within our ranks—"

"No!" cried someone, and several jumped up, calling out, but Riordan merely waited till they quieted down of their own accord.

"No, not any one of us in the Army—you misunderstand me, gentlemen. I meant someone Irish born and Irish bred, calling himself, thinking himself, an Irishman. I meant the ranks of our people, for we are all engaged in this war . . ."

A great sigh went through the room and I realized with some surprise that I was not the only one of us who had feared, and, indeed, half expected the informer to be found out one of ourselves.

Riordan's eyes narrowed as he took in the reaction, and, unexpectedly, he slammed his fist down hard on the table.

"Damn it, gentlemen, that is our greatest weakness. That is what hampers our movements and endangers our every activity—the fact that you can wonder, nay, that you *must* wonder and be cautious, even with each other, never knowing what man you can trust. That is the real danger the informer does our cause, to plant mistrust and suspicion amongst men who, to be most effective in their work, must depend upon each other wholeheartedly! The mouse nibbles; the rat knaws away from the inside, gentlemen, till the whole of our endeavor remains only a standing shell, only too easy to be toppled over by our enemies from the outside. Thus, between them both, we are destroyed!

"Now, you know we have been carrying on an investigation concerning the shameful betrayal of Martin Daley and Brian Cavenaugh this June past. We have been investigating other, similar cases, all without much luck, until last week. At that time, certain intelligence was obtained which led us to the man who will shortly be brought before you, charged with informing in the Daley case and three or four other such cases. This intelligence, together with the results of the investigation we have made, was sent up to Dublin with a request for orders as to how we should proceed. Occasionally a known informer is not brought in, but merely watched for some time in the hope of obtaining useful information. Such, however, was not the recommendation in this situation." He paused and looked rather pointedly at the empty chair, and I could not tell whether it was anger or sorrow that showed most plainly on his thin face.

"Yesterday morning, we received orders from Dublin to arrest and try the man, and if necessary, to carry out the sentence of this military tribunal. We have the man in our charge; it remains for us now to see that justice is done."

Jamie called out, "Who found out about him?"

Riordan was already shaking his head before the question was finished, refusing to give that information, when Sean Culhane leaned forward at the table and said, "He has a right to know everything we can tell him about this, Captain. It was myself, Jamie," he went on. "I heard some remarks from a young officer who was at my house one afternoon. He didn't say much, and I couldn't ask him much, or show that I was interested at all, but there was just enough, a name, connected with a few other names, just enough for us to have a place to begin, at last."

"You think—you believe it was this man turned in my father, Mr. Culhane?" Jamie cried eagerly, and Culhane glancing at Riordan, folded his hands before him, and, pursing his lips, nodded but said nothing more.

Riordan signaled four men who had remained standing by the door, and quickly they left the room.

"They'll be only a few moments," he said. "We've got the man safe nearby. Johnny, you're sure Rose will stay upstairs?"

Johnny nodded very earnestly. I saw him glance up toward the staircase with a little, worried frown, for he knew quite well what was to be done that night, and none of us wanted Rose frightened.

"I'd give ten years off my life, if he really is the one," said Jamie. "I want it over and finished with."

"We all want to see Martin's ghost laid to rest in peace," said my father. "And thanks to Sean Culhane for the doing of it. We've good cause to be grateful to you, Sean, and not just for tonight." The others murmured their agreement.

Culhane looked embarrassed. "Thank God there are a few compensations for keeping strange company," he said diffidently.

Everyone laughed, too loudly, to cover up their nerves, for the time seemed to be going by too slowly, and we were all so terribly conscious of what was about to happen. Riordan began talking in a calm, normal voice about the schedules of future drills, and the distribution of arms, which was going very slowly. Not one in five of us had any kind of weapon, and few of us had even had the chance to learn the working of a rifle or hand weapon. There was also the problem of where to keep them, for any Irishman found with weapons of any kind was subject to immediate arrest and internment without any trial or hearing of any kind. Any house could be searched without warrant, at any time. As we yet had no permanent camp, even in the hills, for security reasons, that was no answer, either. A few rifles had been hidden away in the church basement, but no church was safe from search and seizure, and even those few weapons were a constant threat to us.

Culhane said, "There's only one place for them, and that's Culhane House."

We were stunned. "What?" cried Johnny. "Your house, is it, with the English in and out the doors like blowing leaves? Are you daft, Sean?"

"It's precisely because they *are* in and out—may the good Lord keep them coming—I've never had the house searched to this day. Even four years ago, when it was a general thing, you all remember? One day, when I was entertaining as usual, a detail of soldiers did come to the door with that purpose in mind. And my guests were so outraged they ordered the soldiers to be off and away without their getting so much as a look at the wallpaper!"

Riordan was obviously weighing the possibilities. He said slowly, "It's true enough, it would be easier for you to handle the money as well as the weapons. You've many dealings with various banks, have you not, Sean?"

Culhane nodded.

"Aye, you're a man of business, and fairly large sums pass through your hands pretty often. I'd feel better if that end of things was operated by one man, such as yourself, for I've been wary up to now, and keep changing the couriers, but it wastes time, for I must instruct each man as to procedures, and that leaves too many knowing too much. But the trouble is, how to get the weapons from you when they're needed? You know we can't meet at your house, and even one or two of us showing up there and coming away with a bundle wouldn't look so damned innocent, you know, Sean."

Culhane was about to speak, when James called out, "Why not let Kevin or Margaret take them out, in the donkey cart, say? They'd not be bothered, no more than yourself."

Culhane's head turned swiftly, and his eyes grew deathly cold, his voice tipped with frost as he snapped, "That's out of the question. I won't have my children involved in this—"

"No, no, Sean, don't worry yourself," said Riordan hastily. "Jamie, we'll find some other way. But the cart is a good suggestion, nevertheless. A load of hay on the back would hide the guns well enough. Wait, now, how's this: Who do you get your hay and oats from, Sean?"

"In town, Gilhooley's," said Culhane, still angry.

"Well, then, but you could order from the Daley place just as well, couldn't you? They'd be glad of the money, and Jamie could deliver it to your barn every so often, and come away with a load of, oh, say, horse manure for his fields."

Culhane's anger dwindled, and he nodded eagerly, saying, "Yes, yes, I see. He could bring the money and pick up whatever I've been able to arrange for. That might work very well, Captain. If it's agreeable to Jamie?"

Jamie was all for it. "But how do I get the money you're talking about? And what do I do with the weapons after I leave Culhane's?"

Riordan was making notes quickly. He glanced up. "The money will be delivered to you by one of us, and when you get it you will know that you are to deliver your hay to Sean within twenty-four hours, leaving the money covered, in the barn, and taking the guns out with you. There will be no need to go near the house, nor to contact Sean himself. After you leave Culhane House, drive over that old dirt road, where Kilgannon's house used to be, before it burned down. Unload the cart. Put the guns in back of the stone chimney, it's still standing, and drive home at once. From there, others will see to them."

Jamie nodded. "Aye, that's good. It'll work, if no one talks."

"How long will it take before we're ready?" asked Culhane. "I know there's half the country to train and equip, but it goes so slow! Who is our fellow that travels back and forth to America? Can't he move any faster, then? Or, maybe, can you send a few more along, too? Jesus Christ, Riordan, the war will be over soon, and they'll have to be doing something about the Home Rule Law. Ulster's mustered up two hundred thousand to fight against it, and I've heard they're all armed and ready. What about ourselves?"

Everyone began talking at once, but Riordan quieted them down. "We'll be ready," he said, but Culhane was quite worked up.

"Damn it, Riordan," he flared up, "don't be so cool,

man, will you? We've got to do something more, don't you see? All the training's been fine and the few bits of things we've done so far are good practice, but we're like dogs nipping at their heels—we annoy them, we slow them down, but we don't cast them out! Things are coming to a head. I say, now's the time to get ourselves together and rise up all over Ireland. What are we waiting for?"

"Are, right you are, Sean!" cried more than one man there, but my father muttered under his breath, "Fool talk, fool talk!" and Riordan shook his head.

"Not yet. We're not prepared for that kind of action. Would you ask for another Easter Week, so soon after the first?" he cried, and shouts of anger and frustration filled the room.

"I know, I know, we're all eager for the one last great push, so is the Army everywhere, here, and in America, and up in Dublin. But don't underestimate what we've got to contend with. Our orders for the present are what they have been: train, distribute arms, raise money, recruit more men, and wait."

"Wait!" snorted Culhane. "It's bad enough that our enemies scoff at us and treat us like a band of jungle apes, for the love of God, and not an army at all, without us acting bloody well like! Ours is the only goddamned Army in the world, I guess, where we don't know how many men we've got altogether, or who they are, outside our own company, or even who the hell is running it all! Oh, I don't mean De Valera and all those highups. I mean—well, for instance, who is the Riordan in Clonmel? Or Cappogh? or Kilmac? How many can we count on even in the next village over? Now, *you* know these things, Riordan, you'd have to. You're in on all the top-level conferences. You're the one who talks to Dublin. Well, you see, we don't even know who it is you talk to up there! Where the hell is the money coming from? Where are the guns landed? Who picks them up?

"You're the only one who knows all this. And if anything happens to yourself, why, we all fall apart. We don't have our fingers in it. I'm not saying every man of us needs to know how the whole operation is run, but, by God, someone besides yourself must be in on it; can't your friends in Dublin see that?"

Riordan had gotten to his feet, his eyes narrow, his mouth tight. "You know I can't answer any one of those questions, Culhane," he retorted.

And Culhane answered right back. "You're damned right we know that very thing," he cried. "And we know all the reasons for this secrecy. Pray God tonight will bring an end to our doubts of each other, for I tell you this, and you all know it's the truth: England will soon turn on us like the mad dog she has always been in Ireland. Her returning troops, seasoned, experienced troops from France and Belgium, will pour into our country, and we can expect only treachery and civil war from the north. We've got to join ranks now, we've got to know who we can depend on, who's with us, how it's all put together. I say the time for keeping it in the dark is over, and it's time for putting all the pieces of this great Army you're always telling us we are *together*. Why let them come at all? March to the docks in Dublin and burn the ships as they anchor there!"

Amidst mingled cheers, shouts, and cries of dissent, Riordan's voice now rang out louder than Culhane's at last. "That's the kind of wild rhetoric that has kept Ireland down these six hundred years!" he argued. "Sean, you swore an oath to obey orders as they come, from whom and however they come. Every man who carries the kind of information you would have is a potential bomb in our midst. If it's only myself, and it must be, those are the orders, make no mistake, Sean or any of you, those orders will be carried out, and the first man to object I shall personally lay in his grave with my own hands!"

"Talk, Riordan, talk," returned Culhane sarcastically. "What's to become of us if they take you? They had you once—"

Riordan's eyes flashed dangerously. "Aye, they did. And they learned nothing. Tell me, Sean, would you care to hear how hard they tried to persuade me to open my mouth?"

And the room suddenly became very quiet again. Riordan leaned forward eagerly. "All of you have families. Many have small children, Lomes, farms, stores to lose. I? I don't exist. I have no one, nothing to lose. All I had to lose is long gone. There is not a living soul they could use to force my tongue. And," he dropped his voice so low we had to strain to hear him, "at the last, if there was no other way to keep silent, do you think they would find me alive?"

"We all applaud your courage, Captain," declared Culhane stiffly. "We just want the chance to test our own."

"Aye, Mr. Culhane, you're right!" called out Jamie enthusiastically.

Riordan sighed. "Daley, impetuosity never won a war." But other voices interrupted, taking sides, some with Culhane, some with Riordan, and a minute later I found myself on my feet, shouting as loudly as the rest, backing up Sean Culhane, wondering why Riordan could not see he was right.

"Gerald, sit down!" My father seized my arm and pulled me down next to him. Then, a most unusual thing for him, for he was such a quiet man, he stood up himself and called for order, in a voice so loud and harsh that it cut through all the rest. Everyone looked at him in surprise, and Riordan in gratitude. They milled around a bit, but soon were fairly quiet once more. Still my father remained on his feet.

"I want to ask only one question, and someone should have asked it, I think, before this," he said.

"And what would that be, Desmond?" asked Riordan.

"Just this: I assume, I hope correctly, that our commanders in Dublin or wherever they are have thought ahead to the possibility that yourself may be killed or captured, and have already made some plan or two to cover such a contingency, without leaving ourselves floundering around like fish in a barrel?"

Riordan smiled and nodded. "Of course." And my father sat down again. Culhane was still quite worked up, and I thought he looked over our way with an oddly special malevolence, but then I told you he was a peculiar man. To tell the truth, I would not have believed, had I not seen it myself, that he was capable of such a great burst of emotion, but people were always misjudging Sean Culhane, the poor man!

Now we heard a sudden, low knocking on the front door, and every voice ceased at once. We hardly drew breath, then the knock came again, and then again. It was Frankie's signal. There were headlights on the road and we heard a motorcar approaching. The car turned in by the house, continued on around back, then the lights cut out, the motor died.

"It's them," said Riordan softly. "Johnny, turn off some of the lights in here, will you? Everyone, sit down now, and be quiet."

Quiet we were, and quiet we stayed, settling down in our chairs once more as the triple signal was repeated, this time at the back door. Johnny went into the kitchen to let them in. A minute later two of our men entered, leading a stranger between them, with the other two, followed up by Johnny, behind.

They shoved the strange man down into the empty chair and stood back against the wall, watching him. He had been blindfolded. Riordan gave a signal, and Johnny removed the blindfold as we all stared curiously.

The man was short and heavyset, wearing thick eye-glasses, which the blindfold had evidently pressed hard against his face. He sat rubbing his eyes and blinking, but not looking around at all; he wiped his glasses over and over with the end of his tie, and, watching his hands moving nervously, I wondered why they had not tied him up. He had a broad, reddish face and was breathing very heavily, almost wheezing, and still he looked down, at his glasses, at his hands, at his feet, at the floor, but not at anyone at that table.

"What is this?" he demanded in a high, froggy-throated voice, and for all the bravado in the question, it was easy to see he was thoroughly terrified.

Ignoring the question, Riordan, his own voice quite remote, asked, "You are Timothy Gallagher, are you not?"

The man nodded several times. "You know who I am," he quavered. And it was then he looked up and stared around him. "Why am I here?" he asked.

"You have been accused of informing against your own people," said Riordan, his words like hot lumps of lead dropping onto an icicle.

Gallagher cried out incoherently, tried to jump up, but someone pushed him down from behind.

"You have no right to do this," he sobbed. "This is no court. You're just a pack of murdering shinners!"

"Be still!" warned Riordan.

Gallagher sank back in his chair, wheezing heavily and murmuring unconnected snatches of prayers under his breath.

Riordan began to read from the papers in front of him, pages and pages of sworn statements against him, involving him in incidents going back ten years or more. I did not know any of the names that were mentioned. Whoever had put it all together had been thorough. Gallagher was a dairy farmer from outside Cappogh. He traveled about more than the average farmer, delivering his milk in several villages, and to the two hotels in Dungarvan. He also supplied milk to the police barracks there, as well as to British Army installations in the area. Gallagher had done very well for himself over the years. He employed eight regular men in the dairy, and four delivery men besides himself.

"Why have you continued making milk deliveries personally, in spite of the fact that all four of your main delivery routes are well served by your own employees? Why is it yourself, and not any of your men, who takes the milk to the police barracks and to the army installations? Twice each week you make regular stops at each of those places, lasting upwards of half an hour at each."

Gallagher squirmed, tried to explain that he had old friends in those places, customers who had stayed with him from years before, and he enjoyed spending a little time talking with them. "I'm a busy man," he said. "You don't find Timothy Gallagher lifting a pint with his pals in the pub of an evening. But a man's got to have some company, don't he? I work hard. I pay my debts. I owe no man and I mind my business. And it's my business who my friends are."

Riordan nodded. "That's true enough," he agreed. "But now it's become our business, too." He pulled out a large folded sheet of paper, which he held up, opened, to show us it was covered with small figures. "This was taken from the business accounts of Mr. Gallagher," he explained. "You do well, extraordinarily well, don't you? You've no need to lift a finger for the rest of your life. Accounts in three banks in Dungarvan, one in Dublin."

"Since when do you hang a man for making money?" cried Gallagher.

Riordan laughed curtly. "It's been known," he said. "But we don't envy you your just earnings, Mr. Gallagher. We're just curious about where they came from. You have noted down here the receipts from the farm, and the milk routes. Those monies you have deposited in Dungarvan. But we wonder where did you get the money you sent up to Waterford City once a month, by post, to your solicitor, Mr. John Leonard, with instructions, written in your own hand, to deposit to your account? Will you tell us where that money comes from?"

"Where did you get that stuff?" shouted Gallagher, once again jumping up. "That's my private papers, you've no right to steal them out of my own house!"

Quickly Riordan put the papers aside, without answering Gallagher. Then, waiting till the man had been forced to sit again, Riordan said to him, "When did you first come to know Martin Daley?"

A look of bewilderment crossed Gallagher's red, sweaty face.

"Martin Daley?" he repeated, shaking his head. "I don't know the name. Who is he?"

"Liar!" cried Sean Culhane, jumping to his feet. "You knew him. You knew a great deal about him. You informed on him, confess it!"

"Culhane, sit down!" snapped Riordan, but the other men were exclaiming angrily now, and it would be hard to quiet them.

"You're not that far from Dunknealy, Mr. Gallagher, that you would not have heard of Mr. Daley's unfortunate death this June past, along with one of the Fenian organizers from Dublin, by the name of Brian Cavenaugh. Search your memory, Mr. Gallagher, surely the tale was talked about, here and there, on your travels?"

Gallagher's brow puckered, then suddenly he threw back his head and began to speak quickly. "Oh, oh yes, now I remember. Him that was hanged, wasn't it? For hiding the other man out? I never knew him. I just heard the name, like you said, as I went about."

"And did you, by any chance, also happen to hear the name of Leftenant Robert Dudley, Royal Kent Brigade, stationed in Dungarvan?" called out Culhane. Gallagher's expression changed swiftly. He stared, openmouthed, as Sean went on. "Mr. Dudley is that fond of buttermilk, isn't he? Orders a couple of quarts every week, sometimes more often. Says he could get it more cheaply in town, but there's something very special, very special," Culhane repeated slowly, "about yours. Leftenant Dudley was the man responsible for the hanging. Now, how did he know about Cavenaugh? How did he know who was hiding him? How did he know about the secret room behind the parlor wall? How do you suppose he knew all those things, eh, Gallagher?"

"God in heaven," shouted Gallagher, "how do I know how *he* knew them? I never heard them before this night. I had nothing to do with it. You're trying to say I informed. I didn't. I didn't. I never knew Martin Daley or the other one. I don't know you. I don't know what I'm doing here!"

"Where did your travels take you the third week of June?" asked Riordan, referring to yet another paper. Without waiting for Gallagher's reply, he answered it himself. "Twice into Dungarvan. And the evening of the second time, you sent one of your men by train up to Waterford City, carrying two hundred pounds sterling, to be delivered by hand to your solicitor, the same John Leonard! Two hundred pounds, a nice round figure. And the very next night Martin Daley was dead."

"I—someone owed it to me," cried Gallagher, for the first time turning and looking round at all of us watching him. "You can find out yourselves, ask. Ask Dan Thompson at the barracks. He had gambling debts. He used to get into card games with the wrong people. He had to pay them, last year, or they were going to hurt him. I loaned him the money, and it took him the year to save it up to pay back."

"Hmmm," remarked Riordan thoughtfully. "Frugal man, Thompson, saving two hundred pounds in only a year, and him only drawing corporal's pay."

"I—I think he had a lucky run of the cards!" cried Gallagher. "I don't know. He just had it for me and—and I took it, that's all there was to it!"

"Where did you hear about Martin Daley?" my father called out.

Gallagher squinted, trying to see where the question had come from.

"Who told you about him?"

"What?" gasped Gallagher, peering around wildly. "I told you. Everyone was talking about it, everyone I met. It was all over, every town, every farm, every village. That was the first I knew of it, you've got to believe me!"

"Sean," Riordan said quietly, turning now to Culhane, "tell this court what you heard concerning this man, and from whom you heard it."

Culhane stood up. "As you heard before, I had several of the officers and their wives over at the house for tea. Among them was Leftenant Dudley. During the conversation, there was much talk about our—the Army's—activities. It was Dudley's opinion that we would never come to anything, that soon our old problem would defeat us again, as it had before, and he said, 'All we have to do now is wait for the informers to appear. They always have, and we have always reaped the benefit.' I answered him, pointing out very carefully that there had not seemed to be any such goings on in recent years, not in Waterford anyway, not even after the business at Eastertime. And then Dudley laughed, and spoke in high praise of Mr. Gallagher here, and he said wasn't it lucky for England that the tinkers liked buttermilk almost as much as he did!"

"The tinkers!" cried Jamie, horrified. "No, that's not possible. 'Twas them that brought Cavenaugh to us. 'Twas them cared for him, and hid him at risk of their own lives!"

"One mad dog is all that's needed, Jamie, and all dogs get a bad name," said Riordan.

"You're lying!" exclaimed Gallagher, staring terrified at Culhane. "He—he's lying. He's making it all up, every word. Dudley couldn't have said any of it, for none of it happened!"

"Gallagher, be careful. We've got enough on you here, without taking Martin Daley into consideration, to hang you three times over," warned Riordan, tapping the pile of papers before him.

Gallagher slumped back in his chair, a choking sob in his throat. "Why are you bothering with this farce? This is no trial. You're going to take me out and murder me, aren't you? Oh, my God, you come stealing into a man's house in the night, drag him away from his fire and his family—"

"You've no right to enjoy that fire, that house, or even that family!" called out my father fiercely. "Ireland is at war. You've been given a chance to answer our charges, but you won't or you can't. Legally we could have shot you where you stood! There's many a good man gone from his fire and family this night because of you, you low bastard, and others like you!"

"War!" cried Gallagher, with a choking laugh. "Ireland has always been at war. It's a regular condition of life. Well, I'm sick of it. I'm sick of being pounded down. I'm sick of taxes I can't pay and troops and police marching in and out of my house whenever they take a notion to! I found a way to make them leave me alone. I found a way to live, in spite of everything. And there's not one of you here wouldn't do the same, given cause!"

Riordan rose carefully from behind the table, so carefully he moved that it seemed the furniture and the very floor under his feet were made of glass and he feared to hurt them. He came and stood in front of Gallagher. Without the slighest warning, he lifted his open right hand and slapped the cringing man contemptuously across the cheek. I shall never forget the look of loathing on his thin, drawn face, as the lamplight caught on the silver close-cropped hair, the deep brown eyes, the long thin pale scar that wound its way down one side of his face from temple to jaw. Gallagher reacted to the slap with a moan, jerking his head away, but he could not keep himself from staring into Riordan's depthless gaze.

"Cause?" repeated Riordan. "There is only one cause in Ireland, and it is shared by all of us." Then, without turning or taking his gaze from the cowering man before him, he said, "What is the verdict of this court?"

"Guilty," said Sean Culhane.

"Guilty,' said Liam McLoughlin, at the same moment several other voices said the same word. "Guilty as charged."

One by one, and swiftly now, the men were answering, and I saw that soon it would be my turn, and Jamie's, and I was troubled. I could see something eating away at Jamie too, and when it came time for him to speak he hesitated, so that everyone turned around to look at him impatiently.

"What do you say, Daley? Guilty or not?" asked Riordan.

"I don't know!" said Jamie slowly. "Oh, I know we've got all the evidence and the testimony and witnesses and that, but he hasn't said it. I want him to say it himself."

The men called out to him, many of them angry now, for the thing was dragging on that they wished to be over.

"Did you not hear the man tell of a way he'd found to keep them away from him, Jamie?" asked McLoughlin patiently.

Jamie nodded. "Yes, but let him say more. What about my father? That's what I'm here to witness, my father's killer brought to justice."

Gallagher was watching Jamie intently, hanging on his words, and now he cried out to Jamie himself, "I never harmed your father, boy! I never heard the name of Daley before the hanging. I didn't inform on him, I swear to Christ and His Blessed Mother!"

"Daley, this is not a private argument—" Riordan called out.

But Jamie didn't even seem to hear him. "What good will it do you to confess the rest and not that? What will you gain by it? You do confess to those other things, the things they read out to us? Do you? Speak up!"

"Daley!"

"Yes, yes, it's true," Gallagher's brief fling at bravado had departed for good. Now he fell down on his knees, sobbing, beating his fist on the table. "I passed along information, now and again—"

"For money?" persisted Jamie, paying no attention to Riordan's stern gaze.

"Yes, for money—and protection. But I *did not know* about Martin Daley!"

Jamie stared at him for a few seconds, whilst the rest of us watched him, and I saw emotions fight one another in him, till at last his features became very stiff, his eyes remote, and he called out, like the rest, "Guilty!"

Then I had to speak. I watched every move Gallagher made, hoping, even now, that he would break down and say the rest. But I realized that whether he had turned in Uncle Martin or not, he was guilty of the other charges anyway. "Guilty," I said, wondering, as I said it, why I too suddenly felt so guilty.

And finally Riordan. "Guilty. Take him out."

Gallagher attempted to stand, but fell down again, hanging on to Riordan's legs and screaming, but they pulled him away.

Johnny darted forward. "Shut him up, for God's sake, or they'll hear him over to Dungarvan!"

Allie Clarke produced a handkerchief, and was in the process of trying to tie it around Gallagher's mouth, when Rose ran downstairs, her long hair plaited over her shoulder for the night, a robe pulled over her, and her eyes, looking around the room, were wide and full of horror.

"What is it, Johnny? Captain Riordan, what's going

on?" She glanced at Gallagher, being held up between Allie and Joe Clarke.

"Missis, missis, help me!" shrieked Gallagher, trying to grab her hand. "Missis, I didn't do what they think I did. They're going to—"

"Get that man out of here!" ordered Riordan abruptly, and the boys quickly dragged him into the kitchen.

Rose turned to Johnny. "Johnny, what is it?"

He patted her shoulder and tried to lead her back up the stairs, but she would not go. None of us would answer her, though she looked from one to the other of us. I thought Johnny a fool for not having told her what might happen. But Jamie, standing by Sean Culhane, was paying no attention to what went on. He seemed to be arguing with Culhane, both speaking in low voices, and Culhane shaking his head vigorously. Rose sank down onto a chair. Riordan gave Johnny the eye, trying to get him to take Rose away, but again she would not budge.

"Captain Riordan," said Jamie, his face quite angry, "I want to go with them. I have a right."

"I told him it was out of the question," said Culhane.

Riordan shook his head. He took a revolver from his pocket, and for one horrible moment I thought he was about to put it into Jamie's own hands. Jamie thought so, too, and I saw him shrink back from it a bit. But Riordan handed the weapon to Culhane instead.

"Take him with you," ordered Riordan, and he would not let Sean talk him out of it.

"Jerry and myself will come, too," said my father.

Rose stared at him, then flung her hand up to her mouth, her teeth biting the knuckles as she cried, "Oh, God, you're going to kill him!"

Riordan spoke gently to her. "The man's an informer, Mrs. O'Donnell. He was charged, found guilty, and will be executed. That's all there is to it."

She searched his face trustingly. "An informer? You're sure he was that? He confessed it?"

"Most of it," Riordan said. "There was much evidence against him. He was directly involved in three cases we are sure of, and seven men connected with those cases are dead, because of him. And we are also convinced he was responsible for Martin Daley's death, although he denies it."

"God, God, think of it!" she murmured. Then she closed her eyes. "It's still murder you're doing," she said flatly.

"Rose—!" cried Johnny, but she would not let him finish.

"I know. It has to be done. I know an informer is a danger to us all," she whispered. "But, still, there'll be a reckoning someday, you'll see. You do what you must do now, but we'll all pay for it somehow. I don't think God will bless this night's work."

"It has nothing to do with God!" said Riordan darkly, a pained look in his eyes. "None of it has anything to do with God. It's all in our hands, can't you see that? God's not on one side or another. It's ours, it's whatever we make of it. And paying is something that starts before we're born, Rose O'Donnell. And it goes on and on, before, in the middle, and at the end—but there's no end to the paying. One day, a man will find the way to stop it all. I've no doubt it will be a simple way, so simple we might have found it long ago. And on that day, the whole mad business of man's fear and hatred of other men will be finished." His voice grew harder, and his eyes closed for an instant, infinitely weary. "But that day isn't here yet. We're in a circle of darkness, Rose, don't you see? And we must all keep plowing the same stony field, round and round, till we find a way to break the circle. Now, maybe when that happens, God will be glad of it, but I don't think any of us will know that."

There was a pause, and my father said, "Come on, let's go," and he, Jamie, and I followed after the Clarkes and Gallagher.

We went out the back door, around to the side, where the car was parked. Joe got into the driver's seat. Next to him was Culhane and Jamie. They pushed Gallagher in back with my father and me. Allie shut the doors, gave a look to the road, and signaled us to go ahead. Then he watched us. I looked out the back window and saw him looking after us, and then he walked slowly back into Johnny's house.

Chapter X

We had no moon, but the sky shifted with restless, hurrying clouds that seemed to be propelled endlessly from someplace to someplace else, never getting anywhere. The car sped along, too, and ourselves in it, silent, thinking our own thoughts. Joe drove north, then headed east, up along the coast to Blind Cove.

Timothy Gallagher sat between my father and me in the back seat, huddled all to himself, his arms clasped tight against him. I thought maybe we ought to have tied him up, but there wasn't any fight left in the man. My father was watching him, and Sean Culhane, up in front, was sitting half turned around so he could keep an eye on him as well. After a bit, Sean took out some cigarettes, lit one for himself, and was about to put them away when he changed his mind and held out the box to Gallagher.

But Gallagher seemed not to see them at all. Sean nudged him, and offered them again, and Gallagher blinked, as if he were having some trouble focusing his eyes. Then he looked at the cigarettes, and at Sean, and at the cigarettes again, so obviously bewildered that Culhane shrugged and put them back into his pocket. Gallagher kept looking at him, and finally Culhane turned full around front and started to talk to Joe about the road and how far we had come.

I wondered what Jamie was thinking, if he was remembering the night his father died. Of course, what else would be in his mind as we raced along there? Well, and it would all be over soon. I kept telling myself that, for comfort, though damn little comfort it did me. I had begun to realize already that nothing ever is really over, it just thins out as time fills in. I wondered why I felt no hate for Gallagher. Indeed, there didn't seem to be any feeling of hatred about any of us. Just coldness and a feeling of unreality. Was that the feeling of justice being served? It surely was different from hot hate, or even cold hate, a curious feeling, one I had not experienced before.

Whilst I was still beguiling myself from what was happening to me, we had reached Blind Cove. It looked a most desolate place. Not a house in sight anywhere, not a light to be seen. Were it not for the sound of the waves rushing in, you could hardly tell we were on the shore.

Joe parked the car behind a big outcropping of rocks away from the road. We had to drag Gallagher out of the back seat, for the moment he felt the car stop, he had begun to weep afresh, and he clung now with both hands to the back of the front seat. God, how I hated putting hands on the creature and forcing him to his own death! I think I would gladly have shot him myself, there, right in the car, just to have it finished. I knew he would talk, talk, talk to the very end, and I knew, without despising him for it, that he would crawl and beg and plead for his life, and that we would kill him nevertheless.

We walked past the rocks, down to the edge of the water, stumbling a bit on the stony beach in the dark. Gallagher was praying under his breath, and he was still crying all the while, but he made no move to run away. And, as last, Sean Culhane said, "Here." And we stopped.

Sean took the gun from his pocket and checked to make sure it was loaded properly and the safety catch was off. Gallagher fell back a step, flinging his arm in front of his face, and he looked for Jamie, who had stayed a few feet away.

"Daley," said Gallagher, "Daley, listen to me, will you listen, then?"

"I am listening," replied Jamie evenly

"I've done a lot, you understand? I've done what they

said, all of it, but that. Not that. You've nothing against me, I swear it. What do those others matter to you? Or to you, or you?" he turned and looked quickly at me and my father. "You three are here because of one man, Martin Daley. You don't care about the rest of it. If you believed I did not harm this boy's father, would you let them kill me anyway? Why would I lie to you now? What else do I have to lose?" His voice was rising hysterically, and I could see he had gotten through to Jamie.

Culhane saw it, too. He pointed the gun at Gallagher's heart, motioning the rest of us to stand away from him.

"You've got a family, Gallagher," pointed out Culhane in a dispassionate voice, a voice that had nothing to do with the gun he was holding.

"Yes, yes, God help them!" cried Gallagher, but Jamie was listening to Culhane, a puzzled frown on his face.

"Those others you turned in, that was finished business a long time ago. There isn't anyone left from those affairs who could harm your family. But here you have the man's son, and his brother-in-law and his nephew, and there are others in the family besides them. I think you're trying to protect your own family, Gallagher. I think you're trying to keep Daley's people from carrying on the payment after your death."

"No, no, what are you talking about?" Gallagher cried wildly, appealing again to Jamie. "He's crazy! I know you wouldn't go after my wife and son—I never thought— Daley! For the love of God—" And now he broke and ran, blindly, his feet splashing in the shallow black water. He shrieked a dumb, inarticulate cry as he moved. Culhane did not follow. He stood quite still, raised his arm straight out in front of him, and fired twice.

Gallagher jerked back, coughed and flung his arms forward, as he fell, head first, into the water. Culhane watched for a second, the gun still poised, then walked over to the body and fired once more into Gallagher's head.

"Best make sure of it," he explained, coming back to the rest of us. He glanced up the beach, then down the other way, to see if the shots had attracted any attention. But we saw no one. And quickly we returned to the car.

"Are we just going to leave him there?" asked Jamie. "They'll find his body in the morning."

"They'll take a bit of time figuring out who he was," said Joe. "That's why we came so far from home. There's nothing to connect any of us with this place, or with him."

"I don't know," mused Jamie. "I think, somehow, we're all of us connected with Gallagher forever now."

"It's over and done with, Jamie," said my father gently. "Don't say anything to your mother tonight. I'll bring Anne over in the morning, and she can tell it all."

"I don't want her to know we were here," said Jamie.

"Of course not, don't worry," my father answered.

And there did not seem to be anything left to say then. Culhane was very quiet, and we were all tired. We reached home near to four o'clock in the morning, and, even when we parted, Jamie hadn't a word for anyone. I didn't feel like talking myself.

I supposed we would grow hardened to what we'd seen and done. I hoped we would, for I knew that had I to go through a night like that another time and feel the same way, I'd never make it, never. My mother let me sleep past breakfast next morning; it was kindly meant, but I'd far rather been awake than the way I was: tossed between sleeping and waking, the face of Timothy Gallagher intermingling with the dead faces of my Uncle Martin and Brian Cavenaugh slowly strangling as their bodies turned round and round on the ropes. I kept hearing Riordan's voice repeating, "Take him out, take him out," and it being done, and me having a part in the doing of it. I knew, in my sleep, that the shots Culhane fired were already ordained, and had just been hanging there in the heavens waiting through all the eons of time past to be fired at that one wretched man.

I thought, or I dreamt: Did you know, Tim Gallagher, you poor, lousy scoundrel, did you know, when your soul wasn't yet inside of you, did you know that bullet would be waiting? And did you cry as you lay in your mother's arms, trying to make your young soul forget what it knew

—and did it finally remember before the end? Was there one split second, when we stood with you there on the bleak shore, that you finally remembered? Too late. Too late, little crying baby, little soul terrified with knowing of the bullet, stupid, stupid man living a wasted, treacherous life! The shots came, and each of us, perhaps, remembered things only our souls knew and feared.

I had said to my father, before we went off to bed, "I wish the world would figure out another way to win a point. I wish God wasn't so cruel. I wish he'd show us another way."

"Some say he has, and often," replied my father softly, but there was scorn on my face, and fear too. "When one thing is very easy and the other is very hard, which will a man choose? No, he'll have to take away the liking for killing, the seeking for it, the pleasure of it, the assurance of it, before love will take its place as a solution to anything."

And with that he left me in my bed, remembering the faces of our friends, the men we worked with and trusted, the men we hoped to join together with to build a new Ireland, and I wondered, before the nightmare took me over, where was the talk of building? For I had heard only of killing and driving the enemy out, and that was fine, I was sworn to it myself. But what of us afterwards?

So it came to us, in the midst of our growing days, that we learned to be cutters-off of other men's lives, reapers in a field sown forever with new living crops. It was a hard way to become a man. But all ways to do that are hard.

When I awoke, it was nearly noon. My mother was waiting for me to go over to Aunt Ellen's with her. She was very pale and she said little, that was her way, and she asked me to take Jamie and the girls out, away from the house, while she told my aunt about Timothy Gallagher.

"I will cry a lot, I expect," said my mother as we walked through the fields. "And she will, too. There's been enough tears in my sister's house, and too many of them for Kathleen and Janet to see."

I agreed with her, though I thought perhaps Jamie would want to stay with his mother that day.

"No," she said. "Take him out in the air, in the fields. We've a stray lamb that got loose yesterday sometime. You go and find the creature, and bring him home while I talk to Ellen."

Jamie met us in the yard, and he called his sisters to come out for a walk. The little girls came running, barely stopping to hug my mother, for usually they were discouraged from following us about. But today it would be us following them, for they skipped off ahead of us, laughing and chasing each other along the side of the fence, whilst Jamie and I followed slowly, not having much to say even now.

But when we reached the stream in back of the house, there was Margaret waiting for us, all alone, on foot, skimming rocks into the water. We went along, she naturally falling in with us, and, after a bit, she said, "Did you hear Rose O'Donnell's down sick today?"

Jamie looked at me quickly, then he said, trying to be very casual, "No, I didn't know. What's wrong with her? She seemed fine enough last—" And he stopped in confusion.

"Last night, you were going to say," flashed Margaret, her voice rather strained.

"Yes, it was last night," I put in quickly. "Some of us took a walk down to Johnny's, you know. I saw Rose myself. She offered us some tea but—"

"Jerry!" snapped Margaret sharply. Kathleen and Janet, who were not far ahead, turned around in surprise. Margaret smiled at them and waved them on. She watched them, still smiling, till they disappeared into a thicket of trees, then the smile faded fast. "Rose called the priest to the house today. Kevin heard news of it at early Mass, and he saw old Father Donovan on his way there afterwards. They say Johnny came into town half out of his head; Kevin said she was up all night, in a wild condition, crying about killing and informers and revenge!"

"That's odd," mused Jamie uncomfortably, but Margaret ran ahead of him and turned to face him.

"Is it? Is it odd, Jamie?" she demanded. "My father took a walk down to Johnny's last night, too," she went on, forcing him to stop where he was. "He didn't get home till past four in the morning. There was a killing, wasn't there?"

"Oh, for God's sakes, Margaret, do you have to make it sound like the end of the world?" exploded Jamie. "We can't talk about it."

"Why not?" she cried. "Isn't it supposed to encourage the rest of us, just our knowing there's some of you out there protecting our precious rights? My father said the man was an informer."

"Let's forget it, please, Margaret, will you?"

"No, let's not forget it. Tell me about the 'trial.' That's what they called it, wasn't it, a 'trial'? Now you're all not only God's duly appointed army of saviors—now you're the police too, aren't you? And the jury, and the judge, and the executioners? Tell me, did you arrest him, just like proper police? Did you read out the charges against him? How did he look when you shot him?"

"Your father shot him!" I told her hotly. "You've no right to talk this way. He was doing his duty, so were we all. And the man was guilty. He was probably the one who informed on Martin Daley!"

She turned deadly pale and stepped back, as if she were expecting to be hit. "I'm sorry," she said, her voice suddenly dull and lifeless. "But what's the difference, anyway? Informers, police, armies—it's all death and destruction in the end!"

Jamie looked at her sternly, his mouth set. "There is some difference, Margaret," he said quietly. "You've got to get it sorted out in your mind."

"Oh?" she returned. "And you've got it sorted out, have you? You've got everyone put into his proper little place, good and bad, right and wrong, have you, now?"

"God, no!" answered Jamie heatedly. "I wanted to see the man pay for my father's death. I swore I'd do it myself, if I ever found him out. But when I saw him, and heard him, and stood by and agreed to his death, I knew it wouldn't serve any purpose beyond keeping him from betraying someone else sometime. My father will not come back to life because Gallagher is dead. I don't even hate the stupid little bastard! Your father did the shooting because he was ordered to do it. Margaret, our people, all of them, the good ones and the lousy ones, they're all suffering! One of the main causes of their suffering is this everlasting informing. And there wouldn't be any of that if the English were not here. I know they have no right to be here. When they're gone, my people will still be themselves, good, bad, ignorant or brilliant, lazy or ambitious, and then it'll be up to themselves to become something better. If they can. If they want to. If they know they're able to.

"But now they can't do anything for themselves. So, first the English have to go. And they don't want to go. And I don't like the job of making them go, and neither does Jerry or your father or anyone else. But that's the first job we've got to get finished, if we can. And then, afterwards, let the world blame Ireland squarely, on her own, if she can't get along and prosper and live in peace."

"And then, if she can't, the hell with Ireland!" cried Margaret.

Jamie shook his head, exasperated. "Not the hell with Ireland!" he said bitterly. "Ireland was here before we came; she'll be here after we're gone. No, the hell with us then, I suppose. That's all."

Margaret nodded her head. "That's all," she repeated mockingly. "How simple you make it sound. You're all the same! You talk in speeches out of books, or you make them up as you go along! In between, there's people and living—where do you fit all that in?"

"It keeps going," answered Jamie simply. "There's naught to stop it that I know of. I guess people just have to grab at life in between the dying."

"Oh, that doesn't answer anything!" she muttered and fell silent, walking along with us, pulling pieces of leaves and grass from the stone fence and tearing them apart in her fingers.

A bit later she asked, "Where are we going?"

"There's a lamb missing," answered Jamie shortly, not looking at her.

"Oh," she said. We crossed the stream, calling out to Kathleen and Janet to stay closer to the rest of us. They waved back gaily and ran ahead again, calling the lamb in every direction.

"Oh, Jamie!" Margaret burst out, catching hold of his arm so he would slow down. "Jamie, why don't we all go away to America?"

"America?" said Jamie. "What would we be doing in America?"

Margaret spoke quickly and though we thought she might have been joking, she was quite in earnest. "Living, that's what we'd be doing. We could get far away from here. We could forget all the fighting and the anger and the killing!"

I was surprised to hear her say it, for usually she pretended those things did not exist, and when we were with her they did not, for a while.

"Well, but you can't just run away from things, just like that, just for the wanting, can you?" asked Jamie.

"*Why* can't you? Tell me, why can't you, Jamie? Can't we ever do anything we want? Do we always have to keep everything going along just the way it has been?"

"No. We can stay and change everything," cried Jamie. "Don't you understand that's what we're fighting for—the chance to change it? Running away doesn't change anything."

Margaret's voice was faint and hopeless. "That's what everyone says. And they stay and nothing ever changes. It just gets worse."

"It will change, Margaret, you'll see," promised Jamie, his hand on her shoulder, and he forced her to raise her eyes and look at him. "I promise you things will be different. Someday we will forget all this. Try to believe in it, won't you?"

"Yes," said Margaret halfheartedly. Then, abruptly, she threw down a handful of torn grass, and she ran off ahead of us, calling the girls.

By this time we had gone more than two miles, looking

high and low for the little creature, and we kept on going, although I never thought the lamb would get so far from home on his short little legs. Strange Good Shepherds we, judging between the one lost lamb and the other, condemning the one and seeking out the other!

It was over at Declan's Crossing we found him at last, out in a fine, sunlit meadow that they were letting go to grass for a year or two. The meadow was surrounded on all sides by young sapling trees, so you wouldn't even suspect anything was there at all, but it burst upon you suddenly from the thickness of the woods, like a little round emerald on a dark finger.

Margaret spotted him first; she went softly along, cautioning Kathleen and Janet to be very quiet or they would frighten him off.

"There, listen," she whispered, stopping. We stopped right behind her, listening carefully ourselves.

"There it is again. It's crying!" she said, running ahead lightly through the high grass. "Where are you, *acushla?* Keep calling out, there's a pet, there's a sweetheart, keep calling, keep telling us where you are!" She was running and stopping, running and listening, turning her head all about. Then she nodded, very pleased, and beckoned to us.

"Over here," she called. "He's over this way." She went bounding ahead again, holding her long skirts up to her knees as she went.

Jamie and I pounded along behind her, clodding through the meadow like giants treading a spider web. We found Margaret quite hidden from sight, on her knees in the grass, holding the lost lamb in her two arms, crooning and rocking it gently against her body.

She gave us a warning look as we came near. "Be quiet," she said. "He's that terrified, the darling! Look how his little tongue is hanging out. He's not eaten nor drunk since yesterday, I'll wager!" The lamb bleated pitifully, nuzzling Margaret for nourishment and, disappointed, bleated again, breathing very hard, his eyes wildly rolling in his head.

"Hold him there, I'll be back," yelled Jamie, racing

away. I didn't know Declan's Crossing very well, but evidently he'd been there before and knew where the well was. In five minutes' time he was back again, carrying a pail of fresh water.

"Here, try to get him to take some," said Jamie, down on his knees next to Margaret. She dipped her finger into the water and rubbed it gently on the lamb's nose. He licked it, all right, but it was cold and it wasn't milk, and he didn't like the whole business at all! She tried again, but he shied away, still bleating. Finally, between herself and Jamie and me, the two of them holding the lamb whilst I steadied the pail against his flying little feet, we nosed him into the water and forced him to drink a few mouthfuls. Then we let him up, and Margaret sat down with him on her lap, smoothing his wool, which was all over twigs and snags. He settled down well enough then, cozying up to her, and she held his little face against her cheek and kissed him warmly on his black nose. And that was Margaret, too.

Jamie had been looking at her all the while, not saying a word. And then I saw him do something I never thought to see: he reached out his hand and touched her cheek as softly as she touched the lamb, his eyes wistful and wondering, and on his face a look of joy and sadness together.

Margaret felt his hand on her face. Startled, she looked up, saw his eyes, caught his expression. And an answering, indefinable sadness filled her own dark eyes, but still she smiled, and her own hand, with its lovely long slim fingers, crept up slowly and took his hand and pressed it harder against her cheek.

Till the day I die, I shall not forget the sight of Margaret Culhane sitting there in the grassy meadow, her long dark skirts flung out around her, with the wee small lamb nuzzling her girl's breast, and Jamie touching her cheek with his big, strong, gentle fingers, wondering at the loveliness and tenderness in her sweet gypsy face.

It was then I knew that Jamie loved her, and that she loved him, and suddenly, from four dear friends, there were only the two of them in the entire world. All else might fall and fade and die away in that instant, but there

were those two, with the lamb cuddled between them in
the warmth of their close bodies. I turned away, my eyes
full of sudden tears, for what was there for them, for me,
for any of us? Love as we might, hate as we must, "tomorrow" was a word for politicians and generals, and today was all we had.

I felt a door shut on me then, but, strangely, I didn't
seem to mind it. I felt a part of this new thing that was
happening to them, though neither of them yet knew it. I
was in love with her myself, I'd known that long enough,
but I'd also known that nothing would spring to life between us. It made me sad, sometimes, but I knew I could
not be the man for Margaret. Only Jamie could give her
what she needed to breathe, to be alive and free, for only
he, other than Kevin, truly understood her. Jamie with a
look could calm her. Jamie with a word could quiet her.
And now it was complete: Jamie, with a touch, could
shut the whole world away from her.

No, I was not shut out, but it wrenched me to see their
love so touching, so new and so vulnerable that day, for
we had not time for love. We had idled the summer away
into autumn and the world was turning around us, and
everything was changing. Too late, I thought, too late.
Though they were still so young, it was too late already.

I wandered away through the meadow, taking the girls
with me, and played with them for a long while till they
were hungry and asked to go home. Then I took them
each by the hand, and, singing all of us, we went back, to
find Jamie and Margaret already on their way toward the
trees, Jamie carrying the lamb in his arms while Margaret
held his hand, still talking and petting the creature as they
went, half dancing in front of Jamie, and half clinging
shyly to his side. There was a smile upon Jamie's face
would have shamed the noon sun for brightness, and one
glance at Margaret showed me I had been right, for everywhere upon her pale face I saw the shadows had disappeared. Yet I knew well, for well I knew them both, that
they had not said one word about what had happened
and did not yet realize that it had happened at all!

We took the lamb back to my place, home to his mother, who rewarded the lot of us by butting and kicking and acting so much like the ram it was funny to watch, nor was she finished when she'd laid into *us*, but seemed entirely of two minds about the lamb. One minute she'd be licking and nuzzling him as he drank his dinner greedily, then, the next minute, evidently remembering the trouble and worry he'd caused her, she pushed him away and scolded him severely till the poor fellow didn't know what to do.

"Oh, go on with you, now," chided Margaret. "First you raised bloody hell because he was gone and now that you've got him back with you, safe and sound, you raise bloody hell because he went away!"

"That's mothers for you, I guess," I said, and it's true, isn't it? They'll be at you and at you one minute, then grabbing you and hugging you the next, and screaming about something trivial without taking time out between for a breath.

"I'll see the two of you tomorrow," said Margaret suddenly. "I've got to get home, it's almost time for tea."

Jamie was for walking her home, but she said, suddenly a bit shy, "I'd rather go alone. After the other night . . ." she let it trail off unhappily.

"What? You mean what your father said?" laughed Jamie, but then he stopped laughing, for she was quite somber now.

"Och, he's a fool." She tried to toss it off lightly, but it didn't work. "But just until Kevin goes. He makes things—hard for Kevin. I don't want to add any more. It's only a few more days now, and he'll be gone. And," she added, her chin jutting up defiantly, "then I'll do what I want and see who I want, he can't stop me."

"He's your father, Margaret," said Jamie, very troubled. "I'm glad it's me you want to see, but—" As he looked at her, his heart was once more in his eyes.

She caught the look; she could not have mistaken the meaning. And, with a sudden, anguished cry, she said, "Oh, damn you men, damn you all!" And she ran away from us, down the *boreen* toward Culhane House.

Jamie looked after her as she went, scowling darkly, and I saw him mouth her name silently, but Jamie was a proud man, and the sound of it never touched his lips the rest of that day.

Chapter XI

Now September had come, and with it steady cold rains that would chill you to the heart. Kevin was to leave us. In a week's time he was going away to the seminary.

We begrudged the earth its rain, for we wanted to spend those last few days as we had spent so many others, out on the land, free, pretending nothing was coming to an end. We could not be together at Culhane House, nor could we be comfortable either at Jamie's place or mine, for both of our mothers were so anxious to be kind to Kevin and Margaret that they never left us a moment to ourselves.

And then, three days before Kevin was to go, the autumn sun broke through the clouds in such a madness of brilliance that everything took on a new, tawny glow, and the warmth of it drew us outside once again, as if neither summer nor ourselves could bear to leave each other yet.

Now it seemed only natural that Kevin and I rode together, while Jamie and Margaret roved far afield of us. We went back to all the old places we had made our own, trying to find that they were just the same. But they were not the same, for we were not.

We went up to our hill, Running Hill we called it, and told Kevin how Jamie and I had first met Margaret when she'd come home from school. Nothing would do him but that he climb up to the top with us, and Margaret as well, laughing, loping long-legged up through the green with the sun flashing on her skin, as she danced in and out like a witch among the bushes and briers, swinging one-armed around the tree trunks, darting out at us, racing ahead, whilst we trudged along behind her, for it was steep to the top, and the Blackwater River winding dark and silken below.

She stood against the sky, far above us, and reached up her arms, stretching hard as if she would grasp the sun itself, and my heart caught for the sight of her. I moved, without knowing I moved, noticing Jamie lift his head to watch her. She saw him coming and held out her hands to him, and he gave a low cry and leaped ahead of Kevin and me, running up to meet her at the top. He picked her up in his two arms, whirling her about and laughing with her. Then the sun dazzled me and seemed to envelop them together, so that I could scarcely see them anymore, but just a blurr of shining motion.

Still I climbed, but I felt a hand on my shoulder. I stopped and leaned against one of the trees. Kevin stood with me, and he was smiling.

"Stay a while, won't you?" he asked, motioning to the two on the hilltop, and his eyes were very joyful and his voice was very warm and glad.

I followed his gaze, nay, I did not want to look away from them, as I saw them running down now through the grass, hand in hand together. I caught Kevin watching me then, and I shrugged and laughed a little.

"She loves him," Kevin said, and I nodded dumbly.

"And himself?" asked Kevin gravely. "Has he said anything? Do you know?"

I turned to him, spread my hands out. "What does he have to say? It's on his face; it's in his voice."

Kevin seemed to consider this, saying nothing for a bit. Then, "It's in your own, too," he said.

"Oh, well, now, it couldn't be helped, could it?" I tried to say it lightly, but it didn't work. "She's a girl men will love."

Kevin shook his head. "No, you can't love Margaret if she doesn't want you to love her. She will put the world between herself and strangers. She always has, even when she was small. She would do everything, anything, for someone she loves, someone she trusts. Margaret woos with her whole self. She gives all—and she asks for all. Not many men can match it. And not a few would fear it. She is easily hurt."

I said nothing. I could not imagine anyone ever wanting to hurt Margaret.

"She loved our father, long ago." He paused, his words coming uncertainly. I would have stopped him then, for I thought he said things he did not want to say but felt he must say.

"You must have heard. He was not—kind to our mother. Poor Margaret." He sighed. "She thought everyone loved everyone in the world. I was older. I knew better. I had already begun to hate him when Margaret was born. He never wanted another child—God, he hardly wanted me! But I was a son, a Culhane son; that made some small difference, for a while." He closed his eyes, leaning his head back against the tree. "Oh, my mother was such a fool! She tried so hard, so long, to make him love us. But he couldn't. He couldn't love anyone. He's a man obsessed with dreams, but all his dreams have been only nightmares to us. He's a man who thinks tenderness is weakness that drags you down. He only feels safe when he feels nothing. He has driven all feeling for anyone else out of his heart, and in it he keeps to himself and his dreams, oh, all those great, grand dreams that keep men from seeing the small happinesses that come in minutes!

"I remember Margaret running downstairs to meet him when he would come in; as children will, she'd be full of a hundred things to tell him, her face lit up with delight to see him. And he would order her away, or tell her to be quiet, and the light would die out of her eyes. She'd come quietly back up the stairs, trying not to cry, because that annoyed him, too. And if she'd see me and know I had seen what had happened, she would hit me and hit me, and then she *would* cry. But she wouldn't let me say a word against him. What kind of a man is it that fears a woman's tears? He had such great power to be kind; we needed kindness, but he feared that too, I suppose.

"She tried to please him in a hundred ways. She used to make little flower crowns and leave them on his desk for a surprise and he would pick up his papers and let all the little crowns fall to the floor, and never notice them. But she said nothing. It was not until she began to hear him quarreling with Mother that she grew afraid of him. Mother was all the love either of us ever knew then. And when Margaret realized that, for all her love, Mother could not stand against him, and we had no real protection at all, then she began to run away.

"Oh, she went a hundred times! We found her in barns, walking on the roads, cold and hungry. Once she was gone three days, up somewhere in the hills over the sea. She told me she was going to jump down into the water so she would never have to go home again. And I? I took her back. I didn't want to, but what else was there to do?

"Afterwards, he beat her. I think he beat her so many times that she stopped being afraid of him. It sounds odd, but then she really began to defy him, openly. When he would hit her, she never flinched nor cried, but called him names. And when he made the tears come to her eyes, she would hit herself, with her own fists, till she stopped.

"When he beat Mother, it was Margaret who tried to stop him. Not me, for I had been through it and knew it was no use; it only made things worse. But Margaret used to run into their room when she heard Mother crying and him shouting and swearing. She jumped right on the bed one night and wrestled him, trying to drag him away. He shook her off like a dog would shake a rat; she went flying across the room and hit her head on the hearth. Mother was screaming. She ran over, tried to carry Margaret away from him. And that was when she had the first heart attack." His voice died away.

I said not a word, for I believed he had more on his mind. But the silence grew and grew between us, and my head was so full of pictures of the awful things he spoke of that I almost forgot he was there. Then, at last, I asked him, "Do you still hate him so much?"

He shook his head. "I don't know. I'm not supposed to hate. I'm supposed to 'love my enemies and do good to those who hate me.' He's my father. He's a strange, disappointed, angry man, a man that takes love and trust and despises them. He can't hurt my mother anymore, thank God. He can't do much more to me now. But Margaret . . .''

"Well, she can leave him, can't she, like yourself? She can go someplace else, or marry, never see him again, if she wishes. There's nothing that chains her to him, is there?"

Kevin looked at me with that same, familiar, unfathomable sorrow I'd seen in him so often. "That's what I've waited for, and prayed for. But there are going to be—difficulties ahead. And she will need someone. Someone strong, who can help her stand against him. Someone who will stand between herself and the world. I won't go away, Jerry, if I can't leave her protected."

"Well, and here comes her protection right now," I said very loudly, for the two of them, out of breath and red in the face, had come running up to us.

"What happened to you two?" asked Jamie. "It's a grand run! Oh, God, but I'm winded!"

They threw themselves down on the grass, panting like hounds after the hunt, and we began to talk, about not much of this and even less of that. I noticed how Kevin was watching them, never taking his eyes from them. Margaret was chattering away and didn't see it, but, after a while, Jamie began to look puzzled. He had caught Kevin at it several times. I thought he was angry, for he lifted his chin defiantly, as though he thought Kevin disapproved.

Suddenly I realized that no one had said a word in several minutes. Margaret was staring at us, tapping her bare foot impatiently.

"Well, are you all dead or what is it?" she demanded. "I've asked the same question three times and no one has answered me. Jerry, what is it?"

I smiled. "I guess we're tired, that's all."

"Huh, tired from what? And Kevin, you've got eyes that big on you, you look like you swallowed a gospel! Kevin, say something! Jamie?" She looked over at him in exasperation, but he was still staring at Kevin, meeting his eyes with a steady gaze.

"Well, the hell with the three of you! I might as well have stayed home and talked to the cat; I'd get more conversation from him!" She jumped up in a pique and stalked away down the hill, but for once no one watched her going or remarked on it.

"All right, now. What is it, Kevin?" Jamie put it to him coolly.

Kevins' glance dropped to the grass at his feet, and he began idly picking blades of it and piling them up together.

"Jamie, will you do something for me?" Kevin began, and at once Jamie's temper flared out in the open.

"It's about Margaret, I expect," he said sarcastically.

I opened my mouth to speak, but Kevin said quickly, "No, Jerry, it's all right. Jamie, you don't understand me. Will you listen?" His voice was urgent, pleading. Jamie said nothing, but folded his arms and waited.

"When I've left," Kevin went on, "Margaret will be all alone. More alone than you might think. I want to put a heavy burden on you, Jamie. I want you to swear to me —no, don't say anything yet—I said *swear,* a vow before God. I am in earnest, Jamie! Swear that you will always be her friend."

Jamie looked relieved, bemused, starting to laugh, then he saw how deadly earnest Kevin was. "Is that it? Is that all you know of me, Kevin? I don't have to swear to that. I am her friend. I'll always be her friend. But there's more you don't—"

Kevin interrupted him swiftly. "No, don't add any more to it. Whatever you're thinking, whatever you're feeling, has nothing whatever to do with what I'm asking of you. I'm asking you to stand by her, to protect her if it comes to it, against anyone, anytime, who would hurt her. I'm asking you to do this without a reason and under all circumstances. Will you do it? Will you swear that to me, Jamie, and let me go away in peace, for the love of God?"

Jamie grasped his hand. "Kevin, Kevin don't you know

we've wondered about you all these weeks? Always something on your mind, always something you wanted to say. Is that what it was? Oh, Kevin, why didn't you speak up?"

"I had to wait. I had to be—sure." Kevin whispered.

"What is it you fear for her?" asked Jamie, but Kevin whipped away, his face contorted with emotion.

"I beg you, don't ask me any questions. I can't answer you. Will you do the thing or not?"

"Of course I will, gladly, if it will set your mind at rest." Jamie said it easily, but I knew he was sorely troubled. He sought my eyes for some explanation, but I had no answers myself.

Kevin then said sternly, "Say, 'I, James Daley, swear before Almighty God that I will always be a true friend to Margaret Culhane, and that I will never turn from her or speak or act against her, and that I will protect her from all those who would do so.' "

Jamie repeated the words, phrase by phrase, which evidently Kevin had thought out with great care ahead of time. When it was finished, Kevin shook his hand and thanked him.

"But it's little you'll be thanking me, I fear," he added. "I hope to God things will go well for you, and that all that vow will ever mean is that you'll keep from losing your temper over some outrageous thing she does. But, Jamie, if a day comes when you have cause to doubt her, remember what you swore today. If a day comes when all hearts and hands are turned against her, remember what you swore. If a day comes when you believe I tricked and trapped you by this vow, remember it anyway, and keep to it!"

"Kevin, you've lost your mind! What is this all about? Have you or Margaret done something to bring trouble on yourselves?" cried Jamie, pulling him around hard.

Kevin took no notice of Jamie's grip upon him, but simply said, "Margaret hasn't done anything to harm anyone in all this world. As for me, I have done nothing. Nothing," he repeated with a queer, scornful twist of his mouth. He looked at Jamie and started to speak again, then pulled back and shook his head.

"I'll be gone soon," he said. "Don't think too badly of me."

And, with that, he left us, heading quickly down to the road.

Jamie and I lingered there on the hill, as I told him all that Kevin had told me before. He listened, his eyes growing very cold and remote, but he said little. An hour later, we went our separate ways.

My mother had planned a little farewell supper for Kevin the night before he would go, just ourselves and a few old friends from school, but it was never held, for the next morning Margaret appeared, in a driving rainstorm, drenched to the skin, her clothes sticking to her, her face white and great shadows under her eyes. Jamie was over at my house. She had been to the Daley's first, looking for him. Now she stood at the door and would not come in, the rain pelting on her face. I thought she was crying, but I could not really tell.

"Come out, please," she whispered. Without a word, without so much as jackets or caps, we went out to her. We must have looked like three fools, walking along together in that great rain, paying no heed to where we went, but Margaret knew where she wanted to be. After a bit I saw we were heading toward Bearsey's Bridge. Mind you, now, nobody talked—it was that kind of a storm that if you opened your mouth to say anything, all you got for your trouble was a gush of rain straight into it.

It was not until we were sitting on the rocks under the bridge, somewhat safe from the downpour, that Margaret would speak.

"He went away last night," she said.

"Kevin," said Jamie. "Why did he go ahead of time?"

"There was an awful row," she whispered, shivering. "Kevin and Father. I was asleep when it began, but the sound of their voices woke me. You'd think I was used to it by now; God knows they've been years at it, but I listened at the top of the stairs.

"He called Kevin terrible things. Terrible. I never heard

such things before. He—he said Kevin was running away from the world and trying to hide himself in the seminary because he couldn't love a woman . . . in that way, you know?" She wouldn't look at us, but stared at the rushing water and hurried on. "And all the time he was saying those things, Kevin just stood there listening and—and laughing at him! It was so awful, that laughing. And when he stopped laughing and Father was so angry I thought he was going to strike him, Kevin said that, like every thing else he'd ever believed, Father was wrong about that too. He said he had loved a girl, and she'd loved him too. He said he'd love her forever, because she made him believe that there really was love in the world, and he had made up his mind there wasn't any. He said she showed him what fearful things it does to people who aren't loved, and he began thinking of all the people, all over, who live their whole lives through without love.

"Father sneered and shouted, 'Priest talk!' and then Kevin grabbed him by the arm and said, 'I learned about love in her arms, Father, not in a church.' He said he knew what he was giving up, and it was because he had found out what a man's need for love is that he was going away, to try to help others find it, too. He said you can only see God's love when you find it in other people.

"And then Father screamed at him what an ungrateful son he was—I've heard all that before. But Kevin just turned around and walked out of the room. He came up the stairs, but I ran ahead of him, into his room, and I got his bag that was already packed, and his hat and coat, and I met him with them at the head of the stairs. He kissed me goodbye and said there was no sense to waiting anymore. He asked me to say goodbye to you two, and then he just took his things and walked out the front door, without even closing it behind him. And he was gone."

She stared unseeing at the gray rain, a tiny smile on her sad mouth. "Fancy Kevin loving a girl and none of us knew it! I'm glad he did! I'm glad he had a little happiness in his life. Poor Kevin. How good he is, how much he's had to bear!"

Then Margaret wept, burying her face in her hands, and

we let her cry it out, sitting there watching the rain, watching her tears trickling down beneath her slim fingers, and we could do nothing.

"What will I do now?" she moaned. "Oh, God, what's to become of me now?" There was a note of terror in her voice, and she looked up at us wide-eyed.

Jamie patted her shoulder and tried to say something comforting, but she cried out, "You don't understand! He's been like—like a strong root under me, something holding me in place. Until this summer, Kevin was the only one in the world I could depend on. He was always there, always the same. He knew what to do, I didn't! I kept telling myself that he wouldn't always be here. He was going away, and I was happy for him. I'm still happy for him. But I'm afraid for myself now."

'Margaret, Margaret, what makes you afraid?" asked Jamie, smoothing her wet hair gently.

She leaned over and took his hand in hers. Then she looked at me, and took my hand too. Her grip was hard, her hand was cold. She cradled our two hands to her throat and sobbed over them, and kissed them! She gazed past us, across the water and the fields beyond it, a distant look in her face that I'd seen before. I didn't like that look; it scared me, somehow, as if we were losing her even as we held her with us. I wondered if we could truly hold her if she slipped away from us, and her words, spoken now so softly, tumbling out so quickly and urgently, only strengthened my fears.

"Don't ever go away from me, Jamie!" she begged. "Jerry, don't leave me, will you?"

"Hush, now, where would we be going?" whispered Jamie, but she didn't seem to hear him.

"Kevin knew it," she said sorrowfully. "There isn't really any me at all. Nowhere. I don't seem to be a person all myself, not like other people are, not like the two of you, or Kevin, or anybody. I—I slip off, out of myself, sort of *away*, all melting and disappearing to me, bit by bit, and I can't stop it. I start to—go away. I can see myself, as if I were someone watching from outside. I start to talk like the last person I talked to, I think the last thought I heard, and everything I know and care about, everything that is me, is going and going every minute. I try to reach out for it, but I can't see it anywhere. Oh, it's like being a ghost, and talking and trying to touch people, but there's nothing left of me to do it.

"I've got to be held, held *here,* into myself, do you see? Somebody's got to want me and call me and reach out to me, hold me, say a word. Say, 'Stay, don't go away, Margaret,' and then I'm all right, I'm here again and all the shadows have gone away. I'm me." She huddled between the two of us, all of these strange things pouring out of her, clutching our hands so hard I wondered at the strength of her own.

"Margaret," said Jamie at last, "that's not true. Oh, I know you feel it, you believe it. But it isn't. There's always been something remarkably *enduring* about you."

She laughed bitterly. "Enduring?" she repeated. "Aye, you think that, and you've called me strong and proud, too, and you've liked those things in me. I knew that. And it's all been for you that I made myself that way, because you wanted it. I'm a chameleon, you know. Whatever it takes to keep me alive in people's minds and hearts and lives, then that's what I am, that's what I'll be. I know myself by what I see in other people's eyes, and if they stop looking at me, I'd disappear into the air. Whatever it is that makes me anything at all, would be gone. *I'd* be gone.

"Now I've lost Kevin. If you ever leave me, who will there be to see me? And without you to see me, I won't *be* at all! Promise me you'll never leave me alone! Promise me, promise me!"

We both promised her; sure we would have promised her the moon for a bracelet, wouldn't we? And we put from our minds the oaths we had sworn for Ireland's sake, and the fighting that was coming, and the thought of separation we might have anticipated.

So the three of us sat there, holding each other very tightly, thinking about ourselves and about Kevin, and saying goodbye to more than the summertime. When the rain finally let up, I left the two of them and went on home to tell my mother she could call off the dinner party. I had nothing more to say to them, and I thought they might have much to say to each other. . . .

Jim Daley tried to open his eyes. He wanted to say something to Jerry. What was it? Why couldn't he do it? He heard someone talking low to the doctor. He wanted to thank them for everything, for looking after him, for . . . He was astonished to find that he had forgotten what he was thinking.

Getting old, he told himself wryly. Then, recalling where he was and that officially, he supposed, he was dying, he felt like laughing. Not getting *much* older, he thought, not much more.

Margaret. He hadn't said her name, in his mind or with his lips, since the day he'd left Ireland over fifty years ago. Why did he have to think about her now? He had managed to push her out of his mind, and keep her out, except in the darkness of his night's dreamings.

Margaret. A long, gasping sigh escaped his dry lips, and the doctor, he knew, would at once be leaning over him like a hawk, with the stethoscope, looking for more signs of life. He tried to laugh again, but it was no use.

There was Margaret, and Jerry had brought her back again. She stood before him, just as she had always looked, her eyes gazing deep into his own, seeking and finding what he had so dearly loved to give. Go away, Margaret Culhane, he shouted feebly in his heart. Go away, my love. But she would not go. . . .

. . . Jerry was gone home. The rain had stopped and a bit of warm sun was working its way along the ground to them, and twinkling on the swelling stream. Margaret stirred, stretched, and got up, bending over low to walk out from under the bridge.

He had gone after her. They walked along the water's edge, then Margaret had stooped and taken off her soggy shoes, and wiggled her feet comfortably in the muddy grass.

"Oh, that's good!" she sighed. "Try it, Jamie."

He had done so. They waded into the water, splashing a great deal, and he had laughed, hoping the storm was really over.

"The rain wasn't wet enough for you?"

She shook her head, climbed up to the other side of the bank, sitting down on an old log to put her shoes back on. He had sat next to her, watching her, thinking she was always new, always fascinating. Then, out of the corner of his eye, he saw a pair of pointy ears and two bright little eyes, not three feet away, looking at him.

He nudged Margaret. "Shh, look, there's a fox."

She had looked up, startled, "Oh!" she exclaimed in a small, high voice. Then she laughed as the fox's impudent face considered her a moment, and he raced off.

Jamie heard the word and the laugh, saw the look on her face, and, for the first time, understood what the excitement was he was feeling. He reached out, suddenly, not quite knowing what he was going to do, but that he must touch her.

"I love you," he said, his hand caressing her hair gently. "I love you, Margaret."

Her eyes grew very wide, her mouth parted, and she scarcely breathed, her look drinking him in entirely. His hand fell harder on her small head, slipped down the shining black hair, cupped the nape of her neck and drew her face close to his own. She hadn't said a word, her eyes never left his as he kissed her, and the hot press of her lips against his own fired through him an awakening. Dazed, he drew back and searched her face, saw her eyes closed, the lids trembling. He looked at the lips in wonder. They were a magnet. Impatiently he pulled her to him again, and once more the touch of her soft, firm mouth overwhelmed him. He felt her arm about his neck. He began to shudder at the strange powers working in him. Convulsively he grasped her in his two arms, pressed her against him, wildly kissing her eyes, her cheeks, her hair, ears, throat . . . When he feverishly touched his lips to the hollow of her bosom he could hear her heart beating very fast.

He was amazed; he could hear her life, he thought, and Margaret sighed, almost a sob it was, and clasped his head against her breast and held him there, rocking a bit. From the fearful trembling through her, without looking at her face, he could tell she was crying. Troubled, he turned his head and did look up—to see a wide and radiant smile on her pale face while the tears tumbled down her cheeks!

"Margaret, why?" he asked. Her answer was to look down at him, to kiss him over and over. He held her to him again, knowing instinctively it was the right thing to do, because he loved her, he loved her and love made everything right.

"Ah, Jamie, Jamie, I love you so!" she cried, and now he pulled her down into his arms, cradling her, smelling the sweet freshness of her hair and skin, murmuring her name over and over and "Hush, hush, there, now, love," and she said, "I'll never have to go away again. I'll always be me, I'll always know who I am now. And you'll never, never leave me alone, will you, Jamie?"

He had pressed her to him, holding her head against his shoulder, feeling so very tender, and so very violent all at the same instant. He wanted so many things, suddenly, all to do with Margaret. He wanted to kiss her, to comfort her, to lie with her, to hold her rocking and safe, to somehow make her small and put her in a pocket next to his heart, to joke with her, to run down the hill holding her hand, to ride with her, racing the wind, to touch her secret girl's body, to kneel at Mass with her, to eat dinner with her, to watch her and talk to her and listen to her.

He loved her. Now he knew where the weeks and days and hours had been taking him, the dreams and nights without sleep, the restless rides, the quarrels and impatience, the sudden sadness and the long, slow wanting gnawing at his inside. And now he understood where and how they all belonged in him.

They had sat there, not talking or moving very much, till sundown, and evening streaked the sky and the geese called overhead. Then they had gone home, each to a different place, but nothing would ever separate them now, neither place nor time nor people nor death itself, and they believed the world was waiting, bowing low before them, because they loved each other. . . .

Chapter XII

Now winter came upon us at last, with the peace and promise of new snow. What had brought us low was past and passing, so many tears shed that year, heavy and drear as the autumn rains, but hope and even bits of joy began to touch us again. And Margaret bloomed fairer than any rose in spring, full of love and a new gentleness that became her well. Kevin wrote that he was happy and working hard, and Margaret brought his letters with her to Jamie's house, where everyone would sit about the big kitchen table, whilst she read what he had written, and the smell of fresh-brewed tea warmed the air.

Margaret spent much of her time those days at my aunt's house and she was more than welcome. She begged to be taught cooking and sewing and many of the womanly things she had scorned before. Of course, she understood none of them, and had little patience learning them, but she filled the house with laughter and livened many an early dark afternoon for everyone. She seemed but a third and older daughter at the Daleys', and I often wondered if my aunt suspected that there was a special kind of love between herself and Jamie. If she did, she said nothing, but the love she had always felt for Margaret as a child grew fonder and deeper as time passed.

Jamie and I came in with a load of peat for the fire late in the afternoon when the first snow fell. We found Margaret stamping around the kitchen, a vast white apron shrouding her dress from neck to toe, so much flour in her dark hair she looked like a lady in an eighteenth-century powdered wig. She was cursing like the best man I've ever heard at it, waving Aunt Ellen's wooden spoon in the air as if she were like to beat something, whilst the rest of them were lost altogether between laughing and yelling, and mopping up and soaking out and rinsing off, for Margaret had been making Chrstmas bread, under my mother's careful tutelage. Only somewhere, God alone knows where, she had left out a step or two of the procedure, and there were now pans and pots and bowls of pale bread dough that had risen and risen and finally spilled over onto the floor. Everything was dotted with raisins and currants and caraway seeds that, as you watched them, flowed steadily toward the doorway with the mucky dough beneath them; Margaret had tried to mop it all up with a cloth and had burned four fingers doing it, for she'd set the dough to rise almost on top of the fire.

My mother had tears down her face with the laughing, which interfered greatly with her assistance in the clean-up job, and little Janet was shrieking and playing sliding pond on the doughy floor, whilst Aunt Ellen did a bit of fancy swearing herself, chasing Janet and screaming at her to stand still and take off her boots, and there was poor Kathleen burning her own fingers trying to scoop up as much as could be saved.

"Oh, Jesus in heaven, it's no use in the world!" roared Margaret poetically, and she not yet seeing James and myself standing dumbfounded in the doorway, letting in the drifting snow about us and that much of a chill that the fire began to act tizzily.

"Who in hell's bottom pit has gone and left that door open *this* time?" shouted Aunt Ellen. "A-hah, missy!" She pounced on Janet and threw her to the floor, wrestling the black boots off her little feet, which had been thwucking like the suction cups on an octupus' arms as she walked about.

"Close that door!" yelled my mother, turning to see Jamie and me. "Well, what are you gawking at? Set that down somewhere and take yourselves right out again till tea's ready!"

"Oh, no!" groaned Margaret, stopping in mid-turn to find herself right in front of Jamie, and him with a puckish smile you'd love to slap off his bold face. Her hand went to her hair, her eyes wide with shock and dismay, as he grinned at her and gently removed a fat raisin that was stuck to her cheek with a bit of dough.

She tried to find a smile handy but couldn't, and only watched himself with high indignation as he chuckled and ate down the raisin. Then she took her spoon to him, and to me too, which wasn't fair, and she chased the two innocents of us out into the cold snow once more, slamming the door behind us with dire warnings not to come back. So we hung about, wrestling in the wet, revenging ourselves by throwing snowballs at the windows, till my mother came to the door and beckoned us inside.

Generally speaking, which is all I intend to do on the subject, mind, the place had been made respectable again. We were very careful not to refer to what we had seen before, and Margaret, with her hair brushed out and tied loose around her shoulders with a bit of red ribbon, poured tea with the elegent grace of a duchess—but the tea cakes were a bit flat, and specks of dust here and there on them told the story, and I noticed a large, sooty blob bubbling unnoticed on the burning peat in the fireplace.

"Margaret will make a very tidy housewife someday," announced my mother, and Aunt Ellen nodded away quite nobly.

Margaret's cheeks were blazing, but she managed a smile and passed around the cakes again. I was quite willing to let them pass me by, but Jamie kicked me very hard under the table, so I ate two more to be agreeable. I was hoping they'd put off the marriage a year or two, just till Margaret had gotten it all in hand and straight in her mind.

And after tea we all lingered around the room, talking and playing with the girls, and we ended up singing old Christmas songs, with Margaret proving herself the perfect mate for Jamie, as her high, shaky soprano wobbled feebly up and down the measures only a small bit flatter than his own grandiloquent "instrument," as he was very fond of calling his voice—he made it sound as if some doctor had grabbed hold of him and opened him up and planted a flute in the middle of his throat. But he knew all the words and never had to go "mmmm-mmmm-mm!" in the middle of a line, like the rest of us. Yes, I'll say that for him, Jamie knew all the words.

And it was that voice of his that got the two of us into a new line of business, would you believe it? Business for the Army, the drumming up of it, I mean. And this was the way of it:

Things were very quiet for weeks and weeks. Four or five times, Jamie got a parcel of money delivered at the door, sometimes by a deaf mute that traveled the roads doing day work for a meal and a bed. The next day Jamie would take the wagon over to Culhane House, straight to the barn, with a load of hay. Old Patrick got so used to him coming and going he hardly looked up. And, hidden in an empty stall, there would be a few ancient guns from what looked like the time of Wolfe Tone, six rifles, and once a submachine gun without ammunition. And he would leave the money in place of the guns, drive out past Kilgannon's burned-down house, place the guns in the stone chimney, and come home again without incident.

But now there was a tightening up of organization all around, and a big drive on to recruit new men all over the country. Some of our officers who had been taken after the Easter Uprising were beginning to return from prison. They were sent to various places, as Riordan had been sent to us, to train and prepare new companies for the Army and the fight ahead. Those of us who had more or less completed our training, and at least knew which end of the gun to point away from us, were in demand here and there, to speak at meetings and to explain a lot of what the new men would be doing, as well as to exchange information wherever it would be helpful.

Now, I'm not saying this to be troublesome, but I never had the thought in my head that Jamie or myself would be trusted in this end of things, for neither of us had ever been out of Waterford before, sure, we weren't seasoned travelers. But it was all Sean Culhane's scheme that we did indeed become tangled up in the things, and when we heard about it Jamie looked at me and I looked at him, and we both nodded our heads and said, "So that's the way the wind blows!"—or some such original observation. Sean Culhane put it into Riordan's head to send the two of us off around the country to these other groups. He'd been very quiet about Margaret for all this time, and we'd been waiting for him to pounce. Now it came, and what could we do but obey Riordan's orders?

It all happened one night at a holiday party in town, and we were all feeling high and hearty with the music and dancing and a drop or two against the night air. And then some of the boys called out, "Give us a song, Jamie boy!" and they all laughed and stamped their feet and banged the glasses on the tables till himself would stand up and sing.

I thought Riordan would die on the spot when he heard Jamie rendering "The Tricolored Ribbon" twice straight through with time out for swallowing. He was murdering it altogether, and I couldn't stand it another minute. Up I jumped by his side and sang along, whilst Culhane looked thoughtful and Riordan quickly drank down a double something. I didn't think it sounded half bad with myself holding up the tune of the thing, except we got into a —what would you call it today?—a clash of personalities, at the end there, to see who could carry out the last note longest. The boys began counting aloud and clapping in time whilst we both gasped and turned purple in the face and refused to give in. And I won! By full half a second, for Jamie, in a fit of coughing and wheezing, sat down very suddenly in front of a convenient glass of beer, and waved it graciously at me, acknowledging my victory.

"Hurrah!" they all shouted, and asked for more, and, God help me, but when I got my breath back, we stood again, and gave them three more straight, including all of the verses of "Paddy McGinty's Goat" and the Waterford version of "Tread on the Tail of Me Coat," which you'll find is somewhat different from the original.

Riordan gave us a great send-off and bought a round for everyone, and I've never seen spirits higher or hope more at home than that night with everyone clapping and stamping and even dancing as we sang. And finally, when we were tired and it was late, Jamie looked all around at our friends, and began to sing "The West's Awake." He and I had fooled around with the old words to that song and changed them a bit. It's a real rouser, and when we'd done it once and again, by Heaven, they asked for it a third time, and some of the boys had picked up the words and sang it with us:

> When all beside a vigil keep
> The West's asleep, the West's asleep—
> Alas! and well may Erin weep
> When Connacht lies in slumber deep.
> There lake and plain smile fair and free
> 'Mid rocks, their guardian chivalry.
> Sing, oh! let man learn liberty
> From crashing wind and lashing sea.
>
> And if, when all a vigil keep
> The West's asleep; the West's asleep!
> Alas! and well may Erin weep,
> That Connacht lies in slumber deep,
> But hark! a voice like thunder spake
> "The West's awake! the West's awake!"
> Sing, oh! hurrah! let England quake,
> We'll watch till death for Erin's sake!

I saw Culhane and Riordan with their heads together then, and, sure enough, we got our orders the next day. We were sent off to Touraneena, to a camp meeting in four days' time. Of course Jamie took it for a high honor and recognition of our talents, but we both knew that whatever Riordan thought, it was just Sean's way of keeping Jamie from seeing Margaret. Though, knowing the man's general way of doing things, I did not understand why he was treading so lightly and why he simply did not forbid her to see Jamie at all.

"Maybe he hopes we'll get shot," offered Jamie to me cheerily as we wound our way along the slushy roads. I was frankly glad to hear him say anything, for Margaret had given us both hell for going at all and he had to promise her that we were not going there to blow up something or to get ourselves arrested or to become two more dead Irish heroes. Her attitude had somewhat dashed Jamie's high spirits, but our experience in Touraneena restored them at once.

The meeting was held out in the open, with a huge flaming fire blazing away. There were a couple hundred of them waiting for us, big, tall lads with old guns and eager eyes, and a lot of young townies got up in one-pound uniforms with the double shoulder belt and the turned-up hats, thinking themselves very smart, but having to hide the uniforms under winter coats when they went home again.

Many of the lads had never learned to fire a weapon or make a bomb or even, though it wasn't important at that point, march straight together. They were unsure of what lay ahead, but they only wanted unifying, and unifying was what we were there to do. We answered their questions as best we could, and heard what their own problems were, and met their leaders. We told them what Riordan had told us and discussed the way of the big war in Europe.

I think me put a little heart into them, and then, at the end, we got them singing the songs that keep the spirit high, standing in the midst of them all with the fire flickering on their faces. And, at last, the two of us would begin the song that speaks best of what we longed for, what we were trying to do, and why we were there at all. After the first few notes, they would jump to their feet, with smiles broad enough to fill an empty heart and join in with us:

> I'll sing you a song, a soldier's song,
> With cheering, rousing chorus,
> As round our blazing fires we throng,
> The starry heavens o'er us;
> Impatient for the coming fight,
> And as we wait the morning light
> Here in the silence of the night
> We'll chant a soldier's song.

Soldiers are we, whose lives are pledged to Ireland.
Some have come from a land beyond the wave.
Sworn to be free, no more our ancient sireland
Shall shelter the despot or the slave;
Tonight we man the *bearna baoghal**
In Erin's cause, come woe or weal;
'Mid cannon's roar and rifle's peal
We'll chant a soldier's song!

Well, it seems we were a success, and that was only the beginning of a winter-long series of meetings in Waterford and Cork and even up through Tipperary and Wexford, across the mountains, anywhere we could gather a group of men together. Sometimes we were gone only for a day or two, sometimes for a week.

Riordan was pleased with us. We'd report back to him at a small meeting of the officers, with only himself and Culhane and McLoughlin and a few others. We told them all we found, how many men we had seen; we told them what we thought of the leadership in each place.

And every time, when we were free to go home again, there would be Margaret waiting for us, wrapped in white furs shining as the January snows, her black hair flying behind her, her face glowing with happiness, running down the road to meet us, throwing her arms around us, with grand old Byron snorting and puffing in the cold air, stamping from one foot to the other. But, once the joy of seeing us again was past, Margaret grew angrier each time.

"It's all his doing," she cried, slapping her hands together to keep them warm. "He keeps sending you away—"

"And we keep coming back," said Jamie lightly, winding a strand of her hair tightly about his finger. "He'll have to get used to it, for, with you here, we'll always come back."

"He hasn't talked of sending me away to school," pondered Margaret. "I wouldn't go anyway, but he was so determined that I should. Half a dozen times I've been

* The gap of danger. Pronounced "*bar*-na bweel."

ready to have it out with him, but I hardly see him these days. He's been down to Queenstown five or six times, something about shipments of guns from New York City, and now he's together half the night with Norwood."

"Norwood again?" said Jamie. "Has he learned anything?"

She shook her head. "What would I know of that? You'd hear it before me. No, no, it's something new about his property. His damned everlasting bits and pieces of property. To hear him talk, we must have owned half of Ireland once!"

"Well, if it keeps him from bothering you, I hope himself and Charlie darling will stay at it a year and a day!" cried Jamie, grabbing her in his arms and kissing her, whilst she trickled a handful of snow down the back of his neck.

"This will be over, Margaret," he said very earnestly, holding her close while I bestowed my full attention on old Byron. "Soon. We've got a big fight ahead, next year probably, and then we'll really be free to live our lives."

"Will we, do you suppose?" she asked doubtfully, but he pushed her off and held her at arm's length, tightly, looking straight into her eyes.

"Can't you feel how things are moving, and changing? Can't you feel a new spirit in the air, Margaret? Oh, will you for once just believe something, just believe it and feel it; don't doubt it and nibble and gnaw away at it till there's nothing left. Our day is almost here, *mavourneen,* do you know that? Do you?"

For a few seconds she searched his eyes, then a small sure smile spread across her face and she nodded. "I see what you see, Jamie. And I'll believe it, every minute, I swear it!"

He pulled her back to him and began to kiss her so that I knew they had forgotten I was there. I led Byron away and made up my mind I'd best be asking Kate Crotty to a dance with me the next week.

Chapter XIII

But we were not there the next week, nor another beyond it. We moved north to Clonmel and then to Slievenamon, traveling through the dangerous V gap in the Comeragh Mountains on foot, sleeping out at night in the little stone shelters the shepherds used to use long ago. Our journey was successful; we spoke to a great many men in different places and returned home without incident.

We stopped first at my place, but no one was home, and sure enough we found my mother and Aunt Ellen and the girls having a late-morning cup of tea together, holding one more in a series of premature wakes for us, for Kathleen told me later that all they had done since we'd gone off was talk about what good lads we were and how we'd be missed.

Kathleen was sent off at once to tell Margaret we were back again, and we sat down to eat surrounded by mothers and sisters and pet dogs clucking and kissing and barking and wagging and dabbing their eyes. No sooner had we eaten than Jamie insisted on having a look round to see how everything was doing.

And it was out in the fields behind the house that Margaret found us. She dragged the two of us back to the house, to the big wooden table outside where we used to eat in summer sometimes. Up she sprang on top of the table, folded her legs under her skirts like a Turk, and demanded to be told all we had done. But, at that same moment, we spotted a man on horseback coming quick along the road, raising the dust so hard we couldn't tell who he was. He turned in at the Daley's front gate.

"Jamie Daley! Daley, are you at home?" we heard him shouting.

Jamie and I jumped up and ran around to meet him.

"Who wants me?" called back Jamie.

It was O'Rourke, not much used to the backside of a horse since he and his wife had bought the shop and lade-da'd themselves into a motor coach besides. Sweaty, dusty, and all of a thirst, O'Rourke nevertheless did not dismount, but pulled over to the side of the house, glancing down the road ahead of the house, which was empty.

"What's up?" asked Jamie.

"Riordan wants you to get right over to Culhane's. He sent word this morning. There's a delivery—"

"Only now?" asked Jamie, puzzled. "That shipment was due in at Queenstown three weeks ago. Or is it the same shipment at all?"

O'Rourke looked concerned. "There's been some mixup in the whole thing. I don't know much. We were expecting a big one, two hundred rifles, new; ten thousand rounds of ammunition, grenades, besides. And six crates of medical supplies."

"What went wrong, then?"

"I tell you, I don't know!" O'Rourke shook his head. "Sean was three days in Queenstown trying to find out. He came home empty-handed and swearing fit to crown a martyr. That's five thousand pounds! Five thousand, gone to hell for all we know, and nothing to show for it."

"Ah, maybe he heard it was come at last, and that's what we're getting today," I put in, but again he shook his head.

"No, something small, that's all there is. But he might have heard something from Flynn. He's our man on the boat, a stoker, I think. All we know is that, so far, he hasn't been arrested. They checked with New York from Dublin, that's what's been taking so long. Somewhere between here and America, our five thousand disappeared. They won't deliver without the money. Some of our people are trying to put it together again over on the other side. The big shipment is still available, but I don't know how long. Oh, it's all in a tangle. Get yourselves over to Culhane House and find out whatever else you can."

"Will you go in and take something to drink?" invited Jamie.

O'Rourke looked longingly at the house, taking off his hat and wiping the sweat from his face. "No, I've got to get back right away. And listen, you two, be very careful. They've doubled up on the patrols now. Everyone's very nippish with the new troops coming in next month; they're expecting us to give them trouble."

"They're so right!" Jamie smiled grimly.

O'Rourke looked doubtful. "Not much, not without those guns," he said glumly. "Well, I'm off. Remember me to your mother, will you?" He turned the horse's head about and rode away back up the road.

Jamie and I ran for the barn to hitch up the hay wagon. And there was Margaret, running toward us.

"Well, did you forget all about me?"

"Margaret, I'm that sorry, but we've got to leave. There's something come up," answered Jamie, leading two of the horses out.

"And how long do I have to wait this time, a year?"

"Margaret, will you move?" She had planted herself in front of the horses, whilst I was trying to get them to stand still and be harnessed up.

"Tell me where you're going."

"Over to your house. There, are you satisfied? And you can't come with us," said Jamie.

"Lovely!" she cried, eyes twinkling. "You'll just let me trot along behind you, is that it? Won't that look grand, now?"

"Margaret, this is business. Your father doesn't want you involved in it. You know that."

"Ah-hah!" She smiled in triumph, and quickly climbed up and seated herself amidst the hay in the back of the wagon. "That's all you had to remind me of, Jamie dear!" she smirked.

Jamie groaned and looked at me, as if I could do anything with her!

"All right, all right, stay there," he gave in. "But the minute we get to the gates, down you go, understand?"

She nodded very agreeably, scrumbling herself into the hay and poking her head between the two of us on the seat, plaguing us as we turned up the road by tickling the backs of our necks, stuffing hay down our shirts.

"Say, Jerry, did you notice anything queer about O'Rourke?" asked Jamie, one hand on the reins, the other reaching out behind him to push her away.

"O'Rourke?"

Jamie grinned. "I never heard him say so much at one time. He must really be upset. You'd think it was his own money!"

"It's an awful lot of somebody's money," I said, "Margaret, stop it this instant, now!"

"What are you doing after you see my father?" she asked, ignoring me altogether. "Oh, let's go and have a good long ride!"

I glanced at Jamie. There was an uncomfortable pause.

"We'll have something else to do then, sweetheart," said Jamie ever so softly. "I don't know how long it will take—"

"Oh, something else! It's always something else these days!" she cried in exasperation. Jamie sighed. Then, an instant later, she said very contritely, "I'm sorry. Truly, I am. But I missed you so!"

She knelt up straight behind Jamie, throwing her arms about his neck suddenly, and nestled her face against his hair. I saw him bend his head and press his lips to her arm. As I watched, and remembered a bit late to look away, I was surprised by the sudden lurch of my own heart, and I thought I'd best be finding other things to occupy myself from now on, for I loved them both too much to push myself in on the little time they had together.

"We're here," I warned them, as the big black iron gates loomed up ahead of us.

"All right, down you go, quick," said Jamie, slowing the horses.

Margaret kissed him again lightly, then jumped down

to throw open the gates for us. We drove past her, straight beyond the house to Culhane's big barn.

Patrick was not there. The place seemed deserted as we backed the wagon up to the barn door and went inside. The empty stall that was always used for the guns we picked up was empty that day. Though Jamie poked around the straw quite thoroughly, we found nothing. He straightened up, puzzled and wary, just as Sean himself came in from the side door, looking nervous and thin-edged.

"Glad you're back safe," he said rather perfunctorily. When we would have said thanks, he cut us short. "Did they tell you what's happened?"

Jamie nodded. "Some. The money's gone and nothing seen from it."

Culhane grimaced, yet, though it was obvious he was disturbed, his voice sounded as remote as always, as if he were listening to something someone else was saying from a distance. "That's it. I don't know what to think. I've worked with Tom Flynn twenty years, more than twenty, and he's never let me down yet."

"Five thousand pounds is a big temptation," said Jamie.

"Never!" Culhane flung back at him. "Never, not Flynn. I'd stake my life on that man. No, no. Something's happened to him."

"Well, you can't blame yourself for it," said Jamie kindly. "The only thing that matters now is that shipment. O'Rourke said they're trying to put enough together again to pay for it."

Culhane ran his hand through the thick, unruly shock of brown hair, pushing it back from his wide forehead. "God knows how long that will take them. The first five took over a year."

"What about De Valera? They say he's raising millions over there," I pointed out.

Culhane looked at me briefly, then away. "De Valera can't do everything," he drawled, a vague frown drawing together his two pale eyebrows. "Now, I managed to get hold of one crate of rifles, and a hard fight I had to put up for it, too. There are only eight guns, but they're pretty new. They were marked for shipment to France, but a friend of mind set them aside in the back of the post office, and somehow their ship sailed without them."

"From America?" inquired Jamie.

Culhane laughed. It sounded contrived and somehow artificial "From a few of 'ourselves,' not fifty miles away. British sympathizers, all of them, out for democracy and 'making the world safe' again, and so forth. They are eight of the finest hunting rifles I've ever seen, a noble sacrifice for the boys at the front, I understand. Well, we can make better use of them, eh?"

"Sure," said Jamie, and he seemed suddenly anxious to finish up and be off. "We're to take them to the same place, I suppose? Or is it changed? O'Rourke warned us they've tightened up on their security lately."

"They have, and it's going to get a lot worse before we're through, I'll wager," answered Culhane, his pale eyes seeming to jump out from the sallow face like darts from the darkness. "You'll have to wait. They're still up at the house. Things have been so chaotic here I haven't had time to do anything. I'll be back in a moment."

He left quickly, bending his head to pass through the doorway. Culhane was a tall man, a very tall man with wide shoulders and large hands. Somehow I always felt better when he left, perhaps because he always gave the impression that his being with you was a favor to you, and that can grow damned uncomfortable. Oh, maybe it was just that I felt uncomfortable anyway, working with the man and knowing so much that was unpleasant about his own family and himself.

While we waited for him to bring the guns, we went round to have a look at his horses. There were twenty in the barn then, fine-looking animals every one. Culhane bred hunters mostly, sometimes a few racing horses and a jumper now and again. And there was old Sailor, Kevin's chestnut, nickering and tossing his head, very glad to see the two of us again.

"Poor old fellow," said Jamie, rubbing his nose. "We'll have to take you out soon, like the old days. You miss Kevin, don't you, old boy? Don't you, Sailor?"

"Are you finished yet?"

"Margaret, will you stop sneaking up on us like that?" I had almost jumped out of my skin when I heard her voice there, suddenly, in the quiet barn.

She sauntered in, grinning. "Don't you worry about Sailor. I've been taking him out every morning, and Byron's in that much of a fit, he bit the horse in the stall next to him yesterday." She laughed, scratching Sailor's ears.

"Margaret, you're not supposed to be here. Go back to the house, will you?" ordered Jamie, quite put out with her.

"I'm not afraid of *him*." She tossed her head. Then, with a quick smile at me, she wheedled, "Jerry, do something for me, will you? I think I've gone and lost my hair ribbon in the wagon. Just take a look and see if it's there?"

I went outside to the wagon and searched around a good three or four minutes, but I could find no ribbon. And then, as I went back in to tell her the same, I stopped in the doorway, and tried to back out again quietly. For there they were, and the world could have slipped away under their feet and they'd never have noticed. Jamie was holding her in his arms, one hand pressing the back of her head against his own, kissing her as if he would hold her with him forever. They hadn't seen me, and I meant that they would not, but, at that moment, in from the side door walked Sean Culhane, lugging a heavy wooden crate in his arms.

I tried to signal to Jamie, but he couldn't see me, which fact I had been so glad of only a second before. Culhane said nothing, but stood watching them, as I did myself, and the look on his face would take a book to analyze.

At last Margaret pulled away a bit, and ran her fingers tenderly over Jamie's face. "I missed you so," she whispered.

"Margaret!" Culhane said it in his usual low voice, but she jumped away from Jamie and stood with her back against one of the stalls, her face red with anger, her eyes flashing.

Jamie stood his ground. "I'm sorry, Sean," he said

evenly. "There's no secret to it. We haven't had much chance to speak to you."

Culhane set the crate down carefully, wiping his hands free of dust. "And if you had spoken, what would you have said?"

"Father!" broke in Margaret, but Jamie quieted her with a reassuring look.

"That I love your daughter very much, and that she loves me, too. And that we will be married."

Culhane spoke in a slow, precise drawl, drawing the words out beyond their intrinsic worth. "Daley, I told you once, I do not want my daughter mixed up in what's going on here," he said, not looking at Jamie at all.

"She's not, Sean, I promise you," answered Jamie a bit hotly. "The one thing has nothing to do with the other. You know that."

"It seems, actually, I know very little," retorted Culhane, his large mouth curling scornfully. "It seems I do not know what I should have known."

"It's no use going on like this, Father," cried Margaret. "I love him!" Her breath came and went in short gasps, and she clutched the top of Sailor's stall with white-knuckled fingers.

"Really, Margaret, the scene is impossible," said Culhane flatly. "I am cast in the part of the wicked father, while you and Daley are the innocent young lovers—I presume you *are* innocent still?"

There was no mistaking his meaning. Margaret uttered a little cry, and Jamie sprang forward, about to strike her father, but he stopped himself with great effort. Culhane's expression never changed.

"Oh, Sean, you know me! And you know Margaret. Don't talk like a fool!"

"I see. You're a very honorable, even a noble young fellow, then?" Culhane smiled insolently. "Then you'll understand me when I tell you that my plans for Margaret's future do not include you in even the remotest fashion. Surely, since my daughter is so very honorable, like yourself, she has told you what those plans are? Surely she told you that she is going away to school again, and then she is to be married, when she marries, *if* she marries, to a man of her own station, whom I shall choose for her? She did tell you that, didn't she, Daley? Yes, she did. I can tell by your face. So I must ask, are you being entirely honorable in interfering with my family?"

"I won't go away, I told him that too, Father!" cried Margaret. "I'll live my own life and you'll not stop it!"

Culhane folded his arms and considered the two of them for a long moment. "I see, I see," he murmured, and I could not read the expression in his eyes at all. Then, to my astonishment and theirs, he smiled, a bit stiffly, but a smile nevertheless, and gave them a little, ironic bow. "You're very serious, I see," he said, and I wondered how he could say it so lightly, for it was obvious to me he was far from reconciled.

"Yes, we're serious." Now it was Jamie's turn to be sarcastic, and, as he spoke, he reached out and took Margaret's hand in his own.

Culhane's light eyes, flickering ever so slightly, rested on the two of them an instant, then darted away again, to fix their gaze at some spot beyond them.

"Then I'm sorry, James Daley. I'm not going at this at all right, I realize that. What we have to do is try to be reasonable—"

"No!" cried Margaret vehemently, pulling away from Jamie and stepping between him and her father. "No, we must not be reasonable. That's your favorite word, isn't it, Father? Reasonable! That means do everything your way and don't make a fuss about it. That's how you tried to keep hold of Kevin, and he listened to you, for years he listened, until he learned there's no being reasonable with you! And he went. You couldn't hold him, and you can't hold me!"

"Kevin was of age," answered Culhane slowly. "You are not."

"I don't care!" shouted Margaret. "I don't care about anything but Jamie—"

"Stop it! You're becoming hysterical! Don't make any more of a fool of yourself than you already have!"

"Sean, this isn't doing any good," began Jamie, and

Culhane again shifted his gaze to stare at Jamie for a second.

"You're quite right, of course," he said quietly. "This kind of talk never does. As I said, Margaret is too young to think of any marriage whatever now. If you were only willing to wait, at least—"

"Of course we'll wait," said Jamie. "We don't want to, but we've our whole lives ahead of us. I've work that has to be done before I'd ask any girl to share my life. God, Sean, you're in the thing yourself. Don't you know me any better than that? You were my father's friend. You've known me since I was a boy. I'll do what's right for Margaret, and I'll never hurt her or give her cause for grief. Can't you see that, man?"

Margaret listened, pale-faced and defiant, but when he'd finished, she flung herself into his arms.

"Jamie, stop it!" she begged. "How long will we have, do you think? Till a bullet stops you? Till they catch you and hang you like your father that awful night?" She was crying, holding his face in her hand so very tightly. "I want you for that long, as long as I can be with you! I don't want to wait till it's all safe and proper and convenient! That will never be. It's never convenient to love people! There's always something stopping happiness. Can't we just have our bit of it now, before we can't have it at all? Jamie?"

"Your lover has a much better grasp of the situation, Margaret, it would seem. Whatever your feeling are about each other, if they are true, they can only grow in time. We are at war, or have you forgotten that? Jamie wants to do the right thing, why can't you respect that and do as he wishes?"

"Because it's not as he wishes!" Margaret hurled back at him. "It's as you wish! It's always as you wish! And don't talk about feeling growing in time! I'd caught on to that one by the time I was ten! No, no, Father, it's time that changes feelings, and changes people, and takes their love for each other and kills it! I don't believe in time! I believe in now, right now, while I am what I am, and Jamie is Jamie! Who knows who we'll be in five years or ten? Maybe we'll be us; maybe we'll be two other people; maybe we'll be dead altogether. We've got to love each other now, or it'll be too late and we won't even have anything to remember when time's done its murders."

"You don't seem to have much faith in the future, or in yourself," said Culhane distantly.

Margaret simply shook her head then and fell silent, for he would not understand what she said.

Again he pushed his hair from his forehead. His neck held up his head like a flagpole, stiff the neck and straight the head, and both unbending. He turned again to Jamie, who returned his cold gaze just as coldly.

"I was surprised by all this. I am surprised still. My daughter has been raised for a very different sort of life than what you offer her. I do not doubt your sincerity, but the suitability of such an arrangement. However, I am not the Almighty. We can only hope our children will do the right thing. After that, they must choose for themselves. Still, Margaret must abide by my decisions for a few more years. So I will ask you not to see her—"

"No!" Margaret cried out, but he went on smoothly.

"Not to see her, or communicate with her in any way, until she is of age to choose as she wishes. You will be fair enough to give her this chance to find her way free of you, if that is what is to happen."

"That I cannot do, nor will I," answered Jamie shortly.

Culhane sighed. "Then only disaster will happen," he said. "Loving each other, seeing each other every day, how long will that honor you boast of endure? You're a man grown, Daley, and Margaret is no child. No, no, human nature is what it is."

"Most of the time, the three of us are together," I finally spoke up, and instantly wished I'd stayed out of it.

"How long will it be before they find ways of leaving you behind?" asked Culhane curtly. And I fell silent, remembering how Margaret had sent me for the ribbon before. My eyes went to the bright-yellow band around her hair. She caught the look, flushed, and looked away.

"We don't need a guardian angel, Culhane," said Jamie. "It's little enough we see of each other now."

"Yes." Culhane nodded. "And each parting harder, each reunion more poignant. You merely prove my point."

"That's enough of talking!" said Margaret feverishly. She stared wild-eyed at Jamie. "What will you do? It's all in your hands. What will you do about me?"

Jamie smiled gently at her. "I'll love you, and keep you always, Margaret. You didn't have to ask. But I'll not bind you with it till my job is finished. I did not want to go against your father, but that's the way it is. Go up to the house, now, *acushla,* and don't worry."

She looked at him and knew he spoke the truth, pressed her lips quickly to his hand, then, without another glance at Culhane she ran off out of the barn.

"Look, Sean, I know you're upset, and I'm sorry," said Jamie uncomfortably. "But it's all very new and we're not used to it ourselves. That's the way of it, though, and you cannot change it, believe me. You have my word that no harm will come to Margaret. I've not broken my word yet. Will you accept that?"

"Yes, I will," said Culhane, sounding almost as if he had forgotten all about Jamie. He was still staring at the doorway where Margaret had gone running out. "And we'll have to leave the rest to time."

"That suits me." Jamie shrugged. Let Sean trust to time to spoil it all; let him think what he would, if it comforted him.

At last, I pointed to the wooden crate on the floor and broke the silence. "Those the rifles?" I asked.

"What?" asked Culhane, startled by the question. "Oh, yes, that's the lot. Take them over to Kilgannon's, but be careful. Try to get away from the place before dark, if you can."

"Any message? They're hoping for some word on the other business."

"No, I can't tell them anything. I'll be in touch. Now you'd best be off and on your way." He looked for a moment as if he would say more, but changed his mind, turned away abruptly, and left.

Silently Jamie and I loaded the crate into the wagon and piled the hay high on top of it and around it. And silently we drove away down the road. There was no sign of Margaret. Jamie sat slumped against the back of the seat, the reins slack in his hand, a dark look on his face.

"I wish I'd laid him out there," he muttered.

"For a minute, I thought you were going to," I said, but he shook his head.

"That's the whip of it," he pointed out. "He's her father. I can't treat him like any other man."

"Jamie, she hates him. That makes a difference."

"No. No, it doesn't. He's her father and I cannot lay hands on him, no matter how he opposes us. Ah, well, it'll all come out." And he tightened the reins, sat up straight, and tried to look as if he believed it.

Nearly an hour later, we drove slowly up to the old burned-out house by the twin birch trees leading off into Ballyteague. It was very quiet, not above an hour and a half to sunset, a kind of peaceful glow settling over the old stones and new grasses, softening them. Ireland's rain and sun don't leave anything raw or ruined-looking very long.

We looked around. There was nothing in sight; no sound save the busy nesting cries of the birds in early evening. So we got down and carried the rifles over to the old stone chimney. Inside of it was a long, straight, hollow space, perfect for what we were hiding. But, just as Jamie began to break open the crate with his knife, I got a terrible itchy feeling around the back of my neck. I never moved at all, but I said to him, "Don't move. I think someone's watching us."

Very slowly he set the crate down, keeping the knife open in his hand. "I can't see anyone," he whispered to me, glancing over my shoulder.

"It's just a feeling. Come on, finish up and let's be going," I urged him, for the itchy feeling would not go away.

And then I saw them, emerging from the trees ten feet behind Jamie, six British soldiers, with their rifles pointed straight at the two of us. A small sound of breaking twigs told me there were more of them at my own back.

"Raise your hands, slowly, now," cried out one, a corporal he was, crisply enough. Born leader type, *had* to be with such a snappy voice.

Jamie's face mirrored my own disgust. He palmed the knife and we both raised our hands. Then they came in closer.

"Now, what would two nice Paddys like yourselves be doing out here in this deserted place, I wonder!" said the corporal in what he evidently thought to be some kind of foreign accent. He noticed the half-opened crate, the shiny steel of the rifle barrels showing out distinctly.

"Hm, fancy that, guns, is it? Imagine! And you chaps never heard there's a law against Irishmen having guns. My, my, you've a bit of explaining to do."

He ordered one of the men to take the rifles. Another two were told to search the wagon. One of them used the butt of his rifle to knock through the seat and the wooden bottom, searching for a false bottom where more weapons could be concealed.

"All right, now, let's have your names, smartly, now!" snapped out our corporal. What *is* it about corporals anyway?

Of course we said nothing. I think he was about to press his point, but one of the soldiers came over to have a good look at us.

"I know these two," says he. "This one's Daley, and that's his cousin, Noonan; they're from Dunknealy."

"Wrong by a mile," quipped Jamie.

But he stepped closer to us, smiling nastily. "You don't remember me, do you, Daley?"

"Should I?" sneered Jamie right back in his face.

"Might," said he. "I was at your house last year, the night we hanged your dad. Thought you might remember that."

Jamie's face turned livid with anger, and all at once he kicked out, landing a hard slam at the fellow's groin. He knocked the Englishman off balance, but missed his target. We waited for nothing. I grabbed the corporal by the neck and swung him around, twisting his arm till he dropped the gun. But Jamie's opponent was determined to have it out, and the two of them were locked together in one hell of a struggle. The fellow had got out his own knife, a wicked-looking thing at least eight inches long. The two of them circled around, looking for an opening. I saw the others come running, and quickly picked up the corporal's gun.

"Back off!" I shouted to them, just as Jamie and the soldier closed with a thud you could hear clear to Roscommon. There was a twisting and flashing; I could hear the soldier swearing, and then he fell to the ground, Jamie's knife buried in his chest. Again the others moved in, so I shoved the corporal in front of me, and they stopped cold when they saw him in their line of fire.

"D-don't shoot, boys," quavered the hero of the day, and I could feel him shaking as I held him.

Jamie quickly picked up the rifle belonging to the dead man. "Put the weapons down, nice and easy, now," he ordered the others, and they did what he said, backing away from the guns as if they would go off by themselves. "Now start running, back the way you came. I'll send your commanding officer here along in ten minutes or so, provided you're not on the way back. Otherwise you'll not see him alive again. Now go on!"

They turned away, but only straggled along not too fast, looking back uncertainly, till Jamie raised the gun and fired after them. Then they took off indeed, and as far as I know they're running still.

"Well, this was a great day's work!" I exploded, looking at the soldier on the ground. "What'll we do now? They know who we are!"

"Couldn't be helped, I suppose," sighed Jamie, looking suddenly rather strange. He fetched a bit of rope from the wagon and began to tie the corporal's hands behind his back. Then he removed the man's boots and threw them into the bushes. "Start walking," he ordered.

"You won't get far," said the corporal, setting off across the rough ground in his stocking feet. "We'll find you, and we'll hang you two just like we did your old man."

I saw Jamie raise the gun toward the middle of his back, but then, reluctantly, he lowered it once more.

"Go on, you son of a bitch!" he shouted, and turned away.

"What should we do with him?" I gestured toward the dead man.

Jamie stared down at him thoughtfully. "They'll be back here later. They can have the pleasure of burying him. We've got enough of our own to worry about. Come on, let's get busy."

We had no time to lose. Quickly we worked together to unhitch the horses from the wagon, which was ruined anyway. We jumped up bareback, with only the bridle and bit and the small sense of two very surprised workhorses who had rarely been ridden in all their lives.

"We've got maybe an hour, then they'll be out after us with the dogs," cried Jamie. "We can't go home. Best make for Riordan in the hills and see what he says."

We rode the reluctant horses by back roads and dirt roads and no roads at all up into the hills, hoping we'd find Riordan in the same place, for they moved around a lot to avoid notice. We were in luck. He was there, all right, sitting pulling on his pipe by the fire, a cold evening wind coming up as we rode in.

The men came running to us; there were more than twenty-five up there full time now. Wasting as little time as possible, we told them what had happened.

Allie Clarke and his brother Joe came over to us as we took some tea and supper, and Riordan sat thinking out what was to be done.

"God!" Allie shivered, rubbing his hands together nervously. "The two of us were just about to go pick up the damn guns!"

"Thank God you didn't go. They'll be as thick as ants there by now. You can't use Kilgannon's place again," said Jamie.

"Aye, and we can't let you two go home again, not now," brooded Riordan. "You'll stay here. There's plenty to do, but I would have liked you out free better."

"So would we, Captain," quipped Jamie. "Can you get word to our families? My mother's been worried before.

Now they'll be after her and the girls, and Jerry's folks too."

Riordan nodded. "I'll see to it they know you're safe away," he promised. "The charge will be murder, you know. That's bound to upset them."

Jamie's lip curled. "Tell them he was one of them that came after Da that night."

"Ah!" Riordan nodded, and Joe slapped Jamie on the back. "Did Sean have any word, by the way?"

"Oh, he had a lot of words," said Jamie, glancing at me with a smile. "But not anything you'd want to hear. He said he'd keep in touch."

Riordan shook his head, sucking on vain on the dead pipe.

"Damned luck," he said in disgust. "Eight gone today, and the whole damned shipment we were counting on. How do they expect us to fight a war without weapons?"

"How did we ever?" Jamie pointed out, lighting himself a cigarette he'd got from Allie. "We'll manage. We've got to."

Chapter XIV

So the posters were run off on the two of us, can you imagine it, us up in print and a reward to boot, just like those Wild West cowboys off in America! We were wanted, is what we were, to the tune of fifty pounds apiece, on a whole lot of charges the best of which was murder. O'Rourke presented us souvenir copies of the posters; poker-faced and wordless, he put them before our faces as we were trying our best to shave one morning. Ah, God help us, camp life may be for Germans and boy scouts, but it didn't suit Jamie and it didn't suit me one

bit. The shaving water was that cold you could easier
freeze the whiskers off than cut them, and damned if anyone could find the last sliver of soap to be seen in the hills.

"So that's us?" remarked Jamie, looking down at an
awful picture of himself, which we both recognized was
one taken about three years back at somebody's wedding
party. "I wonder how they got hold of it."

"Never mind yourself, look at this, will you?" I pointed
with great disgust to myself there on the paper, looking
like a wild-faced kid of eight or so, with a grin on me that
made the words printed below seem idiotic: "Wanted for
Murder, Smuggling, Possession of Deadly Weapons, Re-
sisting Arrest, Assault on person of British troops," etc.,
etc.

Jamie only nodded and went back to scraping the skin
off his neck. "I told you you were drunk that night. You
don't even remember when they took it. I had to prop you
up and you kept smiling and telling all the girls to get in
line to kiss that mug of yours. Well, there it is now—any
wonder they didn't?"

"I suppose my mother's seen this by now," I thought
aloud, crumpling up the posters. "I wonder what she'll
think."

"She'll know what happened," Jamie said. "It's not
murder to kill an English soldier on Irish soil, never forget
that."

Well, of course we waited anxiously for news from
town, and soon enough we heard that they'd been to both
our houses and threatened the hell out of everybody and
taken poor old Will into headquarters twice. If they got
any sense out of him, they'd sure be the first in a lot of
years, more luck to them. More than once Jamie and I
begged Riordan to let us slip down and see the folks, but
he wouldn't hear of it. Time had to pass, he said, wait till
they had someone newer to think about. Meanwhile we
had enough to keep busy. The new troops arrived with the
new moon, and both about as welcome. These were tough
veterans, over from France and grown mean in His Majesty's Service. They looked upon duty in Ireland as a rest,
and they enjoyed no longer being confined to dirty little

trenches, but could roam around causing trouble whenever they wished.

We saw to it that they did not enjoy their new job too much. Despite Culhane's pleadings, which we heard about endlessly from O'Rourke, Riordan refused to stage any daylight massive raids, but stuck to what we knew best, night attacks, surprise terrorist strikes, and other discouragements.

Jamie spent his spare time smoking like mad and composing long letters to Margaret. He would not trust even O'Rourke to deliver them, for O'Rourke worked too closely with Culhane, and Jamie feared she would never get them once the father caught wise. From Margaret herself we heard not a word, not for weeks, though O'Rourke always made a point of telling Jamie very formally that Miss Culhane was looking well and hoped he was the same.

Mostly Jamie worried about the farm. It was all up to Will now, but with no one there to keep him straight, how long would it be before he let the place go to hell altogether? Aunt Ellen was a wonder of the world for work, but she and two small girls could hardly keep up the place by themselves. Then there was the money for Norwood. How long could they hold the place if Will let it all slip away from him?

Months went by and rumors reached us, although Riordan tried to hush them, that Will Daley was hardly ever home, but spending more and more time in town. Where did he get the drinking money? Someone said one of Norwood's lads was slipping it to him pretty freely, and he'd run up a bill at the pub would keep a family going for a year, but it was paid one day, no questions asked. To all this bad news Jamie said nothing, but I could see he was working a way out of it in his head and I left him alone to do so.

More time passed, and we heard that Charlie very abruptly had stopped paying Will's drinking bills, had, in fact, dropped Will altogether, and still the rent was paid on time. Nor did the Daley place go to weeds, though there was much speculation on just how it was being cared for.

Up the road like a hound sniffing out his rabbit would come Charlie. Into Daley's front yard came Charlie, right to where Aunt Ellen would be working in her garden. Off would come that fine hat from Charlie's head.

"And how is your family this fine day, Mrs. Daley? Any news from Jamie on his travels?" would smirk Charlie, for that was the prideful little lie Aunt Ellen always used to explain Jamie's absence from home.

"Oh, I expect he's halfway to South America by now," she would say, staring Norwood deadly narrow in the eyes. "Will you take the rent now, Mr. Norwood? I've work to do."

And poor old Charlie, thwarted once more, would grab the money and ride off with his cohorts behind him, whilst my aunt stood nailed in the doorway or the garden till the last of them was out on the road.

Poor Charlie, week after week he came, on weekends, on Sunday even, morning and evening, and the farm never bloomed so fair. Even when he himself had just left the pub in town, and knew for a solemn fact that Will Daley was sleeping one off in the corner and not in this world at all, there was the work of the farm, far too much for the womenfolk to handle, going on as if a crew of ghosts were hard at work.

Well, it wasn't ghosts at all. It was Jamie, aye, Jamie, the only man in the world mad enough to try his hand at night farming. Oh, all the almanacs going back hundreds of years could tell you at a glance that, for most things, night farming was better and much better luck. Hell, half the crops they speak of are supposed to be planted at midnight by the light of the moon or the dark of the moon or some such. But Jamie was the only one to take them up on it. He knew Will would do nothing, and Will did nothing.

Jamie, you see, took to disappearing from camp three or four nights a week, very late, sometimes past midnight. I wondered for a time where it was he went. I thought maybe to meet Margaret, and I didn't say anything about it. He never asked Riordan for leave to go and Riordan never seemed to notice he was gone. I did think it odd that he never assigned Jamie night watch, not even once. I often got stuck with that duty, and many's the cold black night-time I'd be stamping my post back and forth, my shoulder aching from the rifle, peering into the darkness down in the valley, thinking spiteful thoughts about my dear cousin.

Sometimes Riordan would stroll along by me, his pipe in his mouth, the moon shining off his silver hair. He'd walk out my way and stop for a bit of talk and a smoke together. I often had it on the end of my tongue to say something, or ask him about Jamie, but I never did. Until, one night, long after he usually came back to camp, there was no Jamie. I fretted and marched and stamped and peered a good two hours beyond the time, but I heard nothing, and he never came. Riordan strolled along up to me and startled me blind.

"Not back yet?"

I jumped, staring at him, but he paid no attention to me, just frowned worriedly, looking past me, down the trail.

"What?" I blurted out, almost dropping my rifle. Riordan tamped out his pipe impatiently against a tree.

"Jamie. He's past two hours late, isn't he?"

I avoided his keen eyes. "Uh, sir, he is." What else could I say?

"Let me know when he comes in, will you, Jerry?"

Oh, there'd be a reckoning then, I could see it in my mind's eyes: Jamie blistering and agonizing under Riordan's rare golden tongue-lashing and maybe a court-martial to boot!

"Sir—"

"Yes?" He turned back.

"Sir, I was wondering. I mean, it's that quiet tonight, you know, and I thought I could—"

"Don't ask me anything!" he snapped quickly before I could get the words out. "You know I can never sanction a man leaving his post, now, could I, Jerry? Not for any reason. And, of course, a man would be a fool to ask permission for such a thing, now, wouldn't he?"

I dropped my head. "Aye, he would, sir."

Riordan stared down toward the valley again, relighting the pipe very slowly and deliberately, it seemed to me. "It's a pleasant night, isn't it? Just the kind of night a man would like to sit outside a while and relax from the troubles of the day. Oh, not for long, mind you. Just as long, say, as it would take you to get down to Daley's and find out where that lunatic of a cousin of yours is!"

He said the last most emphatically, bit into the pipe stem very hard, grabbed the rifle from me, breathing cold air into the night, and began marching my post dramatically, stamping his cold feet against the frozen ground. I didn't waste time thanking him, but took off on the run down the hills the shortest way I knew, to Jamie's place. Something must be terribly wrong to make him so late, I knew it. They'd caught him, of course. I ran, puffing cold air into my already half-frozen lungs, heart pounding at the thought of all that could have happened. My two feet were numb with the cold and dampness; my face was windburned and itching, and the wind ripped the clothes about my body with no respect at all.

The damn fool, why hadn't he told me? Oh, sure, because then I would have insisted on going with him. I ran along, jumping back fences and ditches, almost spraining my ankle with it all, and I was cursing the bonds between me and Jamie altogether.

I suppose it was record time that I arrived outside the house, sneaking up slowly like a weasel by the chickens, I was that sure the place would be surrounded by soldiers. I could see smoke curling up from the chimney, and a light burning brightly in the kitchen window. That was normal enough. Aunt Ellen always kept a light in the window for Will to see his way up the road by. It was one of her more romantic notions that Will could see at all after drinking the day and the night away, but no one ever tried to dissuade her from the custom.

Like a criminal instead of a nephew, I stole alongside the house, crushing into the bushes, until I reached the kitchen door. Then I listened and waited, but there was no sound inside. Finally, believing I was as good as hanging myself, I reached up and knocked on the door. There was no answer. I'd have to do it again, damn Jamie Daley! I knocked once more, and this time I heard my aunt's voice calling cheerfully that she was coming. Her footsteps approached the door, and I heard Kathleen's voice too.

"Who is it out there at this time of night?" called my aunt very loudly.

"Shh, for God's sakes, it's me!" I answered faintly.

There was a silence, then the two voices whispering just the other side of the door, then again she called out. "Identify yourself, you out there!"

Oh, God, Aunt Ellen, I thought in anguish and me in peril of my life, didn't I hear her laughing when I gave my name. In a moment she undid the latch and let me into the kitchen.

"Jerry, lad, you're quite a stranger," says she, grabbing me and kissing me heartily. "Kathleen, set another place for tea. Come over by the fire, boy, and have a good warm for yourself. Look at him, will you, half dead with the cold. Jerry, I was talking to your mother only today. She's well, and so's your Da, and I was saying to her—"

"Aunt Ellen," I broke in, trying to look around and see where himself was hidden. "Where is Jamie?"

Her eyes widened, flew to Kathleen, then back to mine with an innocent stare so I knew right away she was going to lie to me.

"Jamie? Isn't he with you, then? Didn't you tell him to meet you here?"

I looked carefully around the room. Both she and Kathleen were fully dressed. There were dishes and the remains of a meal on the table.

"You're up late, aren't you?" I said. "Now, you *know* Jamie's not with me. The damn fool is missing from camp, Captain Riordan is freezing his ass off standing my watch, and if you don't fetch out that maniac of a son of yours at once, you'll have the whole Army down on all of us!"

"Whisht, listen to the tongue on the boy!" she chided, grinning, and even Kathleen laughed at me. They pressed a cup of tea into my cold hands and set a plate of ham and potatoes on my knee.

"Didn't you know where he was, then?" she asked me curiously. I shook my head, still staring about, ready to spring at a moment's notice. Then, as I stuffed my mouth

with good ham, doesn't the door open and in walks himself, big as life. And didn't he give me the grin as he went
over to the sink to wash two very muddy hands!

"I didn't know we were expecting you, Jerry," says he.
"Ma, that's all of the potatoes and turnips. Kathleen,
you'll have to cut the eyes tomorrow and store them the
way I showed you. Does Riordan know you've abandoned
your post of trust?"

That last was for myself. " 'Does Riordan know?' " I
mimicked him furiously, slapping down the tea and the
plate and jumping to my feet. "Riordan sent me after you,
and I'm to bring you back at once. Oh, he'll have you up
in front of a wall in the morning, you can depend on it!"

"I don't think he'll be that drastic," drawled Jamie.
"Now, just take up your tea again, for I'm having another
cup before I go. Now, Jerry, close your mouth, will you?
Everything's just fine, and the farm's blooming."

"Oh, yes, yes," said Aunt Ellen gaily as she poured him
out some tea. "One of the cows has gone quite hysterical
with the novelty of it. She's never given so much milk, and
as for the plow horse, I think Martin bought him from a
tinker, he's that fond of working at night! The rest of the
jobs get done as usual, and we're managing famously,
thank you very much, and Mr. Norwood can stuff it!"

"Ma!" cried Kathleen, blushing furiously, as Jamie and
I burst out laughing to hear little Aunt Ellen talk so.

I did not ask about Will, for there was something rather
fierce in her gaiety and I think she could not bear to let
herself dwell on the fact that one son risked his life for
something the other son cared nothing about, and she
loved them both.

Then Jamie quickly got into his jacket and cap and
kissed his mother and sister tenderly. "I won't see you for
a few days, now, but there's nothing much to be done.
Take care of yourselves, and give Janet a hug for me in
the morning."

"We will that, Jamie dear," said Aunt Ellen, holding
him very close to her for a moment before he opened the
door. "And I'll see Margaret on Sunday. Mind, the two of
you, be careful going back. There's spies and patrols all

over," she added, as if I weren't all too aware of just that fact.

The door closed behind us and we moved swiftly across the back empty field, a wide-open stretch. I covered it with my eyes closed. I'm the boyo you never see in the picture shows, not the one with the firing squad facing him that stands up bravely and refuses to take the blindfold, but the other one, the one they have to drag out between two soldiers, whimpering and yelling all the way. And I'd want the damned blindfold, oh yes I would. God, I don't want to see it coming! I don't want to know where's it's coming from. Just kill me quick and don't tell me your intentions, thank you very much all the same!

I was ready to strangle Jamie, but I couldn't say a word to him till we were almost back into camp, for fear our voices would carry to the wrong ears. But I gave it to him as we came close.

"One night you won't come back," I told him. He grinned. "No, listen to me, now, Jamie. Have a little sense. You're a wanted man. They'll shoot you on sight, and where will the family be then? Worse off. Will you listen?"

He shook his head, as we slowed down, spotting the small fire in the near distance.

"No, I can't stop it now. Even if Riordan orders it. I'll obey every command he gives, but I can't and I won't let them fend for themselves."

"Oh, stop being noble," I snapped. "I heard your mother mention Margaret's name. Have you been seeing her, then?"

"Four times," he said. "She slipped over to the house for a bit. I'm worried about her. She has no one to talk to now, even my mother and the girls aren't much help. You know how Margaret is. I worry what she'll do. God, I wish I could get her out of that house! Believe me, I'm not being noble, Jerry. It's just that they all depend on me, and so does Riordan, and sometimes I don't know what to do first."

He looked so miserable and tired and downhearted I instantly felt sorry for my angry words. "Jamie, whatever you do, you'll have to be careful. Riordan will have your skin stretched for a flag this night. And suppose some night, if he does soften up and let you off, one of our own men shoots you by mistake? The whole thing is crazy!"

"We might do just that, Jerry, if I don't get the password this minute," came a low voice from behind us. Jesus Christ, on top of it all, we'd walked right past the sentry post without a thought!

"The West's awake," I said, fuming at Jamie, whilst Riordan appeared from the shadows behind us.

"Now let England quake," said Riordan, giving the countersign briefly. "Turn around."

You never in all your life saw two grown men spin around in their tracks quite so flexibly as Jamie and I did then. Riordan, his ears quite red, threw my rifle at me.

"It's damned cold out tonight, sentry," said he, ignoring Jamie as if he weren't there at all.

"I—I thought you said it was pleasant," I stammered.

"Me? I never said such a thing. Continue your watch, damnit. Noonan, good night to you."

"Good night, sir and—thank you," I called after him.

"Good night, Captain," said Jamie.

Riordan never turned, but I heard him say in his customary clipped manner, "I didn't hear that, Daley. You're in your blankets, aren't you, soldier?"

"Yes, sir!" snapped Jamie, grinning, as Riordan went off out of sight.

"Well, you heard what he said," Jamie yawned. "Time to get some sleep."

I shook my head, wondering. "He knew all along, I suppose."

Jamie shrugged. "I suppose he did. He's a fine man, Riordan," he mused.

"Huh, small thanks to the poor bastard who risked his life to come down for you," said I, blowing on my hands to warm them up.

Jamie came close to me and took my arm, holding it like steel. "Listen, Jerry, don't do that again, do you hear? Don't ever come for me again. No matter what happens, don't look for me. Do you understand what I'm saying, Jerry? Don't ever come for me again."

But I wouldn't answer him. I pulled the rifle across my shoulder and marched away. When I returned on my rounds of the camp, he was gone. Next morning he was his usual cheerful self, and it was as if nothing had ever happened. Riordan caught a blistering cold and croaked his way in a glowering rage through camp for the next two weeks, but he never said a word to either of us about that night.

And so, as far as Jamie knew, it was forgotten. He still left camp when he could and went down to the farm for a few hours, despite the patrols, and they were everywhere. I never, never went after him again, as he had warned me. But, ah, Jamie boy, many and many a night when I didn't have the watch, I sat on a hill high above the farm, my rifle poised for firing, watching you moving fearlessly across the fields, silhouetted in the moonlight, with the plow and the horse before you. And you never knew there was a rifle at least, aimed to guard you from your enemies. Full many a night I cursed the brightness of that big moon and loved Ireland all the more, because of you there, stubborn, proud, foolish man of Ireland! He loved the land, did Jamie, and, at the end, he has returned to it. . . .

I never knew that of you, Jerry, I never knew that, and the insides of the dying man across the room wept for finding out that he had been guarded and remembering once again, with fresh pleasure and old pain, that he had been so much beloved.

Jim Daley wanted to put his arms around Jerry and thank him then, but there was no moving left in him and he knew it. We'll set it all straight one day, Jerry, he promised in his mind. When there's time because there isn't any time to worry about anymore, then we'll sort it all out and we'll all know how much we really loved each other and needed each other. That's a promise, he repeated to himself firmly, that's a promise I'll keep if there's anything of me that remembers afterwards. I hope there is. It can't all have been for nothing, can it? Not like bugs, not like germs and small, insignificant things. God, let it all have been for something! I don't even ask to know *what,* I'd be happy enough just to know there was a cause, there was a reason for it all. And a small pang of fear went through him as he recalled that very soon now he was liable to be finding out for sure.

Think of the land, he told himself. Jerry's voice had stopped for a bit. How long the night was, this last night, and how much, oddly, he was enjoying it. He had done what he feared most, he had let Margaret slip into his thoughts, and, beyond the first agonizing moments of memory, it had not been painful. It had been a release, he realized. Now, after long years and another life in another world altogether, he could think about her, yes, all about her, all that Jerry had not yet told, and his only agony was that he might not live to hear it all to the end.

He thought of the land then, and the feeling of it, damp and grainy-dark in his hands, full of small things he did not recognize, seeds, pieces of rotted wood and leaves, a hundred things that, along with itself, made up his country. Had it looked or smelled or felt so very different from the earth in America? He had picked up dirt by the handful in different places. It looked the same, but merely knowing it had its own place and did not belong to Ireland made it quite different to him.

He thought of the sweet-sour earth lying in his hand, dark and rich against the warmth of his palm, and he thought again of Margaret, Margaret lying asleep on the earth he loved, waiting for him near Bearsey's Bridge an hour before sunup, Margaret weary and pale, curled up under a tree, the sinking moon casting a wan, pearl-like glow on her skin.

It was during the time he had been farming at night. Later than Jerry spoke of, nearer to mid-spring, 1918. He had been coming down for the plowing and sowing. A week earlier, his mother had sent Margaret a message to meet him. But which night it would be, no one knew. So Margaret had come every night for a week, and waited till the sun rose, then rode home chilled and forlorn, only to return the next night and wait another.

He could not linger long. Quickly he leaped from the horse and gave him a little push, so that the creature good-naturedly trotted off to stand and drink under the bridge and out of sight. Then he had gone to Margaret's side, knelt down by her and watched her sleeping. He leaned over, kissing her cold cheek; instantly she was awake and in his arms, shivering as he closed her against him tightly, kissing her hair, her lips, her throat, whilst she cried his name over and over.

"I thought you'd never come to me again," she moaned.

"Never think that. Never believe it, for it isn't true," he told her. "I'd come to you from hell. Margaret, you're all there is to come to."

She smiled at that, nestling herself against him there on the new-grown grass, and pulled his two arms about her as tightly as she could.

"I'll hurt you," he murmured, but she clasped his hands locked with her own.

"Then I'll know you're here, and I'm not dreaming it," she smiled.

There seemed little to say, so they sat that way for a while. Underneath his hands, Jamie could feel the soft breasts of her pushing up to meet him, and he could feel her heartbeat like the heartbeat of the whole earth. He closed his eyes, buried his mouth in the soft curve of her neck and shoulder, and her response was quick and thrilling. As he kissed her very hard, she moaned again, throwing her head back.

"God, Jamie, God, God!" she cried, pressing him against her. And he looked with surprise at her face, her eyes wide, intense, longing. He pulled away from her, against his will, feeling as if, somehow, his own flesh was being pulled from his bones.

"Margaret, please, please—" he didn't even know what he was asking of her. He struggled with himself, feeling what was happening to him, powerless to prevent it, but knowing he must. He felt fear of it and joy in it and anger that the fear would not let the joy be in peace. Somehow he had not realized that a woman could want a man as much as he could want her. The knowledge of her passion, the urgency of it in her eyes, her voice, the straining of her body, filled him with delight. It was not a taking after all, but a giving and a taking, both for both.

"I love you," he said very simply. "I want you, Margaret." And she smiled, with tears on her cheeks, and pulled his head down to her.

"Yes. Yes," she said. "Oh, my darling, yes!"

But, even as she spoke, the morning's gray dullness spread across them, and the sound of horse's feet in the distance wrenched them apart. They crouched, like two thieves caught, low spread on the open bank, waiting and listening. Jamie's breath came and went in great raw gulps, his head pounding with a sudden sharp pain, and there was a lump in his throat that would not let him swallow.

"It's only one man," whispered Margaret. "He's going to cross the bridge. Be still."

On came the lone rider, looking neither to the right nor to the left, but came and crossed the bridge, apparently having seen nothing. Still they remained as they were till he was gone and out of sight, and the hoofbeats of his horse sounded tiny and distant, like little drumbeats far away.

The grayness was slowly changing to dull yellow and rose, and the air felt suddenly colder. They no longer had the friendly night to hide in, and, without having to say it, they knew the moment was gone, for the time being at least. He helped her to her horse, after whistling in vain for him for five minutes, only to see him come trotting up very calmly from beneath the bridge where evidently he had been renewing old acquaintances with Dan.

Margaret's face was tired and strained, but her eyes were shining as she looked down at him from Byron's back. And he had held the horse's head, his hand resting on hers on the reins, reluctant to let her go even now.

"It's all of it now, isn't it, Jamie?" she breathed softly. And he had nodded, kissing her small hand fiercely. She bent over and kissed him, too, on the head. "It's perfect now, we've got it all," she repeated. "There'll be another night, don't fear, my darling, darling Jamie."

And then she nudged Byron in the side with her foot,

and the two of them raced up the bank and away across the fields into the brightness of the sunrise, while Jamie had stood looking after her, feeling the world burst into bloom in his heart. Only when he could see her no more did he mount Dan and head back to camp. And when Jerry had spent half an hour lecturing him, he had smiled and taken it kindly, all the while, behind his eyes, remembering the touch of her lips and the heat of her body against his face. . . .

Chapter XV

Well, now, nothing can go on forever except God, and I'm not so sure of that, so, on that premise, let me tell you that Jamie's nocturnal escapades down to the farm couldn't go on forever without someone catching on. And late that same spring, after Riordan had finally had to say a word about it, which word did him little good, Jamie was gone one night to his home. I had the watch, worse luck, so I was of no use at all.

You see, he'd come back long after sunup a few days earlier, looking for all the world like he'd just come into a million. I figured he'd seen Margaret, so I held my tongue, but Riordan didn't. So Jamie had behaved himself for a bit and stayed in camp. But then, the next thing I knew, he was gone again.

Whilst he was out in that far field of theirs, the one Martin never liked because it was so much trouble to get to, separated as it was from the main part of the property by a stream, well, Jamie thought he'd go ahead and put in the cabbages that night. He was that far from the house he couldn't see it at all.

Aunt Ellen and Kathleen were cooking a meal for him,

as usual. I'd said a few words to them when I was there, about their being full dressed so late looking very suspicious, and they'd taken a lesson from it. They were both in their nightclothes, hair down and braided as if they were on their way into bed. There seemed nothing amiss but all peaceful, until Aunt Ellen thought she heard some kind of unusual sounds outside. Thinking it might be myself again, she went to look around. Kathleen stayed by the stove watching the milk didn't boil over. And then she heard her mother cry out. She looked up to see my aunt close the door quickly and lean against it weakly.

"Ma, what is it?" says Kathleen, scared to death when she saw two big eyes and the dead-white face on Aunt Ellen. And my aunt, she couldn't seem to get her breath; her mouth was working but no words came out, and, for the effort of it, her eyes were streaming tears.

"Ma!" cries Kathleen, running over to her.

Aunt Ellen plucked at the girl's long robe. "Listen!" she gasped. And Kathleen heard a sound that struck her to the heart. Cars, and lorries, many of them, heading toward them.

"Jamie! Get Jamie away! They're coming for him!" whispered Aunt Ellen, her eyes pleading with Kathleen. Kathleen snatched up her shawl and slipped out the back door. "Tell him not to come near the house tonight. Go on, Kathleen *ashthore,* for God's sakes!"

Kathleen raced, stumbling and tripping, through the darkness, falling over brambles and stones, climbing fences that were easy by day, but she seemed to have forgotten their whereabouts in the blackness. The moon was down, but the way was not easy to find even when it shone full. Every moment she was running, she fancied she could hear the cars coming along, though she was far from the road.

Back at the house, Aunt Ellen stood for one long moment more without moving, looking distractedly about the kitchen, where all evidences of a meal being prepared were spread out around. Then, drawing herself up with a deep breath that she said later she could feel to her toes like a swallow of whiskey, she began to clear away the food, the dishes, and even the cloth on the table. But already she could hear the sound of the motors turning up the quarter mile of the *boreen*. She turned out all the lights but one in the window, for Will, naturally, was not home. Then the footsteps of many men came pounding up to the door and, closer by, she heard others approaching the back door as well and circling about outside the house. Then came the banging on the door, sure with the harsh, hollow sound of it she knew no human fist ever knocked like that, but only the stock of a British rifle.

"Now, sweet Jesus and all the rest of you up there," says my Aunt Ellen, forcing herself to walk slowly to the front door, "guide my tongue well this night!" And suddenly, as she went to unlatch the door, a great lump came choking into her throat, as she thought of another walk she'd taken to open her home to the intruders from over the sea. But, as hard as she shoved back the latch, just so hard did she force down the memory, for in such a memory is weakness and error always.

There they stood outside. She blinked and swallowed as she saw the numbers of them. Two lorries full of soldiers, and an officer's car as well. And there he stood, impatiently tapping one gloved hand with his baton, the English officer, already peering inside as the door was opening.

"James Daley," said the officer, a captain no less. "Deliver over James Daley at once."

"And how will you have him—broiled, pickled, or baked?" inquired Aunt Ellen, coolly looking him in the eye, and she not budging an inch from holding the door three inches, no more, at the open. The man blinked, looked down at her—remember, she was hardly as big as your thumb, a tiny woman was my aunt, with the heart of a queen.

He surveyed the lay of it all for a second, then, without answering her, he snapped his fingers and two of his bully boys came running up, guns pointed straight at her, and he says, "Open this door at once."

"Certainly," says my aunt, letting it fall open so fast the two soldier boys almost landed inside. "Won't you walk in, yer honor?" says she broadly, and stands out of the way.

In walked the soldiers and in walked the officer and another one too, who had just run up from the side of the car. My aunt stood over to one side as they looked around the front room and into the kitchen. Then the captain turned to her again.

"All right, Mrs. Daley, there's no point to your little games. We have information that your son is here tonight. It will go harder for you if you attempt to hide him or interfere with our business. You should remember that. Now, where is he?"

Aunt Ellen ignored his questions entirely, as she darted past him to a doorway just beyond the hallway to the kitchen.

"Will you lower your voice?" she scolded, closing the door shut.

"Who's in there?" snapped the captain, for nothing in this world will so easily follow where he's pointed at than a regular-army officer! One of the soldiers came after her, and my aunt turned on him, stamping her foot.

"My little girl's asleep, if it's all the same to you," says she. "And I'll not have her frightened by the likes of you and your cutthroats!"

The captain glared at her, motioning to the soldier to check, and the soldier threw open the door to little Janet's room and looked around inside.

"If he so much as touches her, I'll kill him," spat my aunt nastily, noticing, however, that the soldier tiptoed past Janet's bed, opened the cupboard very quietly, poked around with his rifle, then tiptoed back to the door and closed it as softly as he could.

"Nothing in there, sir," he reported, and my aunt folded her arms and smiled coldly.

"We're wasting time," said the officer, turning red in the face at just about the time it usually takes them to do so, and my aunt nodded very agreeably.

"That you are," she said pleasantly enough.

"Where is your son?" roared the captain, advancing a step toward her.

"I don't know!" roared my aunt right back at him, advancing a step forward herself, till the top of her head was almost at a point with his chin.

"Search the house," says he to his men. "You, sit down over there and be quiet. Who else is here besides you and the child?"

Aunt Ellen settled herself daintily on the sofa, spreading out the long skirts of her robe as if they'd been satins, but in her heart she was terrified. For, you see, if she said Kathleen was there, they wouldn't find her, and they'd demand to know where she was. Yet Kathleen might come walking back in any minute, and they'd demand to know where she'd been at such a time, and in her nightclothes, too.

"I have another son, you know," says my aunt, trying to think carefully.

The captain sneered. "We know where *he* is, at least."

My aunt sniffed. "Well, I'd be that obliged if you'd kindly tell *me* where that might be? I've sat up half the night for him, poor lad; he sometimes takes a drop too much. Where did you say you'd seen him, then?"

The captain was watching impatiently as his men walked from room to room, opening chests and drawers and cupboards, poking the ceilings and walls with their rifles, throwing things about.

"Oh, do you think my Jamie would be in there, now?" called my aunt, as one of them flung her good silver out of the sideboard drawers.

The soldier stopped and stared at her a bit puzzled and slow, and the captain angrily rebuked him. "Get on with it!"

Then he leaned over to light a cigar with an ember from the fire. "Mrs. Daley, if you don't tell me what I want to know, I shall have to take you to headquarters, you and the child, of course, for further questioning. It could be unpleasant."

"Yes. I've no doubt it could," murmured my aunt. She could think of no other way of stalling him. What was keeping Kathleen? She heard the men outside, all over the yard front and back, calling to each other, and the flickering of their torches glancing through the windows made her nervous. What if they caught Kathleen as she came back?

"Who sleeps in there?" demanded the other officer, coming out into the living room again. They were standing before the door to Kathleen's room, and it was locked from inside. They turned the doorknobs several times, but it remained shut.

"That's my other daughter's room," said Aunt Ellen.

At that moment there was a sound of shots fired far off that hit her ears like death's own whisper, and a great tumult ensued. The officers ran for the door, which still stood open.

"What was that?" called the second one.

At once, a sergeant came running, saluted quickly, and shouted, "They've spotted him near that little stream, trying to get across. I think we hit him. We'll soon know."

Aunt Ellen's knees gave way, and she quickly sank back on the sofa. Was he dead, then? Oh, Jamie, Jamie, she thought, suddenly feeling very tired and empty of thought.

The second officer ran off with the sergeant; they jumped into the car and drove away quickly. The captain looked back at my aunt, who sat perfectly still. Then he called in one of the soldiers from the back of the house.

"Stay with this woman. Don't let her out of your sight." And then he went dashing off, calling more of the men searching around to go with him.

My aunt sat, and the soldier boy stood nervously between her and the door, trying to watch them both, which is a hard thing to do. She moved a bit on the sofa and he jumped a mile, pointing his weapon straight at her. She laughed in his face.

"Don't try anything, please, missis," says the brave fellow, and my aunt answered him with great contempt.

"Oh, don't worry yourself. I wouldn't want to upset you."

Just then, the door to Kathleen's room opened slowly. Now it was my aunt's turn to jump. The soldier's eyes almost popped from his head when he saw Kathleen, and he moved sideways about so he could keep my aunt in his view and still watch what was coming out of the room.

"Ma?" called Kathleen very sleepily. She entered the room blinking and rubbing her eyes. "Ma, is there somebody here?"

My aunt quickly hid the smile that came unbidden to her mouth and she said calmly, "It's all right, Kathleen. There's been a bit of a fuss. I've got a great hulk of a soldier boy guarding me from my desperate deeds."

"Soldier?" cried Kathleen, purposely stupid, as she walked slowly into the parlor and pretended to be terrified at the sight of the Englishman. She had taken off her robe and stood there in her nightgown, and did a lovely job of screaming and running away.

"Uh, miss . . ." says the soldier boy cleverly, not entirely sure of his procedure, for she wasn't yet of an age to entice him, being only eleven and flat as a board in all prime parts. But clearly his officer would expect him to handle this new situation with imagination and initiative, as they say in the armies of the world.

"W-what?" parries Kathleen, wide-eyed and trembling, and my aunt went over and put her arms about her.

"You stay here with her," says the soldier boy, even more inventively, and my aunt had just the opening she needed. Lightning in her gray eyes, so like Jamie's, you know, she thrust her daughter behind her and faced the beast of England, who was perhaps all of nineteen or twenty, with pale straw hair, nervous blue eyes and that pasty English complexion they get in their cities of soot.

"My child will not stay in your foul sight dressed as she is!" stared Aunt Ellen ferociously. "Shoot me if you will, but this little girl will go and put on her robe this instant. And if you lay a finger on her, I'll kill you with my bare hands, you murdering, whore-mongering bastard!"

The soldier blinked several times rapidly, and stared down at the furious little woman. He even seemed to consider her threat a valid one, forgetting it was he who held the weapon. Finally he found his tongue.

"All right, all right, she can go and get dressed. But you stay here."

Aunt Ellen started to say that was fine with her, but Kathleen pulled at her sleeve hard, and when my aunt looked at her, Kathleen shook her head ever so slightly.

"You're welcome to come with us," says Aunt Ellen grandly, "but her robe is with the clean wash in my bedroom."

The door to her room stood wide open and obviously empty. Hesitantly, the soldier nodded and waved the rifle at the two of them. He stood where he was, never taking his eyes from them, but at least they were twelve feet away. Under pretext of taking out the basket of ironing and sorting through it, they were able to speak a few hurried words.

"Is he alive?"

"Yes, but he's hurt."

"Where is he?"

"In the turkey house. Ma, he's bleeding!"

"Jesus, how bad is he?"

"Hurry up, there!" called the soldier, advancing a couple of feet toward them.

"Oh, be patient!" shouted my aunt. Then she whispered hastily to Kathleen, "Can he be moved?"

But Kathleen could only shrug her shoulders, fear all over her young face.

"Ma, what will we do? They'll look there any minute."

"No, they think he's headed across towards Lambert's."

Kathleen shook her head. "No, no! That's where he *was* going when they saw him and fired. I'd left him and I was heading back across the fields when I heard it."

My aunt patted her hand. "You did well, child."

"I don't know what else to do."

Aunt Ellen sighed and closed her eyes briefly. "I don't, either. We'll see."

"Come on!" yelled the soldier, his eyes narrowed with suspicion, and he came to the door.

"It's not here!" snapped my aunt, turning around on her heel in a great pet, as if it were all his fault. "It must be in her own room."

"Can I get it, please, sir?" asked Kathleen timidly.

Gruffly he let her go. Aunt Ellen walked just in front of him to the parlor, her mind whirling, not knowing what to do next. With Jamie in the turkey house, wounded and helpless, it was just a question of time till they found him. She uttered a perplexed little moan as she sat down once more on the sofa, her head leaning back, trying not to picture Jamie hanging from the same tree that had held his father.

At that instant, she thought she heard an odd little sound. Instinctively she started up, then recollected herself and sighed instead.

There it was again, a soft little thud, a dragging sound. No one knows every small movement and sound of their own house like the person living in it, and this was a sound she had not heard before. The soldier turned his head quickly. He'd heard something, too. He strode to Kathleen's room, just in time for her to walk out again, closing the door behind her. She was in her robe now, just tying the sash about her, and she walked by him, edging sideways, pushing the end of the rifle out of her way with her fingers, and went to sit down beside her mother.

There they remained, whilst the minutes ticked by, not talking, not moving, the fire playing on their still, numb faces, the soldier watching them, never lowering the rifle for an instant. Three or four times Kathleen moved as if to speak, but Aunt Ellen pressed her hand firmly, and she stayed quiet.

Through the night's stillness, they heard the car returning from the other direction. Kathleen and my aunt held their breath. The soldier went to the open doorway to watch them approaching.

"He's in my room," whispered Kathleen, her eyes on the soldier as she spoke. Aunt Ellen stared at her in horror. "Through the back window," said Kathleen. "He's hurt bad."

The officers came stomping in again, their faces angry. "No sign of him here?" snapped the captain.

"No, sah!" snapped back the soldier on guard smartly enough. "It's all been quiet."

Then the captain caught sight of Kathleen. "Who's she?"

"The other girl, sah! She was asleep before, in there." And, as Aunt Ellen and Kathleen watched with horror, he pointed right to the door of the room where Jamie lay wounded inside.

"Hmph!" snorted the officer, greatly irritated. "Wonder she didn't wake up before with all the noise!"

" 'Twas the noise that woke her, you *shivereen!*" muttered my aunt through her teeth.

"What about the barn, sah?" suggested the second officer.

"We have three men there now, sah!" another soldier barked out.

"Well, he's got clear away, it would seem!" said the captain. "We've trailed him along the edge of that stream for a bit—your son's lost quite a lot of blood, Mrs. Daley." Aunt Ellen swore he enjoyed telling her! "We'll renew the search at daylight. He's liable to be considerably weakened by then."

"Are you sure, now, it was my Jamie after all?" inquired my aunt boldly. "We've not seen the boy in months. All I know is that you've broken into my house, frightened my daughter half to death, kept us all up, and for what? Because you say someone told you Jamie was here! And now you've gone and shot some poor devil, some poacher, no doubt, or maybe a tinker, yes, most likely a tinker, and you say it's Jamie. Pooh! I think you've been taken, sir. I think someone's been having a grand joke with you. Do you think my son would be fool enough to show himself around here, wanted as he is?"

"It's well known in these parts, missis," says he, all frosty and smug, "that your fields and crops and animals are well tended, though such work on a farm of this size would be difficult for you and two little girls and a man who spends most of his waking hours off on a drunk in the local pub!"

"Aye, God has been good," said my aunt piously, raising her eyes to heaven.

The captain turned his back on her and issued new orders to the soldiers. Then he prepared to leave again.

"We'll station a patrol about the house tonight, and return in force after daybreak. Meanwhile, I suggest you remain here, inside the house, you and your children as well. I'm leaving a guard on duty to make sure you do. Jenkins," says he to the same boyo who'd been stuck there all along, "Jenkins, you guard them well, and see they do not communicate with anyone, understand?"

"Sah!" snaps Jenkins smartly, saluting as they left.

My aunt watched them go, in a fever of rage. She ran to the door after them and shouted, "Are you leaving that swine alone here with me and my daughters, are you, you monster? If anything happens to us, the Army'll cut your fat throat!"

"Inside, lady," said Jenkins, trying to shut the door, but my aunt wrenched the knob away from him and slammed the door hard shut herself. Whirling around, she spoke vehemently.

"Don't you set one foot closer to either of us, hear?"

Jenkins sighed a bit and nodded wearily. "Yes, ma'am. Don't worry, I wouldn't lay a hand on you!"

"If you do," smiled my aunt coldly, "you'll draw back a stump!" And, with that, she marched straight into her kitchen and lit a fire under the teakettle as cool as you please.

"What are you doing there, ma'am?" called Jenkins, instantly nervous again.

"Drawing a cup of tea, if it's all the same to you, you *twerpeen*," rejoined my aunt in her usual tone of voice. "Kathleen, darling, come here away from that man and set out the cups for tea. There's not much sleeping we'll be doing tonight, with armed guards around our home and a raping white slaver in the parlor—"

"Ma'am, please!" called Jenkins, very hurt by her remarks, so much so that he lowered his rifle and allowed Kathleen to join her mother.

Well, and if they didn't make a bustle and a clatter and a great commotion altogether, rattling the dishes and slapping them down on the table, and Jenkins cautiously eased himself into an armchair, resting the rifle across his knees.

"This is what we'll do," whispered my aunt as she moved about, and in a few seconds Kathleen had heard her plan and understood what she was to do.

"Ma, I'm tired," she spoke up in a plaintive little voice. "Can't I go back to bed now?"

"Bed!" screeches my aunt with all the horrors of hell implied in her voice. "With that creature of evil squatting in our very midst?"

"Ma'am?" called Jenkins, somewhat plaintively himself. "Let the little girl go to bed. She'll be better off getting her sleep."

"Oh?!" answered my aunt, suspicion darkening her voice as she stood, hands on hips, glaring at him through the doorway.

"Please, ma'am. I'm not going to hurt her, honest," assured Jenkins.

Aunt Ellen remained unconvinced, however, and, I suppose to show his good faith, he set the rifle next to him, alongside the chair.

"Very well. Kathleen, you go and tuck yourself up in bed, child, and I'll come along presently and bring you a nice hot cup of tea to warm you before you sleep."

But that much Jenkins would not allow. To have both of his charges out of sight for an instant seemed to him the rashest folly, which, of course, was true. However, Jenkins was a good soldier. He'd go far enough to show he was just as human as the next fellow, but he always knew where his duty lay at the last.

So it was all up to Kathleen, poor lass, from then on.

"I'll take my own tea on a tray, Ma," she says, looking very aggrieved at Jenkins, hoping he'd reconsider, but Jenkins remained adamant, so she let it go. Quickly they fixed up a tray, including half a loaf of bread and the sharp breadknife to slice it with. With an eye out for Jenkins, she decided to risk a great chance, and slipped a half-filled bottle of whiskey on the tray, covering it all quickly with a clean tea cloth.

"Go along, now, darling," says Aunt Ellen, giving Kathleen a little shove into the hall.

"I'll just have a look at that tray," says Jenkins, always in there trying.

At once Aunt Ellen stepped between him and Kathleen, her hand out, as if warding off some great evil.

"Not another foot, I warn you," says she, and carelessly she picked up one corner of the cloth so he could see the tea and the bread, but not the whiskey bottle, which was lying on its side.

Jenkins glanced at the food, sighed, for he would mightily have liked a hot cup of tea himself, and signaled Kathleen to go on. Aunt Ellen waited till she was safely inside the room, and the door closed behind her, then she returned to the parlor and seated herself with enormous dignity across from Jenkins, with her two small hands folded on her lap, eyeing him with disdain, her ears straining all the while to hear if there was a suspicious sound from the bedroom. If Jamie still lived to make a sound at all. She sat immobile, upright, her straight, stiff back never touching the back of the chair, listening, watching, praying and wondering, God, wondering if her son lay dead or dying not twenty feet away from her, and she not even able to go to him.

Meanwhile, Kathleen scurried into the room as quick as a spider, and lit the lamp. There was Jamie on the bed, barely conscious, his left leg hanging uselessly as if it didn't belong to him at all.

"Jamie, are you all right?"

He tried to smile at her, she looked so pale and full of terror, but his head was whirling dizzily and he kept drifting in and out of consciousness.

Kathleen had a look at the leg, his left one, of course. There was a bullet just above the ankle and another lodged in the heel, and the blood running down over the shoe, dyeing the bedclothes dark red.

"Is he still out there?" Jamie whispered, nodding his head toward the door.

"Yes, they're all around the house. Not close, about fifty feet, I guess. The rest are coming back at sunup."

He closed his eyes, weary from the pain and the long day and night behind him, and he tried to think. Meanwhile, she gave him a straight drink of the whiskey and held his head up so he could get some of the tea into him.

"I can't move with the bullets still in," he said at last, and Kathleen looked at him helplessly. He took her hand in his. "You'll have to take them out, sweetheart," he told her, and when she would have pulled away, out of fear, he held her tightly and soothed her.

She went and looked at the foot again, kneeling down on the floor, so he could see the two big eyes of her, wide with terror and uncertainty.

"I think one's gone through, Jamie," she said, pointing to the ankle wound. "It's just a big hole there, on both sides."

"That's good," he tried to encourage her. "Then you only have to do one."

"Oh, Jamie, it'll hurt bad!" Her eyes filled with tears.

"I'll be brave, I promise," said he, forcing the smile now, so she wouldn't falter.

"You're always brave," she chided him, already busy with the things she'd brought. In a moment she lifted the foot onto a clean, folded sheet from the linen press in the corner, so it extended well over the foot of the bed.

"Good," said Jamie, stretching a bit to look down at his foot. What he saw made him sick, for the wounds were ugly and gaping black, with crusted blood drying on them, mingling with still oozing sticky fresh blood. "Kathleen, do it fast, for God's sake," he muttered, choking, and she drew her little self up, smiled her best at him, and held the knife deep down into the whiskey bottle. Then, as an afterthought, she set the knife down and poured some of the whiskey over the two wounds. Jamie, feeling the frightful sudden sear of it, moaned, throwing his arm over his mouth not to be heard.

Kathleen found herself saying Jesus, Jesus, Jesus, over and over again, as she took his foot in her hand, the breadknife in the other and, with a quick, painful pinch of her other hand to keep from fainting, she dug hard into the wound. The bullet moved, and Jamie went white, his eyes rolling up, his two hands holding tightly to the bedpost. She stopped, backing away from her brother, trembling.

Jamie groaned. "Kathleen, please, for Christ's sakes, will you get it out!" he begged, the sweat pouring from his face and head.

Resolutely, not looking at his face again, Kathleen wiped her hands on her nightgown, and picked up the bloodied knife once more.

Outside, in the parlor, in the midst of the deadly silence and the clock ticking slower each minute for not having been wound up at its proper time, Aunt Ellen stiffened— she'd heard Jamie groan. Her eyes darted to Jenkins, staring morosely into the dying fire in the hearth. No, he hadn't heard it. But there might be more sounds, who knew, screams? She prayed he'd faint before it got to that. Oh, if only she might go to him and help him!

She coughed a little, experimentally, and cleared her throat. Instantly Jenkins' head turned toward her, his fingers reaching a bit toward the rifle. No, nothing wrong with his hearing, though he might be more alert.

"You're not much more than a boy, are you, Mr. Jenkins?" says Aunt Ellen in what was, for her, at the time, a conciliatory tone of voice.

Jenkins looked stunned, but did not seem suspicious. "I'm goin' on nineteen, ma'am," says he a bit proudly.

My aunt shook her head sadly. "Not yet nineteen," she says mournfully, "and already a murderer, and who knows what else besides? My, my!"

"Ma'am, please, I—I wish you wouldn't think so hard of me," said Jenkins wretchedly, never having thought of himself in quite those terms before.

My aunt nodded once. "Aye, I daresay you do," she said ever so much more loudly. Jenkins jumped at the sound. "I daresay you'd like me to think well of you, and you with a weapon of death pointed at me in my own home, threatening me and my children, whilst those killers are outside there, waiting to murder my son in cold blood!" Now she was speaking quite loudly, and beginning to work up to a nice weep too, and Jenkins looked more and more discomforted.

"How many mothers' sons have you laid in their graves?" My aunt wanted to know, and, without waiting for him to protest, she went right on. "How many widows and orphans are starving and shivering in their cold houses because your finger pushed the trigger—"

"Pulled, ma'am," put in Jenkins respectfully, listening to her with a sort of fascinated horror.

She ignored him. "Didn't you ever have a mother yourself? And you hardly old enough to grow a beard! You let them put a uniform on your back, you let them put a gun in your hand—"

"Rifle, ma'am," Jenkins said, biting his lips. He was quite downcast now.

"Aye," she repeated it witheringly, "a rifle indeed! Look at you! Look at you! The sight of you this night would break your poor mother's heart! Why did you do it? Why did you let them make you a murderer? Your hands are full of innocent blood, boy! There's got to be a reckoning, you know that; you are a Christian, I suppose? You call yourself a Christian? You go to a Christian church? You whited sepulcher! You blackhearted fiend!"

Now she was on her feet, one hand leaning majestically on the mantel as she spoke on, sure you could hear her a mile off! But she didn't care who heard her, for whilst she was talking, Jenkins couldn't hear Jamie, and that was all that mattered.

There was a very brief silence as she ran out of breath temporarily, and Jenkins took advantage of it to inquire wistfully if she might be so kind as to make him a cup of tea?

"TEA!" screamed my aunt, as if the very word were corrupt. "Never, in my house, will a drop or a bite be served to the likes of you!"

"I'm sorry," whispered Jenkins mutely, and resigned himself to what followed.

She kept at it for quite a while then, till she had him

writhing and so accustomed to her ranting and raving that he never even looked at her as she gradually began to stride around the room, in wider and wider circles, getting closer to the door to Kathleen's room each time. Once or twice, she paused to listen and heard nothing. Good.

But then Kathleen appeared at the door, startling her mother and scaring Jenkins, who jumped up, rubbing his tired eyes, then saw it was only she and sat down again, looking sheepish.

"Kathleen, what's the matter?" asked Aunt Ellen, her heart in her throat.

But Katheen did not seem unduly upset. She yawned and frowned and spoke thickly. "Ma, I was asleep again and you're yelling so loud in here, you woke me up!" And she did indeed look grumpy and sleepy.

"Listen to the child," wailed my aunt. "See what you've done to her. She'll never be the same after this night!"

Jenkins looked at her, openmouthed with honest indignation, but she had caught Kathleen's signal that the operation was over.

"And look, Ma," complained Kathleen, pointing at the window. "It's coming on to *morning already*. If I'm going to get any sleep I'll have to do it before the sun comes up and all those men will be back tramping around again!"

Aunt Ellen followed her gaze toward the window and saw with dismay that the sky was aready lighting in the east, the stars were all but disappeared.

"Come and tuck me in, Ma," pleaded Kathleen, and this time, without consulting Jenkins, Aunt Ellen turned on her heel and headed toward the bedroom. Together the two of them might get Jamie away somehow.

But the ever faithful Jenkins, bloody but unbowed, was still on the job. With a bound he was out of the chair and after them. "I'll just go with you," says he.

Neatly my aunt sidestepped, pushed Kathleen back into the room and slammed the door. Jenkins couldn't help what happened: he was so close and moving so fast be bumped into my aunt.

"Help!" screams she, throwing up her hands and beating him on the chest. The poor fellow was so amazed he damn near dropped his rifle. Aunt Ellen reached for her broom, and a hearty one it was, too, handmade by a traveling broom expert, and very tough. She flailed at Jenkins with it, screaming bloody murder all the time.

"You waited all night till we were worn out and weary!" she accused him. "You waited to pounce, you hawk! You low, lousy, insinuating, degenerate son of a bitch! Back, back, out of my house! I don't care, let them kill me, I can't stand any more of you, you leper, you scum, you Englishman!"

With every word a regular flood of blows descended on his head. Back and back stumbled Jenkins, holding his hands over his face to ward off her furious slashes. God, my aunt was no bigger than the breath of a sparrow in wintertime, but she terrified that lone, lanky English soldier; she turned into a raving shrew, and Jenkins fled before her as she chased him through her parlor, the broom high over her head.

In Kathleen's bedroom, Jamie kissed his sister and praised her, and gave her the bullet for a remembrance of the night. He grinned weakly as he heard his mother's voice.

"Ma's really giving it to him," he said.

Stooping down so she would not be seen, Kathleen peeked out the window. The two guards out back had heard the commotion and were running toward the front of the house.

"Now, Jamie, it's clear now. Go fast!"

Jamie climbed stiffly and painfully out the low window. Kathleen handed him out a small bundle she'd made of his torn boot and the blood-soaked sheets and cloths. She'd had to change her nightgown as well, for it was covered with bloodstains.

"I'll get rid of them far from here," he said, tucking them under his arm. "Goodbye for a while, now, darling!"

Limping heavily, leaning low, he crept along the side of the house, then, with a swift look to either side, he ran as fast as he could across the open yard, out past the barn and the chickenhouse, over a small hill and out of sight.

Kathleen watched him till he disappeared from view,

then got to work tidying up the small room. She had wiped the blood spots up with some of the cloths and one sheet. Now she hid the whiskey away, cleaned off the breadknife and put it back on the tray by the untouched bread, made her bed with fresh covers, and carefully looked herself over in the mirror. She was pale and tired, but there didn't seem to be any blood on her now. She went to her door again and opened it cautiously, peering out to see where Aunt Ellen had got Jenkins to now.

Well, Aunt Ellen was in fine shape. She'd gotten him into a corner behind the front door, wedged in he was, both hands over his head, moaning and yelling for help, and her beating him still with the broom, and screaming still louder. The laddybucks who'd come running in answer to their put-upon comrade's desperate calls for help were hammering away at the door. It wasn't locked at all, but you see, with Jenkins and Aunt Ellen pushing against it, sure a battering ram would have been a help, instead of ther.. standing outside shouting and banging on the door with their rifles. You know, the average English soldier, in his time, and it has been a *long* time he's had at it, why, he must've been responsible for costing the Crown a pretty penny in damaged weapons. I was taught the hard way, in the school of scarcity and lack, that a rifle is for shooting, but then the English were never too bright to begin with and I guess banging down doors with rifles seemed reasonable to them!

However that may be, I'll have you know that they were not able to get inside, and Kathleen was able to stand in her little hall and admire the sight quite a few moments before it stopped. Now two things entirely put an end to my aunt's personal touch in the fray. One of them was that her broomstick went flying across the room. And the other was the sound of the convoy lorries and the motorcar returning up the *boreen*. The fellows outside the door left off banging and shouted for them in the lorries to hurry up.

Jenkins had tears in his eyes, of relief, no doubt, but when he realized that he was about to be discovered at the mercy of a woman half his size, with his rifle on the other side of the room altogether, he turned scarlet, which ill became him, and looked around in wild confusion, trying to spot the weapon and straighten out his uniform at the same time.

"Here's your rifle, Mr. Jenkins, sir," says Kathleen sweetly, for she had picked it up the moment she'd entered the parlor and had been holding it aimed at his heart for quite some little time, never intending to shoot him, of course, but still dallying with the pure pleasure of the thought.

Jenkins grasped his rifle from her in two quick strides across the room, whilst Aunt Ellen, calmly and blessedly quiet, picked up the broken ends of her broomstick and shook her head over the ruin of it. Jenkins' mouth opened and closed a few times, and Kathleen said later she thought he really might be getting ready to say a word or two, but, fortunately for all of us and posterity, the door was broken open by two soldiers. They had believed it to be locked securely, and now, supervised by their officer from outside, which, of course, made all the difference, they came at it in unison with their shoulders, flying through handily and keeping right on going, almost into the fire. Eyeing them in utter disgust, the captain strode in straight at Aunt Ellen. She stood there innocently holding up her broken broom, looking sorely put upon.

"Anything up, Jenkins?" asks the captain, nose directed toward my aunt, who smiled primly back at him.

Poor Jenkins, now standing at rigid attention, shouted out at once, "No, sah!," saluting as if his life depended on it.

Well, once again the whole dreary business was got through, every room was searched afresh, every inch of the grounds was gone over by the experts, and nothing was turned up or under or over that could show Jamie had been there. My aunt and Kathleen sat quite still when they went into Kathleen's room, but she had done a good job of cleaning up. There wasn't a trace of anything except the whiskey, and when they waved that before my aunt, she simply snatched it from them, saying, "So that's where he's been hiding it!" And they all knew she meant Will, of course, so what could they say?

The captain, meanwhile, smoking another of his dreadful cigars, clenched tightly between his big, yellow, horse teeth, marched back and forth in the parlor, hands behind his back, every once in a while stopping abruptly before Kathleen or Aunt Ellen.

"Did these two communicate with anyone during the night?" he finally demanded of Jenkins, who gulped and answered, "No, sah!" Then, as an afterthought, he gulped again and murmured, "O-o-only with me, sah!"

"Aye, that we did," said my aunt dryly.

"Be quiet!" roared the captain. My aunt's faint smile faded, her chin went up and she looked through him as though he weren't there at all.

Just then the door to little Janet's room opened slowly, and she appeared, barefooted, in her long white nightgown, her blond curls tousled and streaming down her back, blinking and smiling.

"Mama," says Janet, watching the captain with great curiosity, "did the soldiers stay all night long?"

Aunt Ellen looked about her. "No, no, they've just come back for a bit, Janet. Now you go back into your room and stay there till I call you, dear."

Janet pouted, and, instead of doing as she was told, she advanced farther into the center of the room, blinking up at the captain.

"Hello," says she with a smile. "Did you find Jamie for me?"

There was, as they say in the cinema, an electric silence in the room. The captain removed his cigar from his mouth and leaned over with what I assume he assumed was a smile fit for a six-year-old child.

"No, I'm afraid Jamie's rather hard to find, little girl."

Janet nodded with utmost satisfaction. "I know. He hides real good. He said he'd show me how to do it next time he comes."

The captain's smile grew broader. He shot one knowing glance at Aunt Ellen, who now sat on the very edge of the sofa, her hands clenched into fists, wondering what Janet would say next.

"And when will he come again, do you suppose?" asked the captain carefully.

Janet considered, screwing up her nose thoughtfully. "Why? Do you want to play with him, too?"

Jenkins, in his corner, snorted. The captain ignored him and answered her, "Why, yes. I'm sure there are a lot of things your Jamie could tell us about."

Janet looked at him with a tiny frown. "No. He only tells *me* things."

"Janet, you'll catch your death of cold standing about in bare feet; go into your room," said Aunt Ellen severely, but the captain told her again to be quiet.

He sat down and drew Janet toward him. She was now the center of several people's undivided attention, which pleased the child no end. She blinked her big blue eyes at the captain in unconscious flirtation.

"Jamie tucks me in to sleep when he's here," she confided to him. "And he sings to me. Someday he's going to sing on the stage, he said so."

"And did Jamie tuck you in to sleep last night?"

Janet thought hard. "Is that tomorrow or when?"

"No, no, last night," said the captain, trying to conceal his impatience. "When you went to sleep, before you woke up today, was Jamie here then?"

Janet opened her mouth into a large pink O, and Aunt Ellen almost stopped breathing.

"Oh, no," said Janet very sadly. "He hasn't been tucking me in for a long time. I don't remember the names of the days much yet, but it's been years and years, when I was just little. But he's going to," she added defensively, and hopped down off the captain's lap. He let her go, looking much disappointed.

Janet followed the soldiers about the house, helpfully opening closets and doors for them, chattering gaily with them all the while, and the captain sat staring ahead of him, furious, the cigar gone cold and forgotten in his mouth. Then Janet accompanied two of the men back into her room, where they looked under the bed, as she giggled and peeked down at them from the other side. Aunt Ellen was furious with her, but did not dare to interfere with what went on.

"Nothing anywhere, sah!" reported the sergeant finally.

"All right, sergeant, all right. Search them for weapons and be quick about it."

As they approached my aunt, she backed away, spitting at them. "Touch me or my girls and I won't be responsible for what happens to you!"

But they did not listen to her. One of them held her still whilst another passed his hands over her body, then they went on to Kathleen, who screamed and cried and kicked at them with all her might. They found nothing, of course, for no Irish household was allowed weapons of any kind, just the finding of them meant immediate arrest.

Now, little Janet was watching all this with great interest, sitting swinging her feet on the sofa, her long nightdress spread out around her, like a little princess. The captain rose and headed for the door, followed by his men. Janet watched them, puzzled, then called out, "*I* got a gun!"

They turned swiftly, and she put up her little hand in a gun shape as kids do and cried merrily, "Bang, bang! I got you."

The captain slammed out the door with the others behind him. In a moment they had piled into their lorries and cars and headed back to town.

Kathleen was crying, exhausted and sickened. The night had been long and full of danger. She buried her head now on Aunt Ellen's bosom. My aunt comforted her the best she could, but she had her eyes on Janet.

"Janet Katherine Daley," she cried in vexation, "how could you act that way with those men?"

Janet jumped up and ran over to her mother. "Don't be angry, Mama, look!" And from underneath her heavy long skirts she pulled a long and ugly thing, Jamie's revolver. Aunt Ellen screamed. Kathleen just stared at it.

"Jamie left it by my bed, on the floor, when he tucked

me in last night," said the little minx. "I been hiding it from the bad men."

"Oh, Jesus, darling, darling!" cried Aunt Ellen, grabbing her and hugging her till the little girl squirmed for breath.

Chapter XVI

Now, as it happened, I got off my watch at dawn, and when I came back into camp everyone was very quiet. Riordan was downcast, for Jamie had not returned at all. This time he knew there must be something wrong. I didn't even wait to hear him out as he ordered me to steal down and reconnoiter. I was on my way in a second's time.

He's dead, this time he's really dead, my mind shouted as I made my way recklessly down through the hills. If a patrol had been on the alert, they might have had me a dozen times, but no one saw me at all. I stayed above the farm and circled around, but saw nothing. By that time, the soldiers had been and left, and the place looked deserted. Even the damned cock was sleeping late; you can never depend on a bird for anything, don't ever do it, no matter what you hear of them.

Seeing nothing, whilst lying flat on my belly for half an hour, I started back up again, not knowing what the hell else to do without any help. I must have been walking and climbing for an hour, when, way off ahead of me, I spotted a man lying face down on the rocks, one of his legs bent queerly under him. Without thinking at all, I began to run toward him.

As I reached him and he not moving at all, I started crying, which is a weakness I've noticed in myself and a great source of shame, too, crying whenever I've thought my heart was broken from some new sorrow, and sure my heart is as strong today as when I first looked about me and cried in this life. But, oh, and he's dead, he's dead, I thought, and I pictured myself trying to tell Aunt Ellen, trying to tell Riordan—Christ, I thought in horror, trying to tell Margaret!

I fell to my knees by his side, noting that the twisted leg was oozing blood from two places at once. "Jamie! Jamie boy!" I cried, turning him over. And damned if he didn't open his eyes and wink at me. It was weak, but it was a wink. And he pressed my hand savagely hard.

"You crazy man!" I told him. "Riordan's waiting to bury you this day," I said, struggling to get him up on his feet, with his arm around my shoulders, for we could not linger where we were another minute, and the glorious golden day itself pointing us out for anyone to see.

"Not this day, I think," he gasped, the breath coming ragged and hard, and I didn't bother to make an argument of it then and there. This way, we struggled together back up the long trail, after I'd made sure the blood was not leaving a trail of its own for the hounds in uniform to sniff out.

It wasn't till long after I'd brought him in and they'd finished patching him up and sent off for a doctor to do it up right, and everyone had stood around him scolding and threatening and congratulating and admiring his sister's handiwork and she only a slip of a girl of eleven, and all that muck, that Jamie suddenly recalled his revolver. A search was made at once, but it never turned up, as you know already. We covered every inch of ground along the way he'd come, hopefully, even finding where he'd hidden the bloody bundle behind a clump of rocks out of sight, thinking maybe, in her haste, Kathleen had made the mistake of rolling the weapon up with the other things. But it wasn't there either. And Jamie, weak as he was, was beside himself, remembering at last, after he came to again, that he'd placed the gun on the floor when he had said good night to Janet, not wanting to frighten her with it.

Riordan took this piece of news grimly, and sent a fast

message to town for little Ted Joyce, our best runner, a bold, fresh, ruddy-faced kid of twelve or thereabouts, to nose around and find out what he could. We put in many anxious moments and hours, but at last Ted turned up with word that nobody had been arrested, and evidently the gun had not been found.

And, indeed, the gun was never found, not to this day has it been found. If you go where it was put, you may yet dig it up, I've no doubt. For, the very next night, once the moon was low again, Aunt Ellen and the two girls dressed themselves warmly and took the gun away from the house.

Through the darkness and shadows and the sudden, startled shrills of the night birds they went along swiftly, till they were off Daley land altogether and into a stretch of wild country near the hills, where many trees grew close together, bending and winding around each other in one direction, blown to grow that way as they were pushed all their lives by the wind from the sea.

And there my aunt picked out one large yew tree with its branches bending down low to the ground. Quickly, without making a sound to attract attention, she dug a deep hole by the tree and put the revolver into it. Then, after replacing about half of the dirt over it, packing it down good and hard, she took from her pocket an old, rusty tin soldier, one of the boys' old toys she had saved, as mothers will, you know. And she laid it gently in the hole, straightening its small arms and legs till it looked proper fine. This she covered with dirt also, but not so carefully, and she mounted up all around it a pile of small stones Janet fetched, and a larger stone at the head.

"There, now, little brave soldier boy," whispered Aunt Ellen, patting down the earth, "lie still and guard well what's beneath you. And if anyone finds this place and digs you up, why, they'll think this is just the grave of some child's favorite toy, and look no further."

Then, just as quickly and quietly as they had come, the three of them stole back to the farm, and waited word from Jamie that he still lived.

He lived, indeed, but for a long time that was all that

could be said of him. We thought he must lose the leg at last, but it was saved. Yet he had lost so much blood. He lay, gray-faced and delirious, the sweat pouring off his wasted frame, for days and days, and the deadly coldness of his hands seemed to be a grim promise of what the future would bring.

Aunt Ellen came up when she could, for there was a suspicion that she was being watched. She brought bandages and broth, whiskey that did the rest of us more good than it did Jamie, and she sat through the long, awful nights, listening to him speak his own, poor private thoughts for the world to hear, crying out Margaret's name over and over, and once we had to tie him to the cot, for he would insist on going to her. It was then that my aunt understood for the first time what was between those two.

She and I were sitting by his side, across from each other, both of us half dozing, for he had fallen into a feverish sleep at last, and we were exhausted keeping watch over him. Then suddenly he began to move about, his arms reaching out beyond him, and when Aunt Ellen would have tried again to soothe him, he moaned, "Margaret, Margaret, I'll never leave you!"

Aunt Ellen looked at me questioningly, and I nodded without a word. She smiled a bit, took his two hands and held them in her own, and whispered, "Jamie, listen to me. Jamie, I'll have them bring Margaret to you."

His eyes opened then, and he tried very hard to focus them. "What? What did you say?" he asked in confusion. My aunt smiled at him and leaned close so he could hear without effort.

"I said, darling, I'll get Margaret to come here to you, soon now, don't fret yourself—"

But his eyes went wild, and he struggled pitifully to raise his head. "No! No, don't, Ma. Keep her away. Keep her out. . . . I promised . . . Sean . . ." But the tremendous effort proved too much for his poor strength, and he fainted again, his hands going slack in hers.

After, over a hot cup of tea, I tried to explain what had happened between Jamie and Sean Culhane. Her bright eyes clouded as she heard, and she nodded several times, murmuring "Tch, tch" every so often, and drawing in her breath with a sharp hiss as I described Sean's accusations.

"Oh, God, Jerry lad," she sighed finally. "That man! That man! Why can he not leave people alone with their lives? I've seen him at it, over and over, these twenty years now, and I'll never get used to it. And, now it's Jamie too. You know how I love little Margaret, and she like my own daughter all these years! I couldn't think of a better lass for my Jamie, if only the father . . ."

She let it trail off helplessly. What could she say? But as she stood to leave us, her mouth tightened stubbornly. "I don't care about Sean Culhane. Let him say what he will. I'm going to get Margaret up here. She'll do Jamie the world of good, poor lad, and that's all that matters to me!"

I stood looking after her as she went off with O'Rourke, smiling to myself, for she had told me, by bits and pieces, all that had happened the night Jamie was hurt. Well, I thought, the woman who could beat poor Jenkins to a blind, deaf, and dumb halt can surely handle Culhane!

So Margaret came to us, up there in the hills, so thin, so drawn and pale, with the shadows deep on her hollow cheeks. I warned her ahead of time that Jamie would look poorly, and she tried to be prepared, but when I held aside the tent flap so she could go in, and she saw his face yellow against the white linen pillowslip from home, she uttered an awful little cry, and pressed both hands hard against her lips. Her eyes, welling with tears, roved back to me and she shook her head from side to side.

"Oh, my God, he looks so bad!" she whispered through fingers wet with tears.

"Margaret, try to be calm. It won't do himself any good to see you like this," I said gently, and dug around in my pocket to find her a handkerchief. She blew her nose and wiped her face, and put on a good enough smile, unless you knew what her own smile looked like. Then she went in, pulling me behind her by the hand. Swiftly she knelt down by the side of his cot, and put her hand against his cheek.

"Jamie, Jamie, it's me, I've come to see you," she whispered faltering. "Jamie, it's Margaret. Love, love, open your eyes, please, Jamie!"

His hands moved; she took them both in her own and kissed them tenderly, and slowly he did open his eyes, in wonder and disbelief, as if she might only be one of his dreams of her and not real at all.

"Margaret, is it you?"

She smiled then, really smiled, just to hear the sound of his voice at last, and she kissed him lightly on the lips, on the face, and on his forehead. "It's me, darling. Rest easy, I won't go away."

He frowned, shook his head, but held her all the tighter by the hands as he cried feebly, "No, no, you've got to go away. You're not supposed to be here. Your father—"

"To hell with my father!" cried Margaret so vehemently that Jamie managed a small, fond smile. But mostly he stared at her, unwilling to sink back into the sleep he needed so badly, afraid she'd go away if he closed his eyes.

Seeing this, Margaret firmly entwined her fingers about his, and bade him sleep at once, and said she would not move until he awoke again. Once or twice he opened his eyes briefly, to rest them on herself, with her head on his chest, and then, finally believing her, he fell asleep again. For three long hours she never moved, while he slept on and on, the longest he had managed yet. And when he awakened again, the fever had broken.

I was having the first peaceful smoke I could manage since the whole thing had happened, sitting by myself a bit away from camp on a clump of a rock overlooking the valley. And Margaret came to talk to me, and to tell me that Jamie was asking for something to eat.

"Thank God!" was all I could think of to say, and I was surprised that she remained quite silent then, staring away over the hills, a troubled frown gathering itself on her pale face.

"He nearly died," she said flatly in a very small, tired voice. The tone of it went to my heart. I got hold of her about the shoulders and gave her a hearty hug.

"Aye, but 'nearly' is over. We've got him back again, that's what matters, girl!"

She pulled away from me, shivering. "This time we've got him back," she whispered. "What about next time? And the next after that? One time he'll leave us and he'll never come back, never!"

I thought of many things I might say to cheer her or comfort her, but I had not Jamie's way with words, and I did not know how to make her feel easy about reality. She was right; the war was far from over, the odds were against us, the chances of our living through it a bit remote. So, with all I thought to say, I said nothing, but stood there helplessly as she cried silently in the night, letting the tears fall down her cheeks unchecked.

"Margaret," I ventured finally, unable to bear it any longer, "Margaret, lass, couldn't you—couldn't you try just to think of this day, just this one day that Jamie's alive and not dead? Maybe it would help a little if you took things a little bit at a time, instead of trying to swallow them all down, today's troubles and yesterday's and to-morrow's as well, all at once?"

She sighed and shook her head. "No. I can't think of anything but that it will go on and on and there will be no tomorrow for us. I'll always be wondering and waiting to hear the worst, dreading every hour I don't see him, mis-trusting things he will have to tell me because he doesn't want me to worry. No, Jerry, I don't think I can stand that."

"You will have to, for his sake," I reminded her un-easily, for as she spoke I got the feeling that something had passed us by and was gone without our noticing. I couldn't put my finger on it, for I knew nothing would ever change the way she felt toward him. I was deeply troubled and it galled me not to be able to fathom it.

She pressed her hand on my arm, tried to smile and nodded ever so slightly, then she was gone from me, back inside Riordan's tent, where I could hear Jamie's voice as she appeared.

Margaret stayed with us two days, though Riordan was against it, for he did not want to antagonize Culhane. But when he saw Jamie sitting up, drinking soup and obviously on the mend, he merely nodded approvingly toward Margaret and said nothing. She was strangely quiet for Margaret, except when Jamie wished to talk with her. The rest of the time she busied herself about caring for him, or sat in a corner of the tent, her hands folded and still, watching us all coming and going, listening to everything that was said.

When Jamie felt stronger, Riordan and O'Rourke and myself tried to puzzle through what had happened the night he was shot. We wondered if the soldiers had been tipped to find him, or if maybe Charlie Norwood had taken a desperate chance, since nothing else had worked anyway, and hoped they'd hit on a night when Jamie would be there. The captain had told Aunt Ellen he had "information," but that didn't necessarily mean anything. They always said they had information; often enough it was made up out of their own heads.

Still, in the backs of our minds, we thought sickly of the possibility that there was another informer about. Since the night we had killed Timothy Gallagher, we'd all tried to forget the whole subject of informers. And, of course, there was always a chance that Will Daley had blurted out something when he was drunk. There were a million possibilities and no way of proving any of them, unless, of course, it happened again. Informers work fairly steadily, you see. They rarely hit or miss. If it were one, then Jamie's situation would be only the beginning. All we could do was wait it out.

Now Jamie finally realized that his night farming had to come to an end, and he fretted about the farm until O'Rourke came up with a darling of an old fellow from Killarney looking for work, and later he proved himself one hell of a dandy farmer at Daley's.

Now that Jamie was able to think straight and clearly at last, it was he himself who insisted that Margaret go home. She did not seem to protest too strongly, but muttered a promise that she would be back when Riordan should send for her, and then she was up and off on Byron, not looking back toward camp at all, and I misliked the rigid set of her back as she rode away from us.

I knew she would have a devil of a row with her father once she got home, and tried to tell myself that she was tired and under a great strain and not looking forward at all to one of Culhane's tirades. And I remembered suddenly that I might be just a bit edgy myself, and damn tired as well, and likely to be reading all kinds of meanings into things that didn't exist.

And so, with Jamie mending and myself telling myself I'd best get some rest now and again and hardly doing it, either, we headed at last into the blue heat of August. But then August turned cool and damp and rainy of a sudden, and it was soon enough that I found myself having to serve Jamie a wound far worse than any bullet that ever tore his leg, and it was a wound I shared with him, although he did not know it then.

Chapter XVII

I received a short note from Margaret, delivered to me by the hand of my own father. I didn't even glance at the writing on the envelope, but headed for Jamie to give it to him, till my father stopped me and showed me my own name there. Now, why would Margaret be writing notes to me? I wondered. It must be that she's worried about Jamie and wants to arrange to come up to see him again. With that thought and no other in the world in my mind, I put the note away until I would be free later on. Then I read it, but it explained nothing and left me once again with that vaguely uneasy feeling. All she had written was this: "Meet me at all costs on Running Hill, dawn tomorrow."

And she had not even signed her name. But my father

assured me that he had the note from her own hand and no
other.

I spent a sleepless night, tossing about by the fire, wondering what was up. I supposed Sean had found out she'd
been to camp, and had given her trouble about it. Perhaps
she wanted me to explain to Jamie that she could not come
again. Yes, that was it, I decided, about an hour before I
had to get up to meet her. Sean was spoiling the broth
again. Well, and we'd just see about that!

It was dawn and past, and still she had not appeared. I
waited for her at the top of the hill, where I had a good
view of the road below. There was no one in sight. The
day was dank and dismal, sticky hot and drizzling on and
off. Then, even as I thought she was not coming after all, I
heard the quick, galloping hoofbeats of Byron down below.
I thought she would dismount and let him wait there by the
road as usual, for the hill is quite steep and hard on a
horse's legs. But no, as I watched, she dug her heels into
his sides and urged him up toward me. He tossed his head
and protested strongly, but she kept him tightly reined, and
at length he gave up and concentrated on not breaking his
handsome neck.

When she was ten feet away, I stood up so she could
see me, and the look of her frightened me sick. She wore
a black riding habit, which trailed down the horse's side,
and her hair was loose about her face, like a black veil of
mourning. She was soaked to the skin, her face and neck
wet with raindrops, and the look on her white face was
past knowing.

"Margaret, what in God's name is the matter with you?"
I greeted her, running up and holding Byron's head. She
shivered continuously all the while we talked, which was
not long. And she stared down at me, her face like a stone
statue, hard and blank, and she spoke in an odd, strained
voice I did not know.

"I've come to say goodbye to you, Jerry," she said, not
meeting my eyes at all.

"What?"

"I'm going away. To school. In England. You know, as

my father said." She talked in short, choppy sentences, staring ahead of her without expression.

"You're crazy!" I cried. "Margaret, what about Jamie?"

She drew a terrible, deep breath and closed her eyes, then she opened them and looked at me levelly. "It's all over. I won't see him again."

I reached up and pulled her from the saddle, forcing her to stand and face me. "Margaret, don't do this. It's me, Jerry, I know all about it. What are you trying to do?"

She swallowed, caught my hand in her icy fingers, and spoke convulsively. "I promised, I promised, do you understand? I can't explain it. He's right, that's all I know, he's been right all along."

"And you're saying you don't love Jamie?"

"I love Jamie," she said, biting her lip hard. "I'll always love him, I expect. But I can't marry him. I can't see him again, ever. I promised."

"And when Jamie asks me why, what shall I tell him?"

She leaned against the horse's damp flank suddenly, and pressed her hands to her face. "Tell him I've found I cannot live this way. Tell him I'm not made for waiting and hiding and being afraid every minute. Oh, he knows, he knows how I feel about it! Tell him, whatever mistakes my father has made in the past, it turned out he knew me best."

I stared at her, incredulous. "You want all the things he spoke of, then? The money? And all the fancy folks and that kind of life? Are you telling me you want all that?"

Her eyes flashed at me and I thought she would speak, but she closed her mouth and pushed me away from her. In a moment she was back up on Byron's back, and not till then did she say, "Yes, tell him I want all that. I want *something* out of this life of mine. I'm through living on dreams, Jerry. I should have realized long ago I've only been fighting myself. It's what I was born for. It's what I was raised for, don't you see? And I can't live through another time like this, wondering if he's alive or dead, waiting and waiting—"

"It's a bit hard on himself too, I think," I said very coldly, standing back out of her way so she could pass.

She threw her small head back into the rain, the muscles of her pale throat straining. "Goodbye, Jerry," she said. "We'll not meet again, I don't think."

And she was gone, Byron flinging himself in great leaps down the hills, her with her back straight as an arrow on top of him. And I stood and I stared and I thought I must be going mad, for, if this could happen, then the world made no sense whatever and nothing was worth the pain of living, nothing, nothing, nothing at all!

Fool that I was then, for I didn't think till later, that was not really Margaret at all; that was Margaret lying in grand style and for some purpose. He had forced this on her, I realized when I thought it through and sorted it out from my benumbed feelings. Somehow Culhane had gotten to her. But what had he said? What strange, twisted logic had he used to convince her he was right after all? Or perhaps her fears for Jamie and her desperate loneliness had driven her right into his corner by themselves. Margaret was not the one for living alone within herself; some are, some aren't. Some can make a life for themselves untouched by any other human being, and live very snugly alone with it. But not Margaret. To the extent that she was separated from someone she loved, to that extent was she diminished, and she herself knew that fearful fact better than anyone. And now 'twas she had done the separating; God, what wild and terrible grief would wrack her soul in all the empty, endless days that lay ahead! What had brought her to it, I could not say. Nor could I find a way to tell Jamie she was gone.

Three or four days passed. He talked of her all the time, and then I realized that of course someone, sooner or later, would say something about her. I myself heard from home that Margaret Culhane had sailed for England to attend some fancy academy in London, with several other young ladies who were daughters of Culhane's English friends. Soon everyone would know about it. I had to tell Jamie.

And I did tell him. The light in his eyes went out as I spoke, and, though his hand trembled so badly he had to throw down his cigarette, he spoke calmly enough. I thought, Oh, Jamie, Jamie, say what's in your heart, I'll

understand it well enough, God knows, for she's gone from
me too, and I don't understand it, either. But he did not
speak a word then. He grasped the cane he had carved out
himself and, leaning heavily on it, dragged himself away
from the fire where we sat alone, off to stand over the cliffs
jutting out on the sea, and whatever pain he was enduring
then was between himself and the watching stars.

Yet he did have it out with Culhane, weeks later, when
he was fit to travel about again. There was a meeting at
O'Rourke's, some news about the lost five thousand
pounds. We'd never got that shipment at all, and were
desperate for supplies. Culhane looked tired and grim as
he reported that Tom Flynn had given notice to the shipping lines before he picked up the five thousand pounds,
and an agent of ours in New York had found out from
Flynn's landlady that he had packed his belongings, paid
his back rent, and disappeared.

Riordan's face was etched in weary disappointment.
That was the end of it, then. No one would ever see Flynn
again. He knew he was a dead man if he was spotted. And
all our waiting and planning had come to naught, the
lousy, greedy bastard!

We were about to return to camp with our cheerless
news, when Jamie, still very pale and thin, drew Culhane
aside. Sean looked impatient, but stayed behind. And I'll
spare you the lie, I listened as hard as I could outside the
door, for I had the feeling this was one conversation Jamie
would not repeat to me or to anyone else.

"You think you know my daughter, Daley," Culhane
was saying, "but, you see, she *is* my daughter. That's what
drives her. She hates me. Oh, yes, I've always known that.
But she is very like me. She hates that too, and tries to
fight it. But she cannot fight it."

"No, I don't believe you, Culhane," broke in Jamie, his
voice harsh and bitter. "What did you do to her? Beat her?
Scare her? Tell me. Tell me, or I'll kill you! I'm like to kill
you anyway! Why did you have to do it? What perverse
thing in you is it that must hurt and spoil and destroy
everything?"

"She's hurt you by this, I see," murmured Culhane clinically. "She's always been a willful girl, impetuous, capricious, even you know that, despite your feelings for her. Often she does not know her own mind. Her duties have not come easily to her. She strains at the leash. She longs to keep her freedom. And she has never been able to bear the slighest touch of restraint upon her life. Perhaps that's it, Daley. Perhaps she feared that what had happened between the two of you threatened that freedom of hers."

"Don't be a fool! She loves me!" cried Jamie.

Culhane nodded slowly. "Perhaps she does. Or did. But it had all become too real, I suppose. She was badly frightened at what happened to you. I think it shocked her awake. She wanted no part of this struggle. And suddenly she found herself committed to it, unwillingly, through you, because of you. I don't think she could bear that."

"No, it's you, it's *you* that's done it!" Jamie rushed at Culhane wildly, but he was still weak, and Sean merely stepped aside, so that Jamie nearly fell and had to grasp the table edge for support.

"Believe what you will," said Sean coldly. "It's over. She's gone now."

Jamie's face was twisted with bitterness, and with sorrow. He half turned toward Culhane, leaning on the table, and said, "You were my father's friend," so hurt, so surprised, my heart ached with pity for him then.

Culhane paused at the doorway. "Whatever I was to your father, whatever I have been to you in our work together, I shall be again when I am needed. I have tried to make you understand, one thing has nothing to do with the other. That you love my daughter presents only unpleasant complications to me. It does not flatter me; it does not please or comfort me. I have no such fond feelings toward her myself. She is a means to an end, that's all. Margaret has known what would be required of her as my daughter since she was quite small. I have given my life to hold what belongs to my people, and at last, apparently, whatever her personal feelings, Margaret has decided to do her part."

And then Culhane came outside, not noticing me standing there. He paused again, drew himself up, and then walked to where his horse was tethered. A moment later,

Jamie came out and, though, as I had expected, he did not say a word, he was trembling from head to toe and the look of murdering hatred was stamped on his face.

In months to come, that look settled in on him and became part of him so that, except for brief, rare moments, I hardly saw him as he had been before. In silence he did his work; in silence he kept his thoughts and feelings, and I had not wit nor words to comfort him nor, indeed, myself.

Now through the remainder of 1918 we waited, little happening except that we were prepared for much to happen and that very soon. And then, in November, what the world had been awaiting finally happened. On November 11, 1918, the First World War, or, as we called it then, the Great War—God help us!—was ended and we in Ireland waited anxiously.

Immediately there had to be a new election. Because of the war, the elections had been put off longer than usual. Now we went about campaigning for Sinn Fein candidates to Parliament. We were in a very tight spot, for it would have been easy enough to give in to the Ulster Conservatives up north and let the land be divided as they wanted. Ah, God, how they clung to their mother's skirts and shunned the very thought of independence!

Sure we could have let them go and had an easy end to it, but we of the Sinn Fein party, now, we weren't about to let ourselves be weakened forever. What kind of a victory would that have been? Ah, well, now you see, fifty years later, what a mockery it was after all!

But 1921 and partition had not come yet. We were young and felt power very close to our hand. We were determined, come what may, that when Ireland was free, it would be *all* of Ireland together. We were accused in the press of being fanatics, of endangering our country's position by insisting that all of Ireland come out together when the north did not wish it so. They wondered, in print, how we could talk of justice and independence when we would not allow those six small counties the right to make their own decision. For Ulster long ago had been "settled," as they put it, by Scots and British, so long, in fact, that they were generations on the land and felt it theirs. Well, but we had no quarrel with that as it stood. Though what right anyone had to "settle" a land which was already owned and occupied by another nation of people altogether I cannot tell!

Then, in December, the long-delayed elections were held, and we found that 1916 had not been in vain or forgotten by our people. We elected seventy-three Sinn Fein members to Parliament, which considerably shocked both England and Ulster. De Valera was elected to Parliament, too, although he could not yet return from the United States to take his seat.

But seats in a British Parliament were not what we wanted. What had we to do with a British Parliament, anyway? Let Britons govern their island any way they wished, as we intended to do with ours. Our seventy-three newly elected members refused to take their seats, and can you imagine the roars of laughter in all the pubs in Ireland when word got out that our men refused to recognize that there *was* a British Parliament at all? No sooner was that bit of madness and delight found out than the next came to light and we in Waterford caught our breath in joy and amazement, for, by God, didn't the seventy-three of them thumb their noses at England and declare, as poor Pearse and O'Connell had done first three years before, that Ireland was now a republic—*all* of Ireland, of course! Then they went about setting up the first modern Irish legislative body themselves, and they called it the Dáil Éireann. That was in Dublin, January of 1919. In April they declared their constitution and they elected Eamon De Valera, still exiled in America, mind you, the first President of the Republic of Ireland!

Well, and by God, that did it at last! There we stood on the mountaintop, republicans all, and more than ready to forget the past and get on with the future. We had a government; we had a constitution, God, we even had a President! We had all these things, but, like your little lad at Christmastime pressing his nose against the glass looking at the toys inside the store, there was that between us and enjoying it. After the wild jubilation came the sober moments and the bitter second thoughts.

England, in deep debt from the war, full of ills like inflation and labor strikes, yet wearily swung her whole attention to us again, like the man who's had to keep kicking away the dog biting his foot whilst he fought off a robber, but once the robber is gone, around turns the man, and the little dog has his full attention at last, woe to the little dog!

Lloyd George poured troops into Ireland like water through a sieve.

"There'll be a fight of it," said Riordan, but we were prepared for it. Thousands and thousands of English soldiers were being sent west instead of east to fight, and I guess they were as sick of us as we were of them.

I don't know what the rest of the world thought about us way up here in Ireland. I suppose there were some who admired the nerve of us, and some who shook their heads over the gall of us, and many who laughed at the entire idea of us. Riordan was very much on his mettle right after the Republic was declared, very nervous and waiting for trouble, though some were foolish enough to say England might just shrug it all off after all and let it go.

He called us all together out at Aherne's place, which was so far from the main roads and the patrols we dared risk it once in a while. We drank a stout toast to the Republic and to her President across the seas, God grant him home safe and soon, and then Riordan stood to speak to us. He'd a funny wry smile on his usually thoughtful face and an old twinkle in his eyes.

"Gentlemen," he began, looking around at us all, "this beloved Republic of ours wants introducing to the world. She stands shyly against the wall, like your young sister at the Saturday night dance, neither eyed nor spied by the boys. Well, now, lest she be passed over and forgotten without a single dance before she goes her way, I say, take her by the hand out to the middle of the dance floor. Let others make way for her. Let her call the tune she'll dance to best, and then let all eyes notice her. Make the stiff necks in the crowd, one by one, be forced to bow to her as she goes by. In short, my lads, saying we've got a republic is not having a republic. Padrhaic Pearse, God rest his gentle

soul, Pearse proved that to us. We've got to show all the
world she's here at last and will never be content to stand
by while the dance whirls about her. Let's show them she's
no old maid, gentlemen, but a young maid and pretty and
welcome among us!"

Risk or not, we stood to the man, and cheered Riordan,
and thanked him in our hearts for putting us straight, as
always, to our next immediate task.

I saw so many British soldiers and armored cars and
lorries and what have you arriving in Ireland that I wondered if we'd sink from the sheer weight of all of them.
Now, said Riordan, now was the time to push and push
and never let up on them. Now was the time to build the
pressure until it became unbearable and they would be
forced to act upon the Home Rule Law, for law it was.
But Ulster had gained more time. England refused to talk
or discuss anything until there was peace and things about
this so-called Republic of ours were settled.

But there was something coming we hadn't figured on at
all. I think it made the whole thing drag out much longer
than it should have. You see, with all the agitation and the
declaration of the Republic, all the policemen in Ireland
walked off the job. They were republicans too and would
not aid an enemy invasion in any way. Now Ireland was
left entirely without a police force, and the English solved
that little problem in a most ferocious way. For police
there must be, they thought, theirs or ours, it made no difference.

So they sent in their own. Ah, but what police they
were! England put together a Special Auxiliary Police
Force with unlimited police powers, responsible to London
and not under the command or authority of the regular-
army units. We'd heard something about those devils before they arrived, and a sullen, quiet mob of Irishmen
gathered in clusters along the streets to watch the first
batches of them pull into town.

These were the Black and Tans, or, as we called them,
simply the Tans, and you'll hardly find more hated words
in Ireland even now.

I'm going to tell you about the Tans once and for all.

They were, since the time of Cromwell, the foulest plague of all to hit Ireland. Winston Churchill, a great man for his country and death to ours, sent them along to us. If you've read or heard that they were made up entirely of retired army officers, you've not heard true. Oh, there were old army men among them, no doubt, as well as the scourings of army prisons, did you hear that too? I think not. Indeed, to be accurate, the crusted scum off the lousy prison walls of every jail in England: degenerates, arsonists, murderers of every speciality, a fine group of highly talented and skilled men, a cutthroat crew of killers perfectly suited to the work ahead of them, that was the Tans! They wore black pants and khaki army blouses and black beret hats and were easy enough to spot. They had orders to straighten out Ireland once and for all, in any way that would work. Well, and that opened up doors undreamed of in hundreds of years, did it not? Those fellows didn't need to wait to have infinite power before they were infinitely corrupted—sure they were that before they ever saw Ireland.

Into Waterford they came, day after day, lorries full of them, ships of them, acres and oceans of them, swarms and flocks of them, they the crows and Ireland the cornfield! They had powers to arrest without warrants, to torture and kill without trial or recourse—well, why go on listing the thing, there wasn't anything new about them at all, only the name. The English swore they were being forced to fight terrorists with terrorists, whether that be true or not is for someone else to say, all I know is that, compared with the Tans, your average English soldier soon came to look like Prince Charming.

Now, at this moment in our capricious history, I must call back to your mind, with tremendous apologies for even mentioning the name, himself, Charlie Norwood, the agent of the landlord, his brother, Lord Norwood himself back in England. What do you mean, was Charlie still around? And where would Charlie *be* but around, collecting his money, hiding behind his bodyguards, cursing the Irish and lashed into latherings of rage when the Republic was born, for, if we won, now, where would that leave him? They wouldn't hold a shilling's worth of land in Ireland, you can be damned sure.

So far, Charlie hadn't suffered too badly from our goings on, but now he knew war would spread across the land from coast to coast, like a flame, and many a thorn in the side of Irishmen like himself could and would easily disappear in its smokey trail.

So the Tans appeared to Charlie like an army of angels in black berets. As an English citizen and property agent, doesn't Charlie up and demand their protection at once? And nothing could have suited them better, for Charlie's house was big and comfortable, so fifty assorted devils of them billeted themselves there, along with his regulars, at his expense, mind you, and protected the hell out of him. Now when Charlie rode out to collect and inspect, you couldn't see him at all, he was that deep in Tans! They soon took over the little villages nearby, drinking what they would at any pub and never paying. God help the man who asked for payment! They conducted house-to-house searches, looting what they would of personal property as they went. More than one young Irish girl soon enough had reason to hate them, but I will say, from what reports on such activities we got, not one man who had attacked one of our girls escaped with his life, or himself whole and entire to repeat his error.

Now public feeling against Charlie grew as it never had before. From being a creature of ridicule, he became a target for open hatred. With the Tans swarming all over town, Sean Culhane was squirming, for there was little enough he could tell us about, no one ever knew what they were going to do next; they had no regularly scheduled drills or patrols, but simply descended unexpectedly as the whim took them. They were fair to eating Charlie out of house and home, too, from what I heard, to say nothing of the quantities of hay and feed their horses consumed. Not that they rode overmuch, they preferred motor vehicles, but they had the horses just the same.

So there was a noose around our throats, and we had to be ten times more careful than ever before. Now we soon had yet another damnation to put up with, and that also had to do with Charlie Norwood, sure his was a name would be more in our minds than most the next couple of years, as it turned out.

You see, besides himself, Johnny Rob back there at home, and Charlie, there was yet another son of the Norwoods, younger than Johnny Rob and only a year or so older than Charlie. Sydney Norwood was *his* name, knew nothing, had nothing, did nothing all his life except wish Johnny Rob might be carried off of a sudden by the fits, and spend his father's money as fast as he could.

I guess Sydney knew his older brother pretty well, and didn't figure to enjoy life so much as long as Johnny Rob held the purse strings. And he was right, was Sydney. The new lord was The Lord, as they say, and he had no obligation to support Sydney. The father, of course, had left Sydney a handsome sum in his will. When the old man died, Sydney, out in the cold as ever from the title, ran through his inheritance in just over a year's time and, pockets out, went crawling home to Johnny Rob for more.

"Not bloody likely!" says Johnny Rob. "You'd best go see Charlie in Ireland. Maybe he'll take you on and teach you a trade."

And that, as far as Lord Johnny Rob was concerned, was the last of Sydney, sink or swim with the Irish as he might. But a trade was the last thing in the world to suit Sydney Norwood, as he had already tried a few in his search for prosperity, such as gambling, embezzling a bit here and there (just to keep body and soul together), and a few unsuccessful forays into the blackmailing game, which nearly got him killed. Some said he'd had a soft thing going with a wench of a cousin of his up in London for a while, such were his pandering ambitions, and was finally arrested and convicted of pimping. They do say, don't they, that the middle child has it hard, adjusting?

Now, why do you suppose I am telling you all this in the midst of our great war with the Tans? Whisht, now, what do you imagine Sydney thought of when he finally finished his eighteen months and was let out of jail, that being about June of 1919? Ah, weren't they desperate for men, the Tans? And weren't they offering all sorts of inducements of the sort that would appear to Sydney, such as money and power and women by the flock, all the basic values of life, don't you see? So, along with a few others who'd shared his solitary life behind bars, Sydney joined up for the hell of it, and because he hadn't a shilling, and because he remembered he had a brother of some little influence in Ireland.

Well, the way of it was that shortly after that fateful decision, in on Charlie Norwood and his fine house and his contingent of Tans moved yet another black beret, his loving brother Sydney, two trunks of clothes and two gold-handled pistols to his name. And, if Charlie had been the blight of the land before, once slick Sydney arrived, there was a pair of them there, each shoving the other in turn and shoving the Irish double-handed together. I guess Charlie had an inkling time was running out. It was their only point of agreement: bleed the tenants white and then do it again.

The first thing Sydney did was to show Charlie how to fulfill a lifelong dream. How kindhearted you are, Charlie darling, but you cannot think of leaving these people on the land, don't you see? They're all republicans and enemies of the state which I, happily, now represent. Push them off, Charlie darling, I'll back every move you make; raise the rents till they can't pay; now there's two of us and Johnny Rob still gets his, come what may. Let's up the revenue while we can and make a good profit.

Charlie was a little nervous at first, but, with Sydney behind him, he soon became outright *courageous* about throwing his people off the lands, out of the cots, and forcing his farmers to the brink of bankruptcy and many over the brink and down.

"My, my, Charlie my brother," says Sydney to Charlie, "just to think what a cushy life you've had of it all these years. I never knew!"

"I had to be careful when Father was alive," admitted Charlie with a bold smile, "but Johnny don't care what we do, as long as the money keeps coming in."

That was very true, as Sydney well knew, but even though Charlie said it, he didn't quite believe it himself.

He was too used to being careful, and the poor creature didn't have Sydney's natural, easygoing, openhanded spirit of cruelty to begin with. And, too, he was handicapped by the lack of dash, which Sydney possessed in overwhelming amounts. Charlie was just mean, which is well enough for a small boy only beginning a lifetime of crime, with years of learning ahead of him before he's the polished perfection of badness. But that was all Charlie was. He was stunted: mean little child, mean boy, mean grown-up man. He just didn't develop right.

But Sydney, now, was the very essence of gentlemanly vice, which is saying a lot when I think of some gentlemen I've known in my day. Another thing: as I told you before, Charlie didn't have much going for him in the way of looks. But Sydney was a rogue to set eyes on! Taller than Charlie, but not too tall to be graceful, fair hair, slicked down, small ears and hands, dark eyes, a manner of style about him, ah! and clean, polished boots—sure was he a brother at all?

He was. In fact, to show you how *much* of a brother he was, I'll tell you that one of the first things Sydney undertook in Charlie's house was to win the loyalty and affection of every Tan Charlie kept by him. In a couple of months' time, do you know, those bastards would just as soon have served Sydney as Charlie himself? Now, if that isn't friendly and fraternal of the man, I ask you, what is?

The Tans knew their own, and Sydney was the man for them. Charlie was a drudge. Money was his meat, and he had an orderly mind. He treated them like the curs they were, and kept a pretty tight rein on their natural inclinations, which ran to thieving, pillaging, raping and the like. I imagine they found service with Charlie pretty confining and conditions in Dunknealy too quiet to suit them. 'Twas no wonder Sydney took such of their fancies as they still preserved. They called him "Yer Gryce" and "Lud Sydney," and began to treat Charlie with a subtle kind of unspoken insolence.

Sydney took to the military life with great ease, and to the Tans with affinity. He went drinking with them, and whoring with them, and, when they weren't too busy with

all that, he went exploring the countryside with them,
looking over every piece of property the Norwoods controlled, familiarizing himself with the lay of the land.

We made no move against them for the time being, but
we kept a close check on the messengers up from town as
to what was going on there. We had little real information
and, for once, Culhane couldn't help. We desperately
needed to know what was being planned, but the trouble
was, no planning seemed to be done at all. This drove
Culhane wild and he continually pressed for some united,
big action throughout the county, but Riordan always refused. Ours was a guerrilla war; we had not the men nor
the arms to fight pitched battles, nor was that our way.
Our intention was to harass them any way we could, to
seem to be everywhere, to give them no peace to draw
breath. We'd show up at Dalton's Cross with a sack of
grenades (when we could get them), whilst fifteen miles
away we'd raid Tierney Barracks within the same hour,
and blow out a van on the road the other side of Kilmacthomas five minutes on top of the two.

This kind of wild hopping around damn near drove the
Tans mad. We'd have them routed out of their bunks all
hours of the night, sleepy and swearing, struggling into
their pants and blouses and trying to get the lorries started,
only to find that our lads had just drained all the petrol
from the tanks, or let the air out of the tires, or pulled a
few wires in the ignition. How we could have used those
lorries ourselves, if only we'd had the means of hiding
them and bringing in supplies to keep them running. But
keep in mind, we were a force spread thin at best, two or
three dozen here and there, that was our great strength
and safety. Few of us knew our counterparts in other
areas. Therefore, if we were captured, how many could
we bring down with us? Riordan made that very clear to
Culhane so many times, and, whilst Sean could see the
reasoning behind it clearly, this kind of fighting galled
him, struck him as unmanly and furtive, and made him
harder to get along with than ever.

Yet it was, all told, a grand scheme and worked very
well on the Tans, although we were exhausting ourselves

as well. Not a night's sleep straight—that was a little motto we thought up, and all it meant was that every night, in every military establishment in the area, the Irish Republican Army (that was us now, surely you've heard the name?) would try to provide a bit of diversion to keep them stirred up. Some of our lads had a neat way of pitching a bomb through a door or window as they might be sitting at their mess, or just settling down for a doze. We moved fast and light; all we carried with us was our weapons, those who had weapons, and whatever we could pack on our backs.

Well, do you know, the English didn't take at all kindly to our efforts to move them out? No, they did not. Can you stomach the nerve of them, but they called us a terrorist organization and not an army at all! Terrorists, from them that brought terror with them seven hundred black years before from over the water, and then stuck around to see it perfected generation after generation! Coming from them, of course, it was a compliment laced with high flattery, but, if we *did* strike terror into them and maybe ground our heels around in it, too, why, man dear, all they had to do was pack up and be off—same as today, don't you see?

Chapter XVIII

Have you ever noticed that in the midst of wars and famine, plague, drought and downfall, Christmas continues to come? Who there was to think of Christmas in Ireland the year of 1919 I cannot venture to say; God knows 'twas not us! I think I read somewhere that truces used to be declared on such holidays; knights used to quit fighting; armies would leave off besieging castles; everyone broke it up and went home to celebrate even on weekends.

Who wants to kill a man at Christmastime? It doesn't sit right in the gut, that's the hypocrisy of it, don't you know? Kill the poor devil with impunity next day, but let him enjoy his Christmas. I think Christmas should be indefinitely postponed. The only good thing that ever happened of a Christmas Day that I can recall was the birth of Jesus, little good the day did him, poor creature, himself. But all chaos and disaster haunts that blessed day; it is a focus for evil. Maybe the Church had something there, maybe on special holy days the forces of wickedness try extra hard to spoil whatever good there is. But, you know, they succeed with such consistent regularity, it leaves you wondering about the relative strength of moral right in the world. Christmas should be *granted,* like the Nobel Peace Prize, only when the world uniformly deserves it. Yes, by Christ, there's a thought for an editorial. Don't let the day be commonplace, expected or dreaded as the case may be. Let Christmas be declared when the world has been at peace, men really decent and proper to each other, for one full year. Then, go ahead, put up your trees and blazing logs, prepare your geese and turkeys, up with the lights and out with the toys and candy. By God, Earth, you've done it; people, you haven't killed each other, nor lied nor stolen nor cheated nor betrayed your children nor drunk or drugged your honest senses. If a year has passed, world, and you can look yourself proud in the mirror, then you deserve Christmas, more power to you! But till then, stop the horrible lie of it, the peace on earth, the men of good will, the lovely, meaningless songs; stop dragging that poor man's sublime thoughts and hopes for you through the mud and blood of your insanity. And, man dear, I say this to you looking you straight in the eyes, for, above all other things, for all reasons and for absolutely none, I love Christmas with my whole fool heart!

I loved it in 1919 too, I suppose, when I remembered it, when there was time or energy to remember anything but that, behind my back, there was always an imaginary

bullet Heaven-directed to hit me just through the heart
and lung. I had got into the curious habit of always turning and looking over my shoulder to see if it were coming
yet. I remember I was hungry most of the time, and cold,
and very tired. I suppose the same could be said of any
shopper in any Christmas queue in any department store.
But I was scared too. I suppose those are more in keeping
with the real story of Christmas as it did happen according to all reliable reports. Surely little Mary, not much
more than a child herself, was cold and hungry, tired and
very, very scared that long, strange night. But Mary got a
present out of it. The Christmas of 1919, there was no
present, and we were cheated once again.

All through December, a freezing snow had fallen sullenly and deliberately on the ground. The sky hung low
and very dark and there seemed to be no sun at all. At
night, the temperature fell and froze what was there; the
next morning brought the snows again, till there were
layers of ice everywhere. Tree and bush were bare and
black and deadly-looking. Christmas Eve brought an end
to the snow; its place was taken by a thick, freezing sleet.

Some of the men were sick with fever and coughing
hard. Willie Cassidy had the pneumonia in both lungs,
and lay in his blanket near the smoking, sputtering small
fire, coughing and shivering, his great dark eyes staring
across the hills, his fingers never still but constantly pluck-
ing at the blanket threads.

The rest of us tried to sleep, though it was only six in
the evening. Riordan, as usual, marched nervously about,
looking at his pocket watch every five minutes. He had
sent Joe Clarke and little Johnny O'Donnell off to Cork
that morning early, in a lorry we'd managed to find petrol
for. Ever since Culhane's contact, the ship stoker, had
lifted that five thousand pounds, we'd been hard up for a
way to bring in any more shipments from the States. Then,
as luck would have it, Johnny O'Donnell's brother in
Boston agreed to send along some rifles now and again,
written down as cases of old clothes, heavy boots and the
like. He wrote that his first "Christmas present" was arriving on the twenty-fourth, so Joe and Johnny had set out

to get it and they were due back by eight o'clock that night.

Jamie was sitting on the wet ground near poor Willie, trying to keep up his spirits, with his own sodden blanket over his shoulders and head to keep out the rain and sleet, singing some old carol in his dreadful, hoarse voice. But Willie seemed beyond hearing or caring, and Jamie wasn't really putting much of an effort into it. Yet, when he would pause for even a few seconds, Willie's wandering, feverish eyes would seek him out and Willie'd whisper, "Ah, give us a song, will ye, Jamie boy?" And Jamie would smile and begin again, and Willie would stare once more across the gray, wet hills, and cough, and shiver, and pluck the blanket to shreds.

I could not stand to see them, after a while. I took the watch and went up to join Riordan in his march through the mucky ice.

"Two more hours, if all goes well, and we'll have our Christmas present," remarked Riordan, trying to smile as he saw me coming.

"Aye, all our pretty toys," I murmured.

Riordan clapped me on the shoulder. "Cheer up, then, Jerry," says he. "It'll be over soon enough."

But I didn't feel like talking. I turned away and walked slowly to the edge of camp. When I reached it, and turned once again to come back, I saw Riordan still where he'd been, in the driving sleet, squinting down at his watch, then trying to see down through the wet and the darkness to the road below. 'Twas then I heard a faint "Hallo" in the distance. It couldn't be them. I whirled and splashed my way in the direction. Then I heard it again, and someone calling, "Riordan, Ian Riordan, are you here?"

"Who goes?" I shouted as I was supposed to, holding up my rifle. Really, it was idiotic, for I couldn't have seen a regiment a foot in front of me.

"Will you put that damned thing away, Jerry Noonan, and find me Ian Riordan?" came a voice behind me. I turned quickly and there was himself, old Father Donovan from Holy Rosary, wrapped round and round in a long black cloak he must have dug up in the rectory attic, like

a black mummy, on a mule which, instantly he saw me
clearly, bared his lip and brayed unpleasantly, the water
dripping dolefully down his ridiculous long eyelashes, like
a camel's they were, and Donovan spoke a sharp word to
the beast as I led him back to Riordan.

Donovan got down stiffly, taking his saddlebags from
the mule's back and tying the creature to a thin tree.
Riordan came sloshing over to him.

"Father Donovan, it's a warm sight you are!"

Donovan was looking around at the miserable lot of us,
and shaking his head, then he caught sight of Willie and
went over to him, and knelt down in the ice by his side.

"James, will you leave off the damned music for one
minute!" yelled Donovan, glaring at Jamie.

Jamie looked offended but did stop singing, and at once
Willie focused his feverish eyes on him and tried to speak.

"Ah, there now, Willie, there, don't try to talk, lad,"
crooned Donovan, taking his restless hand and starting
from the terrible hotness of it. His eyes met Riordan's,
who stood above him, and Donovan shook his head very
slightly. Riordan's mouth tightened, and he looked away.

"Father Donovan, is it you?" wondered Willie, smiling
weakly.

"It's me," replied Donovan heartily. "James, run and
get my saddlebags, will you? Willie, me lad, I've brought
you two things that'll set you right in a trice and have
you on your feet by morning. Jamie, hurry there, will
you?"

Jamie came running back with the bags.

"And what's that, Father?" smiled Willie, trying to prop
himself up on his elbow. But the effort brought on the
coughing again, and he lay back, racked with it, the rain
pouring on his hot face and coldly into his raw throat, his
hand clawing the air helplessly for breath. Alas for Riordan's bit of a tent that had so nicely sheltered Jamie
once; it was long gone, burned to ashes, along with the
captain's spare clothes and four excellent guns.

Donovan whipped off his cloak and folded it quickly,
laying it under Willie's head. "There, that'll ease it a bit,

Willie. Now, here we are, lad. I've brought you Communion and a bottle of good Irish whiskey."

"Ah, that's grand of you, Father," gasped Willie. Donovan blessed him and gave him absolution, although Willie tried to say he hadn't been to confession in a while, but Donovan fiercely shut him up and swiftly put the Host into his mouth before the rain would dissolve it. Then he took the top off the whiskey and filled it with liquor, and lifted Willie's head to pour it into his mouth.

"This'll warm you, Willie," says he, but the whiskey poured down the sides of his mouth, and Willie's head fell back. Donovan, cursing and swearing, handed the whiskey back up to Jamie and put his hand to Willie's chest. "Thank God, he's not dead," he said after a few seconds. "But he will be by morning, if you don't get him off the ground and out of this weather."

Riordan looked sick himself. "Where can we take him?"

Donovan stood up, leaning heavily on Jamie, and spoke harshly. "I'm taking him back to the rectory with me," he said. "Don't argue with me, Riordan."

"I was only going to ask, do you think the Tans will respect the church?" asked Riordan midly.

Donovan snorted, and, hauling up the skirt of his soaking cassock, he pulled out a heavy, old-fashioned revolver from his pants pocket. "No, but they'll damn well respect *this,*" said he.

Riordan's eyebrow rose and a faint smile appeared on his thin mouth. "Would you really use it?"

"I hope to God I'd use it!" vowed Donovan stoutly, then he added, in an infinitely sad tone, "I don't know."

He stayed to give Communion to any man there who wished it and, after saying a short prayer, shook hands with each of us. I helped them wrap Willie up as best they could and got him up on the mule, but we had to tie him on, for he had lapsed into a coma. They started off down the mountain then, Donovan on foot leading the mule slowly behind him, his thin cassock clinging wetly to his bent old frame. I watched them till they were quite out of sight. A while later, I thought I heard the mule braying, and then I wondered if I'd heard Willie coughing, and I prayed they'd make it into town without being picked up. As I stood there, Riordan came to me with the watch in his hand. He showed it to me wordlessly. It was eight-thirty, and the boys were not back.

"It's just the weather," I tried to reassure him, though I didn't believe it myself. "You know the lorry's no good in this muck. Like as not, they've pulled off the road to wait till it stops."

"And be picked up carrying four boxes of rifles?" He shook his head. "You know better. No, something's happened to them."

"What do you want to do?"

He thought a moment. "We've got to get those weapons. I'll wait another half hour, to be sure, then you and Jamie and Andy, and Allie Clarke, go after them—"

"On foot?"

He shook his head again. "No, you'll have to make time. Go by O'Rourke's. In back is the car. Here are the keys. Stay off the main road. You know the route they took to Queenstown?"

I nodded. We'd been there when they were briefed.

"Good. And take your weapons," he added.

Jamie and Andy and Allie and I got ready to go, and sat waiting in a small cluster, hoping like hell any minute we'd hear the lorry come lurching and protesting up the road, but we heard nothing. Riordan came to us then.

"You'd best go," he said curtly. "Be careful. And try to bring the lads back, will you, now?"

We set off quickly through the snow and ice toward O'Rourke's. It was about two miles away and, as we came through the trees, we saw the lights were out. Jamie ran behind the house, then emerged and waved the rest of us in. In a few more moments, we had piled into the car and Jamie was driving down the road, sitting hunched up over the wheel, staring hard through the glass, for the windshield wipers barely moved at all, and he was driving at top speed.

"We'll find them, won't we?" asked Allie in a strained voice. 'Twas his brother we were after, and they were very close.

"Sure we will, take it easy," muttered Jamie. I sat looking out the back window, to see if we'd been spotted. Jamie drove like a madman, around hairpin turns, through a couple of wooden fences, into and out of ditches—sure the car almost lost its back wheels half a dozen times, skidding and sliding back and forth on the road as he tore along.

"Take care, or they'll have to come looking for *us*," warned Andy anxiously.

Jamie paid him no need whatever. Mile after mile we roared along, meeting no one out on the dark roads, and seeing nothing by the roadsides that might have been a wrecked lorry.

"They could still be in Cork," said Allie. "Suppose they had trouble finding the boxes? They might still be waiting at customs. Are we going all the way there?"

"I hope not," said Jamie darkly, with a glance at the petrol gauge. "We don't have enough petrol to get back if we do."

Gradually, as we drove through the now pelting rain, we could see the sky up ahead clearing in fits and starts, small breaks in the black clouds, a star poking out here and there. After a bit, the rain began to slow down, and fell in larger drops. Then, a while later, it let up altogether.

"Bad luck," muttered Andy. "The patrols will be out in full force now."

"Jamie, where the hell are we?" I wondered, for I hadn't seen a road sign since we'd started.

"Just outside Clashmore," answered Jamie. "At least we ought to be, if I'm on the right road at all."

"Wait!" cried Andy abruptly, sitting straight up and leaning forward in his seat. He pointed out the window. "What's that up ahead? Stop!"

Jamie almost landed us in another ditch, so quickly did he slam on the brakes. "What? I don't see— Ah, yeah, there it is," he said, peering ahead through the wet glass, cursing the rain that still dripped down from the roof. He pulled over to the side of the road and drove straight into a field. We had the doors open and the guns in our hands before we'd fully stopped, and came piling out fast. Ahead, around a sharp curve in the road, we could hear gunfire from several directions. It was so loud and there was so much of it they could not have heard us yet.

"Quick, keep to the side and stay together," called Jamie under his breath. Crouching low, we ran along the side of the road, then, around the bend, we dropped to our bellies and watched.

It was the lorry all right, on its side in the middle of the road, the back end of it blown to pieces, the metal twisted and smoking blackly. Beyond it was parked a patrol car, empty now, but its occupants not far off, for we could see four or five men fanned out along the left side of the road. From somewhere off in the field shots were being fired, and they were all returning the fire.

"They've got them pinned down," whispered Jamie. "We'll have to come up behind them and get them between us and the field."

We moved out again, running now as fast as we could, bent over not to be seen or be shot at by mistake from the field, for they could not tell who we were at such a distance. We had to pass by the lorry, for the Tans were about twenty feet up the road beyond it. As we crept by the wreck, Allie stopped.

"Wait. For Christ's sake, wait up!"

I turned around, for I was closest in front of him. He was staring at something in the road. Just standing there, staring, his mouth open in horror, the gun in his hand hanging forgotten at his side.

Jamie, who had run on ahead, thinking we were just behind him, suddenly looked back and, seeing we had stopped, came back cursing. "What the hell is holding you up?"

The rest of us ran over to Allie, and then we saw what he was looking at. It was Joe, lying on his back in the road, and if I told you that heaven had sent Ireland a rain of blood that week, then that would account for the pool of it around Joe's head, and under his whole body, streaming out in thin, scarlet rivulets into the mud puddles in the road. He had been screaming when he died, I judged, for his mouth was twisted open and his staring, dead eyes were full of terror. His hand had been digging into the mud of the road, and I saw sickly that someone must have deliberately stepped on his fingers, for they were crushed and pulpy, with pieces of bones sticking out through the torn skin.

Allie gave a low moan and picked his brother's body sitting up in his arms. "God," he said, "look at his face!" And he hugged Joe's poor face against his chest, turned against his own body to shut out the look on those eyes and the sight of the bayonet cuts all over him. They'd evidently killed him slowly, perhaps to make him talk, perhaps for the fun of it. Every tooth had been knocked out of his mouth and both of his arms had been broken in several places. He was all apart inside his skin, and Allie, hugging his brother to him, suddenly realized this. He couldn't help it, he recoiled with revulsion, dropping Joe's poor corpse down into the bloody mud again, retching and shaking terribly.

And suddenly we became aware again of the gunshots nearby. Jamie looked away from Joe's body and shook Allie very hard. "Come on, let's get the bastards!" he whispered. Allie shook his head, sobbing, his hand across his mouth, but Jamie shook him harder, and at last he stood up again. I thrust his gun back into his hand, and we moved off away from the lorry.

There were six Tans, all told, and even as we came up behind them four moved ahead, sliding quietly over the low strong fence, while the other two kept up a steady round of covering fire. If it was Johnny O'Donnell out there in the field, he was running out of ammunition, for he had stopped shooting rifles; now he was using his revolver and not returning shot for shot as he had been just a few minutes earlier. The two Tans on the road were firing blindly, and the four in the field now waited in silence, not firing themselves, peering about in the darkness, for he had not fired in a while.

Slowly they crept forward, till we could hardly see them. Jamie signaled silently, with his hand, and he and Allie headed for one of the two still shooting, and Andy and I for the other one. We came up so closely behind them they could have reached out and touched us. When we were ready, all together we fired at point-blank range into the backs of their heads. Scarcely seeming to notice it at all, they fell forward within seconds of each other, their upper bodies jackknifed across the fence. At once, the other four whirled about and began shooting at us on the road, but we ducked down behind the fence. Then from the field came another two shots. I heard a loud cry and ducked my head up in time to see one of them flung to the ground. There was a pause in the shooting. Evidently they were at a loss as to what to do, caught as they were between ourselves and Johnny out there, but at last we saw two of them crawling slowly back toward the fence, pushing their rifles on the ground ahead of them. The third one moved out across the field, beyond the range of our pistols. We trusted him to Johnny's care, and turned our attention to the other two.

Jamie and Andy were out of bullets. I had two more, and Allie was cursing and jamming bullets into his gun as he sat by the fence, leaning against it as they came on. Unconsciously we were all listening for the sound of Johnny's pistol again, but it did not fire.

I signaled Jamie I was going to circle around and follow up in the field. I ran down the road, keeping very low, for about fifteen feet, then hopped the fence and into the field. Suddenly it was very quiet. A moment later, I heard a loud yell. Looking back, I saw the two Tans up on their feet and leaping toward the fence, then Jamie and the boys stood up and met them as they charged, hand to hand, cursing, shouting, hitting. I almost forgot the man I was after, but a gunshot fifty feet away brought me sharp around again, and I saw him standing up quite clearly. I stood then, too, and shouted at him. He turned and raised his gun, but I fired first. He dropped down on one knee, raised his arm to try again. Then I shot my last bullet into him and he dropped with a short scream and moved no more.

I went to look at him, to make sure he was dead and would present no threat to my back, then I stood up and looked over to the road. Jamie was waving to me. I waved back, calling them to come ahead. And I began to call and search for Johnny as the three lads behind me came running.

"Johnny!" I shouted. "Johnny O'Donnell, are you here?" There was no answer. "Johnny, it's us, get out of it, for God's sake! There'll be another patrol along any minute." I tried hard to remember from which direction the gunshots had been coming when we first arrived, but I was all turned around out in the middle of the dark, icy field.

"O'Donnell!" "Johnny, answer us!" the others were calling, spreading out and running about. We kept looking back up at the road, where the dead bodies, the patrol car, the lorry and our own car were so plainly to be seen.

Finally, just up ahead of me, I spied a few low bushes and a man's leg sticking out. "Johnny," I called more softly as I made my way forward cautiously. "Johnny, is it you?"

"Jerry? Over here," came Johnny's voice, and in a moment I found him. He was sitting propped up against a wooden crate, sprawled out like a marionette, his two arms spread out limply at either side of him, his legs spread wide apart.

"Jesus, Johnny!" I dropped down by him, so damn glad to see him alive I could have kissed him! "Come on, Johnny, we've got to get out of here," I whispered urgently, and tried to help him stand up, but he groaned terribly and begged, "Don't touch me, Jerry. I'm hurt bad. Oh, don't move me, don't move me!"

"He's alive!" called Jamie, who had just come up and was yelling back at Andy and Allie.

"Jamie, look at him," I said. Johnny's head had fallen back. Jamie knelt by him, and Johnny gripped the edge of his sleeve and spoke very low, as the rest of us leaned over, trying to make out his words.

"They followed us the last five miles, from Youghal. The lorry couldn't take the speed. The throttle went dead and we were just able to jump out before it turned over. I was okay. I got round to the back and started pulling out the crates, but I could hear them coming in behind us. I didn't see Joe. I kept hauling on the damn crates and calling to him, but I didn't hear his voice at all—"

"Johnny, talk later. Come on, now," urged Andy, with an eye to the road.

Johnny's eyes closed, his eyelids fluttered. His face was ashen white, his lips thin blue lines, and already, when his eyes opened again, there was a cloud over them. He stared unblinking up at the sky, still clutching Jamie's sleeve, and spoke again.

"No, no, I'll tell you now. I was only able to get one of the crates out when I saw their headlights. I dragged it away to the side of the road and took my pistol and fired at the case of gunpowder inside the back—it made a grand explosion—" He smiled a ghastly, openlipped gash, the muscles of his mouth had little power left them and his lips remained fallen back away from his teeth. "They were startled by the fire and while they pulled up, I dragged this crate here into the field—but one of them spotted me and shot after me, got me in the legs, both legs, I guess. I can't feel my legs anymore, so I guess it was both of them. They started shouting and coming after me, then one of them found Joe. Oh, Allie, they—got Joe!" His eyes filled with tears as he tried in vain to see Allie.

"Someone shouted, 'We can get the other one later, he can't go far,' and they went back to Joe. He was alive. I guess he'd been thrown to the other side of me when we went over. I don't know. I kept crawling along, dragging the crate, till I got here, and I couldn't move anymore. I opened the slats; there were six of the rifles and a box of shot. I don't know what I thought I was doing, but I remember I loaded every one of the rifles and I put them out here on the ground beside me, and my pistol in my lap. I forgot what I was doing some of the time. I wondered why they hadn't come after me. Then I thought, maybe they've gone away, or I was asleep and dreamt it, I can't remember. But I pushed the crate here and leaned up against it and I heard them shouting and swearing, and I heard Joe— Oh, God help him, Joe, Joe—!"

"What happened to Joe, Johnny?" asked Allie, his voice choked.

Johnny closed his eyes again, tears running down his gray cheeks. "I—I guess they tried to make him talk," he faltered weakly, and we had to put our heads down almost to his lips to hear his words. "They beat him, I heard him cursing them, and then, after a while, I heard Joe screaming—"

"Oh, God, God," moaned Allie, jumping up.

"I thought they'd leave him alone if I shot at them," whispered little Johnny. "I kept firing the rifles one after the other. Finally, Joe stopped screaming. I used up all the rifle shot, and then I waited for them to come at me. I fired five times with the pistol, then one last one, and I thought it was up with me." He opened his eyes and for a moment they were clear and unclouded, and he looked fondly at us, smiling a bit, as Johnny always used to smile, trying so hard to get a bit of the devil into it, and he breathed, "It's a hell of a way to spend Christmas Eve, isn't it, then?"

I was holding his head. He cried, "Rose, Rose!" and he never moved again, but died like that, his eyes fixed on us, that bit of a grin still clinging to his bloodless lips.

"Johnny?" said Jamie softly, watching the quiet face.

And from the direction of Clashmore, a scant mile away, the church bells began to ring suddenly. We all jumped up, looking around wildly, as first one set of bells started pealing, then another and another.

"It's Christmas," said Allie tonelessly, staring down at little Johnny O'Donnell's body.

Then, through the midst of the bells' gay notes, like a falcon's shriek in the midst of a lark's song, we heard the roar of motors and the ring of a siren on the road.

"They're coming," said Andy.

"We've got to get out, come on!" I picked up my empty gun and started off toward the car.

Jamie did not move. "We've got to take them back," he cried.

"Jamie, come on. We've no time," Andy urged him.

Jamie shook his head and shuddered, looking down at

Johnny, lying there still clutching his pistol, his head falling over now on his left side. "But we've got to bury them!" he said, in a daze.

I pulled him away, without trying to argue, and we ran back through the icy wet field, slipping and falling and running again till we reached the car. The bells were still ringing loudly. We climbed in, praying the motor would turn over. It did, and we drove away at top speed, Jamie staring blankly through the glass window in front, Andy's hands directing his every turn of the wheel. I had picked up three of the rifles by Johnny's side, and Andy had the other three. And that was the shipment: out of twenty-four rifles, only six were saved.

We left them there, our brothers, our friends, dead and fragile and broken, like birds in a dog's mouth, there in the field of snow and ice, under a skyful of stars with the Christmas bells ringing all around us. A week later, as the New Year lulled our foes into a brief laxity, we went back there, oh, yes, we did, and we found Johnny's body, just as we'd left it in the field, frozen now, and covered with a light blanket of new snow. We took him home to his wife and daughters and buried Black Johnny O'Donnell, but we never saw Joe Clarke's poor tortured remains again. I hoped someone had buried him too, in some unknown little grave somewhere, I hoped they'd thought about him a little, and maybe wondered for a few days what kind of man he'd been and why he'd spent his last Christmas Eve giving up his life for Ireland.

Chapter XIX

Father Donovan was not able to get up to see us since Christmas Eve. Toward the end of January, poor Willie Cassidy died in the rectory. The priests buried him in the graveyard at night, quickly, with a short prayer, their heavy black woolen cloaks wrapped tight against them as they shoveled in the half-frozen earth themselves, with Donovan holding the lantern and keeping watch for the Tan patrols.

Not one of all Willie's large family was with him when he died, not even Frankie, and none there at the grave to watch and witness and say a prayer.

The news of his death came to us two weeks later, but by then we had grown so used to the idea of his dying that it was like a tired echo when we heard about it. Guilty or not as it made us feel, we were too tired to mourn. Sorrow for the dead is not rage; it is not fury and helpless disgust and anger, is it? I mean, I'd always thought of sorrow for the newly dead as a gentle, hurting, private thing. But what we felt when we heard about Willie's dying was not gentle at all. It was a rage that ate like acid through what was left of our hearts. I remember I was actually angry at Willie. Christ, Willie, you poor bastard, will you let yourself be just a memory, Willie, like Joe and Johnny? I had it going round and round in my head: Willie, I thought, Willie, get up, you blithering lazy-ass, you're not dead at all, and you know it! To hell with what the priests said; what do priests know about life or death? Get up, Willie Cassidy, I was crying out in my mind's voice. But, you know? Willie never answered me at all. And he didn't get up either, poor damned Willie!

That winter dragged itself out and out without end, it seemed. We saw nobody from home for weeks at a time, and there was little news but bad when we did see them. I don't remember much of one day or the next, except we lived like jack rabbits in holes in the ground, sleeping out at night in the hills, rain or snow, wind or fair, with what weapons we had grasped in our hands.

There were ambushes on the roadways, vans and lorries blown to bits, quick raids and fast, flighty skirmishes that left the Tans jumpy and sick to death of us. Our force was small enough, God knows, too small for the job, but we did the job anyway.

Yeah, it was fighting all the way that year, devil a chance for much of a rest, mud to the armpits, up, down, and across the green fields of Waterford. Jamie and I spent a few weeks on a mission for Riordan up in Wexford. The job was to have taken only a week at most, but we were seen and driven from place to place and had to hide out till we could slip through and get home again.

I began to lose track of who was winning, or how many men I'd killed; what was worse, after a while I lost track of caring about it. We were through with grief. We fought wildly and grimly, with the skull of death grinning from each red eye, and we never thought about what we did in the daytimes, for we thought of nothing else in the nights. We lost brothers and friends, cousins and fathers, lumped all together in the backs of our minds to be properly sorry for one day, but we had to keep on going.

Then, all in a morning and picked down at last and forever by the English harvesters, my father died with seven bullets in his body, coughing up his heart's blood into his mouth, still trying to stand and fire his rifle. 'Twas in a thicket of pine trees outside Kilmac. We'd blown up a small van in the road, not knowing a lorry loaded with Tans was hell-bent the same way ten minutes behind it. Besides my father, we lost four good men that same day, all for a barrel of gunpowder and a couple of tommy guns. No man's life is worth only that, least of all my father's. Oh, God in heaven, but we were sick of war! No more the green lads we used to be, crowding up with the men on the mountains, dying to be part of them.

How had it happened? Now *we* were the men; a week's growth of beard, sometimes two, on our faces. Hard faces, tight-muscled, jaws aching from clenching our teeth on a mouthful of terror. Not one of us who hadn't been wounded—myself with that long of a scar down the side of my neck from a bayonet. Scraggy, red-eyed, hairy, careless, dirty, swearing hard men we became. The oldest of us, aside from Riordan and O'Rourke, was twenty-five. The youngest claimed to be seventeen, but he was a great liar, almost as great as myself. It seemed that most who had been there before us were gone, taken, time after time, hanged or imprisoned. Others were shot down in their tracks or beaten to death by the Tans and thrown into the rivers and streams to rot. I didn't think of my father anymore. I know Jamie didn't think of Martin either. We would think of them again, and the full impact of their loss would thrust itself like knives into our insides, but we couldn't think of them then and survive.

The young lads coming in to us now, passing off dirty faces for bearded ones, straggling up one or two at a time, they were only boys, fifteen and sixteen, with a good deal to say, and all of it bad. They weren't interested in the possibility of peace worth a damn. They didn't believe in peace. They didn't know or remember and couldn't imagine peace whatsoever; try as well to describe color to a blind man or music to the deaf. They were going to fight for the Republic till they died, and they fully expected to die. And, for a few minutes, listening to their hard words, some of our own youth came back to us and we were amazed to hear them and see the bleak haunted faces and the cold eyes of them, till we remembered the looks of our own.

Christmas came and went again. All I recall of it is that I had a chance to see my father's farm again. We passed it heading back to camp from some action or other. It was empty now. My mother had left to go and live with Aunt Ellen until I would come home again, if I came home again.

It's funny, the farm was the one thing that didn't make me sorrowful that winter. I suppose, with the snows and the silence, it looked pretty much as it always had in wintertime. But I hated to think of it in the spring. Once, just a couple of years ago, and, mind you, time was bending and stretching itself red in the face then, and two years before seemed a century to me—but, just those two years earlier, spring on my father's place was the way it had always been: busy, bustling, rushing, like an army, I suppose, in its way, for it's nothing but hurry to get the seed in, hurry to get plowing, hurry to get it all ready, then wait while nature took over the job and made it grow. I hoped I would not see the farm that spring. Sometimes I felt so bad, I hoped I'd not live to see it thick with weeds, strange and silent without the creatures on it, and the house falling to ruin, and the flowers wild without love to care for them, reaching out in all directions for the voices they knew and the hands they knew tending them into shapes of pridefulness and glory.

It was very early in that spring of '21 when my little cousin Billy Kilpatrick, barely twelve, came struggling up against the wind through a howling March day, with news from home and a sack of food my mother and Aunt Ellen sent.

I hadn't seen Billy since he was two years old, I guess; his folks lived over in Cappogh and I wondered idly, not really caring, why he was in Dunknealy. You know, come to think of it, I never did ask him, either. I'd never have known the boy at all but for him seeking me out and telling me who he was.

"Well, then, is it yourself, Little Bill?" says I, looking him over. He had gotten taller than his father already, I thought, trying to remember my cousin Pat, but I couldn't get him fixed in my mind somehow. Billy turned red in the face and scuffed his boots against the snowy rock he'd found me leaned against half asleep. He stared about him wide-eyed and excited. I looked where he looked; God knows there was nothing to get excited about.

"I saw your mother," says he absently, still not able to take his eyes from Riordan and a few of the others who were huddled about the fire, talking as they blew warm breath on their fingers and held their ragged blankets around their shoulders. Riordan had his blanket tucked in here and there into his belt against the bitter-cold mountain air.

"She's well," Billy murmured, though I was just about to ask. "And so's Aunt Ellen and the girls. Oh, I was supposed to tell you and Jamie— Say, where's Jamie?" He peered around curiously.

"Busy," I said briefly. Jamie was out with two men setting up an ambush for a lot of Tans being transferred up from Cork. He hadn't thought much of the ambush, for we'd only three grenades left altogether, and, while your grenade will do great damage quickly, it must be planted just right or it's all a waste of energy. A moving lorry is not an easy target; we didn't want to destroy it entirely, for we needed the guns and ammunition they would be carrying, as usual, and didn't want it all blown to kingdom come.

"Is he fighting, do you mean?" cried Billy, his eyes sparkling at the thought.

"I suppose so," I answered him very shortly, for I didn't want to talk to the boy about it, any of it. I really didn't want to talk at all. I was cold and tired and worried, and his enthusiasm made me uneasy. We had grown remarkably quiet. Nobody wasted strength speaking unless he had to. Sometimes, just breathing from one minute to the next seemed too much trouble.

Billy was looking at me sidelong, then he turned away, embarrassed, and fell silent himself. I was sorry in the instant.

"Well, well, then, Billy." I summoned every last ounce of energy I could find in me. "Well." And I couldn't think of anything to say to him, until, very lamely, I asked, "How are you doing in school these days, then?"

God, even in the midst of the end of the world, grownups will still ask kids how they're doing in school! Why don't we ever ask them anything important, like how are you doing in life? Are you hanging on? Have you begun to go mad yet? What do you *think*?

He shrugged, disappointed, I could tell, with his heroic cousin. I expect he hadn't thought to find me wrapped in a blanket but marching around with a dozen medals flapping on my chest, poor kid. "Okay," he answered. Then, glancing at me shyly, he added, "It's hard to think about school when you're waiting to get into it."

"Oh, it'll be all over before you're of an age to fight," I said quickly, and his sudden look of dismay and anger angered *me*. Damn-fool kid, didn't he know when he was well off? I said no more, finding myself fidgety and wishing he hadn't come and that he'd go away. I didn't like to think of him alone going down the mountain again, dodging patrols, going hungry, catching cold, ah, what's the use of talking? I just wished he'd go away.

As if he knew my thoughts, he got up to go. "Oh," he said suddenly, "I near forgot. Aunt Ellen says to tell you and Jamie somebody you know is back. Somebody named Margaret is back. Well, take care of yourself, Cousin Jerry." And he looked at me for another moment, as if he would like to say more, but then, to my surprise, he hugged me very hard and ran off.

"Yeah, thanks, Billy." I found I was talking to myself, standing abruptly and looking after him in astonishment, his last words finally reaching me in their full meaning. Margaret was back! That's what he'd said. But when? Aunt Ellen had probably told him a lot more about it which he, boy fashion, figured was just frosting on the cake, and had only bothered to remember the main part of it. Margaret Culhane. I hadn't heard her name in nearly two years. Jamie and I never spoke of her.

I sat down again, leaning my rifle against a rock, and, my hands annoying me because they'd suddenly become unsteady, I reached inside my coat and pulled out a package of cigarettes. I looked at them, considering. There was a whole one and a half I'd pinched out about a week ago. I took the half. No doubt there'd be worse moments ahead.

I wondered if I should tell Jamie. I sat and puffed and thought hard. It had all been a long time ago, I reasoned. What with one thing and other, I had forced myself to put her out of my mind. Jamie never mentioned her, but Jamie never talked about things that hurt him. I wasn't even sure if it still did hurt. But he'd find out sooner or later. There was only one way to see how he felt. So, thinking it over till the end of my half a stale smoke, I decided I'd best tell him after all, come what may.

Later that night, after he'd been back and had a meal and a rest, the two of us were over by the fire, trying our damnedest to keep warm.

"Billy Kilpatrick was up today," I said casually.

Jamie frowned, trying to remember who Billy was.

"Oh, yeah, Pat's kid," he answered indifferently. "He must be big now."

"Tall," I nodded. "Nice enough kid."

Silence. I hesitated, then went on. "He saw everyone. They're all right."

A brief smile crossed his face. "That's good."

"Yeah." I forced a laugh. "He thought we were a damn regiment in clover up here. Couldn't take his eyes off the rifles."

Jamie nodded. "What do you expect?"

Then I blurted it out, because, the way we were going along, it would have taken me ten years to lead up to it!

"Jamie, Billy brought a message from home. You'll never guess who's back from England." I suppose I couldn't have put it worse if I'd tried. I watched his face and waited.

He shifted around a bit, and poked a piece of wood that had fallen on the ground into the fire again. Then he looked at me from under half-closed eyelids, and his look was a dangerous one.

"It could only be Margaret," said he, starting to hack away at a bit of pork with his pocketknife. "Is she well?"

"I guess. Billy didn't say much, just she was back."

"Back with the father?"

"I don't know. Where else would she go?"

"I don't know," he answered laconically, and began chewing his pork.

"Well," I said, a little piqued. I don't know what I'd expected him to do, but I expected him to do something! "I'm glad to see you're so quiet about it, then."

"What did you think I'd do?" he asked, very quietly.

"I don't know what the hell you're liable to do, ever!" I shouted hotly. "The last I knew of her, she broke your young heart. Did I know for sure 'twas mended long since? Or is it?"

He looked so long and so thoughtfully at the logs turning to ashes before us that I knew the answer without him saying a word. But then he did answer me, and it was not the one I knew was in his heart.

"It's been nearly three years, Jerry. I've known a couple of girls since then, and one or two I felt very warm for. I haven't thought much about her."

"And you're a liar, Jamie Daley!" I threw it back in his face. "You've thought of her. I know every girl you've met these three years, and they all had something of Margaret in them. The one had dark hair, and another brown eyes, and another was slim and rode well—and I saw you turn away from each of them after a couple of nights when you found Margaret there no more!"

I rather thought he'd hit me then. Jamie had hit men for less. He'd brook no idle fingering of his feelings, would Jamie! But no, he smiled instead, and said wistfully, "Do you really know me so well, then, Jerry?"

"I think you love her still, no matter what she did to you, that's all I know!" I insisted, blinking at him belligerently, for the smoke was stinging my eyes.

He shrugged a little. "Ah, let it go, let it go. It was all over before it began. I wish her luck. I wish her peace—what else can anyone wish for anyone else? And there's an end to it."

He sighed and looked away, past me, when I would have said more, then he turned from me and stretched out on his blanket.

"Luck," he'd said. "Peace." I wondered. I remembered Margaret and loved her still, unchanged one whit for all the passing time. I watched Jamie lying on his back, sleepy, bone-aching like myself, staring at the bright sparks flying up in to the chilly air. He still loved her, too.

I wrapped myself up and lay down, my arms folded under my head, trying to imagine what she would be like now. Had she cut her hair short as they were all doing, and was she a lady, whatever that was supposed to be, was she a lady with silk stockings and high-heeled shoes and the rest? I smiled to myself, my eyes closed, trying to picture wild Margaret trimmed down like that. I could no more imagine her in all that regalia than I could imagine her mad horse, Black Byron, a sweet-tempered gelding! I fell asleep with memories of her racing over fields and fences, her long hair flying behind her like the horse's long mane, the rush of wind in her face, the smile and the laugh in her voice and her eyes as she cried out exultantly and leaned forward eagerly in the saddle. . . .

The man dying there was following most of the story calmly enough, but once more the name Margaret raised the beat, that feeble beat that would once have raced, but the years for that were supposed to be over and all the dreary physical chains of things interrelating and acting upon each other that were supposed to make up an emotion were supposed to have long been sternly chilled and stilled into limbo. Yet, somewhere, a great broad smile at the thought spread warmly over the chill, and the feelings stirred. They were not the vague longing regrets the conscious mind holds onto through old age, often wondering, in its secret places, because it could not feel the feelings that gave it memory anymore, what, after all, had it really been? Or had it really been at all?

But Jamie knew, and his remembrance of Margaret and his feelings for her, in there somewhere, still lived, the boy and the man wildly wanting the girl and the woman, wanting in the only complete way there is between man and woman; it had never died, but had only been turned off. Perhaps that was what had preserved it, after all. Perhaps it hadn't had a chance to get used up or worn out, or whatever it was that happened to old men's loves.

That night that Jerry is going on about, his mind told the dying man, I remember that night. It was with pleasure he could say this, his memory was as good, no, better than Jerry's. And that little, young secret laughing smile continued warm as the man thought: Ah, you were right then, boyo, for how close I did come to smashing my great fist into your handsome, bright troubled face! But what was the use of it? Telling me Margaret was anywhere, anywhere at all in the world, was enough for me. Home or away, here or in England, what difference? She was not in my arms, and that is love. If she was not there, held tightly against the whole damned world, then she was lost to me. Walking by my side, even, and not there in my arms, alone just the two of us, the lonely feeling two lovers experience when they are with other people, doing anything, saying anything, listening to anything but the voice, arms, lips, hair, force, God in heaven, the fusion of their love! And Margaret was gone from me, though two hours' ride to the valley would have brought me within sight and sound of her.

You remembered her, Jerry? I remembered, too, and wondered when I'd first loved her, and realized that I'd always loved her, but still I'd been surprised to find it out, and that she loved me. Whom else would she love but me? Jerry loves her, loves her still, never married for love of her, I know that. But it was not to be.

Perhaps we should all have shared one another, but when has love learned to be generous? Perhaps that's where it has failed and should be reevaluated and restated and relearned. Would I have wanted Margaret in Jerry's arms and then in mine? And yet I loved them both so dearly. I wonder. I can think it and feel no jealousy, but put the warm, living woman under my hand and ask me then. No doubt I'd have an answer for you!

He was temporizing now, he realized that, because he knew what part of the story was coming next and he did not want to hear it.

Jerry, don't tell the man everything, he thought a bit desperately; and, if Jerry had been leaning over the bed, he would have noticed a slight, weak flaring of those nostrils, and wondered what chance worry or fear had flitted through Jamie's dying mind. Important messages from mind to mind never get through, only the inconsequential, the stray, the trivial. Or else, how many million telephones would ring of an instant, from the wishes and messages, lonely longing heart to heart? But the telephones remain silent, unless it is the landlord or your broker or a football lottery. So much for mind reading, he thought wryly. It was a good thing he was dying; soon enough the novelty of painlessness would begin to wear off, and then he would be desperate for a pain somewhere, anywhere, to know he was still alive.

He heard Jerry's next few words and suddenly prayed that he would die at once and not have to keep thinking about it. But he did not die. He had to hear it all, it seemed. Perhaps he was in purgatory, that strange place the nuns used to torment children with, or perhaps he was already consigned to hell. But there it was, it had to be heard. Someday he would have to hear it one final time from someone else's mouth and remember it all again in one, finished, perfect piece, exactly as it happened, not in the broken, fragmentary way he'd dreamed it for fifty years. Maybe then he would be finally free of it. . . .

Well, I put Margaret from my mind as best I could and tried to get on with the things at hand. I put herself in with all the other sorrows I was carrying around to pull out and mourn over one day. I hoped Jamie could do the same. He seemed to. He didn't speak of her. But then, Jamie never spoke of things that tormented him, and I counted that a bad sign. Each man has his own hell to walk about in, no less the caged tiger his zoo, I suppose. I could no more reach out from my own to help him than he had the power to leave the cage or to reach me, either.

I did think Sean Culhane had picked one hell of a time to bring her back. Things had never been worse, in my memory. We were fighting as if we were winning, but we were not winning. At best, we were holding them off and praying for a settlement, or, rather, the settlement that we wanted, the only one we could accept with honor. Ah, hell, skip honor and just say the only settlement that ever made any sense. You know, the one we're *still* fighting for!

And now that Margaret's name had come up, and she had come back, whether we saw her or we didn't see her, we were aware of her, if you understand my meaning. And, along with her, her father, for you could hardly separate the one from the other.

We hadn't seen Culhane in over a year. There was little news from him. He still managed to entertain those of his British friends who stayed on despite the trouble, but, when the Tans had come in, many of them suddenly abandoned Ireland until it all "blew over." We were not in that much need of information, anyway. What was there to discover? There were the Tans, more every month, and we had to get rid of them. The political stuff was being handled from above. Our one and only job was to hound them and keep them on the run. Pressure, that's what we were. Oh, some wild fellows here and there seemed to feel it was all tied in some way with the workers' revolution, and there were a lot of new-baptized Communists in Ireland, but what did we have to do with all that? Let them rant and rave as long as they didn't interfere with our job and could create enough chaos to help us along.

Culhane had grumbled and complained and appealed to his high and mighty English friends, all for the purpose of keeping them from billeting any of the damn Tans in his house. For a while it worked, but they got so crowded for space that he had to give in or look the fool or worse. There were ten Tans assigned to Culhane House, and Riordan was worried. Culhane was his ace in the hole; not knowing exactly when or how to use his services, he must yet be kept as free as possible to come and go, to be of help when he was needed. So a message was got off quickly, telling him to lie low and wait for orders, and to avoid all contact with the IRA just then.

We all felt his life in great danger, his so-called connections notwithstanding. Things were too bitter by this time. The English were shipping bodies home every day, and every man in Ireland was suspect. Yes, we thought that Culhane's tightrope was fraying a bit more all the time.

Then came a day in May when a boy came up with a message from Culhane, and we all crowded around as Riordan opened it quickly, wondering what disaster it would take to make him risk such a thing. But we knew no more when he'd read it than we had before. All it said was that he wanted a meeting that very night at O'Rourke's house. He'd get there about eleven and wanted Riordan and some of the rest of us urgently. We tried to imagine, as the day went on, what in God's name had happened. More than one of the men were afraid to go, for if Culhane were followed it would be a death trap for every one of us.

There was an hourly patrol, dogs and all, on the river road which led to a dirt road a mile long, and there was O'Rourke's. His place was fairly safe, yet the road had to be crossed to reach it. Riordan, O'Rourke himself, beaming from ear to ear at the thought of seeing his wife for an hour, Jamie, Allie Clarke, and myself made up the number.

We went on foot and arrived without incident about ten minutes before the hour. Culhane was not there yet. Riordan, a man of great delicacy, took care that O'Rourke had a few minutes alone with his wife, whilst we waited in the dark of the barn till we heard the sharp, driving beat of a horse's hoofs approaching.

Riordan looked out cautiously, then nodded to the rest of us. It was Culhane. We waited till he jumped down from the horse. We could hear the beast panting and wheezing, such was the speed by which he'd come. Culhane went into the house after knocking lightly on the back door. But still Riordan held us back a few more minutes, watching the road and the trees around it.

There seemed to be no one about or following behind. Then we went in, one by one, fast across the moonlit yard, cursing the damned gander ever alert to invasion and positively squawking with wrath at each one of us crouching and running across his territory. Somehow at night he seemed to feel it was even more his than ever, although I cannot say I can ever recall a case of a man being treated with respect by a gander, night or day.

Culhane was sitting by the fire when we came in, with a glass of whiskey in his hands. He looked terrible. Riordan kept his eye on the door, I by one window, Allie and Jamie by the other two. Mrs. O'Rourke had disappeared upstairs, and himself, still beaming, was finishing off a ham bone and beer at the table.

"Well, Sean," said Riordan gravely. "What is it that's brought us all here tonight?"

Culhane drew himself together with obvious effort, lean and slick, but it didn't quite come off that time. He looked haggard. I thought he looked haggard, but it might have been that afterwards, after I'd heard what he had to say, I figured he *must* have looked haggard. I can't recall which.

"There's been a wedding," says he, avoiding Jamie's eyes, which were intent upon him.

"Sean—" began Riordan, frowning, but Culhane acted as if he didn't hear him.

"A wedding, I said, and it will likely have some effect upon our organization. I say *likely*. I hope it will not, but I cannot help but think it very well will."

"Who's the man?" asked Jamie, his voice harsh and grating.

Culhane would not turn to make his answer. "It's insanity," he said in that cold voice of his. "Norwood. Charlie Norwood."

I almost laughed then. It was bubbling up in me, the very thought of fat, pudgy Charlie a husband. But then it washed over me like hot bile in the face. My God, I thought, *Margaret's* husband! I looked over at Jamie. He was staring, unmoving, at Culhane. I couldn't even tell whether he had quite taken it all in. Riordan grasped it at once, of course, and sat down quietly, motioning the rest of us closer around the table.

"There's a few things to talk about, then, it seems," he said.

Culhane nodded. He might have been discussing the weather; so might Riordan, for that matter.

"Did you go to it?" asked Riordan.

Culhane nodded again. "What else could I do? It would have seemed strange. After all, I suppose, in a way, he's a 'catch.' " He laughed ironically.

I saw Jamie's hand tighten quickly on his gun, but he

made no move. His face was drained of color; his lips looked like a thin black straight line in the firelight.

"I thought she was joking when she told me," Culhane said. "I knew nothing about it, nothing. Till last week. She came in to talk to me, with him waiting outside, hat in his fat, dirty little hands. I'd seen them drive up together, and wondered why she'd brought him with her. And in she came, tall and haughty, and told me. She didn't ask. She told me Norwood wanted to marry her. You've no idea how she's changed. She said she was going to do it, no matter how I felt about it. I thought for a moment, just a moment, I'd kill her, but one never does at those moments. She stood in front of me with her eyes flashing and the most contemptible smile on her face, and she told me the wedding would be this morning at ten. Then she turned on her heel and went out again. And that fool"—he grimaced in disgust—"waiting outside my door to get my blessing! Well, I brought it off as best I could. Riordan, this puts me in an impossible position."

Riordan was thinking. "It also puts you in a very good position," he said slowly, and Jamie's head went up.

"Riordan!" he cried, but Riordan ignored him.

"You'll have easy access to Norwood's house from now on, as his father-in-law," Riordan said. "You have an opportunity to find out things, with Sydney living there, too."

"Oh, Jesus Christ!" muttered Jamie. Then he got up and walked away from the table. Culhane still said nothing.

"Can you do it, Sean?" Riordan was asking, leaning forward anxiously.

Culhane's lips started to move, but he could bring no sound out. Instead, he barely nodded.

"It won't be easy," Riordan went on. "I won't order you, but I'm asking you, Sean. I know what a blow this must be to you—"

Culhane looked up, startled. "A blow!" he exclaimed. "I spit on her. Was it for this I sacrificed everything all these years? To see her, my last hope in the world, throw herself away on that pig?"

"Easy, easy does it, Sean," murmured Riordan, embarrassed, trying not to feel the man's feelings with him.

Suddenly Jamie whipped around, bumping into a lamp and knocking it down in his haste. "This is your doing!" He hurled the words at Culhane. "All of it! She'd have done anything to get away from you. And now you'll spit on her! She's betrayed you, has she, then? God damn you forever, Culhane, you've destroyed her! What sacrifices did you make? Was it so hard, then, to have all those lords and sirs and colonels trooping in and out of your house all those long, sunny, sociable afternoons? You told me you were saving her up for one of them—God, you made that pretty damned clear. One of *us* wasn't good enough for her. Well, now she's taken one of your own bloody types. Maybe not quite high up enough to suit you, but one of them, anyway. What are you complaining of, Culhane? She's only done what you brought her up to do, hasn't she?"

Culhane flushed and started to his feet. His words came fast and full of bitterness. Hatred flashed between himself and Jamie, with Riordan powerless to halt the flow of it; like an invisible current it ran across the room. We could all feel it and we all drew back from it.

"I have worked for Ireland's freedom all my life," cried Culhane passionately. "And I've tried, in my own way, to make some kind of life for myself. What does a man like you know about a man like me? Or a woman like her? I was trying to make something better for her. Did you think I'd really throw her into your hayloft, Daley—"

"But now you've thrown her into Norwood's arms," rejoined Jamie, his mouth twisting sickly. "And what will you get for all this? Tell us, how does it change your life, Culhane? How does it make it harder?"

"Don't be stupid, Jamie," snapped Riordan, turning around to face him. "Don't you see? Married to a Norwood, how far have her sympathies turned? She knows too much about her father's work—about all of us—"

Jamie's eyes grew enormous. He leaped at Riordan. Only Allie, stepping between them quickly, prevented Jamie from hitting him. I grabbed his arm.

"Let me go!" he cried.

"Jamie, stop this!" Riordan was saying sadly. Culhane stood still, staring defiantly at Jamie.

"What are you accusing her of?" shouted Jamie. "Informing? It would serve you bloody well right if she did turn you in, Culhane! 'Twas you that froze the heart out of that girl long ago and gave her ideas. Your ideas, your goddamned crazy relics of ideas. You taught her well, you madman. She was to be this and she was to be that, and she'd marry a man of her own station and all that rot! You did it, and I curse you, Sean Culhane. You were never a father to her, no, nor to Kevin. You drove them both from you!"

But this was too much for Culhane. With a snarl, he strode across the few feet of space between them and slapped Jamie.

"You low bastard!" he said, as Allie struggled mightily to keep him and Jamie from each other.

But Jamie broke away and slammed out the door. Culhane gazed after him, rubbing the knuckles of his hand.

"Sean, we can't stay long, you know that. The question is, what's to be done?" asked Riordan.

Culhane ran a nervous hand over his thick hair. "I'll stick close. But don't count on anything. Sydney's no fool. I doubt much if he'll invite me to sit in on his councils, such as they are. I'll do what I can, you know that."

Riordan nodded, rising to leave. He took Culhane by the hand and clasped the other arm around Sean's arm awkwardly. He would have liked to say more, but talking to Culhane was never easy.

"I know we can count on you, Sean. There'll be talk, of course," he added, looking away. "Ugly talk. I'll do what I can. She'd best take care till it dies down."

Culhane sneered. "That kind of talk never dies down. It was such a stupid thing for her to do now, of all times! Where will the Norwoods be when peace comes? What did she hope to gain?"

"Maybe she doesn't believe we'll win. There are a lot that don't, you know," said Riordan ruefully.

"Win or lose, she's thrown her life away for nothing!" retorted Culhane.

"Aye, it seems," answered Riordan. "Well, then, we'd best leave first. Take care of yourself, will you, now?"

Culhane barely nodded. As Riordan opened the door to leave, I could see Jamie standing alone outside, smoking a cigarette, looking off across the valley, his face stony and hurt-looking. He didn't glance around, even when he heard the door.

Poor Captain Riordan; he looked out at Jamie, looked back at Culhane, shrugged a bit helplessly and said, very low, "Sean, I'm sorry. I'm very sorry about everything."

"I know," answered Culhane, bitterness framing his few short words like the black border on a mourning card. "Aren't we all?"

And then he added, "Ian—" Riordan turned inquiringly, and Culhane said, "If she says one word to them about any of us, I'll kill her myself, I swear it!"

Riordan nodded sadly, turned away again. Jamie, who had overheard this exchange, threw down his cigarette, stamped on it, and stalked off into the shadows. Ah, Margaret, Margaret *ashthore,* you left our minds reeling and our hearts sick that night, and dark were the thoughts against you then, love turned into hate and despair at such a few words, my poor darling, you did not deserve words, nor those thoughts from us! But we knew nothing of women, nor do we now.

As we moved along in silence next to the stone fence along the road, keeping an eye out for the patrol, we could see their headlights gleaming from the distance, heading our way. I heard the faint sounds of Culhane's horse going back home, and, though I was torn apart by anger and confusion at what Margaret had done, yet I was sick in my stomach with loathing for her father, nor could I find one ounce of pity for him, though others would find much to pity, but I remembered too well the past, and Margaret sitting with the small lamb in her lap, and Jamie's eyes soft and loving on them both. And, with Jamie, I cursed Sean Culhane to hell forever.

Chapter XX

The reaction among the other men to Margaret's marriage was what we'd anticipated and feared.

"Peg Culhane? That's a good one!"

"Do you think Charlie can handle her?"

"Poor Culhane, all his chickens have come home to roost now!"

"Well, Charlie's got the money. You don't think he's been taking the rents all these years without putting by something for himself, now, do you?"

"Ah, Culhane'll never be the same. I never liked the man much, but he's done his bit for Ireland. I always thought the daughter was as like him as a fingernail. Did anyone go to the wedding at all?"

"What a fool she is, to marry Norwood *now*. Once we've won, where does she think Charlie will be but out of a job? The brother will never look at him twice."

Everywhere there was derision and scorn for Margaret, and many expressed hatred, for what she had done was a slap in the face to her father and, in a way, to all of us. I tried to imagine what it was doing to Jamie, but, as the days went by and gradually the men spoke less and less of it all, he pulled away from all of us and kept to himself. He spoke in monosyllables, did his job, ate alone. He rode away from camp and offered no explanations when he returned. Riordan watched him drag about with bleak eyes and worried about him, but never said a word.

As for me, I plunged myself into what lay at hand, trying not to think about it, but it was no use, of course. The more I blocked it out, the more it would return. Early one morning, after I'd been out all night—for nothing, it

289

turned out, for the messenger I'd been awaiting never came at all—instead of riding straight back to camp for breakfast and a sleep I could sore have used, I rode about aimlessly through the hills, paying scant attention to where I was going or who might be interested in watching me go. As it happened, I found myself near the top of our old Running Hill, over the River Road, too far up, I reasoned carelessly, to be seen unless someone was looking for me, and no one was.

I stayed there, oh, maybe an hour, looking down, not thinking, just remembering pictures from the past. When my legs got too stiff to stand, I sat down on the grass, still looking.

It was spring again, coming to Ireland the same painful sweet wrenching way it always had. Everything around me was so new and fair and tender, from the small green shoots of grass to the nesting birds chirping nearby, I was almost afraid to sit for fear of hurting something. I had become such a great hurter of things; I felt as if everything I would touch ever afterwards would be hurt or killed. I tried to hold myself away, against the small things of the world, when I was not too tired to remember them.

Sometime later, I heard a horse's hoofs on the road. I dropped to my stomach, just peering down over the hilltop. The horse moved into view, far below. It was a big black, a beautiful animal. I couldn't make out the rider, man or woman. It might even have been Margaret on old Byron, but that was just my fancy. I could have called down. The way my mind was working on me then, it's a wonder I didn't call! I saw whoever it was glancing over toward the hill, then he laid on the horse with a hard crop and was gone in an instant down the bend of the road. Margaret with a whip? Margaret beat an animal? But, oh, the world was upside down, anyway: Margaret married to Norwood? It was all the same; if one was possible, why not the other?

The sun was very bright and hot over me. I knew I ought to be getting back. I couldn't seem to get up to leave the place. Instead, I rolled over lazily under a clump of thick-growing shrubs and lit up my last smoke. I told myself that when it was finished I'd get myself together and head back to camp.

But it didn't seem I was fair started on the cigarette, when my ears picked up a tiny sound, so small, so faint, it didn't seem right to call it a sound at all. Yet, there it was. It might have been just a fox or a squirrel, or some bird picking about in the brush, but the hair on the back of my neck began to prickle anyway.

I crushed the cigarette into the earth and very slowly grasped the rifle in my hand, my finger around the trigger, a bit too ready to squeeze. I began to sweat. I wanted to fire at whatever was making that sound; though I could see nothing, my ears had been the saving of me often enough to trust them alone. Then it stopped. I waited. Nothing. I was about to jump up and get out fast, when it came again, off to one side about ten yards. It was a bit louder now, and I could tell it was neither a bird nor an animal. It was someone moving stealthily through the trees, stopping every few feet, and whoever it was was headed directly for the crest of the hill.

Cautiously I got to my knees, still keeping well hidden in the shrubbery. I had the rifle pointed right at the spot where he must show himself, a little natural break between two clusters of trees. There was a small, crackling noise of twigs breaking under the weight of human feet, and a figure appeared in my sights, a man with a rifle slung over his shoulders, one hand pushing aside the low branches in his way. It was Jamie.

I don't know what made me stay quiet then. It would have been the most natural thing in the world to jump up and call to him. But I didn't do that. I stayed where I was and watched him as he stopped once more, listened, looked sharply about, and made for higher ground. He passed within six or seven feet of me and never saw me at all.

He reached where he was apparently headed for and, at first, did what I had done. He sat down in the grass, his arms folded, his eyes looking straight out across the valley. He didn't move for about ten minutes. I felt like some damn spy, watching him that way, but there was something curious about his manner, something that made me want to see what he would do next before I made myself known to him. And I knew, too, that whenever I next spoke words to him, they would have to be about Margaret. I was in no hurry for that.

He sighed very hard—it was more like a weird moaning sound—and his head sank down on his chest.

"That does it," says I to myself, and I had actually gotten to my feet, shouldering the rifle, and a good thing it was, too, for the first thing I knew, Jamie had leaped up from the ground, quicker than I, threw his head back, gave out with a wild kind of a whoop, and took off running down the slope, waving his weapon in his hand, his great foolish long legs seeming not to touch the earth at all. He ran carelessly, heedlessly, crashing into small trees and rocks, nearly falling a couple of times, picking himself up impatiently and stumbling on even faster.

Watching him, I knew the black mood was eating his insides, and there was not a thing in all the world I could do to help him. A man in that condition's best left to his devil, whether it be the bottle or a good fight or just a run for a lick of the wind's tongue till he drops and sleeps. I thought he'd surely stop any minute. He knew as well as I that soon anyone riding along that road would be sure to see him coming. Surely he'd stop. Now. Now he must stop, before he was through the last thick clump of trees—but he did not stop. He began zigzagging as he went, but his general downward direction had not changed.

Then, from beyond the road's bending, I heard sounds that about paralyzed me. Motors, lots of them, and the noises of many men talking, laughing, horns honking. They were coming along quickly. In a moment they'd have come into view. Couldn't Jamie hear them? I didn't know. He must have, but he did not stop.

I lit out after him, praying God take the steps for me, for my own legs at their best were never a match in speed or strength for Jamie's. But I ran on, not even daring to risk calling out to him. I went straight down, leaping over stones, crashing through bushes as if they'd never been there. I had to catch up with him before it was too late. I fell, and I guess it was a good thing, for, before I knew what had happened, I'd rolled straight down a good fifteen feet. I picked myself up, raced on after him. He had reached the thick growth of trees just above the road. Twenty feet more and he'd be on it! With a cry like bloody death I shouted, "Jamie! Tans! Tans!"

He hesitated, hearing me, half turned back, and that was my chance. I jumped upon him and dragged him flat to the earth, just as the first of the cars and lorries turned the bend toward us. We lay there in a heap, face down, our legs tangled. But he kept trying to push me off and get to his feet. I had to sit on him, finally, with my two hands squeezed around his blasted neck, before he relaxed and stayed still. I kept my eyes on the road and counted seven vehicles in all, five of them loaded with Tans and the other two low open staff cars. They were headed for Dungarvan.

Neither Jamie nor I moved for a moment after they'd passed. Voices carry far in the clear air of the hills. When they were finally gone, I got off of Jamie and let him get his breath. He did not move, but lay very still, his arms spread-eagled out in the grass. Not a blessed word did I say, but lay there myself, panting, my arm draped over his back, waiting for *him* to say something. That's two lunatic Irishmen for you every time, mark me. Twenty feet between them and perdition, and who in his least of right minds would not have been running the other way, half a mile gone already?

I waited till he pulled himself up and began brushing the leaves and twigs off his clothes. Then I said, "Let's get out of here," and I picked up my rifle and his together, and headed back up the hill. For a minute I was afraid he would not come after me, but then I felt him reach up and take his rifle from me, and he fell into step beside me as we went back to the sheltered top of the hill.

When we were safely out of sight of the road below, we sat down in the grass and he lit up a couple of his own cigarettes, and passed one to me. All this time, mind you, Jamie had not said one word!

"Are you all right?" I asked him. "Maybe you're not so

glad to see me," I added, the whole thing between us flashing back on me in the instant.

"Whisht, now," he answered, but he hadn't said yes and he hadn't either said no.

"Well, where did you think you were going?" I demanded, jerking my thumb to indicate the road below us.

He grinned, but it wasn't his grin. His eyes and his heart weren't in it.

"I was looking for a fight, I guess you'd say," he answered slowly.

"With them?"

He nodded.

"All by yourself?"

"Aye."

"And after that, when you'd emptied your rifle into them and knocked a few of them about a bit, what did you have in mind to do then?"

He stared stonily down at the dark earth we sat on. "Die, I guess," he said. "Why not?" he added defensively.

Well, but this was not Jamie at all. Die, he says! Die, the man says, him that's spent how many damn years of his damned young life trying like the very devil *not* to die?

"I'm that sorry I interfered with your plans!" I retorted. I mean, what the hell kind of an answer can you give to a fool statement like that?

We sat in silence for a while more. Then he said, "Do you think they'll ever leave?"

The sound of his voice startled me. I'd been busy with a few thoughts of my own. "Who, them?"

"Aye, them," he said with a cut of bitterness sawtoothing his voice. "Do you ever stop and think, Jerry, they've been here for hundreds of years? Hundreds. Is it like they'll leave us now, or tomorrow, or, maybe, ever?"

I didn't know what to say. "There's the peace talks—"

"Talks! There's been talks before! What does it ever accomplish? Here we are, hiding out like criminals in our own country and them riding the roads like kings! What kind of a war is this, I ask you, Jerry?" He stood up, arms folded against his chest, leaning against a tree trunk. "Do you know? You've been in it as long as I have. Hit them and run, disappear into the hills, fade into the night before they can muster arms against us. Steal a decent rifle and feel sick and ashamed when the man next to you falls and dies at your feet because he didn't have a rifle at all, maybe just a pistol, if he was lucky, or a pitchfork, or nothing but his two bare hands! And what good is a stolen rifle when the bullets run out and you can't get any more, unless you steal them at rifle point, and pray none of them you're stealing from will make a move, so you'll be forced to pull the trigger and show them there's no bullets there in the first place!

"We fight and fight and listen to speeches and plan what it will be like when they are finally driven out. Half the time I forget what we're fighting for, and it comes down to just that I stand here, and your English soldier or your Tan stands there, and I know I've got to kill that goddamned Englishman because if I don't he's going to damn well kill *me*. What's it all for? Where's the Army we dreamed of? Where are the thousands of Irishmen, uniformed and equipped, fed and shaved, clean and, most of all, *sure,* so damned positively *sure* of what it's all about? Where's the Irish Repubican Army that was going to stand up as one man and walk like a solid wall driving them back and back until they fell into the sea?

"I don't see it. I don't belong to it. Is it there at all? Why haven't they seen it? Why haven't they been driven into the sea and us lined up around the shores like a wall of stone to keep them there? Do you see it? Tell me, Jerry. Do you see the whole thing and am I blind and raving?"

I shook my head. "No. I see just a war, yes, it is a war, one that's gone on for all these years and we seem to be small pieces in the middle of it. I don't know when it'll ever end."

"End?" he echoed, his voice full of hurt and despair. "What end of it is there? For centuries, all our hopes and dreams, all our thoughts and efforts have been directed toward the one goal. I'm almost afraid to wonder what will become of us if they ever do get up and go home. What will we do then that fills our lives and thoughts and excuses our poverty and backwardness and keeps us from looking to marry till we're old enough to be grandfathers and holds us ironbound from the ways of our past or of the rest of the world? I don't know—war is our father and our mother, our sweetheart and our children. War is our ambition and our pride. I wonder, when we win the war and we have our freedom, will freedom be as sweet to us then as war is now?"

"You're crazy!" I broke in. "You sound as if we love war, we love fighting and killing and dying! That's an awful thing to say, what's come over you? All we want is liberty and peace, that's all we're fighting for now, that's all we've ever fought for! *You're* making speeches, talking about *speeches!* And, with all your gab, you still haven't told me why you're so hell-bent on throwing yourself into a one-way battle with the Tans. I mean, you that's talking so sweetly about peace!"

A streak of anger flashed into his deep gray eyes. "Just once I wanted to come out in the open, right up to them, just me and them, and have it out man to man. Just one time, I had it in mind to let them take a look at my face, before they blew it off, instead of the back of my head running away!"

I jumped up, beside myself with fury, and glared down at him.

"You say it as if we'd been running from them, instead of fighting like we have." But he did not answer. I could not rest or be still till my wrath was spent. "Another thing, come to think of it, where the hell have you been these last weeks when I've loooked for you?"

"Oh, have you been looking that hard for me, Jerry?" His voice was hard; he gazed past me over the valley, and his thoughts suddenly seemed remote and unreachable again.

He had me there. I'd been far from seeking him out, and I guess he knew it. Since I'd heard of Margaret's marriage I knew the two of us would have to talk it out, but it hurt so badly just to think about it I hadn't wanted to take the chance of it coming up.

"Look, Jamie," I faltered, "about Margaret . . ."

His eyes grew black. He turned to me and, in the coolest tone I've ever heard from his mouth, he said, "I know about Margaret."

"I *know* you know about her," I snapped in exasperation. "Leastways, you know what Culhane told you, what the others are saying about her. But I remember that once you promised her brother you'd never desert her and you'd always be her friend—"

"She doesn't need a friend," he cried, with contempt and pain in every syllable he uttered. "She's got a husband now."

"Oh, for God's sakes, Jamie!" I blew up altogether. "Where's your mind at, man? You don't think she really loves that *shivereen,* do you?"

He leaned his head back as if suddenly his neck ached unbearably from carrying it around. "I wish to God she did love him!"

"What?"

He looked over at me, a scornful smile on his face. "I've seen her, Jerry."

"What did you say?" I gasped. "What are you talking about?"

"I've seen her, talked with her, that's what I'm saying."

"Margaret! When? Where? How did she look? What did she say?" I jumped on him. I might have known, if a meeting like that could be managed at all, Jamie would manage it.

"When?" he began thoughtfully. "About ten days ago, in the early evening it was. I hate that time of day: sun gone, moon still only a promise. It's a time I want to go away somewhere by myself or sleep through it, if I can, or be indoors by a bright fire, with yellow lamps lit and steam curling up from a teakettle near my nose. That day there was a rain that lasted through the whole afternoon and stopped with the dusk, no sunshine breaking through the clouds afterwards, not even a minute's worth of rainbow, just that damn bleeding away of all the colors in the world, that *dead* time of day.

"I'd gone down, been going down every day I could, to find her. I had to see her, just once. I rode Dan straight down into the valley—now, don't preach—that's where I've been every minute I could get away, mostly at night, mostly in the dead of night, like some poor Godforsaken banshee haunting the old meeting places, some of them anyway, places where I was pretty sure I'd be safe enough—"

"Pretty sure!" I exploded.

"I told you I was looking for a fight," he said. "I guess I did kind of hope they'd find me, one of those times, and have it out and over with. That's the mood you found me in today.

"Well, that evening I went cross country, through the fields and over the ditches, to the bridge. I tethered Dan under it and let him graze—it's little enough of valley grass he gets these days, anyway—and I sat myself on the embankment and thought about her.

"It was strange the way it happened. I was thinking so hard about her, staring out at the water, and I saw something moving along the bridge, very quiet and very slowly, not a shape at all at first, just something that moved the light for an instant. I don't know why, but I wasn't afraid. I damn well should have been, but I wasn't. I didn't move. I kept staring into the haze, watching the bridge, and in another minute I saw her. Margaret, on foot, and that's a hell of a walk from Dunknealy!

"She was wrapped in a gray shawl, or it might have been black, it was getting harder and harder to see. I could tell she hadn't seen me. She paid no attention to anything, but walked that tall, straight way she always walked, one arm holding the shawl close about her, and she stayed to one side of the bridge, near the water, and kept looking down at it. She looked like you'd imagine that old Irish goddess Erihu might have, all these years walking and weeping alone through the land! I had the crazy notion that she was trying to make up her mind to jump in . . ."

"Och, now, Jamie!" I cried. His voice was miles away, his eyes half closed. He didn't hear me.

"I got up from where I was sitting, quietly, and swung myself up on the bridge. I had to hurry, I thought, I wouldn't even wait to run around to the foot of the bridge, and if she were to hear me and my boots clanking on the wooden planks, she might do it, or at least the sound might frighten her and make her run away from me.

"I did frighten her, what a great clown I was, jumping up just in front of her eyes, out of the fog and the mist when she thought she was all alone! She didn't know me for a minute, till I spoke to her. She looked at me with those eyes—you recall those big, dark eyes on her, Jerry? She looked all about and tried to turn and run back, only I said, Margaret? It *is* you, Margaret Culhane!

"She put a hand up to her mouth, as if she might scream and didn't want to, and she took a step closer to me and looked and looked so long at my face I wondered had I changed so much in just a couple of years that she wouldn't know me at all.

" 'Jamie?' she whispered, and her other hand touched my arm. It did, only just a second, but I felt it light there like a bird, and then it was gone, down at her side, and the fingers hidden away in the folds of her skirts.

" 'Aye, it's me,' I said to her. 'We've met on the bridge as we promised, you remember?'

"She smiled fleetingly and it was gone, like her touch on my arm—there was all of a bird about her, quick-flitting, then gone. Could anything keep her, I thought, while I stood there and looked at a phantom of a woman. Could anything hold her and keep her from leaving that bridge and vanishing back into the swirl of the mist again?

" 'Are you well?' she asked, her eyes taking me all in at once.

" 'Yes, well,' I stammered. 'And yourself?'

"She started to speak, but a shadow came suddenly into her eyes. She drew back from me—can you imagine Margaret pulling herself away from me, Jerry? And I loving her—and she knew it! But she pulled back, and the hand went up and drew the shawl around her throat and she stuck out her chin in that stubborn way she had.

" 'I'm wonderful, thanks,' says she. 'I suppose you've heard I've married,' she added defiantly, as if I would throw it up in her face! I thought she hated me. When did she start in to hating me, and what for, Jerry *bawn?*" he interrupted himself in anguish. I could make no answer, nor did he really expect one.

"All the leaving was on her side, aye, and all the marrying too!" he exclaimed, his voice a shock of anger and bitterness. "When she said that, and looking at me with those walled-off eyes as she said it, and that toss of the head, like she was saying to me, 'And look how well I've done once I rid myself of you,' I believed all they were saying about her, Jerry!

"From that moment, everything they said fitted together, and I was sure and certain she'd sold herself into the arms of that bastard Norwood! A look flashed between us in the darkness there on the bridge and, before I knew what I was doing, I lifted my hand and slapped her proud face with the flat of my hand, a blow that left five red fingers welted into her cheek!"

I closed my eyes, feeling the sorrow fill out and spread through my veins and choke off my breath and clutch at my heart. Ah, Margaret, I mourned, whatever you did, you didn't deserve that blow from those hands.

"What happened then?" I asked dully.

"I stood there, with my hand still raised from the swing I took at her. As I saw the welts stand out on her face and the tears start from her eyes, I thought I had died and was standing in hell and that I'd have to be spending eternity on that bridge hating her and hitting her and loving her all together, without ever being able to tell her or take her in my arms and make her forget it. I thought maybe that was my punishment for all the blood I've been shedding and, oh, maybe just for being born Irish under the sovereign crown of England. I don't know. It was so terrible to see her!

"Any other girl would have hit back or fallen down and drowned down the river with crying, or screamed and run off, but not Margaret. Not Margaret. She never moved, nor put a hand out to feel the weals on her skin, nor lowered her eyes, nothing like that. She threw her head high, like a queen, her face pale around the red marks, her eyes running with tears. She stared at me, her mouth closed, saying nothing. I remember I lowered my arm then. When she saw that—God, I guess she thought I wasn't finished hitting her! But when she saw my hands hanging by my sides, she dried her eyes with the edge of the shawl and drew it around her again, over her cheek so you couldn't see the marks, and she said to me, 'Goodbye, then, to you, Jamie Daley,' and she turned to walk away.

"But I couldn't let her go, Jerry, not if I'd had to throw her to the ground and hold her as you did with me today. I wouldn't let her go like that, a goodbye and there's an end to it. No. No, I didn't know what I could say. I didn't have any right to say anything. But I reached out and took hold of her two arms from behind and I pulled her back against me—ah, the lightness and slimness of her!—and I held her there with her head tight against my throat and the fresh smell of her hair rising up in my face. I said, 'I love you, Margaret Culhane, before God, I love you!'

" 'No!' she cried, and she turned herself around in my arms and tried to look at me, but I held her fast, till she settled sort of warm and drowsy, and I could feel her light breath near my cheek. I think if I'd let go of her then, she'd have fallen down. Her body was all atremble.

" 'This cannot be, Jamie,' she said. I cared not what she had to say, for I had her there where she always belonged, close in my arms, and there was nothing in the world or heaven or hell could've taken her from me then. I took her little dark head in my hand and I pushed the shawl away from her face and I kissed her.

"I kissed the bruised cheek and every red mark I had made. I kissed her eyes where I'd made the tears come, and I kissed her mouth.

" 'You're not his wife, Margaret,' I said.

"She shook her head. 'I am. That's the truth. I am his.'

" 'But you love me, even so,' I said, small satisfaction in that. She shook her head, and looked away.

" 'Tell me you love him, Margaret,' I cried. 'Can you tell me that? Can you?'

" 'Let me go now, Jamie!' she said, and she dropped her arms from where they had crept up around my neck.

" 'Say it!' I cried, before she would fade into the night again and maybe for the last time. 'Say it once. I don't care what lies you've told all this time, tell the truth once and I'll leave you in peace, Margaret!'

"She gave me her smile then, but if it was meant to give a man peace, she doesn't know what the word means.

" 'I've always loved you, James Daley,' she said very simply. 'Didn't you know that? Goodbye.' Just that, just 'Goodbye,' and she turned and ran quickly across the bridge away from me. Jerry, whoever it was invented words can't have known the sorrow and regret and the ending of everything that goes into that one damn word, 'goodbye'!"

He sat now with his face buried in his hands, his voice barely audible.

"It only means 'God be with you,'" I reminded him bleakly. "That's as good a thought for a leaving as any, and better than most."

"And now she's married to that pig!" he went on, paying no attention at all to me. "She'll stay with him. I know Margaret. She went that far to spite her father, to pay him back for all he did to her, to escape something she was afraid of, ah, I don't know. But it's as if she'd gone and killed herself and all there is left of her walks the damp fields of Ireland in the middle of the night like a soul in hell never resting! God!" he cried out remorsefully, "*I* was the one who built her castles in the air about when she'd be married and free of Culhane, and happy. Happy! You remember, she was going to have herself three fine sons and name them for Kevin and you and me—" And then it came out at last. I saw the grief and the longing shake him with a long, shuddering sob. His shoulders shook.

"I've lost her forever now, God help me! And God help her!" he cried fiercely, and he turned his head away, giving me a rough push to go on and leave him alone.

So I simply walked away and left him leaning, trembling, against the tree, his face against the rough bark. I heard him pound the tree with his fists and cry out over and over, "Oh, damn the war! Damn the war!" And, in my heart of hearts, how I echoed those sad words, as I waited for him a little farther up on the hill, my rifle ranging in an arc over the space around him in case anyone might come upon him and he in that condition.

So that was the way it was to end—but I was wrong, as it turned out, for Margaret's marriage seemed to be only the beginning of a great tangle of trouble.

Something was up, right here in Waterford. The hurricane's hot breath began swirling down below us and I soon found out that nothing is ever really over, not war, not hate, not love—nothing ends.

Chapter XXI

Now a stillness hung over us, in which nothing seemed to move; we half dreamt our way through the days. One was like another, perhaps it was all just one endless repeated nightmare, as, perhaps, the world is that dust mote in the giant's eye they talk of. But forces were at work, you understand, that we knew nothing about and had no control over. Whoever of us was brooding about private griefs soon enough found little time for them for grief was building that would soon burst upon us like pent-up waters from a flooding river.

It began with young Mick O'Sullivan. Mick was what people in America think of, I suppose, when they think of a young Irishman. He was good-looking, nice even features, a big mop of hair, a quick smile, a way with words, and all the girls loved him, or so I heard. He was a favorite with everyone. The only thing Mick really hated was Tans and boiled tin beef, and since he'd been up with us in the hills, he'd had more than his share of both.

Mick was from Ballyduff. He'd only been with us eight or nine months. He'd been on his way to sea, but he'd taken a job in Dunknealy, then dropped it quick enough when he had his first smell of Tans and, by ways and ways, he found himself joining up. I think he was just turned eighteen when he came to us.

He was the only good laugh any of us had had in a long time, and that was because of his moon-calfing around about Cathy O'Mahoney. She was a pretty little girl with wheat-colored hair and big, surprised gray eyes and a laughing voice. I met her a couple of times and liked her very much.

It took Mick a long time to win her, for she'd suitors aplenty and he hadn't much time for proper courting, the way things were. But, once he'd won Cathy's heart, well, Mick was a strapping young man, living alone and in misery away from any soft touch of comfort or affection, like the rest of us, and Mick began to pine away, as they used to say, for the sight (and it's not for me to say what else) of pretty Cathy.

Cathy lived with her family in a small village named Clonkill, a mile or two downriver. Sure it was hardly a village at all, really. It had one store and a few decent houses, but mostly cottages clustered about that had been put up God knows how long ago, in rows, by the Norwood family, as they had gone about putting the owners off their lands and taking the farms for themselves. Some of the men of Clonkill made a few shillings at odd jobs and in planting and harvest seasons, but it was a poor, wretched place, all in all, and those in it hardly less so. Still, the rose blooms in the dung heap, and somehow Cathy lived and grew and loved our Mick.

Now, the laugh of it was just this: Mick could think of a hundred different reasons why Riordan should send him off on missions or errands or with dispatches or what have you, anything, you see, so he could get himself out of camp with a chance to drop off for a while with Cathy. Riordan was wise to the thing and, though he felt for the lad, rarely let him off alone, for he was a stranger to the

hills and easily lost. Moreover, he was not wary enough
for his own good.

But, as the months passed, the humor of the situation
began to die away as poor Mick became more and more
sour and sullen. God knows, none of us was exactly
blooming any way you want to look at it, and none of us
had been with a woman far longer than Mick. I can't rec-
ommend that way of life; indeed, I could hardly survive
it, looking back, and I believe half the rage of killing was
just the urge of loving twisted around all wrong. That was
why we felt good after a battle, for a while, just for a
while. It got the longings out of us, in a horrible way;
maybe that's how we might end wars, come to think of it.
Let the world's women open their arms and hearts to the
men gladly and freely; let there be loving, at least, if there
cannot be love. Oh, sure, it's simplistic to the point of
simple-mindedness and there's lots more that should go
along with it, but you recall we are speaking of desperately simple-minded activities, such as suffering and killing
and dying.

Never mind, now, it was Mick we were speaking of.
Well, one week and all that week we could tell something
was up with the boy. He was more than restless, he was
obsessed with getting away. I heard him ask Riordan, and
then I heard him beg Riordan and finally I heard him
demand that Riordan give him overnight leave, and that,
mind you, with every Tan within twenty miles picking
every leaf and blade of grass over for us!

Well, of course, what could Riordan say but what he
had always said, and that was no. I heard Mick's angry
voice, though I couldn't make out his words. I tried to
make a small joke of it to Jamie, who was painstakingly
cleaning his rifle by the firelight, silent as he had become.
But my joke died on my lips, for he was not listening.
Then Mick came stomping out of Riordan's tent, cursing
and swearing under his breath. Someone in his way
laughed and called out, "Better luck next time, darlin'!"
and Mick kicked him aside. There were muffled curses in
the dark, sounds of scuffling. Nobody bothered to get up
and look or try to stop it. Soon enough the sounds died

away; the fire began to die down, and most of us fell asleep. But not Mick. He sat staring down into the sea for a long time. Then, we never knew what time it was, he left camp and headed over toward Clonkill.

He was nearly at the village, going to Cathy's house, which was the last in a row of cots at the edge of the eastern end of town. And he was spotted by a Tan patrol. They caught him walking along the side of the road, the poor damned young fool, in the glare of their searchlights mounted on the back end of a lorry. They called out for him to stop. Mick began running.

They shot at him, and hit him, but he kept on going. He made it to Cathy's house, where one look at him told the worst of the story. There were only four Tans; they came into the village to have a look round, banged on a few doors, routed out a few people, but nobody really had noticed anything. When they saw they were getting nowhere by themselves, three of them stayed to keep watch in case they would spot him again, and the fourth went with the lorry to get help.

Meanwhile, Mick was half conscious, not even realizing the danger he had put his girl and her family in. They tried to fix him up as best they could, but it wanted a doctor to look at it. No one knew what to do. They could not fetch in a doctor. Word of the dilemma spread through the village, despite the presence of the Tans, as word always spreads about from person to person, and no one in all Clonkill knew what was to be done. All they did know was that the Tans would come back, and there would be a lot of them.

Now an odd thing happened there that night in that little, miserable village. Sure, think of it, wasn't it *built* beaten into the ground to start with? What right or reason did those wretched people have to feel or think or plan or *think* of planning, and especially what they did plan, those contemptible, hopeless excuses for human beings? Hadn't the whole world spun round them and they not affecting it or being noticed at all? Where, then, did they get the audacity, do you suppose, to decide as they decided, to defy the Tans?

At any rate, at the first light of dawn, Sydney Norwood and fifty of his best (that's a comparative term, you understand!) entered Clonkill. They came in Sydney's open car and two battered lorries full of men, armed with rifles to which bayonets had been handily attached ahead of time. They headed straight for the small cottages on the east side, for that was somewhere around where the fugitive, Mick, had been spied earlier.

There were the cots, poor old ramshackle, thatched-roof huts was all they were, and nothing much alive in them but poor, old ramshackle leavings of families that had barely managed to find the eight shillings a month for the rent and little more besides.

Clonkill was very quiet as Sydney rode in. No one, not a soul, out on the streets. But they were in the houses and in the store, peering sullenly out at him and his men from behind closed doors and windows. The whole silent village watched the road as Norwood rode in, down the main and only street, out past the stables, to the cottages.

If it had been Charlie, now, and he an old hand at getting what he wanted from people, ah, Charlie would have had sense enough to know that nothing was to be accomplished that day. Charlie would have turned himself right around and ridden the hell out of there. Charlie would have figured a way to get someone to want very much to turn poor Mick over to him, and that would have been that. For one thing Charlie had learned in Ireland, when the people are united together for anything, a whistling wind out of purgatory wouldn't split them.

But Sydney got upset at the sight of the empty, sunlit street, streaked red light on gray stones in the morning light, the windows staring blindly at him, and him a grand big target up there in his open car. And the truth is, you know, that if every eye that stared at him that day had a bullet in it and a muzzle sticking out from it and a trigger handy to it, Sydney would have been ground to a garnish and not much of that.

Up and down the cobblestones rode Sydney and his car, as the two lorries full of Tans, bayonets pricking the fresh sunny air, rode behind him. Perspiration was oozing into his starched collar and fury clawing a scrawny hand up into his prideful guts. When they reached the raw turf of the dirt road that ran alongside the cots, the Tans pulled up and jumped out, stretching themselves out into a double line along side of the roadway. Sydney too got out of his car, and went striding up to one of the cottage doors.

Sydney knocked. No answer. He knocked again, very loudly, and this time a little voice called out, "Who's there?"

The Tans thought that was terribly funny. They almost burst their lungs laughing. Sydney waited till the amusement had died away. He was very loath to answer. His dignity was suffering somewhat to start with. The whole thing didn't suit his style.

"I've come to arrest a fugitive from the Irish Republican Army," he shouted. "You've got five minutes to come out here and turn him over to us. After that, we'll move you out and find him ourselves."

No answer. No answer at all, and, after he'd stopped speaking, the silence was all the more silent for its having had nothing important said into it.

Norwood signaled the sergeant of his troop. The sergeant signaled two of his men. Together the three of them advanced on the small house with their rifle butts raised. The sergeant began pounding on the door, whilst the other two smashed in the small windows. There were screams from inside, and someone quickly unlatched the front door.

"Out!" ordered the sergeant. Out they came, an old lady, two younger women with black shawls drawn over their heads and shoulders, and three small, scrawny children. They clung to each other there in the road, shrinking back from the Tans, not daring to raise their eyes to Sydney.

"Is he in there?" asked that gentleman smartly, and the old lady began to cry.

"We have no more. We have no more! You can't take no more from us!"

One of the younger women put an arm about her, mur-

muring, "No, no, Mother; it's all right, now," and Sydney
bit his lip and walked away from the little group.

'Wait, wait!" called the old woman desperately, breaking away from her daughter. "Yer Lordship, what's to become of us?"

Sydney ignored her. She stared about, confused, then
started to usher the children back inside the house again.
The Tans stood between them and the door.

One of the younger women spoke up. "Our things are
in there. Clothes and dishes and the furniture. They belong to us." Then she too headed for the doorway. One
of the men shoved her back.

"You'll touch nothing," called out Sydney. "Sergeant,
keep those people still."

The poor old lady thought they were being evicted, you
see; she didn't understand what was going on.

"What's he say, Patsy? What's he say?" queried the old
lady, pulling at the girl's arm.

"He says we're not to touch anything that's ours," said
the girl coldly, watching Norwood's progress.

The old lady ran after Sydney and fell to her knees on
the dirt road.

"Lord Norwood, Lord Norwood," she quavered. She
always called anyone named Norwood "Lord." They were
all chicks out of the same egg. She grabbed at the sleeve
of his crisply starched blouse with her two old hands.
Sydney wrenched his arm away, but she wouldn't let him
be.

"Where are we going to go?" she cried, tears springing
from her faded blue eyes. "I was born in that wee cot. My
children were born there. We always paid the rent. It's in
your book. Look in your book. We're down regular every
month, Your Lordship, ain't we? And it was harder than a
big rich man like yourself could know, to raise the shillin's, all those thousands of shillin's!"

Sydney Norwood pushed her away and told her daughter to keep her quiet. He walked on, but she would not be
quiet. The daughters and the little ones came running to
her and tried to lift her from the road, but still she knelt
weeping, keening, with her thin, shaking arms outstretched,

beseeching heaven and God and all the saints to testify to every penny she had bled out all through the years of her life. Heaven was very, very quiet that day.

At the next house there was more trouble. The door was latched; the Tans had to break it down. Those inside came out quickly enough then, hands raised in the air. The Tans searched inside quickly. Mick was not in there. Sydney went to the next door and the next and the next. It was the same. They opened the doors, or waited till the Tans knocked the door from their hinges, and then they walked out quietly. They gathered themselves around the grieving old woman and stood staring stolidly at the Tans. The women did not weep. The children were still, trying to look brave. The only men were old men. They avoided each other's eyes. But now Sydney came to a house halfway down the row. He pounded on the door. No one answered him. But when he ordered the Tans in, there rose a sudden, small sound of laughter and it grew and grew and traveled through the air until it even reached the little huddled group there by the edge of the road. And every remaining locked little house seemed to rock from the sound of it.

Then the children began to smile and put voice to the smile, for children always will see hope in laughter, and their voices grew into and mingled with the other laughter. And the black-shawled, dry-eyed women joined in, and the old men pulled their backs straight and looked at each other and cackled until finally the whole street rang with it, and only the one little old lady didn't seem to hear it at all, but carried on her lamentations, "Sweet Jesus, Lamb of God, don't take us from our home!"

They were at the bottom of the cliff, you see. They had nothing else to make answer with. They fought bare-handed from the pit with black Irish laughter, the kind that people have mistaken for gaiety for a thousand years. But gay it is not, for all the rollicking strong sound of it. It is desperate and lacks a note of joy in all its range.

The Tans, angered by the laughter, moved in quickly. They surrounded the remaining houses. But when they broke the windows with their rifles, hands appeared and threw dishes at them, benches, chairs, pots, a hail of household furnishings, and drove them back to the road. There they gathered and again stormed the doors, and again fell back in confusion, for every stick of furniture inside had been piled up behind the doorways.

Sydney Norwood was panting with rage and frustration.

"Shoot! Shoot!" he screamed hysterically. So the Tans fired into the windows, into the splintered wood of the doors. The laughter ceased abruptly. A silence came into the air and hovered there as Norwood glanced about him, and the Tans waited, eyeing the cots blackly, their fingers still resting impatiently on the triggers. Sydney strode over to his car and took a bullhorn out of it, held it up to his mouth and began to speak.

"You must turn over the traitor to us at once. If you cooperate now, only those harboring him will be arrested. The others may go free. You can go back to your houses. I repeat: Give us the man immediately and we will leave you in peace."

Then he called over the sergeant and spoke to him briefly, glancing at the cots now and again. The little group on the road watched warily now; even the old lady fell silent. Not a movement was seen in all the village.

The sergeant went to the back of one of the lorries, taking four men with him. They lifted out two great ten-gallon tins of petrol. Still, no one said a word.

Quickly they tossed the petrol all over the cottage walls and threw the still-spewing cans up on the thatched roofs. When this was done, Sydney, who had been leaning against the front of his car, watching, his face twisted with anger, came forward, picked up the horn again and shouted.

"For the last time, come out, give yourself up!" he roared, now directly addressing his unseen adversary.

"We'll see you in hell first, Norwood!" called someone from inside one of the cots. Another voice from way down at the end of the row yelled, "Up the Republic!"

Sydney turned deadly pale, smiled his strange smile, and threw a lighted match at the first building. Nothing happened. The match went out as it traveled through the air. He ground his teeth and lit another one. The sergeant, who had served time for arson long before the days of his glorious army career, spit laconically out of the corner of his mouth, stepped forward, and fired one shot into the petrol-soaked wood and straw.

Instantly flames shot up from roof to roof, licking at the corner beams, spitting and sizzling through the few miserable patches of grass and bushes around the houses. Bright, oh, so awfully, dreadfully bright, the little burning houses made a threadbare holiday fire, barely a decent Yule-log blaze, and then, as the fire began to spread, a man called out, "Norwood, wait!"

Sydney turned. Behind him about five feet, out from the last house in the row, staggered a young man, Mick it was, pale as a cloud, leaning with his arm about Cathy, who stared Sydney down with hatred in her face. Mick stood and waved weakly.

"Stop, I give myself up. Put the fire out, quick!"

Sydney looked at Mick curiously for a long moment. Then, almost casually, he pulled out his revolver and shot Mick dead and the girl on top of him. He waved the gun at the Tans, and quickly they began to fire the other houses across the way.

"Too late," muttered Sydney, putting his gun away again. "They had their chance. Now they'll pay."

As the fire leaped through the houses, out they came, screaming, coughing, cursing, tearing away the piled-up chairs and tables and chests from the doorways. Some ran out, their clothing a red shroud of flames, falling down and rolling about frantically in the dirt road.

But Sydney Norwood was not finished with Clonkill yet. As the people came scrambling to escape the fire, the spindly timbers already crashing down behind them, they ran into the face of a machine gun, mounted on the back of one of the lorries, spitting death at them. The other Tans, at a signal from Sydney, opened fire into the crowd with their rifles, close up, every man a marksman and targets aplenty right before his eyes. No one was laughing now, except maybe Sydney Norwood, and he was enjoying himself too much to laugh at all.

They didn't have a chance, but came and were hit and doubled up and fell. Some tried to reach the Tans. Some tried to crawl away. Some women fell shrieking upon the living bodies of their children, but English bullets were made of sterner stuff and traveled easily through the thickness of two bodies, two thin and hungry bodies, without marked decrease of effects.

It was over in five minutes. Twenty bodies lay still, sprawled in the dirt. The fire belched and hiccuped and simmered itself down to leavings. All the good stuff had been burnt up quickly. Sydney Norwood wiped his dripping face with a handkerchief already soaked with sweat. He looked at the ruined cottages. Ruin, all was ruin. Bad business, for he just realized what the old lady had been babbling about. Good God, this was evidently Norwood land, and Norwood cottages, and Norwood tenants! What would Charlie say? The hell with Charlie, what would Lord Johnny Rob back home in England waiting for his rents say? Bad business. A dead loss. He began to giggle nervously, and backed away, stumbled, and fell awkwardly over one of the bodies. He reached about him in the muck, frantically trying to pull himself up.

He had just made it to his knees, when the first stone came flying through the air. It hit him on the ear. Then came another, catching him between the eyes, and down he went again. He looked up, sputtering, to take in the little group of women, children, creaking old men slowly advancing on him, their hands filled with stones. He'd forgotten them, the first ones out. They'd thrown themselves on their faces at the first sound of the gunfire. He had forgotten all about them, damned clods, what did they think they were about?

Now the short space of air between him and them was suddenly dotted with flung, flying stones. Silently the people advanced behind their pathetic barrage. Sydney shuddered. They'd tear him apart! Where were his men?

"Fire, fire, you fools!" he screamed, edging back and back away from the group, pulling himself painfully to his feet, feeling his own blood hot and stinging, oozing from his face and his ear.

There was one more burst of gunfire then. They hadn't had to aim. It was all over. Like pricked balloons, they gasped and burst out air, and died, falling on their dead neighbors' hospitable soft corpses.

The sergeant helped brush Sydney off properly, without comment of any kind. He offered Sydney a fresh handkerchief, and escorted him back to his car.

"They're all crazy!" said Sydney, shaking his head over it. The sergeant was inclined to agree with him, looking back over his shoulder as he remarked.

"Well, that will teach them," said Sydney, pressing the fresh handkerchief to his bleeding ear. The sergeant allowed as how it certainly ought to, it was an example of what could happen to people shielding a fugitive from justice. Sydney liked the word, *example*. That was what he would tell Charlie. He had made an *example* of these people, and, as for the fact that the Norwoods themselves owned the land and the houses on it, why, that should certainly prove to the world that they meant what they said and backed up their loyalty to the motherland with blood, if need be!

With a tired wave of his hand, Sydney signaled his driver to go on. The Tans piled into their two lorries and, at seven-thirty in the morning, they drove out of Clonkill, leaving poor Mick and his Cathy and a lot of other people lying down amidst the blood and ashes.

Oh, man dear, did you ever stop to think what a world of troubles might be spared if only we could be everywhere or know what was everywhere? Each of us can only see his little part in things, and without knowing the whole of the cloth, how much of a misery we can make. Whilst armies fought and died, and far away in England men tried to swallow their pride and sue for peace and other men tried to swallow their indignation and listen to their suit, and far away in Ulster—which, by God, let's not forget, was, is, and always will be the fifth part of Ireland —there we were, and Clonkill its little cross thread of the skein, and things going on to do with us we'd no knowledge of or power to avert. And later, when all the threads were finally pulled together, ah, what difference did it make *then?* The time was all and the knowing came too late. Sure there's a time when having a five-pound note can make the difference between living and dying, as Jamie used to say, and when that time has passed, one way or another, all the five-pound notes in heaven and hell won't help at all.

There went Sydney Norwood after his short morning's work, and the dirty smoke from his grand car's exhaust following behind him like the stench of sulphur they say follows Satan about. Think, in such a small, sweet-smelling land as this, think how great and wicked a cloud the smoke from that small village burning made as it rose up into the fresh morning sky. Think of that morning; you have such mornings in America still, despite all they write of, have you not? Someplace, you still have mornings when you and all that makes the morning are one?

Well, many a time I have seen the milky morning mists waft in from the sea, spreading themselves under the sun's eye, across the treetops soft and billowy, shining like the web of a spider after a rain, in the early, early light of day. And I saw the mists just like any other day, and that was the morning Clonkill was burned to death.

Aye, just like any other morning, the sun and the mists rose from sleep, calling them that were able to rise up, too. And we were able still. Yes, up we rose, stretching and yawning like any other day, hearing the far-off call of the geese in the valley and the cries of love-weary cocks strutting their coops, bragging of what they'd done in the night, one to the other, from sun-slanted farm to farm down below us.

Yes, we had slept that night; did you think we would not be able to sleep, then? We'd slept although the smoke from Clonkill had curled up gray and dim and stinking in our nostrils under the dawn's full shine. But even if the world is weeping and the women keening, the soldier sleeps. Work is for the next day. It is all there, waiting to be done, and the soldiers sleep. Some of us did not sleep so well, it is true, for there was killing to be done, and the night before killing is for sitting up by a fire, maybe, waiting and thinking and cleaning your rifle a couple of times more, waiting and thinking and saying goodbye to everything in your mind once again, till you're tired of saying goodbyes and feel, instead, like saying to hell with them all and what does it matter anyway, because I'm not coming back tomorrow, I know it. And you remember without any smile at all that you said the same thing the last time, and you realize with a bitterness as bitter as the stale taste of the cigarette you're passing around for a bit of a smoke that every time you've said it has only made it more likely to be true the next time. And finally, one day, it is the last time, and you die regretting, after all, that you never had a chance to say goodbye to anyone, knowing all the new things you know and feeling so different and so much closer to them all, and never being able to tell it because you're dead or because, if you did live through it again, they'd never understand anyway and it's best left forgotten amongst the men you shared it with. I remembered faintly when we had all been fond of a fight, but if God had thought up some different ending to a battle instead of death, we'd have welcomed the change.

But you see, now, the night before we'd had no chance to sit and think such thoughts, and perhaps it was just as well. For what had happened at Clonkill was not to be the end of the madness, but the real beginning. Up to then, it had been a war of sorts. From that night on, it was a frenzy for killing that came upon us, with reason or no, there was madness on both sides.

We heard the news late in the day and we went down later that night, at the dark of the moon, to find them still burying the bodies, every man turned undertaker and gravedigger. We searched for Mick and his Cathy. One tired, sooty, grimy old man, leaning on his shovel for a rest, pointed wordlessly toward the end of the row of corpses, and we found them.

They'd laid them out together, their hands clasped, and all of Cathy's small family nearby. There were none of her people left to mourn, so we took the two of them and rode to O'Sullivan's house in Ballyduff. We wrapped their bodies in an old blanket. Riordan got down and knocked hurriedly, the rest of us staying mounted, for patrols were all over and we couldn't even stay to hear a prayer. When Mick's mother came to the door, a shawl thrown over her white nightgown, her hair plaited in two gray braids hanging down over her breast, she found her son and his girl lying across the threshold. Riordan, with tears in his shadowed eyes, told her what had happened, then leaped back to his horse and rode away.

I looked back, fool that I was, and saw the father, tall, like Mick, holding high a lantern behind the mother, as she sank down on her knees and cried out, and smoothed the bloody hair from Cathy's poor, pale face, and picked up Mick's stiff hand and cradled it against her body, rocking and moaning, whilst the father tried to get her to help him bring the two bodies into the house. I turned away then, and rode fast, till I caught up to Riordan. His face was set and grim, his pipe clenched like a new-grown fang between his teeth, and he rode along in silence, slouching low on the brown gelding.

Later we sat around an early-morning fire, whilst everything was still gray and cold as our thoughts, and we watched Riordan silently breaking small twigs one by one in his thin-fingered hands, carefully throwing the pieces into the flames until I thought I'd go mad if he didn't say something soon.

Then, at last, he spoke. "I'm going to send for reinforcements. We can't handle this kind of thing. We are too few here."

A small, suppressed cheer passed through the men. At last, we thought, oh God, for once to fight like an army and have done with it, victory or defeat, life or death, just *once* to fight in the daytime facing the enemy and letting them see it on your face as you came on.

"I know," continued Riordan, sighing a bit, "I know full well that many of you have wanted us to take a different tack all along. But you knew that was impossible. Gentlemen, I must tell you, it may still be impossible. We cannot move without orders. But my orders do not cover this kind of situation. Norwood's gone mad altogether. In other times I daresay even the regular British Army might take a hand against him, but these are extraordinary times and we must do it ourselves. Dublin must be informed of the situation and made to understand what we're up against."

Jamie spoke up. "You'll not risk a man traveling up there now? Will you use the radio, then?"

Riordan shook his head. "No, the radio's out. It's only for short messages at best. This will have to be done in person. I'm going myself. Tomorrow. O'Rourke will take over command till I get back."

"You're crazy—sir!" protested Jamie, and Riordan laughed joylessly.

"Possibly," he admitted. "But that's the way it is, you see. Oh," he seemed to say it as an afterthought, "by the way, Jerry, I've a job for you. Try to arrange it for this coming Friday, if you can suit both sides."

"What's that, sir?"

"Get down to Sean Culhane. Not to the house, of course, unless there's no other day. Tell Culhane that we're asking for help. It will take some time. There will be a big push on, if we're able to get what we want, a large-scale attack on Norwood's headquarters and the Tan barracks. I'm not sure when. As soon as we can manage it. We don't intend to leave any of them alive."

"He'll want to know his part in it," I interrupted, and Riordan glanced at me in quick annoyance.

"Tell Sean that his part in it is to kill Sydney Norwood as soon as he gets a signal from us, and to create any kind of diversion he can think of. Our object is to have the Tans, or at any rate most of them, those not out on patrols, together in one place at one time. That will mean a daylight attack. All the eggs must be in one nest and the nest must be crushed. Tell Sean to wait and watch."

Jamie jumped up. "What do you mean, Norwood's 'headquarters'? His headquarters is in Charlie's house!"

Riordan replied cooly, "Yes, that's what I meant."

"What about—Mrs. Norwood? She's to be got out, isn't she? I mean, before the attack starts?"

Riordan hesitated. Then he said, "I don't think so. We

can hardly warn her, can we, and risk her spilling the whole thing to her husband? And, Daley, before you start swinging again, let me tell you that I'll have you up on charges if I hear another word about Mrs. Norwood. Do you understand me?"

They glared at each other, whilst the rest of us wondered if it would come to blows. "And there'll be no heroics from you, no matter what your personal feelings for the lady may be," added Riordan.

"Yes, *sir!*" snapped Jamie, smarting, and he walked away.

Riordan watched him go, a faint frown wrinkling his brow, and shook his head. Then he sighed, squared his shoulders and turned back to me. We spent several more hours talking then, and eventually Jamie came back. Meanwhile Riordan had dispatched a boy down to Culhane's with the message that he was to meet me at the pub in town, come Friday next in the late morning, if he could.

Kill Sydney Norwood! Now, that was the best idea any of us could think of. It was a dazzling thought, especially since we'd seen Clonkill. There were few who wouldn't have volunteered for the assignment themselves, although we all knew it was probably certain death for Culhane.

Riordan left us the next day, traveling to Dublin alone and on foot. He bade us all goodbye as if we might never meet again, and at that time it seemed the best kind of farewell any of us might make. I saw him disappear over the rim of the hill and prayed for his safe and successful journey.

Culhane sent word immediately that he would meet me as requested come Friday, and begged me to have a care in coming into town. Friday was a good day for such a meeting. It was market day and the roads and streets would be busy and crowded. There might be some chance to slip into town and out again without being stopped. Well, we'd soon find out, and would we not?

Chapter XXII

Early Friday morning I left camp, unarmed for the first time, feeling helpless as a lamb without either rifle or revolver. But to be stopped, searched and found armed would have been sure death.

Friday was market day; there'd be a big crowd headed into town, farmers with fresh produce to sell or a wagonful of sheep or cattle for the weekly auction. So I dressed myself in overalls with a big hat half over my face, hoped for the best, and cut across the hills toward town trying not to look in a hurry. Hurrying didn't do me a bit of good anyway, as the roads into town were full up. I was late arriving and had to come in at the wrong end of things entirely, across from a very large, fancy restaurant on a block of small, elegant shops that catered to rich Protestant ladies and visiting English gentlewomen and tourists over from America keen on handmade lace, woolens and linen.

I was cursing the delay, and me with a good ten blocks to walk back in the other direction to get to the pub. It was already past eleven. I hoped to God Culhane would wait and not think something had gone wrong. I crossed over the road, hurrying and not caring who noticed now, hardly looking where I was going, and suddenly found myself in the midst of a crush of people going both ways at once.

Just as I'd reached the other side, there was a cry from the crowd around me, an angry cry it seemed to me, and I looked up to see a big black motorcar pull up just in front of the restaurant. The people about me stopped moving and hurled themselves toward the motorcar, taking me along with them in the frantic press. They were muttering loudly, and several times I heard the words "Clonkill" and "murderer," "bitch," "informer," and God knows what all.

The car doors opened and out stepped a good-looking chap. Cocky and thin he was, but, oh, in the uniform of the Black and Tans, very natty, not wearing his beret pulled square over his brow like the rest of them did, but over to one side of his head in the French style. He was blondish, with a thin, pale mustache and an arrogant look about the eyes and mouth. He could have been only one man in all the world, though I'd never set eyes on him before. Sure he must have been and he was, entirely, Sydney Norwood in the flesh!

He ignored the people, though I think he was pale with anger; his eyes were narrowed and he avoided looking at anyone, as though he might catch the plague by mere eye contact. He held the car door open and, a second later, who, by Heaven, should step out but Margaret herself. She glanced about her in some confusion, but she soon caught the gist of the trouble. With a tight smile and a raised eyebrow, she stared at Sydney. He held his hand out stiffly to assist her up to the curb, but she eyed him haughtily and turned away, deliberately ignoring his outstretched hand, which he instantly clenched into a tight fist and dropped back down at his side. She was very fashionably dressed in a large white picture hat and a yellow silk summer frock with shoes to match, almost as I'd imagined her, the very picture of elegance.

Margaret's appearance brought more and louder cries of derision and scorn from the crowd, especially from the women. But when Charlie stepped out then, his big, cowlike eyes rolling about apprehensively, the people began to laugh and hoot, screaming filthy words at him.

"F'Gawd's sake, Syd, get 'em away!" panted Charlie in alarm, keeping the open door between himself and them. Then someone threw something. I don't know what it was, but suddenly others began picking things up from the street and tossing them, still yelling for all they were worth.

Charlie was struck on the cheek with a great clod of
dirt, and looked helplessly at Sydney, who remained quite
cool. There was a great surge toward the three of them
then. I was once more carried along against my will. Now
two other Tans emerged quickly from the front of the car
and began beating people back with billy clubs. Many
screamed and tried to back off, but there was nowhere to
go, for the numbers of people behind them. Margaret was
pushed against Sydney and quickly pulled herself away as
she caught his quick, sardonic smile. Then someone caught
hold of her dress and pulled her into the crowd. She
screamed. Charlie reached out feebly to grab her back,
and Sydney, his face never changing expression, pulled
out his revolver and held it up over his head.

A woman had hold of Margaret. When she saw Sydney
with the gun she shrieked, "Jesus, he's going to shoot us!"
She let Margaret go, and Margaret pitched forward, off
balance. She would have fallen under our feet if I hadn't
caught her. She pulled herself together and righted her hat,
then she turned to thank me. I saw the look in her eyes
when she realized it was me. She glanced over her shoulder very quickly, as if she wondered if I had been seen.
Then she looked back. Charlie was already looking about
for her, and Sydney fired the revolver into the air. The
crowd screamed and began to scatter fast. I had to leave
her or be discovered, and Charlie knew me well enough
by sight.

Margaret didn't smile; indeed, I couldn't understand her
look at all. She lifted her chin, muttered, "Thanks very
much," and turned away, going back quickly to Charlie,
who had finally caught sight of her. She turned him around
in his tracks and into the restaurant, sailing past Sydney,
who was talking to the two Tans.

I got away from there as fast as possibly I could, my
mind still whirling from the scene I'd just witnessed, and,
of course, from seeing Margaret again. So that was what
she was like now, I mused. She looked as though someone
had painted her over in porcelain and it had set good and
hard. Perfect clothes, perfect manners, perfect tone of
voice with scarcely any of the Irish left in it. Her two eyes

that I remembered blazing with life were now guarded, amused, bored, whatever you want to call it; they were empty, not her own warm honest brown eyes at all. Well, she'd had a chance to turn me in, if what they were whispering about her was true. But she hadn't.

It was nearly twelve noon when I reached the pub, and only old Cooley at the bar, cleaning glasses, when I went in. He looked up, didn't say a word, but nodded toward a small table in the back.

Sean Culhane was sitting there by himself, staring moodily into a glass of beer, his face dark and set like stone.

"Where in God's name have you been?" he asked very low, barely glancing up at me. "I was just going to leave."

"Sean," I said, sitting myself down across from him, "I've just seen Margaret. The people mobbed her in the street."

He nodded. "I thought it would happen, after what that lunatic pulled off in Clonkill. I told her to stay home, but you know Margaret. She doesn't listen."

"She saw me."

"Oh, did she, now?"

"And she knew it was me, Sean. I'm certain of it."

"And you're here safe and sound," he drawled slowly. "And the point you're so tactfully trying to make is that she had her chance to do you in and she didn't and therefore we can all breathe easy, is that it?"

"Well, it says something," I answered him, surprised. I thought he'd at least be glad to hear it.

"Never mind," he said, glancing at the clock on the wall uneasily. "Get to it. What's up?"

"Riordan's gone to Dublin."

"What?" It was the first time I'd ever seen his face become animated. "When? Why?"

"Keep your voice down. To get reinforcements, a lot of them. There's going to be an attack on Tan headquarters—"

"At last!" he muttered. "I've been after him for years to get it out in the open. Too bad it had to take Clonkill to bring him around."

God, but the man was made of ice clear through. I suddenly found that I very much wanted to say my piece and be away from him.

"Riordan has a job for you. Not right away. He's not sure when. It's to be just before the attack."

"What's the job?"

"Norwood. Sydney, I mean. You're to wait till you get word, then get rid of him and cause a diversion any way you can think of. Something that will bring a lot of them in together."

He pursed his lower lip over the upper, smiling a bit and nodded. "Well, there's an honor to it, I suppose. I don't imagine I shall live long enough to see the success of the attack. But you can tell him I'm ready for my part in it." He fell silent, finished the beer. But, now that it was out, he seemed oddly reluctant to let me go. He insisted on ordering two more beers, one for myself, and began asking eager questions. Who was being asked to come on? Would we have enough men? Was Riordan aware there were nearly two hundred Tans, not to mention regular troops in and about the town?

I assured him, from what I'd heard so far, that we'd have more than enough men, and arms, good arms; Riordan had promised he'd not come home without them.

Culhane fingered the droplets on the outside of his glass. "I'd like to see them," he said. 'I'd like to see it just once. To see an Irish army all together going into battle."

I laughed nervously. He made it sound like a damn chess game. And I thought it ironic that his attitude and Jamie's should be so close, on this point anyway. "God, Sean, it's not as if we haven't been in battle up to now!"

He sneered, retorting, "That's not battle to me!"

His manner appalled me and I changed the subject quickly.

"How are things with you?" I lied, sounding as if I had been concerned.

He shrugged. "Careful, I'd say. The brother's asking questions."

I nodded. "That's him. I could tell it right off. He's the type. He'd have to be doing it. But why you?"

He spread his hands on the table. "Oh, I don't say it's me especially. He's curious about everything. I guess he figures he can piece things together by instinct. God, these 'instinctive' people make me sick!"

I nodded and thought I'd best be off, but again he returned to the subject of Margaret.

"She's quite triumphant now, did you notice?"

"I didn't notice."

"Well, now that she's got what she was after . . ."

"What do you mean, 'what she was after'? *Charlie?*"

He smiled coldly. "No, no. The land. That's where they were going today. To the solicitors'. Charlie's bought her a grand wedding present. She picked it out herself, I heard. A nice piece of land. They're signing the papers this afternoon. It's Culhane land," he added after a pause.

I stared at him. "Your land?"

"Once. Or, rather, my father's. I'd been hoping to buy it, but they'd never sell it to me. For a long time I'd hoped to get it back some way when this was all over. Now it's Margaret's."

"Well, then, it would have been hers sometime anyway," I reminded him.

He eyed me bitterly. 'It's Norwood land now," he said, and we let it go.

I left him sitting there, with yet another beer up in front of him. It was early afternoon when I was off and, for once, I didn't see a Tan anywhere around. Old Cooley waved to me as I left. For a moment I got the impression he wanted me to come over and talk, but I couldn't chance it and just waved back and got the hell out of there.

Nor did I breathe easy till I was out of town and hiking it across back fields toward the trail into the hills. And, as I crossed the *boreen,* I heard a voice calling me low and urgently. I looked about, and there stood my Aunt Ellen, carrying a little white bleating kid under her arm. When she saw me moving toward her, she tethered the kid to a sapling tree and put a bunch of sweet hay under his nose to keep him at peace.

"Jerry, lad, in here, quick," she whispered. I went in with her behind a couple of thick trees, surprised as hell to see her there.

"Never mind me!" she blustered, kissing me and hugging me very hard. "Cooley sent a boy out to the farm to tell us you were in town. Are you daft? Why did you take such a chance? How's my Jamie?"

She said it all in one great breath, but I still looked mystified at the goat, who was munching his hay.

"He's my excuse for being here, in case I'm stopped. Nothing to prevent a poor farm woman from looking for a stray kid, is there?" she smiled warmly. "Now sit down here and let me look at you."

I asked her about my mother and the girls and the farm, and even Will seemed important to me in that moment. And then we mentioned Clonkill, and her face became quite grave, though she said little, for what was there to say, after all?

"There'll be the devil to pay from now on, we all expect it," she said. "I'd love to ask you what Riordan's planning, but I won't. I just hope it's soon. We can't take much more of Sydney Norwood, lad, tell them that up there in the hills, will you?"

"You won't have to. Just try to hold on a bit longer."

She sighed. "Each day is a bit longer than we thought we could stand the day before. Well, God knows, you lads are doing your best!"

"Culhane doesn't think so," I murmured.

"You saw him?"

"I took him a message. And, Aunt Ellen, I saw Margaret too. Do you know what her own father thinks of her? And the other men too? But she never said a word when she saw me."

"Aye, I've heard the same thing myself. Stupid nonsense!"

"Is it, though? I saw her in town, with himself and the brother. There was nearly a riot in the street. People threw things and called her a lot of ugly names."

"And you, Jerry? What do you believe?" She looked at me quietly.

I hesitated. "I don't think the talk is true. But, God, she's changed a lot!"

She poked me hard on the chest. "That's what I was hoping to meet you about, Gerald," she said, and her tone was strangely urgent. "Margaret Culhane."

"You mean Mrs. Norwood." I couldn't help it.

"Aye, Mrs. Norwood." My aunt laughed bitterly. "I thought she was a friend of yours and Jamie's. Wasn't he that much in love with her and not so long ago?"

"We're none of us children any more," I said simply.

"Then start acting like men." She poked me hard again. "Has anyone of you got a notion what's going on in that pigsty of a house Norwood keeps?"

I had no answer. How would we know?

She sighed. "God help us, how quick you are to believe the worst!"

"She married the man, Aunt Ellen!" I protested.

She scorned me with a glance. "Charlie's the least of it! He's not a patch on the ass of the brother. It's Sydney I'm worried about. He's a madman altogether, I'm telling you plain and straight, a madman, and he's planning to get rid of Charlie and have it all to himself: the land, the rents, the Tans—and Margaret along with the rest."

I stared at her, my head spinning, a swift vision of Sydney's sardonic smile as Margaret walked by him, and the hatred and contempt in her eyes as she looked at him.

"Aye, you might well look like that," my aunt went on. "The mad dog's been sniffing around her skirts since the day she married Charlie. And not only him—"

Worse and worse. "Aunt Ellen, what are you saying?"

She shivered and rubbed her cold hands against mine for warmth. "He treats her as if she was his for the taking. Her own housemaids spend the night in his bed and rise up whispering filth about her. Don't you think that murdering pack that laps at his heels hear what's said? Ah, God, if I was a man I'd cut their throats before Sunday Mass and take Communion with a clear conscience!

How long can she keep him off her? And how long before he throws her to the pack to keep them in line?"

"What keeps him from it now?" I asked, my voice trembling with the very thought of it all. "It's not fear of Charlie, sure!"

She laughed shortly. "The day he fears Charlie hasn't dawned, nor ever will. No, Sydney's a man moving slow till he runs. Mad as he is, he doesn't do anything without his reason and in his time. But meanwhile, Margaret is in mortal danger, inside her house and out of it."

I looked away stubbornly, arguing because I wanted so much to be convinced everyone was wrong. "She asked for her troubles. Look what she's doing to her father, for one thing. And it's true enough, Margaret knows a lot about the comings and goings of the Army."

"And what does James say of all this?" She gazed at me steadily, and I felt very uncomfortable.

"He—he saw her," I stammered. Her eyes brightened. "When?"

"Oh, I don't know. A few weeks ago. And he's having a bad time of it. He figures what we all figure, that she married Norwood partly for spite and the rest for what she could get out of him. Jamie says she told him she still loves him, and that's what makes it so bad, don't you see?" On sudden impulse, I grabbed her arm and cried, "Aunt Ellen, don't let Jamie find out what you think about her!"

"And why not?"

"Because you know him, feeling what he does, he'd just march in there and get himself killed trying to save her. No matter what he believes, he swore an oath to Kevin long ago that he would always be her friend and help her when she needed it. He promised he'd never hurt Margaret—"

"God in heaven, child," my aunt shouted at me in exasperation, "I'm not asking him to hurt her! Where are your wits? She's in trouble; we're all in trouble. Saints, it's *help* we're after!"

I sighed, feeling helpless and stupid.

"All right, lad," she said more quietly. "All I'm saying

is this: If Jamie swore such a thing, now is the time he can live up to it."

And now the bitterness I'd been hiding in my heart against Margaret filled me, flashing up in my throat like the flaming taste of bile. "Aunt Ellen, it's Jamie's *life* at stake!"

"Jamie's life has been at stake since he was fifteen years old," she said calmly. "What more can he do for Ireland than lose it?"

"Yes, lose it for Ireland, if it comes to that. But Margaret Culhane *Norwood* isn't Ireland!"

"Isn't she, though?" murmured my aunt softly. And then she drew a deep breath. "Ah!" she cried. I whirled about to see her eyes brimming with tears. "I know, I know," she said, trying to smile at me, but when I would have spoken again, she pressed her cold finger to my lips. "Ah, Jerry, Jerry, poor lads, all of you! Come, darlin', sit down here and rest awhile. It's the Norwoods you'll have to destroy. The Norwoods and their Tans are strangling us. There's only you lads between us and them. The IRA has got to move soon!"

"The Norwoods will be taken care of, I promise you," I said. "We're planning something big, and soon," I told her, but could say no more.

"There's a lot who'll say it's about time," she answered.

"Yes, Culhane said it. He's been saying it for a long time now." I smiled wryly.

Her brow wrinkled and one fine eyebrow rose up. "Has he, now?"

"But what about Jamie?" I asked miserably.

She rested her hand gently on my arm. "Jamie'd not thank you for shielding him in this."

"I know."

She sighed again, still holding me and looked off across the meadow before us, a sad smile playing about her lips.

"No, you're none of you the same boys anymore."

Suddenly I felt so spent, I wished I could throw myself on her lap and cry like a baby. "Ah, Christ, I'm tired of the sight and smell and thought of killing!"

"Hush, don't talk of it," she soothed me.

"Why not?" I answered bitterly. "It's true. There's nothing left of us that went out three years ago, cocky and pushing for a fight! We're all . . . too damn tired even to fall down."

She did not speak. We sat in silence as the afternoon waned. Once in a while the kid bleated, then he fell asleep at the end of his tether. And, as dusk moved across the skies, I had to leave her at last.

Chapter XXIII

Well, now, after what my aunt had told me, and after taking my time to think it all over, I found, as I reached camp, that I was now anxious to tell Jamie about it, figuring the two of us might rescue her from the situation she was in. I guess I had it in mind we might carry her away from everything down below and keep her safe with us up in the hills. Sure it was silly and romantic, didn't I know that myself? But, the more I thought of Margaret living in the same house with the Norwoods, the less I could stand to let it go on another hour.

I found Jamie as usual in those days, quiet and distant, having just come from a discussion with O'Rourke—and a discussion with O'Rourke was bound to be a one-sided affair, for, though the man was a good soldier and even had a thought or two on occasion, he was so damned closemouthed that you had to guess what he might want of you, for all he'd do was hint around about it, never give a direct order. As I came in, hoping to catch a bit of tea and something to go with it, there was Jamie, stretching and yawning. I poured out two mugs and went up to him. He took the tea, thanked me absently, and asked how Culhane had taken his new orders.

"He was pleased," was all I could think of; what with everything else, I'd almost forgotten why I'd gone to town in the first place. "I think he's dead wrong about his daughter!" I blurted out, and Jamie's great black eyebrow went up straightaway, but I just kept on going. The more I spoke of Sydney, the darker his scowl became, and when I told him what his mother had said, he jumped up so fast the scalding tea spilled all over his chest. But he would not stop to have it tended, only threw some cold water on the burns and went to saddle his horse, leaving me to run after him.

"Wait up, I'm going with you," says I, but he shook me off.

"No. I'll go alone."

"Jamie, let me. Please."

"No."

I could have gone myself. I could have insisted. But he had the right and I didn't. So I stood there and watched him rushing off after her as I knew he would, and all I could do then was wonder what would happen.

Wonder or no, I fell asleep later on and didn't waken till morning and then I was cold and stiff and aching all over from sleeping out on the ground, but that was nothing unusual. Jamie had not returned yet. I asked around and no one had seen him. And then, as I pondered to myself whether to go after him now, I spotted him from a distance, riding slowly back, the horse's head low to the ground, himself weary, leaning forward in the saddle. He was alone.

"Did you see her?" I called as I ran to meet him. "Is she all right?"

He began to unsaddle the horse and then to rub him down slowly and deliberately, with long hard strokes, never looking directly at me.

"She's all right," he answered flatly.

"Jamie, for God's sakes, this is too important to keep quiet about! What happened?"

He went on with what he was doing, petting Dan a bit as he worked.

"I saw her. I told her what I'd heard. She said it was

not true and, even if it was, she could handle him, and it was none of anyone else's business but her own. Now will you leave me alone, Jerry? I'm dead tired and Dan needs his breakfast."

And, until a long time later, that was all he would say about it. . . .

The man who lay dying remembered that night very well and now he thought to himself, how could I ever tell you about what really happened, Jerry? I was all mixed up when you kept asking me questions. I couldn't think. I didn't want to think, for it was a night that had its beginnings and its endings, and I was so full of its beginnings that the thought of how it ended made me sick and I couldn't speak of it.

He had ridden down the hills' far slope, down along the rocky pathway to the water and along the beach. It was not the fastest way to get to her, he knew that, but he had to have a little time to sort it all out for himself, before he would know what to say to her, how to persuade her. Perhaps he would not bother trying to persuade her. Perhaps he would simply take her away with him. It would be easier. He smiled a bit to himself. How romantic it sounded.

And then Dan had begun to go lame. He'd dismounted and looked at the creature's big feet, carefully, one by one, while Dan stood patiently, the sea breeze ruffling his long mane about his big thoughtful eyes. There didn't seem to be anything really wrong with the horse, no swelling anywhere. Maybe he was just tired out, like the rest of them.

Then he'd mounted again and decided to run the horse a bit through the shallows in the cooling water. He turned about and gave Dan his head, settling himself back in the saddle, with the waves splashing up as Dan's long, eager legs stretched and pranced in the surf.

It was a time of day when there seemed to be no time at all. Time was suspended; the sun was hanging like a gold ring on a long thin finger of a cloud. His heart told him that here, at last, was the chance he'd prayed for, to

get her away, to keep her to himself . . . Arragh, he knew
it was all dreams and wishes and being tired too long to
think straight—it was just the kind of day a chance patrol
would shoot him, and all that would happen, after he'd
come to his senses too late, would be that he'd die.

Even as he was thinking, he saw another horse and
rider coming toward him through the waves along the
shore, a good distance off yet, coming out from behind
some outcroppings of rocks by the cliffs. He'd no notion
who it might be, but he could not seem to be afraid of it,
although he knew he should be afraid and suspicious and
certainly careful.

They rode toward each other for a moment and he
thought the other rider raised his arm and waved. And he
had smiled and returned the greeting. He thought; If it
should turn out that we are enemies, I'll take the thirty
seconds' ride left between you and me to think you might
be a friend. And, the moment he thought that, a queer
thing happened. His heart lifted and the sudden thought
came surging through him, Yes, by God, today I *will* bring
Margaret away with me and she'll want to come!

As they closed, he saw that the rider was Margaret. She
lowered her arm when she saw it was himself, and reined
the horse in sharply. He did the same, and then they had
sat there, opposite each other, while Dan and Byron remembered each other faintly, and he had not known what
to say.

But I knew what I would *do,* thought Jim Daley with
a sudden, half-remembered pang wracking his insides
strangely after so many years. I always knew it. There is
just so much waiting a man can wait and so much longing
and there's an end to it. All the tender, persuasive words
he'd had spinning around in his brain went by the by, and
he told himself there would be time to talk later.

So, silently, he had reached over and pulled her reins
into his hand and led old Byron up on the beach, amidst
the rocks. Then he had got down and lifted her off the
horse, holding her against him in his arms, briefly, reluctant to put her from him again for even an instant.

She spoke not a word, nor smiled, but sat where he had

put her, down on the soft white sand, and she watched him tether the horses by the rocks and take off the heavy warm saddles from their backs.

Then he had walked back to her, his eyes never leaving her face. And she had spoken at last.

"I love you, Jamie," she'd said, so simply, and reached out her two arms to him.

Oh, God, but how he'd rushed to hold her then, and to be held by her. He felt a sickness in him; his breath choked him, an agony of longing to be at peace after all the time of war and not seeing her, it was all mixed up together in his mind. He'd never given a thought of what she'd been to Charlie Norwood. He'd never allowed himself to picture her married, and all that meant. All he knew was that he wanted her and that she belonged to him, she had always belonged to him.

No woman since Margaret had ever meant anything to him, but they were all like the rest of his life, like the fighting. The quickness of it, take the truck or bomb the barracks, quickly—in, out, and away. Quickness, too, into a woman, one pang that was only deeper longing, out and it was over, and over the hills to the next bomb or the next ambush or the next woman.

Now, thinking of that, it was as he held her fast and dug his fingers hard into her slim back with the soft little bones lying straight along it, that he buried his face in her breast and wept for the dearness of her.

"Hush, hush, darling," she'd whispered, stroking his hair over and over with trembling fingers. "Hush, *acushla,* my own, hush, Jamie."

He looked up into her face and saw that she was weeping with him. He kissed her throat to still those trembling muscles; he kissed her eyelids and her wet cheeks and then he felt the whole body of her lying along his arm, shivering violently, clinging to him. He'd thought for a moment that she was afraid of him and of being there, and he clasped her even tighter. He looked at her and asked, "Margaret, are you afraid?"

And she answered, her eyes wide and glowing, "I have been afraid, so very, very afraid, Jamie. But not now, if you'll not leave me alone again. Don't leave me alone, will you, Jamie? Don't leave me alone now, or I'll die of it!"

"Don't speak of dying!" he'd whispered, pressing his finger on her soft lips to silence the words. "Ah, Margaret," he cried out suddenly, "I'll never, never leave you, sweetheart. Hold fast to me, hold fast!"

They lay there together on the sand in each other's arms, like two small children. All the desire in him had been lulled away for the moment, for the peace of her arms around him made him forget. They might have been any young couple anywhere sitting out on the beach, but then it had come over him again. They weren't any young couple at all. She saw it in his face before he'd said a word, the ease turn into sudden anguish, the perversity of thought that now forced her marriage into his mind where he'd carefully kept it safeguarded before.

"You're thinking of Charlie," she said deliberately, watching his face change before her eyes. He rolled away from her, lying on his back, desperately searching the evening clouds and first bold stars for what to say. She pulled his head around and said slowly, "Listen to me, Jamie. Charlie's had nothing of me that matters to us, do you understand that? Nothing!"

"He's your husband," he answered dully, not meaning it the way it sounded.

She sighed. "There's that," she said, nodding. And he heard her moving. He turned in a panic, saw her start up, look over toward the horses, the shine of the low-slung moon gleaming on her hair. And, above the pounding of the surf, his heart was in his throat at the thought of her.

"Margaret!" He held out his arms to her. He felt so empty, so tired. He just wanted the feeling of her lying against him, just the comfort of the warmth of her, just that. But she would not come to him.

"It's no use, Jamie. You know it, don't you?"

He nodded miserably.

"A bargain is a bargain," she said firmly and, it seemed, more to herself than to him.

"That's an odd way to talk about marriage," he said,

faintly puzzled, but merely making talk, really, to keep her there with him. And she'd laughed, her lips twisting unpleasantly, but said nothing.

"Ah, Margaret, why did you do it to us? Wasn't there enough in the world against us? Why did you?"

She opened her mouth, closed it, shook her head and turned toward the horses. And then, as if resolving some inner argument with herself, she looked at him again, and sat down on one of the rocks. But when he would have taken her hand, she refused, folding her arms, and began to speak, not looking at him.

"I was never able to forget you, do you know that, Jamie? You gave me no peace at all. Do you know how your mind works? Funny, that, it's always there, isn't it, just going along, thinking away to itself, the hell with whatever *you're* up to—it's got a life of its own. And if you look in on it now and again, no matter what you're in the middle of doing, there it is, thinking to itself. Well, every time I'd look into my mind, there you'd be, Jamie. Quiet, but there all the time."

"Margaret—"

"No, no!" She shook her head impatiently. "I'll say it all now and once only. I've had much to say to you, Jamie, all these years, but you weren't there to hear it. And I did that to you, and to myself. I was so alone, Jamie! I've always been in the midst of a crowd of people and, except for you, for a while, I've been so damned alone. There never was anybody else I could tell it to. I've never been like other girls—all eager and ready to share out their lives in lots all around. You promised before you'd never leave me, and, it seemed, all you did was leave me then. Oh, I know, I know, it was the Army and all that, but I'm not a man and it's no use explaining sense to me.

"When I went away, Jamie, I think I went a bit crazy too. Sometimes I'd let myself forget it was me that did the leaving. And I'd wait for a letter from you. I'd pretend you were coming to me. And then I'd get angry and cry because you never did. And then I'd punish myself for being stupid. I'd let myself, no, *make* myself remember the truth of it, and let it all crush me down again.

"And I wanted you to be lonely for me, Jamie. Were you? Were you ever lonely for me? I hope you were, though that's a stupid, rotten thing to have wished.

"But I guess men aren't like that, are they? They don't miss much, and what bit they might miss, now and then, they never say it at all. Or, well, maybe they do, at first, when love's all new and a surprise and the one you love does everything right because that's the way you want to see it—I guess you do then.

"A woman can die inside her, a bit at a time. Small loss, too, but it's painful to her at least, and pain's pain, after all. Except in poems, the world doesn't count that kind of pain for much. But, oh, Jamie, I wanted to hear you talk to me as you used to! I wanted you to long for me and miss me and wonder where I was, how I was, and worry about me. And I'd say, over and over to myself, He must love me still, and still be all of a mind about me and can't think of anything else. And every night I'd lie awake in the dark and cry because your life was still going on, you were living it, whatever you were doing, while I was just waiting, just waiting for you to think me back to life again."

"Then be satisfied, Margaret," Jamie had answered her, his voice edged with anger. "You had it all. I longed for you, dreamed of you, all of it. But why was it necessary? You've not answered that, Margaret. Why did you go?"

"Because I chose to," she said gravely, looking at him for the first time since she had begun to speak. "I can't explain it any better than that, and I won't try. And now there's nothing for us, nothing but sorrow. Oh, God help me, Jamie, I wish I didn't love you! But it doesn't matter if I do or don't. I'm walking a path that leads away from you, and I'll stay walking it. I can't give you love, Jamie," she added in a tight, hurt little voice.

He felt the anger and the bitterness growing in him then, at her, at life, at a hundred things. And he had pulled her down to him again, roughly, harshly.

"Then the hell with love!" he cried. "Give me comfort,

Margaret Culhane. Just comfort and let the love lie dying out of sight. I haven't enough left in me to love. I'm not asking for your love. Just comfort, Margaret. Hold me tight in your arms, this once only. Let me keep my head on your breast, like the lamb, do you remember, Margaret? Oh, God, Margaret . . . !"

And he'd crushed her against him, for a few seconds forgetting she was Margaret. She was a woman. A blinding pain shattered its way through him. His eyes closed; feeling the femaleness of her against him, he thought, I'm deceived again, like you always are with each of them that's not the right one. They all feel like this! He'd though it blindly, with more hate than love in him then: Let me take her, let me have her and have done with it at last.

He fell across her and tore the shirt off of her, with his eyes still closed, wildly, like an animal. He felt the heat of her breasts closing in on each side of his face, closing and wrapping him soft and sweetly, and his lips found the hard little bone in the middle of her chest and he pressed them there. He'd never let go of her, he thought, never, no matter who she was, it was better than nothing, and nothing was all there was anyway . . .

He knew he was hurting her. He supposed he wanted to hurt her. She pushed him away, hitting at him and crying aloud. And, finally, he stopped, and looked down at her, and she was Margaret. She was really Margaret and no other woman in the world.

"Don't let it be so hard, Jamie," she whispered, and then she had taken his two hot hands herself and pressed them firmly on her breasts and she'd leaned close to him and kissed him on the mouth.

And then, because there was nothing for them and that time when there seemed to be no time would soon be gone, they'd loved each other, each other indeed, for the passion and the longing was deep and waiting with them both.

When the first part was over and he lay well within her warm body, he rested her head gently back on the sand and leaned on his elbow, looking at her fondly, with her strong, fine legs wrapped close around him and her fingers tangled in his hair.

"Have you comfort now, Jamie?" she asked softly.

"Yes," he'd said, lost in the mazes of her eyes, and it was true; he knew it with a rush of gladness that flung itself through him like fire.

"Now give me joy, Margaret, Margaret, Margaret darling!"

And at once he was feeling her tightening around him and he began to move on her. She threw her two arms around his back, digging her nails into his skin, and then the madness that cures itself was on him. He felt lost in her, felt the dissolution of his soul and the only true joining there exists, the blending and the hot, precious moment of heaven touched them both, raised them up, held them victoriously dazzled in the wellsprings of the universe for one instant, and, ever so gently, set them down again, saturated in peace and completion.

For him, it was home again; it was peace and all the dead were buried back in England and wherever they belonged, and Martin was plowing the west field with the team. She was peace, he knew, holding her in the crook of his arm, with her hot, flushed face pressed against his chest, their legs still entwined, silent, not needing any words at all. She was peace. She was joy and comfort and a reason for everything. She was all there was, and he would never let her go.

"Leave him!" he whispered against her ear. "Margaret, come with me tonight. Leave him."

She smiled at him, and lifted her head, and traced the outline of his lips with her finger, and she did not answer him. She looked at him, love shining from her dark eyes as he'd dreamed of them, and she suddenly put her slim hands on either side of his face and pulled him against her very hard and kissed him so deeply and so long that his heart sank, for he knew Margaret, and he knew she was answering him with that kiss.

And it was so. She had pulled herself away and reached about her for her clothes, and still he didn't speak but waited for her to say it.

Finally, she had stood up and dressed swiftly. When that was done, she turned back to him, came and sat down beside him once more, hands clasped about her knees, and she spoke solemnly.

"I cannot leave him," she said, and his heart turned to stone as she said it. "I cannot love you. I cannot see you again in this life and I'm not fool enough to believe you'll long wish to see me in the next. No, Jamie, don't say anything." She put her fingers against his mouth.

"This, tonight," she continued, her voice a bit softer, as she glanced around at the sea and sky and sand and then at him again, as if she was trying to memorize every detail of it, "this should have been a long time ago, Jamie. But there was no time. And now it's been and nothing can ever take it away. But it is no beginning, Jamie. It's only the end of it, my dearest darling."

A rage came sweeping over him as passionate as the heat of love had been moments earlier. He rolled away and stood up, facing her, with the horses now between them, and his voice was hard and cold, but the pain was clouding his eyes, and part of him, deep inside, wondered if he might possibly be dying and this was how it felt before the end. But, he thought furiously, it's not *before* the end. She said it *was* the end, and he was not sorrowful but full of hatred and despair.

"You've made a bad bargain, Mrs. Norwood," he said and he noted with savage gladness that she flinched at the name. "There's more than one end upon us, and this is the least of them. Your rich husband won't have a roof over his head much longer. What do you think will happen to him and to you the day the English pull out of here? And it's coming, soon, Mrs. Norwood, sooner than anyone knows. You should have waited to see the outcome. You should have waited to see which side to line up with!"

She stood unmoving, taking it in silence, and her very look drove him to lash out at her in any way that he could.

"You've succeeded in one thing, I'll give you that," he cried. "You've broken your father's heart, or what was left of it. I'm the last man on earth to pity Sean Culhane, and God knows I don't pity him, but he wasn't worth your whole life, Margaret! And you're paying a pretty price just for the spiting of him!"

But her face had grown dark and remote, as he remembered it had long ago. "It wasn't entirely for the spite of it," she answered with a small, infuriating shrug.

"Oh, no," he spat back at her, "we mustn't forget the land, must we, and the money too? As long as that lasts, you'll be the fine lady of Norwood House, and your own people will spit at you in the streets! And, tell me, how do you like Sydney? Handsome fellow, isn't he? I hear he's that gone on you. You're a regular heartbreaker, aren't you, Mrs. Norwood!"

"Don't speak to me of him!" she cried, and Byron whinnied and trembled next to her.

"Why not? Sure the way I heard it, he's not giving you a moment's peace at all! You're in mortal danger, my mother fears it! Poor Jerry fears it, too! It's a wonder he hasn't come riding in for you to save you from your peril!"

"I can take care of myself, thanks very much!" she cried, her eyes masking over strangely. "I've no need of your assistance, no, nor of Jerry's either. You can tell him that for me, will you do that?"

She had thrown the saddle on Byron's back and quickly begun fastening the straps, her fingers shaking. Then he had come and stood beside her, but she would not look up and only hurried the faster.

"Oh, yes, I can see well enough you've got your life organized. And tonight? Well, tonight you were just tying up some old loose ends. You've gotten frightfully neat since I knew you, Margaret," he said quietly, knowing his words were cutting.

She sighed and leaned against the horse for a moment, and Jamie had thought suddenly that she might faint there, but she shook herself, held on to the saddle and pulled herself straight again.

"Think whatever you like," she said, and mounted Byron quickly. She lifted the reins to be off, but he stood there without moving and held the horse's head.

"One more thing," he said carefully, "from this night I care no longer what becomes of you. But be careful what you say, do you understand? There's talk of your informing against your father and the rest of us. There are many who believe it. More than one would gladly see you dead for the lives of the rest of us."

She stared down at him in the moonlight, sitting straight-backed and proud, contempt on her face and in her voice.

"Is that what you think, Jamie?" she asked.

He studied her briefly, the love and the hate struggling within him, and he answered bleakly, "I don't know."

Her voice was icy as she flung the next words at him.

"Then you'd best watch out for me, hadn't you?" And, in a sudden movement, she grabbed the reins, dug her heel into Byron's side. The horse reared and galloped away across the sand as Jamie was knocked to his knees. He struggled to his feet and watched her racing away from him.

"God damn you forever, Margaret Culhane!" he called out into the night, and his words were swallowed up by the crashing of the surf as the morning tide turned toward the shore. . . .

Chapter XXIV

From Clonkill on, we wasted no time, but descended on the Tans like gulls on locusts. We took them from everywhere they could be found: from their patrol cars, from the lorries, from the roads and from the streets, even out through the windows of the places where they slept. Sometimes we'd take just one man from a group of four, snatch him from his sentry post and leave the other three wondering where their mate was and too scared to look for him. We picked them up on night patrol, six at once who'd never report in safe that morning or any morning. And, when we had them, we weighted down their bodies and threw them into the river outside of town, not so heavily that they'd sink to the bottom—we didn't want to be the cause of their remaining in Ireland any way—but just heavily enough so they'd stay out of sight whilst they drifted with the current out to sea.

They poured more troops into Waterford, like ants from a bottle, till it seemed to us there simply was not room enough in Ireland to put up all the troops and Tans and equipment and officers and politicians and visitors and their comings and goings. But we whittled away at them. Days went by quietly enough. We rested up in the afternoons, exhausted and sticky-feeling. When we were not sleeping or killing or looking for something to kill, we lay about the damp ground smoking and staring at nothing, not bothering to talk. We just waited, and hope began to wear out of us. No matter how many we killed, they seemed to spring up as though from dragon's teeth and we had to start all over again. And still we heard not a word from Riordan. We began to believe that he'd never gotten through at all. There was someone by the radio day and night, but we never got an answer to our calls. It was as if we had died there.

O'Rourke, that great hulk, the strangely un-Irish quietness of him was driving us to distraction, and he seemed content to keep things the way they were till Riordan returned. But Jamie was restless as I'd never seen him, restless and spoiling for something big. I watched him as the days went by, and I was troubled for him. He began to seek out O'Rourke. The two of them would talk together in low voices for hours and I knew they were quarreling, for Jamie's voice, low and insistent, was always tinged with anger and O'Rourke's quiet rumble never made a dent in it.

Then we got news that the Tans were sending in reinforcements themselves, into Dungarvan and Dunknealy and some of the small villages about. A hundred and fifty more of them! My heart sank at the thought of so many more coming. If only Riordan was there to advise us! O'Rourke said what O'Rourke always said, we must wait till Riordan returned.

"To hell with Riordan!" Jamie burst out at that, and everyone looked up at him in astonishment.

O'Rourke sighed. "Daley, shut your large mouth, will you, for the love of God!" he begged wearily, but Jamie ignored him and stood up in front of the rest of us.

"Are you going to let Norwood get away with this?" he demanded, his eyes flashing.

There were murmurs. Someone cried out, "Ah, sure, sit down, Jamie, we're too tired," and Jamie laughed scornfully.

"A hundred and fifty more of them, is it?" he shouted. "And, tell me, how many more after them? How many are we going to be able to get together, *if* Riordan got through, *if* he can talk Dublin into it, *if* he can get the men? Look, we're the ones here on the spot. What does Dublin know about us, anyway?"

"There's talk of a truce soon," said Allie Clarke carefully, for the idea of doing something really big was awfully appealing.

Jamie smiled. "There's been talk of a truce for seven hundred years, on and off," he threw it right back at Allie.

Now, looking about me, I could see the weariness and lack of interest beginning to drop away. The others were moving in closer to him, listening, and O'Rourke's impassive face was worried.

"You wouldn't want to pull anything that'd spoil a truce, would you, though?" asked O'Rourke anxiously.

Jamie didn't bother looking at him as he answered. "What do you call what Riordan himself has in mind? An all-out attack, in broad daylight too, on Tan headquarters, murdering their commander, the honorable Sydney? Well, what I've got in mind isn't much more than a quick skirmish compared to that. Now, listen to me, while we're waiting to blow that bastard to his reward, he's setting himself up so nobody'll have a chance to get him, nobody ever. I say, don't let them disperse, ten here and twenty there, making our job all the harder. No, let's get them while they're still on the damn train. Let's blow up the lot together!"

"Blow up a train?" asked O'Rourke slowly. "Where?"

Jamie considered briefly. "Before it gets into town. Out, oh, let's say half a mile out, at the water tower."

"No, wait, then, Jamie," put in Conn Aherne. "Old Kilrossanty's house is right there. We can't take a chance of hurting any of our own. A blast that strong will blow the house along with anything else around there."

"We'll warn them ahead of time. They can get out," said Jamie impatiently.

"No!" cried O'Rourke. "The fire will spread. You know how those old buildings are. Just like what happened at Clonkill. If anything happened, if they didn't get out in time, it would be murder, pure and simple. And that would put us right along with them, doing things their way."

"Don't talk to me of murder, O'Rourke," said Jamie, his voice deadly cold. "And Mick not cold in his grave!" There was a murmur of assent among the men.

"Where will Kilrossanty go, then? You're talking about a man's home now!" persisted O'Rourke.

"An act of retaliation is in order," snapped Jamie.

Conn cried out, "Ah, for God's sakes, stop sounding off like a military machine, Jamie. You're talking about our own people!"

"I'm talking about getting rid of a hundred and fifty military machines!" returned Jamie. "There's only a few of ourselves and we haven't much time. We'd have to take the train while it's stopped, and the only place it stops for thirty miles is there, to take on water. We'll have to have enough time to set the charge; we can do it before the train gets there, and lie low waiting for them. I'll see to it myself that Kilrossanty and the others are got out, I swear it. Now, what do you say?"

There was considerable argument, but in the end O'Rourke gave in to the extent that he agreed to let any man go who wished to. Ten of us were all that was

needed, though many more would gladly have come along.
And Jamie's plan was eagerly put into operation.

Jim Farrell was our man for this job, a hothead all his
life, an army to himself before there ever was any army.
His special interest was railroads, and, at one time or
another, it was said, he'd set a dynamite charge to every
hundred foot of tracks along the line from Killarney to
Waterford City, so the story went. The sight and sound
of Irish trains running English troops and ammunition
into Waterford was too much for him to bear, and bear
it he did not. He'd lost three fingers from his right hand
one time, setting off a great blast near Mallow, but in
three months' time he'd taught his left hand to shoot as
straight and wind all the little wicked wires as nimbly as
any five men's good right hands, better than most.

Now, Kilrossanty's old house, and a couple of deserted
farm buildings whose owners had been long dead or
moved to America, stood north of town, not far from the
water tower. Kilrossanty's had once been a decent-enough-
looking place, when the family lived there and kept it up.
But then the daughters had gone to America and the one
son was killed in France. The old folks moved into town
with Mrs. Kilrossanty's sister's family, but every spring
and summer the stubborn old devil hauled the two of
them back out there and puttered around by himself, putting in a garden and making unending repairs. It's hard to
get growing out of a man's blood, and he all his long life
back-bent with it.

Trying to turn a penny from the property, Kilrossanty
had done up the two upstairs floors into dreary little flats,
three on each floor. But he hadn't many tenants, it was so
far away from everything. And, when the Tans had come
to Ireland, they had thrown everybody out anyway and
often used the place as quarters on their way elsewhere.
There was a permanent five-man guard there, and it was
well known that Kilrossanty had not spoken a single word
to any one of them, though they sat down at the same
table each morning, noon, and night for two years.

So the ten of ourselves in on the job came out to the
water tower before dawn of a Saturday morning, and

Jim Farrell went quickly to his work, with Allie and myself holding a lantern and covering him.

Jamie had grabbed old Kilrossanty out in his garden, where he was every morning before breakfast, watering and weeding and fertilizing and generally grubbing about. The old man seemed to understand, nodding away whilst Jamie explained to him several times that he must get himself and his wife away from the place before noontime. But still, Jamie fretted about them, though he blustered around a good deal, which was so unlike him that I began to get an eerie bad feeling we would not come away from this day's work unscathed. I saw him sit, the rifle propped up between his legs, and stare over at the house, watching the five Tans on duty with a nervous impatience that soon spread to the rest of us. Kilrossanty was plainly in sight, out hammering a plank up on the side of the barn, and Jamie muttered, "Would you look at that, now? Why the hell doesn't he get out?"

Then we saw the old lady feeding the geese and chickens, and, a while later, doesn't she come on out of the house with a great sweep of a hat on her head, gloves on her hands and garden tools with her! She bent down over her flower beds and began digging away.

It was nearly eleven then and Jamie was biting his lips with irritation. Jim had come back, satisfied with his job of work on the track. He looked at his pocket watch, stretched a bit, settled himself down next to the detonator box and fell asleep till it was time to act. I envied him dozing peacefully away there, his hand not a foot from the levers, and I tried very hard to relax a bit myself, but, with Jamie, I kept anxious vigil on the house.

Finally, at fifteen after the hour, when Jamie was just about to go racing up there and drag them to safety if he could, the old couple came out, got into their cart and drove off without so much as a backward glance. For their sake I hoped the house would be spared, but it wasn't likely.

We had set up our positions earlier, and much of our success, once the train would be blown, was in having got hold of two machine guns the Tans had there. There was one Tan on each side of the tracks, about five feet away. Allie and Finnerty were to take the three in the house whilst Jamie, Conn, and I saw to the guns.

One of them was sitting half asleep on the porch steps, about six feet from his weapon, making himself a cigarette, yelling some kind of an argument back across the tracks to the other one. I think he was running short of tobacco; he held up the bag and waved it, and the other one told him to go to hell, he needed all he had. And so it went, as we moved up on them through the tall grass and weeds.

The other one, mine, was younger and seemed nervous, looking up and down the tracks, one hand resting on the machine gun, his fingers tapping the side of it absently. Neither of them bothered to look behind them at all, where we waited no more than three feet away. Then Jamie yelled and we sprang at them the same instant, pulling back their heads and cutting their throats quickly. They fell heavily, mine over his gun, and I had to drag him away. He was a heavy fellow, I suppose he'd played soccer at school. But that kind of thinking is not for wartime. Those are the thoughts that come back to haunt you as you go along through life. Nobody's free of the great machine's arms, are they?

We lifted the heavy machine guns and carried them farther down the tracks, setting them up across from each other but out of sweeping range, so we couldn't kill one of our own men as we fired.

It was a quarter to twelve. The place was very still. Even the birds had disappeared. I looked over at Jamie, who sat like a stone staring ahead of him. At just about five of the hour, we heard the train whistle and quickly crouched down low out of sight. Joe Finnerty and the others were spread out with rifles ranged along one side. Conn and three more were near me, lined by the track. As the train slowly chugged into view, we waited. Twenty feet away, Farrell's hand was poised to set off the charge. It all happened very, very fast. I had a glimpse of their heads through a window, all the rows of black berets. I thought, All those pretty little hats, and then the train blew.

It blazed up brightly and very fast, pieces of wood and

iron flying in all directions. Inside, those that were left were shouting and swearing and coughing, trying frantically to scramble out over the dying and the dead. As they came, we took them. They never saw us, most of them.

A bunch of them from the second car came out running, sure they were safe, yelling with relief, only to stop when they saw us, their eyes filled with horror. They stood unmoving, whilst those coming behind them swore and shouted to them to keep going. From the other side, we could hear machine-gun reports, rifle shots, shrieks and cries.

Allie had his finger on the trigger of our machine gun and I was to feed the cartridges into it. But when the Tans just stood there, looking at us, Allie did not move, but sat as if petrified suddenly, staring right back at them. Those in back came running, firing their revolvers at us, and still Allie did nothing.

"Fire, Allie, come on!" I cried, trying to push him away then and shoot it myself, but one of the Tans took aim at me. I thought it was all up with me then, only Jamie fired first and the Tan fell instantly, his hand still holding his weapon never fired.

The Tans then fell on their bellies, trying to crawl away from us, but Allie would not let go the machine gun and he would not or could not fire at them. Jamie, cursing his head off, threw his rifle to the ground and knocked Allie away from the gun. Just in time he was, too, for some of them who had not been hurt were coming up now with rifles and opening fire on us, spraying the air with bullets in our general direction.

Jamie whipped the gun around and they began to fall down, like tenpins, I thought, just like little tenpins in a row. In a moment I remembered to look and see if Allie had been hit, but he was just lying on his side, dazed, watching the flames eating up the noon air, a look of infinite sorrow on his face, and I trembled for him. But Allie had killed his share of men, God knows; what had stopped him then I could not say. I looked back at Jamie. He was sitting there rubbing the sweat off his face, his right hand still resting on the machine gun. It hadn't taken long at all. The place was quiet again.

"Did we get them all, do you think?" Jamie asked me.

"Enough," I said, beginning to dismantle the gun to carry it away. He helped me with it, for the explosion must have been heard nearby and we knew they'd be after us soon.

"Allie, come on, boyo," I said to him, touching him on the shoulder.

He started violently, shooked his head, then turned and stared at me in a puzzled way.

"Allie," I repeated, "it's over. We've got to go now, hurry up," I said again, and I saw him look around as if he'd never an idea where he was or what had been happening. Then he caught sight of the bodies all about and the wreckage of the train, and he began to shudder.

"Allie, come on!"

He stood up, still shaking. "What? Are they all dead?"

"Yes, yes, they haven't moved. Come away."

He was about to follow me, when, from the other side of the wreck, between the locomotive and the first car, a peal of shots rang out. Allie screamed, spun around, hit in the neck. He slipped to the ground, blood gushing out of him. Jamie and I ducked fast enough, you may be sure, and I crawled over to Allie. From the looks of him, I didn't think he'd live.

"Jim! Joe Rafferty! Conn Aherne, come here!" I yelled. We'd have to carry Allie from the place if he was to get away at all. The boys came on the run, and once again the damned rifle sounded, bullets spattering all about them, but they made it. I was so busy looking at Allie, I'd forgotten Jamie, but I called back to him over my shoulder, "You'll have to take the gun!"

When he didn't answer me, I glanced back, and my heart thudded as I saw him creeping along belly-low next to the overturned first car of the train, pushing his rifle ahead of him. I didn't even dare call after him, or I'd have given him away.

"Where's Jamie?" whispered Allie, and I nodded toward the train.

Jim Farrell groaned. "They'll be onto us in a minute. Can't you hear the sirens now?"

"Go ahead, we'll be all right," I lied, for I thought we'd never see them again. They carried Allie with them whilst I turned to watch Jamie. He'd worked his way around in back of the second car, behind the hidden sniper. I could see them—there were five or six together, with rifles aimed toward myself. Jamie could never take them all without getting killed himself, but surely he must have realized that.

Then, all at once, didn't he jump up in full view and shout at them! Jamie, you fool, I cried to myself, and I began to shoot, to attract some of their fire from him. He advanced deliberately, firing without letup. I know I picked off one of them, but I'm sure he got all the others himself, though how he lived through the thing I cannot say. The last Tan threw down his rifle as Jamie stood two feet from him, and cried out something, pulling back in fear, and Jamie shot him dead. Then he went walking around the others, looking down at them carefully, and he gathered up their weapons.

And he came back my way, a peculiar look on his face, saying, "That's what was wanted. That's what was wanted all along!"

"What the hell are you talking about?" I cried, dragging him away by the arm, for the sirens were now almost upon us and unless we were very lucky they'd have us.

He came along quietly enough, but I forgot the machine gun. I wished I'd never seen the damn thing. We did make it clean away that day and joined up with Conn and the others. Allie was still alive; they'd tied his neck up the best way they could, and he kept cursing and trying to get up till I thought we'd have to sit on him.

"What was it?" asked Conn, looking intently at Jamie, who was now helping Allie along, his own face totally devoid of expression. He didn't seem to hear Conn.

"Five or six of them," I said. "Jamie got behind them and then he stood up, right where they could see him, and walked into them. I don't think he cared whether they got him or not."

Conn whistled, shaking his head. "Will he be all right, do you suppose?"

And I had to say it. "No. I know Jamie and so do you. When he wakes up from this darkness, I guess you'd call it, he's going to start thinking again, and he won't like what he thinks."

Conn kept staring at Jamie as we went along, and when Jamie demanded to know why, Conn flushed and dropped his eyes, mumbling something about "What will Riordan say?"

Jamie looked at him quite coldly. "We succeeded, didn't we? What can he say, then?"

"I mean," continued Conn uncomfortably, "I mean, that bunch standing there, not moving. They weren't armed. Some might call it murder."

Jamie looked at him, breathing very hard and fast, his nostrils flaring, eyes narrowed. And suddenly he began to laugh, low in the throat, a laugh I'd never heard from him before. I turned away, sickened to the heart at the sound of it.

"Murder!" he said at last. "War is murder, isn't it? Murder in round figures. But we're soldiers, are we not? Sworn to kill the enemy. Were you expecting a *fair* fight, eh, Conn?"

Conn stopped dead and cried out, "Tell me, then, Jamie, would you kill *everything* in Ireland because you're a soldier?"

Jamie flung his arm away with contempt, seized Conn by the collar of his coat and pulled him close. "Listen, Conn." His voice was like ice. "If I had to and I was able to, I'd set Ireland afire from Connacht to the Channel and watch her green smolder into blackest ashes if it would set her free!"

"What? Free and dead?" shouted Conn right back at him. "Good to no one?"

"Death is freedom," whispered Jamie hoarsely, pushing him away. "Yes, even dead, if it would get rid of them. And when they were gone, one of us, one of us from somewhere would come back to the land and pick up a spade and turn over the dead ashes. Aye, and keep turning them over until he found Ireland again. Don't mouth 'murder' at me, man, I'm steeped in it! Murder's the air we're breathing; it's our natural atmosphere. Murder is my life—and yours!"

At a half hour past noon of that day, Kilrossanty's old house stood as it had, and no doubt the old man returned from his peaceful ride and went right back to his patching and plastering, for the place was sprayed with bullets and full of holes. Out of one hundred and fifty Tans, not counting the five stationed there, we'd killed all but thirty, so it was only a handful of those cutthroats who set anything but the drag of their dead heels into Dunknealy that day. And I'd gladly have given life back to the lot of them if it would have taken the stranger's face and voice away from Jamie Daley.

Yet, such is the swiftness of the wheel's turning that I promptly forgot my misgivings when we got back to camp to find O'Rourke wrapped round in a rare smile. He'd had a short radio message from Riordan. The captain'd got through after all, and was coming back in a couple of days with good news. The first rousing cheer heard in our camp for many a weary month went up then. For the first time, there seemed a chance that it might really be over soon.

That night we were like men with new spirits, most of us, talking animatedly about what peace would be like, what the world would be like without the English, without the Tans, without the Norwoods.

I caught a sight of Jamie sitting by Allie Clarke. Allie kept a tight hold of his arm and tried to murmur words of apology about what had happened with the machine gun. Jamie glanced up at me and, with a slight shake of his head, told me there was no chance for Allie.

I turned on my heel and walked away. Suddenly the reality of what we still faced washed over me again, and victory was a word without meaning.

Down below us in the valley, there were no cheers for the truce talks going on. Sydney Norwood took the news of the train explosion with rare bad grace; indeed, he broke his baton over the head of the man who broke the news to him. Charlie, sitting by his big fireplace, having just finished going over his account books, was nodding, half asleep, a bottle of old port on the table before him. But he reacted to the news no better than his brother, for Charlie believed fervently that there was safety in numbers. The mood of the people frightened him, and he wanted as many Tans about him as he could get.

So, after Sydney had dismissed the poor wretch who'd reported in, and after Sydney had stalked back and forth around the room, beating the palm of one hand with the fist of the other, and after Charlie had mildly proposed that Sydney had really best sit down, have a glass or two to calm his nerves and together they would talk over what might be done about the situation—Sydney pulled himself together to that extent, at least, and the two Norwoods had a brotherly talk. I daresay they'd never experienced such rapport before in all their scant skulking lives.

The upshot of this brotherly conversation was this: That same night, twenty men were taken and hanged in town, from lampposts along the main street. At one in the morning, the Tans pulled up in lorries and forced their way into certain selected houses. They knew who they were looking for. The houses were not searched. No questions were asked.

The first man they took was our mayor, old Liam McLoughlin, in his nightcap, sputtering and fuming and complaining that at least they could wait till a man got his pants on, couldn't they? But they didn't answer him, only kept him standing outside away from the crowd that was gathering, whilst they continued their business.

The second man they took was Father Donovan, and when young Father Richard, like Saint Peter long ago, made a hard fist and knocked three of them to the ground, uttering some mighty unpriestly, nay, un-Christian epithets at them, Father Donovan quietly told him to stick to the path he'd already chosen in life. Nor would Donovan move from the spot until he'd seen with his own eyes Father Richard, his jaw jutting out stubbornly but sorrowful submission in his shadowed eyes, kneeling humbly for forgiveness at the church altar. Then Donovan shook their arms from him and, with his breviary under his arm, walked calmly down the church steps and stood beside McLoughlin.

By now the whole town was roused, out in the streets, leaning out the windows in their nightclothes, babies crying at the unaccustomed noises, loudspeakers blaring, searchlights cutting ino the darkness. The lorries rolled over the cobblestone streets, gathering their human bouquet together. And, an hour or so later, the twenty men wer; dead, hanging from the gas lampposts, swinging round and round in the bleary spotted little circles of yellow light. There were angry shouts; the people were held back at bayonet point. Women threw stones and jeered; someone up on a roof somewhere began firing down at the troops. A Tan picked him off soon enough, and two Tans were stationed by each new-inhabited lamppost on the ready, for Sydney had issued the order that anyone trying to cut the dead men down was to be instantly cut down himself.

This occasioned more fury from the crowd, which was handled with great dispatch by the simple expedient of firing at close range into the four or five hundred who milled about, sending them running in all directions. And the night was filled with weeping and the creaking of the rope playing the old Irish symphony composed by English troops so long, long ago.

In the church, Father Richard knelt before the altar as he had been ordered to do, and it took every bit of will he had to keep his two hands clasped forcibly about the altar rail. He had stopped praying. Now he knelt, head up, listening. He heard the crowd shriek, he heard the women keening. He heard the shots and the screams and the bits and snatches of frightened prayers shouted into the night by one voice and another. And he knew that Father Donovan was dead.

Father Richard looked dry-eyed at that red, unblinking light above the altar, which he had always been taught signified a certain Presence in that place. He stared at the light and his mind cried out, though his lips let no sound pass, "Why?"

He did not wait for an answer. Wearily he crossed him-

self out of old habit, and walked calmly from the church,
down the street where the bodies hung. The Tans saw him
coming and watched him warily. As he passed by, the
people cried out to him and reached out to touch him, as
if he carried some great miracle with him, but he carried
nothing. Still, his passing along seemed to have a quieting
influence, and groups of them now went down on their
knees and began to pray aloud together. Father Richard
did not stop until he reached the middle of the street, and
paused when he came to the lamppost whereon hung his
late pastor and old friend, Donovan.

He would have reached out and touched Donovan's
foot, but the two Tans there raised their rifles and warned
him away. Father Richard said nothing. But he turned
around and began to pray loudly, so that all the people
could hear his voice. When they heard him, they left off in
the middle of their own words and fell in with his, so
that the street echoed as church never had with the anguish and bewilderment and pain of so many people.

The Tans decided this might be dangerous. Six of them
came down the street toward the young priest. They stood
in front of him, encircling him with a ring of poised
bayonets. And Father Richard fell silent then, staring
them coolly in the eyes. The people caught their breath,
watched in new terror, waiting for him to be murdered
like the others. And then Father Richard raised his hand
—the Tans advanced a nervous step—and made the sign
of the cross high in the air, so that it included the people
praying, and the dead they prayed for, and the men who
had killed the dead. It was a medieval gesture, it was a
warding off of evil, it was a warning and yet a forgiveness
if forgiveness was wanted.

The gesture completed, Father Richard walked on
down the street, leaving the Tans and the people behind
him. He walked to the next street and the next and the
next. He walked to the edge of town and beyond. He
walked through fields and across dirt roads and into the
hills, swiftly now, as his feelings caught up with him and
he began at last to run, hating the vision of himself, a
priest of God running from his church to us, the soldiers

whose activities the Church could never quite condone. Because he was a simple young man, he felt unnerved and angry that the harmonies of his life were so destroyed, for it was his creed that things should have been the other way around.

Now, what happened in town was not all of that night's bloody work. Other Tans had been dispatched to various places throughout the surrounding countryside whilst the urban entertainment section was operating full force. Sydney's other little list, oh, he had many of them, was made up of the names of all of us in the Army. But, you see, we were all unavailable at the moment. However, each man of us did come from a home, and each home, except my own just then, was sitting on a little piece of land, and had in it somewhat of a family, consisting variously of parents, wives, children, the usual assortment of human relations we all have. And Sydney had decided it was about time that these little houses and these people in them who were unfortunately related to us in the IRA would have to be dealt with. Scattered, in fact, so that we would have no place to come back to, that people would be too afraid to help us, to feed and shelter us or sell us foo' and medicines or anything else to sustain life in us.

The Tans he sent to the countryside rode from place to place methodically; having no orders in particular to kill anyone, they simply got the people out and set fire to the building, the fields, and the barns with the creatures trapped and screaming in their myriad anguished dying voices: cows, bulls, horses, pigs, lambs and sheep, goats, chickens, geese, ducks, yes, and even turkeys, all roasted slowly alive as the people begged to be allowed to open the doors and let them escape. Those animals which were still outside were slaughtered by bayonets in a jolly game of tackle, their bodies merely flung aside out of the way.

And the fields of standing crops, six weeks from harvest and ripely rich in the moon's white light and the fire's red light, what an appetite the fire ate them with—sure you'd have thought that fire had the greedy belly of a hungry Irish peasant!

And ourselves? Why, we were sleeping, I've told you

before, what else is there for a man to do alone in the night but sleep? And that night we slept full of cheer and comfortably, for the rain had let up and the night turned warm again. Riordan was coming, and hope was coming with him, and the end of it all was just around the bend of the road. Why shouldn't we sleep?

By dawn's light our little fire had died into fine white ash and a few of us were barely stirring about, thinking thoughts of tea and a bite to eat, just idle thoughts, but it shows you how far we'd come along the road of insanity that hope drives its coaches on.

Someone called out, "Who's there? Someone's coming, who the devil? Could it be Riordan already? It'd be like him to show up now and us not even awake yet, he'll think discipline has died since he left us."

O'Rourke came rousing quickly from his doss, licking his hands and smoothing back his gray slicey hair to presentability, blinking and trying to make out who it was we were all watching.

A small black figure it was, not coming the usual way, but roundabout, climbing hand over hand in places, over the cliffs from down below. And then we saw who it was. Father Richard. He pulled himself over the last pile of rocks and sat gasping, pale, his cassock torn, his face and hands filthy and scratched. We ran to help him up.

"Would you have any whiskey?" he asked faintly, and, of course, we were able to locate a few drops we kept around for serious wounds and such. I'd never seen a sober priest drink so fast before, and when he put down the bottle from his mouth he was shuddering worse than before.

No need to waste words. We had it from him in a few moments, the whole terrible tale of the twenty hanged men, and we listened in amazement as he told off the list of them.

"McLoughlin," he began, still shuddering, and Jamie threw a blanket over his shoulders.

"What, the mayor?" roared O'Rourke in a fit.

"Father Donovan," the young priest said dully, and we looked at each other, speechless.

"John Cooley."

"Cooley?"

"From the pub, yes, him."

"Terrence McMadden."

"Terry Mack!" I exclaimed. "Jamie, you know him—him that was stone deaf from falling off the horse years ago? He used to hang around with Danny Murphy and—"

"Danny Murphy," said Father Richard tonelessly.

"What?" cried Conn Aherne. "Danny wouldn't turn a gun on an elephant if it tramped on both his legs! He never said a mean word in all his life. Why did they take him?"

Jamie said thoughtfully, "Don't you remember that time he was running messages back and forth for us? It was only a few months, then he got the bronchitis and Riordan told him to take it easy."

We knew them all. Old George Monroe that used to room with Mrs. Mullins and played his fiddle at all the weddings. And Tommy Dunn, the clerk at his father's grocery store, and, yes, my God, Tom Dunn himself, father and son gone together in the one night. Joe Rafferty's younger brother. Conn Aherne's father—and Conn turned away so we could not see the tears welling up in his eyes. And, wouldn't you think Joe and Allie Clarke both were enough, but no, they had taken the last of the brothers, young Ned. All twenty hanged, whilst we slept. Father Richard finished his awful message and then fell silent.

It was in the midst of this silence that Riordan appeared up at the rim of the hill, waving to us gaily and shouting, "Goddammit, is there a sentry to be had or have we won the war already?"

He came riding in swiftly, calling to each of us by name, with a note of joy in his voice I'd never yet heard from him. As we looked up, too numbed to answer or even rise to meet him, I saw that there were other men with him, some on foot, some riding horses. They also called out to us as they came in behind him. They carried rifles, and several of them were leading horses loaded with dismantled machine guns and what appeared to be boxes of ammunition and supplies.

Riordan leaped from his horse with a shout, and then he saw Father Richard. I think the saddest thing of all was watching Riordan's gentle face, with the bright spark of new hope dying out of his eyes and his new smile fading away into sorrow again, as he listened to the tale repeated.

But he heard it out, nodding knowingly when he was told the names of the twenty men.

"It's plain. Every one of them has helped us out, one way or another—"

"Cooley?" someone asked in surprise.

"Ah, he kept a few boxes of gunpowder in his cellar a couple of times, and he used to let me know if he heard anything interesting at the pub," explained Riordan.

"But who'd know a thing like that?" puzzled Joe Rafferty.

"Oh, Norwood has his spies, you can be sure," sighed Riordan.

"Yes, his spies," repeated Conn Aherne bitterly, looking around at the lot of us. "It looks like Sean was right to be wary."

Jamie looked straight at him, flushed, about to say something, but Riordan caught the look and said, quickly, "Why tonight, I wonder? I thought they'd leave things for a bit, after Clonkill."

Jamie's face became a study in agony. "It was all my fault," he said. "The hangings, everything. Retaliation for what we did to their train."

"What train?" demanded Riordan.

Quickly O'Rourke and the rest of us filled him in on the train job. When he heard the figures, Riordan whistled approvingly.

"Now, listen, Daley, quit your heroics. The train was a good job of work. A military job. Against military forces, remember? Not against women and children and old men. Keep things clear, Jamie, or you'll not make it through to the end."

"No one's blaming you for anything, Jamie," said Conn

crisply, and the others agreed, but Jamie didn't seem to hear them.

Jim Farrell nodded, "No, we all know who's to blame."

"Jim, let it drop, will you?" I asked him, but he shook his head.

"No, it's no secret. Culhane's daughter, we all know what she's been up to. I tell you, Riordan, if we weren't going to take care of the whole lot of them like you planned, I'd go after her myself for this night's work!"

I looked to Jamie then, and waited for what he would say in Margaret's defense, but he said nothing at all, and would not meet my eyes. The other men spoke openly and loudly their thoughts on Margaret's supposed treachery, and my heart sank at the sound of it, for I did not think they meant to let her live beyond the day of the attack.

"All right, all right, now," yelled Riordan, shutting everyone up fast. "We've no time for the luxury of recriminations. Let's get ourselves organized. I've brought ninety men with me and orders from Dublin to go ahead with the plans as soon as we can be ready. You know, don't you, that there's a big push on now for a truce. Dublin wants sharks' teeth in our arguments and we're very much part of those teeth!"

"Only ninety?" asked Jamie, looking around very disappointed. "Then that's all of them, those there? I thought they were just the first to get here."

Riordan forced a hearty laugh, exchanging looks with one of the newcomers. "Fancy getting ninety fighting men from one part of Ireland to another today, in safety —and the man wants more! Can't be done, Daley. But with our own thirty-seven—"

"Thirty-six," corrected Jamie dryly.

"Who?"

"Allie Clarke."

"Ah!" said Riordan, closing his eyes. "Yesterday?"

"Yes."

Riordan rubbed his eyes and the back of his neck and stretched tiredly. I could see the effort it took him, but when he spoke again it was with his usual cool voice. "I'm glad he didn't have to hear about Ned."

"Yes, isn't it a blessing, though?" murmured Jamie bleakly.

Riordan shook his head. "Please, Daley, not today."

He introduced us to the two strange men who had been hovering by his side since he'd come in. The first was Big Bob Tierney. He was fierce, a redheaded giant of a man, sixty-two then, one leg gone and the stump of it stuffed into a knee-high boot and that strapped tight to his saddle when he rode. Ah, and the sight of his big, bushy red eyebrows clamped down hard into a mighty frown that'd pale Brian Boru himself if he ever came back! Joseph Francis Sullivan was from Rathgormick, over the mountains. He was a blond, good-looking fellow with baby-blue eyes, a good strong chin, firm mouth, and curly hair like a halo about his well-shaped head. He looked anything but what he was, which was the cleverest man in the world with inventing new weapons and fixing up old ones. Sullivan could take a bottle, a rag, and some petrol and make the handiest bomb in the world—I don't care what the Russians call it today, Molotov or not, Sullivan invented it and you can look it up if you like! He traveled around with a wooden case fitted up with an assortment of powders and ground-up this's and that's that stunk to heaven but turned into interesting things when he mixed them together.

Edward Powell was almost a legend, although still a fairly young man. I was surprised Dublin let him go at all. He was a poet, mind you. Published several books, a very good poet. I read some of his things. Years later I published a few of them for a memorial tribute when he died. Powell had been a friend of Pearse's before the Easter Uprising, and he'd only missed being executed himself by reason of being already serving time in an English prison ship in Belfast harbor.

Powell was a tall, thin, slightly stoop-shouldered, dreamy fellow with keen gray-green eyes and a mind like a human computer. He was pretty quiet and let others talk, until an idea was needed. Powell had the ideas, and in his soft, low voice he'd explain whatever was wanted so anyone could understand it and act on it. He was very much sought after by the English these past few years since they'd been fools enough to let him loose in their midst again. They wanted to question him about the disappearance of eighteen different British officers over the two years since the Tans had been among us. Word was that he himself had shot them all, officers only. He was fastidious, and felt that when you killed an officer you were putting a dozen enlisted men out of whack for a good while. Word was, too, that he had buried all eighteen side by side on top of some hill he was fond of. Now, it's not every day you get to meet a man who keeps his own private cemetery, is it?

Now Riordan would not rest until a message was dispatched right away to Sean Culhane, telling him to come up as soon as he could, for it was time to get his order for the attack. We also required a more detailed layout of the Tans' headquarters at Norwood's, the number, locations, and schedules of the patrols.

It was good we had something to do and something to think about then, at once, without a chance to rest and think about what had happened in town. There were new men to be talked with and fed, new supplies to be opened and distributed.

As I watched our own men and the new fellows, I thought how silent and grim the new ones seemed to be. An untalkative lot for the most part, they sat about, ate in silence, smoked. Many went to sleep where they lay on the ground, not even bothering to spread out a blanket. They never made a move if they could help it, and, when they did move, they were quick and quiet, like cats, without wasted motion.

And then, as I kept looking around me, it came over me that they were no different from ourselves. We, too, were dirty, tired, unsmiling, quiet, and did nothing that did not have a good reason and an immediately productive result. I remembered dimly what some of us had once looked and sounded like. I wondered what those fellows might have been like a few years ago.

But we were all the same now. It didn't matter that we still observed the small amenities and used personal names and sometimes even thought of ourselves as individual persons. We were not really individuals at all anymore. We were just one great fighting machine. And so, in that light at least, we were ideal at last, perfect for the job we were doing, the end product that leaders and generals pray for.

And, last of all, I wondered if it was possible for any of us ever to be himself again. I thought of Jamie's cold words as we came away from blowing up the train; how much a stranger he seemed to me. Was I, then, no longer what I had been? It must be true: I could not be the sole exception. And I thought that soldiers should disappear or die away somewhere once they've won the battles, and let the goodness of peace be lived and enjoyed by those who did not fight them and were not crippled and twisted by them. But I was one of the soldiers myself, you see, and I wanted to be let back into the green times like the others.

Chapter XXV

Sean Culhane came to us that same afternoon and we sat down to do the final planning. He said little about what had happened in town, but privately offered his sympathy to those of us who had lost friends or family. And more, much more than sympathy was offered him that day, for there were few among our own men who did not believe that his daughter had been the cause of it all. Yet no man said her name to him or threw it in his face.

His eyes lit up when he saw the new men and we showed him the equipment they had brought along. Then we sat down to talk it all out. It didn't take very long. He had brought with him a hand-drawn map of Norwood's house and the buildings in back of it, and the roads around it. This was passed around amongst the new men who were not familiar with the place. Then Riordan stood and explained once more the plan of attack.

It was set for dawn the next morning. We could not afford to wait even another day. Every hour that passed increased our chances of being discovered and betrayed. All men were to be in position before sunup. The last sentries at Norwood's reported in at five-thirty, before the guard was changed at six, and it was those last we would quietly remove just before the general attack.

Culhane was to kill Sydney Norwood as he slept, if possible, then raise the alarm, calling the Tans on the run from outside. This, we figured, would serve to empty the barracks into the house and enable the rest of us to advance on all sides quickly, set fire to the barracks and be able to turn our backs safely on them and concentrate all our attention on the house itself. Norwood's room was on the first floor, in the back. It had once been the second parlor. He was using it as a bedroom and office as well, convenient to the rear entrance and the grounds across from where the Tans lived. Culhane was to try to get himself out through the housekeeper's quarters just beyond Norwood's room, thence through the kitchen, and join up with us as we moved in. First he was to make sure the Tans heard that the "assassins" were still inside the house.

The telephone lines would have to be cut some time between five-thirty and six. That was essential, for we could not chance the regular army troops being summoned with their armored cars and heavy guns. Our aim was to strike a devastating blow concentrated in one place, wipe them out to a man, and get ourselves away again. Furthermore, if and when London should decide to send in more Tans, we decided to hit them the same way, or as we had on the train. We vowed not another of them would spend a night in Dunknealy again.

Culhane listened very carefully, asking several questions. No one envied him his part in the action. None of

us thought he would come through it alive, and unless you
knew Culhane you would have been amazed and im-
pressed by his cool, detached manner and quiet, business-
like attitude. As far as I could see, he was just being himself as usual.

It was almost dusk when the council was concluded.
Culhane rose to go, reminding us that he was expected at
his daughter's house for dinner that evening and he must
be careful not to do anything to arouse the slightest suspicion this one last night.

"Right you are, then," said Riordan, his arm around
Culhane's shoulder as they walked toward the horses. On
the way, they stopped to take a mug of tea that was being
handed around. "And, Sean, you know what I said, not a
word to—anyone. We can't take any chances now." As he
said this, Riordan looked uncomfortable and rushed
through it, but Culhane understood well enough what was
implied.

"No need to say it," he answered stiffly. Sullivan and
Powell and some of ourselves walked with them to see
him off, and still he lingered and we lingered with him,
talking of this and that, of the truce, of hope, nothing
about the morning's work ahead.

And then, as Culhane pulled on his leather gloves and
seized the pommel of his saddle, about to mount and ride
off, we heard a sound that brought the sentries running
out with their weapons raised, shouting to each other and
back to us.

"Two riders, heading this way," they called. Riordan
looked alarmed.

"You'd best wait now," he told Culhane, who, I remember, turned toward the pass as we all had, his face
calm, showing a trace of annoyance at the delay. In another moment we could hear the horses riding quickly toward camp, the hard hoofs knocking stones and clods of
earth aside as they came rushing straight on.

"Halt!" shouted a sentry. We heard a woman's voice
telling him to go to hell, a shot was fired into the air, and
then they appeared around the rocks.

"What the hell!" cried Riordan.

I saw Culhane's face turn pale. He seemed to slump against the horse. For it was Margaret herself, as she had used to look, the long black riding dress trailing down the horse's side, her hair loose about her face. And next to her, riding an old roan mare I recognized at once, was Jamie's mother!

The entire camp was confusion; our nerves were on that keen an edge that a hare scampering over the grass would have raised us up quivering. O'Rourke reached them first and helped my aunt down. She clung tightly to him, and I could see she was about done in.

"Sean, why is she here?" whispered Riordan to Culhane, but he never answered at all, only stood still, holding the horse, watching his daughter.

Margaret looked about through the crowd of us impatiently, till she set eyes on her father. She seemed relieved to see him. Riordan pushed his way through the mob of men crowding about the two women, with Jamie and myself behind him.

"Ma, what's all this about?" called Jamie, not even glancing at Margaret.

Aunt Ellen could not catch her breath, but stood leaning weakly on O'Rourke's arm, gasping, "Wait, then, Jamie, just a while . . ."

Margaret remained on the horse, looking over the heads of the men as if they were not there at all. Her gaze never left her father, nor did he cease to look across at her. There seemed to be an invisible thread between the two of them.

Riordan turned to Margaret, his voice cold and careful. "What brings you among us, Mrs. Norwood?" he asked.

Her lip twisted up on one side as she gave an ironic little laugh. Then the smile disappeared as she slowly raised her hand with the riding crop she never used in it, and pointed to her father, who still remained immobile.

"I accuse that man, Sean Culhane, of the murder of twenty men in Dunknealy last night!" she cried in a ringing voice.

We were stunned. Indignant cries and angry shouts

spread among the men, who crowded so close to the horse that Byron reared, nearly throwing her. But she quickly controlled him and went on, her voice rising clearly above the other sounds.

"I accuse that man of being a paid informer in the service of England! I accuse him of crimes against the Irish people and the Republic of Ireland. I have come here to you today to see that justice is finally done!"

"You blackhearted harlot!" shouted Conn, waving his fist up at her. "Is that all Norwood can dream up to throw doubt and fear into us now?"

"Listen to me!" cried Margaret, her eyes flashing at the words flung at her. Riordan, his face a blank, raised his hand for silence.

"Thank you," she said.

But he shook his head, answering icily, "If you cannot prove those charges, you will not leave this place alive."

"And if I am telling the truth?"

Riordan bowed slightly, and indicated she might go on.

"I accuse my *father*," she mouthed the word with loathing, "of holding his lands by collaborating with the English, of breaking a solemn oath made to—to his own family that he would, in return for certain considerations, cease all such activities. I accuse him of breaking that solemn oath by delivering the names of those twenty men, and certain information about them known only to the IRA, to my husband's brother, last night, before dinner."

"Liar!" The one word resounded across the hills like a pistol shot. We all turned now to Culhane, who had left his horse's side and stood alone, his feet spread apart, his arms folded, scorn and hatred on his face. "Every word she says is a damned lie!"

The men roared in anger, turned now to Margaret. They closed in about her horse; hands reached out to grasp her until Riordan roared, "I'll kill the first man who moves another foot!"

No one moved further. Riordan glared at us all, then barked out, "Now get down from that horse, Mrs. Norwood, and we'll hear this thing out."

Margaret hesitated, looking about uncertainly. Hostile

eyes met her on all sides. Her chin jutted out, her eyes full of fire, she jumped down right into the midst of them, by Riordan's side, and stood as tall and proud as her father at the same moment.

"Ask him where he was going when he left here," she demanded coldly. "Ask him what were the orders Sydney Norwood gave him before he rode up here today. You're planning some big attack on the Tans, aren't you? And you've brought in new men—" she glanced about her. "Yes, I don't know these faces, or those, or those over there. But you're all riding to your deaths if you believe what he says today, for he rides back only to tell them the hour and the day and the strength of your force. They will be waiting for you. It's all been arranged."

"Enough, in the name of God!" thundered Culhane, striding quickly to her. "You whore!" he spat at her, but she did not flinch, only stood and faced him quietly. "Sydney's put her up to this, don't you see? Somehow the information has gotten out." He looked around, his voice powerful and persuasive, and the men listened, nodding and looking knowingly at each other.

"How does she know the things she says?" he went on. "Where did she hear we have new men, we are planning an attack, where could she have heard all this save from the man whose interests she has served from the beginning?"

Ah, now I saw where he was heading. I glanced over at Jamie, who did not move, but watched what was going on in fascination, his eyes fixed on Margaret's pale, haggard face as if in so doing he might fathom what was really in her heart. Jamie, watch out, I thought, but he never noticed.

"I heard what I heard spoken this day, between my husband and his brother, not three hours past," began Margaret once more, but Culhane laughed and drowned out the rest of what she was saying. He seized her arm and spun her around toward the men.

"She was told all this; she was told more, God alone knows what she was told. For her favors, for her *love,* if you will!" His tone made the word an obscenity, and then, suddenly, he twisted her about once again and threw her with all his strength against Jamie, so that she nearly fell and clung to Jamie to right herself.

"There's her source of information, gentlemen! There's the man she's been meeting secretly and obtaining information from all these months!"

Jamie thrust Margaret aside, his eyes narrowing dangerously. He would have leaped for Culhane, but O'Rourke held him back.

"No, no," said Culhane smoothly, "I'm not accusing Jamie Daley of informing, only of being weak and trusting with the wrong woman. My daughter sold herself into marriage with the scum of the earth, but she was not content with that. She wanted her pleasure too, gentlemen. She wanted everything, the money, the land, the power, and the boy friend too. What *hasn't* he told her, I wonder, as they lay together in hidden places no decent folk would find them, whispering and—"

"Shut your vile mouth, Sean Culhane!" shouted Jamie, pushing O'Rourke away and swinging savagely at Culhane. Upon a nod from Riordan, some of the men grabbed him and held him struggling frantically. "I never told her anything. Never. I've seen her but twice since she came home, and that's the truth of it!"

Riordan looked sick. "What would she have to gain coming here like this?" he murmured.

"She's mad," answered Culhane. "What she has done all along has been one long hideous plan to strike at me. She married that swine to get me. She wants to discredit me in your eyes, to upset your plans, to force you to cancel the attack or to postpone it till they can get in more reinforcements, to keep me from killing Sydney. It's all directed against me, all of it!"

Now the angry shouting drowned out the sound of the churning tides beneath us, and Margaret held out her arms and cried at the top of her voice, "Do you know where I come from?" Tears in her eyes, she searched Jamie's face as she spoke. "I brought with me Jamie's mother. She wasn't at home when I went there to find her. She was over at the convent in Dealish, with the children and her sister, and your wife, Mr. O'Rourke, and your mother, Conn Aherne! Don't any of you know what's happened in the vailey?"

O'Rourke stammered in surprise, and Margaret, now openly weeping, looked at him, and she looked in turn from one man to another; in her voice all the anguish of the centuries seemed to cry out for a witness.

"The hangings were only the first part of last night's treachery. After that, the Tans rode through the countryside, with a list of names, your names, yours, up here! And they burned your homes and farms, your barns— God, the houses are black ruins with smoke curling about them still. The land is burned, do you understand? Not just the houses and barns, but the crops growing in the fields. The stalks are charred down into the earth and which is blacker I cannot say! Ashes lie over your fields; ashes *are* your fields. And your cows and pigs, your horses and dogs are dead. Some were trapped inside burning buildings where the Tans would not let people throw open the doors. And others are lying with their throats cut and their guts ripped out, stuck up across the charred fenceposts, drowning down the wild strawberries with their blameless blood! And my father, your good friend, he did all this to you!"

The men turned again to stare now a bit uncertainly at Culhane, who took a small step backward, but his face never changed.

She told us that O'Rourke's neat little farm and fields were gone and poor old Willie and Frankie Cassidy's mother's place, Joe Rafferty's house, Aherne's put to the torch after his father was taken. And then she shook her head and put her hand for a moment on my arm as she told me my father's farm was gone. Last of all, she stared levelly at Jamie, who had not moved at all, and she said, "The place is burned down, Jamie. There's nothing left of it at all."

Now a terrible chorus of voices cried out. "Where's my family?" "Is my mother safe?" "What's happened to my kids, my wife, my father?"

After a moment, Margaret spoke again. "I heard about

all this only this morning, and I rode straight toward Daley's, and saw it for myself. I found Mrs. Daley in Dealish and I asked her to come here with me, for I knew I would have no friend to speak for me or believe me." She said this last to Jamie alone, her head flung back defiantly, the hurt in her eyes almost unbearable to look upon.

Conn Aherne spoke then, slowly and painfully, looking at Culhane. "Sean," he said, "I've been proud to call you my friend, and my father, that was hanged last night, he used to speak of you as his friend, too. I am ashamed to stand here and listen to these charges against you."

Culhane, his face now bloodless, his mouth a black line in the midst of it, nodded a bit to Conn, and one by one the other men joined in with him, reassuring him that they were with him. Gradually their feelings turned hot again, and Margaret stood amongst them.

Someone picked up a stone and threw it at her. It hit her cheek, and angry red blood spurted out. She uttered a faint little cry and flung the back of her hand against her cheek, backing away in fright. I ran toward her, but I was blocked on every side. They surged in, pushing and shouting, and more stones were thrown. I saw in despair that guns were being brought out and thought any minute they'd kill her.

But suddenly Jamie roared them down and flung them away from her as they charged. He put her behind him, standing there unarmed, with his arms folded against him, and he called out in a deadly voice, "I'll kill the next man who touches her!"

"Get him away!" yelled some of them and once more they surged forward. Jamie put his arms about Margaret, who could barely stand. I made a stand where I was, knocked three or four of the angriest about some, but made small dent in the pack of them.

"Jamie, don't be a fool. She's lied to you! She's lying now!" Conn cried, and Jamie glanced sideways at him, his lip curled in disgust.

"Get back, Conn, I warn you!" he shouted. "I swore I'd protect her. I swore it to a better man than any of us standing here. And, if I die for it, I'll keep that oath! Get away, get away from it, for God's sakes!"

A sharp crackle burst the air. We looked, to see Aunt Ellen holding someone's rifle, we never did find out whose it was; she had fired a shot free, and now she stood, unsmiling, and pointed the rifle into the midst of us.

"Glory be to God!" she cried, shouldering her small way through the tall rough men, elbowing them aside as if they had been so many fleas. "Get out of my way, you ignorant bastards!" cried my aunt. She pushed her way through to stand at Jamie's side, never lowering the rifle for a moment. And she turned on O'Rourke like a demon, crying, "You, you lout, I left Meg praying for you, what a waste of breath! Now shut up, all of you, for I've a great deal to say and you'll listen to me, for I'll speak to you in the name of my dead husband, Martin Daley, and you'll not deny that name a place in your councils!"

Nobody saw Culhane make a move, but evidently Aunt Ellen did or thought she did, for she turned the rifle straight at him and shouted, "No you don't, Sean. No one is going anywhere till this has been settled. Ian Riordan, you're in command here, aren't you?"

"Mrs. Daley, will you please put down the—"

"I will not!" she retorted. "Do your duty, man. Charges have been brought against one of you. You must hear those charges out, and you will do that if I have to stand here like this, at my age, till justice has been done!"

Riordan sighed, glanced about him at the angry, confused faces. "All right, Mrs. Daley. Sean, will you come over here and let's have this thing settled."

"Gladly," said Culhane tersely.

In a moment we had settled down to listen, at least. Our confidence in Culhane was wavering, but his whole manner was so open and untroubled, albeit angry, it was hard to reconcile Margaret's wild accusations with his calm, deliberate answers.

Riordan stood before Margaret. "Has James Daley been your lover?" he demanded.

She looked at Jamie, and at Aunt Ellen, her cheeks flushed, and she nodded.

"Yes," she said. "Once."

Culhane sneered, as a murmur rippled through the men. "I leave it to you to judge," he said to us, and sat back, a look of contempt frozen on his handsome face.

"You'll listen to this girl; you'll hear her out!" shouted Aunt Ellen, brandishing the rifle again. "Go ahead, Margaret, don't let these brave fellows stop you!"

"Ma!" said Jamie, but she silenced him with one eloquent look.

Margaret stood up and advanced timidly into the center of the circle we had made. "There is more. Much, much more, and you will have to hear it all. There are other crimes involved, and, in a way, I am guilty, too, for I have known about some of them these three years past, and I have never spoken. Nor would I speak about them now," she threw it into Culhane's face as she reached the place where he was sitting, "except for a promise made to me and broken. I don't care what you decide to do with me, but you must punish him. Jamie," she wheeled about, "my father is the informer who betrayed your father and that other man!"

What a roar went up then, and I heard the name "Tim Gallagher" from more than one mouth.

"Gallagher was your man. Your convicted him yourself!" sneered Culhane.

"On your evidence, Sean, on your word," Riordan reminded him, and Culhane opened his mouth to say something, then thought better of it and remained silent.

"He was the one who shot Gallagher that night!" yelled Jamie, jumping up. "Gallagher denied the whole thing right to the end, right to the end!" Then he called out to Margaret, "You knew this? You knew it all the time—and you said nothing! You heard me speak of my father a thousand times; you saw me weep for him and grieve for him and for my mother and sisters left alone without a man to protect them! You knew I had sworn to kill the one who did it—and you said nothing!"

"Because I *knew* nothing!" cried Margaret. "Not then. Not after it had just happened. Not for a long time. Kevin knew. Yes, Kevin knew all about him, and never said a word. Not for *his* sake," she cried scornfully, jerking her head in Sean's direction. "Not for his own sake. He was soon out of it and he knew that. But for my sake, don't you see? He wouldn't go and leave me without someone to take his place. And when he knew I'd fallen in love with *you,* he couldn't tell me then, could he? How could we ever marry with blood between us?"

"There was already blood between us!"

"But we didn't *know* that. Everything would have been fine and the secret never known at all, except my father made an arrangement with Charlie Norwood, yes, that far back, then and there, for a piece of property he'd been trying to get hold of for years. He sold me to Charlie, Jamie, he sold me like a whore on the street, oh, *God!*" Her head sank on her breast, and the sound of her weeping filled the hilltops.

But soon she raised her head once more and went on with her story, her voice low and clear, broken now and then with a sob.

"He tried to separate us. He tried everything he could think of. It was his idea to send you and Jerry out all over the country recruiting at the meetings. When that didn't work, and he knew I had come to you here, after he had set them on you like a pack of dogs—"

Jamie leaped up again. "That night, he—?"

Margaret nodded, pointing a shaking finger at Culhane. "He found out I'd been to your mother's house late at night a few times. It wasn't hard to figure out why. 'Twas he who told them where you'd be. All they had to do was watch and wait. But, after that, when I came home again from seeing you wounded here, and so weak and sick— he was like a madman! He locked me into his study with him, and he told me everything. All of it. He went on and on, names and men and what he'd done to them and what he'd gotten for it. Land, mostly the land, and money too. Lots of money. I couldn't believe it. And he showed me the figures. He had it all written out in an account book!" She laughed wildly. "I thought he mean to kill me, after he'd told me so much. But it wasn't my death he wanted. It was yours." She pointed to Jamie, then to the others in the circle. "And yours, and yours, and all of you! He was always their man, from the beginning. And Kevin had found out.

"I told him I'd tell the whole story, and he laughed at me! He threatened to kill your families and burn out your homes and betray where the camp was. And I was the one who begged, yes, I begged him down on my knees, not to go on with it. I said I'd do anything, anything he wanted, if he'd leave you all in peace.

"And that's when he made the bargain with me. If I would go to school for a while, with some girls from the families of English officers we knew, and then come back and marry Charlie Norwood—if I did all that and never said a word about it, then he swore to me he'd spare you all and never give the English any more information. And I—I accepted the bargain.

"That's what made me the harlot you all call me; that's what pushed me into Charlie Norwood's bed and has kept me there. The bargain I made, the promise I swore to— as long as he kept his part of it.

"But Sydney would not let it be. He's kept after my father and after him. And my father kept putting him off. I didn't know of this then. Charlie was holding back on his end of their bargain. The land. Until last Friday, when we went to the solicitor's office in town and it was signed over to me.

"That was what he'd wanted all along, and there was no need to worry about me anymore. I had served my purpose. And last night my father gave Sydney Norwood two lists of names, those who were hanged in town and the families of all of you here. After he did that, don't you see, I was free to speak, and if I can stop what else is planned by him and them below, then it will all have been worth it, I suppose." And, at last, she fell silent. Indeed, we were all silent then, our heads whirling with the words she'd spoken.

"How bloody noble you are, my dear," drawled Culhane, still sitting as he had been. "I have served this land of mine most of my life, and, I think, served her well. I have sacrificed much for this cause of ours, years I might have been rebuilding my estates, feathering my own nest—"

"You have rebuilt your estates, Father," said Margaret very low. "You've done well by your marriage, and by your English friends, and now by my marriage. You've gotten back nearly all the Culhane land. You've a stable of high-bred expensive horses and a good business going from them. And you've got something over five thousand pounds in a bank account in Waterford City—"

Riordan started. "Five thousand pounds? When was that money deposited?"

"Bit by bit, over the years," said Culhane lightly, but Margaret shook her head.

"No, it was one large deposit, made two years ago, when you were all waiting for that big shipment from America, the one that never came because the man my father trusted was supposed to have taken the money and disappeared. He has disappeared, all right, no one's heard of him since. But the five thousand pounds stayed right here in Ireland."

Now Culhane stood up, his face contorted with anger. 'You may talk till the sun comes up, Margaret," he shouted at her, "but these men here know me. They've known me all their lives. And, I'm proud to say, trusted me. Oh, you've woven your story together very well, I'll give you that. But all we have for it is your word. These friends of mine know what you would do to destroy me. Whom do you think they believe, Margaret? Look around at their faces. They had to be stopped before, or I do think they might have killed you. Do you really think you can turn them against me with a pack of lies?"

Margaret stared at him, then lowered her eyes, and her shoulders sagged helplessly. Without a word, she shook her head and turned away, stumbling in the growing darkness.

"Just a minute, if you please!" It was Aunt Ellen, the rifle left aside, entering into the circle. She embraced Margaret and stood facing us, holding both of Margaret's small hands in her own.

"Jamie, Riordan, Jerry, all of you, listen to me. You've

killed the Englishman, but do you know him well, eh? Do
you really think a soul can pay him for his favors with
hospitality and tea parties and high-stepping horses? Ah,
no. He wants more than that. He wants names. He wants
men. He wants *service* in return for his protection, his
patronage, the privileges he condescends to grant his little
bought and paid-for creatures. And I stand here tonight
and tell you, of my own knowledge, *lives* are what he got
from Sean Culhane!"

She pulled Jamie over to her and kissed him on the
cheek and then pushed Margaret at him. "I said nothing
today, but I waited to hear what *you* would say and what
you'd do. I wanted to hear you stand up for Margaret,
and you did, although you believed she was guilty. I know
you're not sure what to believe, God bless you, my son,
my own, for keeping your word. Now I'll ease your mind
and bring peace to your hearts— Whisht, now, lay hands
on that son of a bitch before I speak another word here!"

She pointed majestically to Culhane, and, at once, for
she had the old Irish war goddesses' tone of command
—it always comes out when it's needed, you know, with
all of them, and she was used to being obeyed—Culhane
was seized and held, and only then would my aunt go on.

Her voice now hushed and full of pain, she said, "Almost five years ago, my husband was taken from me and
hanged before my eyes and the eyes of his children, God
curse forever the kind of evil men to do such a deed and
have it seen by children! But hanged he was, and that
good man along with him, rest his soul. And, these five
years, I have known a thing and kept silent—"

"Mother!" cried Jamie, but she silenced him with a
stern look.

"It is the same thing Margaret found out, the same her
brother knew, God help him forget it in his work. It is
about Sean Culhane and the things he did for the English." She looked about at us and fixed her gaze on
Riordan. "You thought he was a friend, all of you. You
felt sorry for him, you admired the chances he took. You
didn't really like him, no, not that, but you felt you should
have liked him because he was such a good man, such a

good Irishman! But he was none of those things. He was an informer."

"You knew all this was true?" inquired Riordan in somewhat of a daze at the turn of events. "Why have you kept your silence all these years, Mrs. Daley? All you had to do was speak, bring charges. You might have saved many men's lives!" He shook his head in dismay.

"Yes, there's that to it. And that will be on my soul forever. But there were reasons—"

"There are no reasons for shielding an informer!" shouted O'Rourke, quite beside himself.

"Och, shut up, will you!" my aunt cried in disgust. "When Jamie's father was killed, I made up my mind I'd go ahead then and denounce Culhane. I heard two of the soldiers talking, when we were still in the house, after they had broken into the little room and they were searching about amongst the books for papers they thought might be there, papers with other men's names on them. They spoke of Culhane, Culhane had said the papers might be found in such and such a place, they were to be sure and not to neglect looking there after they had taken Martin and Cavenaugh. So I knew who our enemy was. And I would have spoken up, never doubt it. We're living by a harsh law, a cruel and dreadful law and we will pay for it, but it seems we must live this way till they are gone.

"Very well. But there were two young children, you see. Not my own, but the children of a dear friend. You ask me why I didn't speak. Margaret was the reason, and Kevin. Oh, I tried to gather what little bit of Christian spirit I still had that wasn't chewed up and spit out for the hope of revenge! I knew their mother. Not well. He never let her have real friends, poor Mary. How she hated that man. She lived in dread for her children and what would become of them when she was gone!

"*Informer* is a hated word in our country, and all those who fall in his shadow are damned and damned through generations, you all know that. Very well, then, was I to condemn these two innocent children to such suffering and shame?" She turned and stared at us defiantly. "Would it bring Martin back to me? Could I do that to a poor dead woman's children, as it was done to mine? When my husband's feet were pulled from the ground that night, I did not look at him again. I looked around my garden and down at the faces of my children, and I saw them watching, watching their father's swollen face. Their young eyes saw *his* eyes bulging out like a mad creature with death's black tongue gagging his poor, open mouth—" She stopped, convulsed with weeping, stretching her hands imploringly toward the men. Jamie held her frail little shoulders against him and kissed her gray head. Poor Aunt Ellen, I thought through my own tears, you must have looked a little!

Then she cleared her throat and spoke again. "I'll not see that look on a child's face again whilst I live and can prevent it. Not Margaret, not Kevin, I told myself. They would not see that or know that it had happened to their father. And you know, if Culhane had been charged and judged then, you would have come for him at home, yes, you would and you still do, and what his children saw, they saw.

"Later on, when Jamie and Jerry got to be friends with the Culhane children, I got to know Margaret and I loved her like my own daughter. I waited all these years, while they grew up. Kevin is safe now, thank God. I waited only for my son and Margaret to marry and for them both to be safely out of this before I would charge that man and see he paid for his wickedness."

And now she walked slowly and stood before Culhane.

"I add my charges to those of Margaret Culhane Norwood, and I demand justice against that man from this tribunal!"

I have never heard a silence so deep in all my life, as we all simply stared at Sean Culhane. There was little doubt left in us now. Whatever might be their feelings toward Margaret, no one could disbelieve my aunt.

"Well, Sean? What do you have to say?" asked Riordan, without much hope in his voice.

"Not much," said Culhane, pulling his arms away from the men who were holding him, though they stayed right at his side. He looked about the circle, at each of us, and nervously pushed back the thick wave of brown hair that was forever falling over his forehead. He looked at Margaret as if he had never seen her before; his eyes swept us all, sitting there with the moon rising at our backs, and then he spoke.

"The land is Culhane land and has been for a thousand years. I swore I'd get it back, all of it, no matter what I had to do for it. I've been cheated out of everything. Everything, can you possibly understand that? My family were Irish nobles and close to the throne, and I meant to see it come to life again.

"Do you think I'd give my daughter, my blood daughter, to one of you? A peasant? A greedy-bellied farmer content with his flock and his cot? Through her I would have had what I wanted, and grandsons to carry it all through after me. One day Culhane House would have echoed with the tread of princes' feet, and my kind would rule again. And they will. They will, I promise you!" With this, Culhane expressed the first passion I'd ever heard as long as I'd known him.

"You think you'll win this time, but you won't. Never believe it for a moment. England stands ready to pour troops and arms in here till Ireland sinks to the bottom of the sea from them! Up in the north, Ulster stands ready to fight for partition—two hundred thousand armed men are ready to strike if it does not go through. And when the Home Rule Law is repealed, and it will be, that is a certainty, where will you be then? No, your day was over a thousand years and more ago. Your wild Celt blood is thin and full of whiskey courage! Your battle axes are dull and bloodless, for all your skulking about in the darkness. Whichever way it turns out, my kind will rule Ireland after me and keep the rest of you down where you belong, and you'll never, never have the guts to tear them out and take up the sovereign rule yourselves again!"

The men went wild with anger. I thought they'd tear him to pieces, but Riordan shut them up fast and then he put it to us.

"How do you find this man, guilty or not guilty?"

One by one the voices said it, calling out loudly.

"Guilty."

"Guilty!"

"Guilty!" . . .

All guilty; as I heard it over and over, the word became unbearable, all the more so that it was being said in the loveliness and innocence of the mountains that were not made to hear terrible things rather than in the place men build for terrible things to be spoken in, and it's a dead room, a courtroom, right from the start, cold and clean for the truth but damned dead from the evil spoken into it day after day, and year upon year.

Guilty it was, then. Culhane was guilty. Jamie gave Margaret into his mother's arms and moved restlessly forward as the voices finished calling out. Culhane stared far away across the hills, as if he didn't see them.

At last Riordan stood up, sighing, and called out, "Sean Culhane, you have been judged guilty as charged. It is the sentence of this court—"

"Court!" sneered Culhane, and, at that, Jamie leaped forward, murder in his eyes, his hands reaching out blindly for Culhane's throat. Sean staggered against the force of the attack, and once again Riordan separated the two of them.

"Let me go, Riordan," cried Jamie wildly, struggling to get free. "I said I'd kill my father's murderer and here he stands, known at last and guilty according to us all. Why do you stop me? You're going to kill him anyway!"

"We're going to *execute* him," corrected Riordan mildly.

At those words, a slight shudder went through Culhane and he bit his thin lips to keep them from trembling.

Jamie stopped his struggles and stared incredulously at Riordan. "He's been charged and found guilty," he repeated slowly, "and he must answer for it."

"But not to you, Jamie," said Riordan.

"Yes, to me, yes, yes, yes to *me!*" Jamie shouted desperately.

"No, Jamie." I had to say it. I had to make him see it. "There was a promise made to Kevin. You've kept part of it, now you've got to keep the rest. There must be no more blood between the two of you!"

"Damn Kevin and his promises! There was a promise made to *me*," Margaret cried out suddenly. "It was not kept, none of it, none! This last I could not endure. Let the man be judged!"

"It's wrong!" Riordan said.

Jamie looked around, blinking, and said in an odd voice, "All my life I've been told and told, you can kill this one and that one. You must kill them, they are your enemies. But they've all been strangers who meant nothing to me, beyond the fact that they were here where they shouldn't be, beyond whatever personal evil they possess of themselves, as we all do.

"I have been encouraged to judge and execute these men, and I have done so—and you said it was all right, it was war, it was just. Now I meet and know the one man on earth I hate with my whole soul, the one I have reason to hate, the one man of all men who has destroyed everything I ever loved—and suddenly you tell me it would be wrong for *me* to kill him!

"The one is not a crime, because it represents the rights and will of the people of Ireland, and the other *is* because it represents only my own will. But am I not one of the people of Ireland? One is called murder, because it is personal. The other is not murder because it is impersonal.

"Why, the hell you say, if it is murder, it is murder, and have done with it. Say it. Look at it. I'm willing to do it now so somebody else won't have to do it later on. Is it morally right to kill and kill and kill strangers, even though the cause is just, and morally wrong to kill one of your own, a trusted friend turned traitor, informer, spy, and murderer?

"Is it morally right to kill at all, for any reason, for any cause?"

He stopped abruptly, looking about him, looking at Culhane, shaking his head, and no one said one word all the while he seemed enveloped in his own thoughts. And then he looked up again.

"Listen to me. It is immoral to kill impersonally. It is *human* to kill personally. And also immoral! And we who kill and live by killing and inherit the knowledge and instinct and passion for killing, we must end it, for killing tinges all. But a race must come after us that will not know killing. Maybe they'll be able to live because of our willingness to finish it and let it die with ourselves. We've been part of a great evil. We do evil things. We are going to have to do more evil things. But the day must come when we are no longer going to ask these things of ourselves. We have to make that day.

"I swore to free my country from foreign oppression. I pray that those who come after me will free my country from their own oppression, all oppression: the gun, the whip, the pulpit, the thought, whatever. We have to take these steps or it will go on and on until all our chances will be thrown away and our last judgment of all will be of ourselves, and our judgment will be hard and harsh, for we'll hate ourselves for killing the earth to dust!"

No one spoke yet. Until at last Riordan said gently, "You're right, Jamie. We might be the ones to do what has to be done and go away and leave the land to the fresh, the fair, and innocent again. But, Jamie, it is a personal thing with *each* of us, this thing of Culhane here. There is no man among us who hasn't lost something precious because of him."

"No," said Jamie. "I swore an oath to kill him, and that oath will be kept." And, at that moment, I knew what I must do.

"But not by you, Jamie," I called to him softly. My pistol was in my hand. One movement brought it up. The man was five feet across from me, his fine aristocratic profile turned toward me.

I raised the gun and shot him through the head.

At once the men cried out. Margaret screamed and turned away. Jamie cursed me, weeping, staring down. They crowded in around, to see what I had done, and there was so much noise and confusion that only Jamie of them all heard me say, as I looked down at the mutilated body at my feet and whispered, "I had a father, too, Jamie."

Riordan looked at me in astonishment. I put the pistol away then and threw my blanket over Culhane's body. Someone started saying a prayer for the dead, asking God to receive his errant son into heaven, and Jamie and I moved away. A moment later, Riordan ordered some of the men to dig a grave. But Jamie sprang forward and grabbed the shovel from one of them, throwing it aside.

"You'll not bury the likes of that in Irish soil!" he cried.

"No, he's right!" agreed the others. Riordan could not stop us. We picked up the body and carried it out to the overhanging cliffs by the sea. Without another word, we threw Sean Culhane from the cliffs. Upon the rocks and crags he fell. The gay white foam leaped away from him; the waves split and rolled to either side to avoid the touch of him, and Ireland pushed her faithless son from her bosom forever, out to sea. And the whirling pools and sizzling, spitting currents below called up old Manannon MacLyr to come riding over him in his great sea chariot and take his worthless body away with him to the underworld. I looked out across the sea and saw it churning up for miles and I muttered to those I knew would hear me, "Keep him and his kind from Ireland this many a day!"

And that was the last of Sean Culhane, who was fool enough to think a man can own the land. He never learned the earth will tolerate no crimes committed on it in its name. He is gone. The land remains. We are here only on sufferance.

Chapter XXVI

We found Margaret alone on the clifftop, looking out over the sea. Below us the men were talking in hushed voices of the strange events of that day. Fires had been built and food was being prepared. We'd said boodbye to Aunt Ellen. Father Richard took her home—no, I forgot for a minute, not home, but over to Dealish, to the Sisters. I was surprised to see him, to tell you the truth. I'd forgotten all about him being there, and I wondered, though I never said it, where had he been during Sean Culhane's trial, and had he seen what we'd done? As a priest, shouldn't he have tried to stop it? I thought he would have. But, then, I wasn't in town the night before and I didn't walk down that street and see them all hanging there, and I didn't see poor old Donovan dead, either. No, no, I guess Father Richard had wandered off somewhere after he'd spoken to Riordan—maybe wanted to be alone to pray a bit. And of course, if he hadn't heard what was going on he certainly couldn't have tried to stop it, now, could he?

I was afraid of finding Margaret, in spite of what she had done herself to bring her father to justice. 'Twas I who shot him; would she ever be able to think of me in the same old way again? I saw her slip away from the crowd of us, but I didn't follow her then. Instead, I looked about for Jamie. I had misgivings about him too. He'd had every right to be the one to kill Sean. But it had been my hand had done it.

"Jerry!"

He had come looking for me. Now he threw his arms

about my shoulders and hugged me, and I felt the months of silence melt away as if they'd never been.

"It's over, Jerry!" he cried, his whole face alight with new hope. "It's all over at last. Let's go to Margaret now."

And, as I said, we found her perched between the sky and the sea. Her eyes were dry, her face composed, as she sat staring off, twisting a bit of curl from her loose hair about her fingers. Jamie and I stood watching her for a long minute before we spoke to her. And, when we did, she turned swiftly, her face full of joy, and, without a word, she reached out a hand to each of us. And we sat down by her side and the years fled away without memory or blame.

"It's all over now, Margaret," Jamie repeated the words to her. She watched him with great wide eyes and she smiled and nodded a bit.

"You'll never go back to that house again," he said. "You'll stay with my mother. We've got cousins in town. And soon I'll come home and we'll build the place again. We'll make it bigger and better—"

"No, no, just the same," she insisted, squeezing both our hands. "I want it all to be the way it was. Promise me, Jamie?"

He laughed then, and kissed her cheek. "Whatever you say."

"And we'll never, never talk of—all this, will we?" she begged, looking anxiously from him to myself.

"There's nothing to talk about. There's been too much of talking," I said. "After the attack, we'll start all over again and we'll swear that it never happened, none of it." But I found what I was saying was just words. I wanted to go down and leave them with each other, for no matter what we agreed about talking or not talking, there were years of words waiting to be said between those two.

"The attack." She shivered a little and pulled closer to Jamie. "I'd forgotten. It isn't really over. Charlie's still there, waiting for me—"

"Margaret, stop it!" ordered Jamie, putting his arms about her. And I stood up, kissed her gently on the forehead, and left them both, for they had little time. Riordan was even then changing the plans we had made. All we knew was that the new attack would be that same night, not in the morning.

As I climbed down, I heard Jamie whispering, "I thought it was all no use in the world!"

And Margaret cried, "You said once, 'Margaret will survive—there's something enduring about Margaret.' Do you remember that, Jamie? But, my darling Jamie, I didn't want to survive. Sure what would I be doing, surviving out the awful empty years without you in my life?"

I heard no more then but the sea's night song and then the firelight's answer, and Riordan's voice calling me over.

"It's set for midnight," he said, almost jovially, pushing over to make room for me to sit down.

"Tonight, then?"

"It's our only chance. They'll be ready for us to come in at sunup. We haven't time to change everything now. Farrell is moving out with a squad of his men in an hour—"

"What for? Where's he going?"

"To plant charges of dynamite about the barracks, if he can. With Culhane gone, we've no way of getting them all into the house now. Norwood'll be there, of course. I'm offering ten pounds—when we get paid, of course—to the man who brings him down. But the barracks will be blown with them inside, and we'll move in right after. I want you and Jamie to cut the telephone lines—you'll see where they're located, if you have a look at that map Culhane brought. Don't worry, it's accurate enough. He never thought we'd have a chance to make use of it."

"Speaking of Culhane," I suddenly thought, "they're expecting him there tonight. They'll be onto something when he doesn't show up."

Riordan sighed. "Right. It's the best we can do under the circumstances. If Sydney decides to go out riding to find him, it will have been for nothing. But I'm hoping we can get things going before that happens. Now, Jamie— where the devil is he off to now?"

"Leave him alone for a bit, will you, Captain?" I said.

"He's with her?" asked Riordan. "What an incredible woman she is, isn't she?"

"Aye, she's that," I murmured, my eyes traveling beyond him to the height of the cliffs, and I thought was it possible that some good could come out of all the changes evil had wrought on us?

It was then nearly nine o'clock. Three hours to go. I hoped we'd give them something to think about, them in London. I hoped we'd set a fire to their fears and force them to see how things really were with us.

And soon I saw Jamie and Margaret strolling back toward the fire arm in arm. I noticed she had three red roses tucked into the white ruff about her neck, and I wondered where they came from, till I remembered the wild rosebush that grew on the very edge of the cliff, a scrawny, tough little thing it was, too, pushed and shoved about by every wind that reached Ireland, but it still stood, rooted, as it were, into the very stone beneath it, and it bore a few rare beautiful flowers.

It was Riordan himself who brought Margaret a plate of food and some tea and gave her his own place by the fire then. And we all sat down and ate and talked and even laughed a bit; so strange it was, as if we few were caught up in an odd little forgotten pocket of time, between the horrors of what had already happened and the terrors yet before us. But we did not speak of those things. Margaret was to spend the night and the next morning there, safe in camp with our two radio men. There would be time then to plan for the future.

Then Sullivan and Powell came to join the rest of us, and talk naturally turned to what we were about to do. Margaret listened idly for a while, then excused herself, saying she must go see to Byron, who hadn't eaten yet that day. Jamie pointed out to her where she could find the hay we kept for the horses. There was always someone there with them, and he could help her settle Byron for the night.

By that time we were all embroiled in last-minute details. Powell was in a heated discussion with Jim Farrell as to just how the charges were to be placed, whilst Jamie and I carefully examined Culhane's drawing to make sure we'd find the telephone lines quickly. We were worried about the radio. We knew they had one somewhere on the property, and a radio was just as good as a telephone if you were calling for help. But Culhane had not indicated a radio room or building anywhere.

"Margaret must know where it is," said Jamie, looking up suddenly. "Isn't she back from the horse yet?"

"No, I haven't seen her," said Riordan.

We called her name, but there was no answer. Then we went to look for her. The man who tended the horses seemed surprised when we asked.

"Oh, sure I saw her," says he, pointing to a spot where a small mound of hay was piled. "I gave her the hay for that black horse of hers. But when I offered to help her with his saddle and comb him down for her, she said no, she had to get back somewhere and Captain Riordan would understand. And then, when he'd eaten a little of the hay, up she jumped on his back and off she went."

"Back!" cried Jamie, grabbing the man roughly. "Back where? She was to stay here tonight. Why did you let her go?"

"Jamie, Jamie, stop it!" ordered Riordan, pulling him away. "It's all right, Kelly, never mind, never mind. Jamie, what the hell is this now? Has she gone down to Norwood again?"

Jamie shook his head. "No, not *to* Norwood. Don't you see what she's doing? She knows they'd be out after her soon, scouring the countryside if she wasn't there. Riordan, she's going to be there when we attack! We've got to get her out!"

Riordan shook his head sadly. "We can't, Jamie. There isn't any way, no way at all. But she's a resourceful woman, don't forget that. She'll find a way to get out before it starts."

Jamie stared at him, all the newfound joy drained from his eyes. "Will she, then?" he whispered.

Riordan put it to him plainly. "You'll not risk this night's work for her, Jamie. Remember, you're staying

right here with the rest of us until it's time to leave. Do
you understand that?"

"Oh, I understand it, Captain," answered Jamie, and
he walked off without another word.

Riordan looked at me. "He worries me, Jerry. His mind
isn't on what he's doing, or what he's supposed to be
doing. Listen, stay close to him now. Talk some sense
into him."

"You think he's going to listen to me?"

Riordan smashed his fist hard into a tree before him,
wheeled about, anger filling his face with a stranger's look.

"I like a love story as much as the next man, but there's
too much riding on what we do tonight! Tell him if he
does anything foolish, I'll court-martial him, I mean it,
Jerry! Tell him that!" I started to walk away to look for
Jamie, and Riordan called after me. When I turned, he
smiled a little and said, "Tell him we'll get her out somehow. I promise."

I looked at him for a second and then I said, "You
can't make that promise, Riordan." And I went after
Jamie.

I found him loading his revolver, over in a patch of
moonlight by a scraggly tree that hung over amidst the
rocks. He was breathing heavily, panting indeed. He had
a killing look to him, by the very stance of him there,
crouching in the branchy shadows. His whole body was
tense, as if he must spring at the throat of something or
suffocate.

"Jamie." I came up to him, ready to fight him out of
what he was doing, if I had to. He didn't bother looking
up, but growled at me in his throat, like a furious animal,
and went on stuffing the damn bullets into the gun and
spinning the chamber about. He seemed at a loss to what
to do with a fistful of bullets he'd caught up in his hand,
fumbling awkwardly about for his cartridge belt.

"Arragh, be damned!" he muttered finally, and shoved
them into his pants pocket.

"You're not going," I told him flatly, pulling myself up
for the fight.

He cast me a red-eyed glance that did not remember

the knowing of me at all, nor the years of trust we'd had between the two of us.

"I am," he said, pretty clearly, his voice thick with swallowing the spit of rage. I knew Jamie all right. He was half off his head then and would do what he would do. But I had to try, anyway.

"And you're not!" I repeated. It sounded like a schoolyard dialogue between two kids. I stood in front of him, blocking his way.

He put the revolver into his pocket, kicking over the half-empty cartridge box with a curse, and faced me squarely. "Get out of it, Jerry," he said, his eyes not truly focusing.

I reached out to lay a hand on his arm, fool of the world and stars I, twice over, to think there was any reasoning left to be argued in words that night.

"I'll not lose her again!" he cried. His eyes seemed to snap together suddenly, and, when he saw my arm raised to him, his own right arm, the large of it crooked in the air, swung out like a pendulum and cracked across my face with the weight of a stone.

The blow knocked me backward, but I kept my feet under me somehow. Jamie never stopped to see whether I'd fallen, but leaped over the rocks and went striding down the pass. I ran after him, feeling the blood streaming down from my nostrils, a queer squeezing feeling in my nose, and my head was reeling.

"Jamie, come back!" I called after him, but he never turned around. I began to run to catch up with him, and I threw myself at his legs so he'd fall down. I got him down, too, and so surprised was he, he never thought I'd go so far to stop him. We struggled in the dirt and brambles, rolling over and over, without a word between us, the two of us grunting for breath. I thought then I had him, but he pulled away and, like a panther, rolled a couple of feet clear of me and sprang up on one knee, whilst I still was looking about in the darkness for him.

"I'm here!" came his voice, like a piece of chipped ice from a winter morning's pitcher. My head turned toward the sound and I found myself staring straight into the barrel of his gun. Whilst I was taking that in, he pulled himself up again, never wavering his steady aim. "I'll go now," said Jamie. "Will you stop me?"

It was no use. I had known all along it would be no use. Who had ever been able to stop Jamie when he had his mind made up? He watched my face and saw I made no further move. I lay there, staring back at him dumbly, just trying to get my breath. Jamie hesitated a second, then put the gun away.

"I'm sorry," he said gruffly. "It's long due and soon over. I should never have left her, years ago. I didn't know that. I thought all this was more important than she was. But I found out something, Jerry. I found out that it doesn't amount to anything without her, not a damn thing in all the world. If Ireland was free tomorrow and everything I've been fighting for was mine at last, if Margaret wasn't part of my life, it wouldn't mean a thing to me. She's all of it, don't you see?" He looked at me imploring me to understand, and I did, God knows I did, and he saw I did. "I'll be back," he said lightly, watching me still lying where I'd fallen, the two big eyes of me fixed on him. He seemed not to want to leave me like that, yet his two long legs were pulling him of themselves; they *would* go down into the valley, it seemed.

"Will you get up, then?" he asked, a touch of annoyance in his voice.

I did not move. I didn't speak. I couldn't speak to him. My throat was choked with the start of weeping, but he didn't know that.

"Will you die there, then?" he exploded wrathfully.

"No," I said, barely managing to cough it out. "But you'll die *there!*"

"Jesus in heaven, and what of it?"

And I heard a weird sound like a wind wailing a moan from a mountaintop, and I found, to my astonishment, that it was my own voice, bereft of words. And what the hell words were there left between us anymore? It was my own helpless voice, calling to him and he never heeded the sound nor the sorrow of it.

I could barely stand. There was a buzzing in my ears

and a terrible pounding in my head. I rubbed the back of my hand over my face to rid myself of the trickling, tickling, useless tears that fell, but all I did was to smear the clotting blood over my wet face and into my burning eyes. I dragged myself up on the perch of a high rock and, now that words had proven no use, I found them and hurled them down the steep cliffs after him.

"Go on, Jamie," I howled bitterly. "Go on and die, but you're not doing it for the cause or for Ireland, not this night! It's all for her, Jamie," I sobbed. The words hurt me so that I thought my heart would burst from my breast to be free of them. "It's for her you're killing yourself, small thanks you'll get from Ireland for that!"

There was no answer, nor had I expected one. I began to shiver there in the damp and the dark, and again I cried out, but now it was just to myself, no one to hear; sure even I wasn't paying much attention. The moon shot brightly out of the clouds of a sudden, and started to creep across the sky, not another cloudbank around to hide it again. Into the light of the stars it crept, like Judas creeping amongst the soldiers to Christ's side, showing the way.

"Aye, Margaret, It's Margaret." I kept mumbling to myself, like a little prayer they used to teach you that would get you free of three hundred days in purgatory, like a free pass, if you say it with meaning. And then I began to listen to what I was saying. Aye, *Margaret*. Don't disembody her. She's not Eve and the whole damned lot of Delilahs. It's Margaret you're talking about, Jerry, Margaret. The proud pale face and the big trusting eyes and the mighty heart of her. Margaret, it's for Margaret he's going.

"Well, then, and he's right after all!" I cried aloud. I pulled myself to my feet and started stumbling after him again, not trying to catch up with him, but just to be with him in it. As I moved along, I saw Margaret's many faces in my mind, and I thought of the years I'd loved her, too, or the phantom of her, and dreamed away the many nights of her sitting her horse, half dead from terror and half dying from decisions, there on the hill above the

Blackwater River the day she had turned her life from Jamie.

I had gone a bare mile down the mountain, trying to run but mostly just stumbling along in a daze, when I spied a man sitting on a fallen log, having himself a smoke all alone in the night. I didn't pay him any attention, but if he'd been a Tan and shot me through the heart that minute, still I would somehow have taken him along to the other place with me.

"Come on, come on," said a voice which was Jamie's. I drew closer as he stood up and ground out his cigarette.

"Jamie?" I gasped.

"It's me. Are you coming, then?"

"Yeah."

He asked me nothing more, but fell into stride with me.

"Have you a weapon?" he asked me presently.

"Yeah," I answered again.

We moved along silently, down the hills past the darkened farmhouses, slipping through the fields on the far side of Norwood House. We kept well into the trees that seemed to shroud the house under the pale dismal moon. The house was bright with light blazing on every floor, and a sound of music filtered out through the still air. Across the way, the barracks were lit up, too, and there was only one sentry at each entrance.

"The gardens, between the greenhouses," whispered Jamie, and we moved on stealthily, keeping very low. The music grew louder and we could hear loud, raucous laughter, the sound of many men's voices. They'd been drinking. It sounded like some of them were singing along with the music. There came a clatter of dishes over the other sounds. Jamie touched my arm and nodded over toward our left. At the side door were two Tans, both of them laughing and talking, their backs to us. One was holding open the door halfway, and they seemed to be watching something interesting going on inside. There was a clear piece of lawn six feet from the bushes to the stone terrace along the side of the house, and the moon was lighting it up almost like day.

"Jamie, the phone line," I whispered, grabbing him

and indicating a black cable that trailed down from the window near the doorway.

He nodded. "Let's get it," he whispered back.

He went to the left, I to the right. Silently we raced from the cover of the bushes and flower beds and trees to the walls of the house. Carefully, hugging the walls, we crept up on the Tans from either direction.

Jamie took his revolver out and I did the same; then, at almost the same instant, we reached our men and hit them a good solid blow over the head. They went down with only a bit of a low moan. Jamie grabbed their rifles fast, before they clattered on the stones.

It took me almost ten minutes hacking and sawing away with the dullest knife you ever held in the midst of a nightmare against four or five dozen ten-foot-tall enemies before I was able to completely sever the phone line, but at last it was done. If only nobody in the house tried to use the telephone before midnight. It wouldn't take them long to suspect something was wrong with the line, and come outside to check on it.

I felt Jamie touch me briefly on the arm, and I pocketed the old knife. I stood with my back pressed against the wall on one side, Jamie on the other. Carefully he pushed the half-open door open even further. He moved his head slightly, toward the opening and I did the same, and we found ourselves looking into the room where most of the sounds seemed to be coming from.

To our left was the great dining room, its double doors thrown open. The stairway to the second floor was in the center, sweeping grandly up in a great curve. The place was alive with Tans, each with a drink in his hand and a smile on his face, drifting about, laughing a great deal. I couldn't see where the music was coming from, but, from the sound of it, it must have been a radio or a gramophone, playing very loudly "A Long Way to Tipperary," accompanied by several loud male voices winding their way in and out of the lyrics at varying intervals.

Jamie caught his breath, pushing the door dangerously open. I followed his gaze as three or four of them obligingly moved off to sit on the stairs, and inside the dining room I saw Margaret. She was sitting at one end of a long table, wearing a low-necked wine-colored silk gown, her hair dressed high on her head as I'd never seen it, twinkling with the touch of diamonds.

At the opposite end of the table sat Charlie darling, for all the world like old Henry the Eighth, gnawing on a chicken leg, it looked like, grasped in both fat hands, and Charlie was staring with a moody frown down the length of the table at his beautiful wife.

Sydney was seated next to Margaret, speaking to her intently, leaning far over so that his lips almost touched her ear, and from the expression on her face I could tell it was talk she did not like. I noticed there was an empty seat, with the silver service and dinner plate still there, on the other side of the table. Culhane's place, yes, he had been expected! But he was dining with the devil at the time, I'd no doubt. Too bad he hadn't had time to send his regrets.

Even as we watched, Sydney's voice began to grow louder, and Margaret's disdainful, frozen smile faded. She stood up suddenly, placing her napkin precisely on the table before her, and said something to Charlie. I saw then, when she turned to speak, that the three wild roses were still tucked into the soft curve of her neck; she had fastened them to a narrow black ribbon tied in a bow about her white throat.

Whatever she'd said, Charlie dropped his meat, pushed aside his chair and jumped up, shouting to Sydney, "Damnit, Syd, that's going too far!"

Sydney simply leaned back in his own chair, his face bland with contempt. Margaret swept past him on her way out of the room, and he casually whipped out his arm and pulled her back to him. Now Charlie knocked over his chair, trundling down the length of the table toward her, shaking a fat fist at his brother. But Sydney held her arm tightly, smiling up at her as she strained to pull away. Jamie swore under his breath and made as if to move inside, but I held him back.

"Wait, wait, what good would we do her like this?" I hoped the brothers would get involved in a nice heated argument and Margaret then could get herself away safety.

Well, argue they did indeed; their angry voices attracted the attention of the Tans who were milling around. The music stopped abruptly as they crammed into the room, watching the family fight with great interest.

"Take your hands off her, Syd, d'you hear me?" shouted Charlie, awkwardly trying to pull Sydney's grip on Margaret loose.

Sydney's smile never left his face. "Oh, Charlie, Charlie, have a care," he said sweetly. And he reached slowly into his pocket and pulled out a small, fancy-looking gun.

Charlie saw it, fell back, sputtering.

"What's this? Syd, don't be a fool, in front of the men! What's the matter with you tonight?"

Never relaxing his grip on Margaret, who was squirming and hitting at him, Sydney stood up, looked around at the now silent men, then back at Charlie.

"It's time, brother," he said in a mild, pleasant voice. "It's really high time, Charlie," he repeated, and, with a thoughtful smile, Sydney Norwood shot his brother through the heart.

I saw the blood spurt out from the tiniest little hole in Charlie's dinner jacket. He struggled to reach Sydney, to grab the gun from him, but then he fell heavily to the floor and lay face down and quite still. Margaret screamed. The Tans said nothing, but watched Sydney, fascinated, as he put away the gun, wiped his hands with a linen napkin and motioned to some of the men to lift Charlie's body out of the way.

"Now, now, Margaret dear," said he. "You are in my debt. Heavily in my debt. I have just freed you from a most irksome relationship. I expect you are brimming with gratitude. And you are confused as to how to show your gratitude—without embarrassing me."

"It's not saying much," said Margaret, rubbing her arm, staring at Charlie's body, "but you've killed a better man than yourself this night!"

Sydney looked annoyed. The Tans winked at each

other, grinning and poking the fellow next to them with their elbows.

"Tomorrow, at dawn, as all in this room know, an end will be put to the irritating situation here in Dunknealy. Once your little band of diehard Spartans is wiped out, a new era in the administration of this land will begin. I will be responsible for the rout, and I'll be thanked on all sides and raised to a position more fitting my talents. Poor Charlie, he never would have fitted in, would he?"

"They'll hang you for murdering him," cried Margaret, at which Sydney laughed, and his roomful of Black and Tan automatons echoed the laugh dutifully.

"I don't think so," mused Sydney softly. "Charlie will have died a hero's death, fighting alongside other English soldiers, against IRA terrorists. Isn't that right, boys?"

Cheers, whistles, and appropriate remarks made the rounds among the Tans. Sydney then pointed to the chair next to his place, so that Margaret would sit next to him. But she pulled away with a muttered oath I could not make out, and started to walk out of the room.

The Tans, with an eye to Sydney, silently parted to give way before her as she came toward the door. I believe she thought he was going to let her go. Her footsteps quickened, and then his voice rang out behind her.

"Stop."

She did not stop, but two of the Tans, grinning, quickly stepped in front of her and blocked her way. She turned; they were all around her.

"Come back, please," called Sydney.

One of them grabbed her, but she shook him off proudly, and walked back to stand across the table from Sydney, looking down at him with blazing eyes, her pale cheeks afire with anger.

Sydney smiled his peculiar smile and shook his head.

"My dear Margaret," he said ever so softly, "don't forget how grateful you were going to be."

"Oh, yes," she whispered. And she leaned over and spat in his face, then stood back with her own peculiar smile and said, "That squares us, I think."

Sydney jumped up, ran around to her, seized her by

her hair and twisted her head till her face was up against his own. Then, even as Jamie nudged me and we entered quickly, Sydney was kissing her, brutally, his teeth digging into her lips, his left hand reaching into the low neck of her gown.

"That's it, Norwood, let her go!" cried Jamie. We both had our guns drawn and kept our backs against the wall as we came.

Sydney whirled toward us, throwing Margaret heavily against the Tan nearest him. His usually cold eyes glared at us redly, and rapidly he glanced in the direction from which we came, to see if there were any more with us.

"Oh, Jamie, no!" groaned Margaret, shaking her head.

"Margaret, get over here by us," Jamie told her. She said not another word but edged around the Tans and started toward us. And then one of them grabbed her and held her in front of him.

"Let her go or I'll kill you," shouted Jamie. Sydney watched eagerly as his man pulled Margaret back again with him, and into the group of them across the room.

"Listen, Paddy-*bawn*," jeered her captor, "you fire once and the lady's finished." Slowly, still holding Margaret securely with one arm, he brought his other up and about her neck, so that we could see the knife in his hand, now pressed against her throat.

Sydney stared at him and began to clap his hands slowly and loudly, as if he were the only audience at a command performance in the theater. "Very nice, Edmonds. Very nice indeed." He turned back to Jamie and myself. "I think you'd best put the guns down, gentlemen, and tell us what this is all about."

Cursing, Jamie threw down his revolver. It rolled and clattered halfway across the polished parquet floor, landing almost at Margaret's feet. Quickly Sydney retrieved it. "You too," he said to me. I dropped my own gun, and one of the Tans got it.

Sydney perched himself on the end of the table and studied Jamie and me with a puzzled frown.

"Now I'd like very much to know why you're here, if

you don't mind," he said lightly, toying with the revolver in his hand.

Jamie and I said nothing. The hands on the great wall clock above the mantel read eleven-thirty. In half an hour the attack would begin. Somehow we had to get ourselves and Margaret out before that. If we were still in that house when Riordan ordered the barracks blown, Norwood would kill the three of us without a thought.

"You called him 'Jamie,' " mused Sydney, glancing with great interest at Margaret, who had been pushed into one of the dining chairs and now sat slumped over, her hands clasped before her on the table. "Then I take it you are acquainted?"

Margaret shot him one swift look of pure hatred, and lowered her eyes again. Sydney shrugged, smiling affably.

"Oh, yes, I think you are. I rather think you are. My poor brother, cuckolded in his own castle, tch-tch! My dear, you *are* a one!"

He strolled casually toward the two of us, a few of his Tans coming round behind us meanwhile. And when he came in front of Jamie he said, "Why are you here, *Jamie?*"

"Go to hell, Norwood!" Jamie smiled at him, but Sydney went all pale and his eyes seemed to glass over. He raised the handle of Jamie's revolver and swung it with all his strength against Jamie's mouth. Jamie started for him, but was grabbed from behind by two of the Tans and held back. Sydney looked at the blood spurting from his mouth and murmured, " 'If thine eye offend thee, pluck it out, *Jamie*. And your mouth offends *me*. Have a care. I want answers. Nothing but answers will satisfy me. Now, why are you here?"

Jamie shook his head to clear it and, in doing so, glanced across the room toward Margaret. I saw his eyebrow go up a bit, and, following his gaze, I saw that she, unnoticed now, was slowly backing away toward the doorway. Another few feet and she'd be out and away.

"Well?" insisted Norwood, playing with the gun again.

Jamie grunted painfully and mumbled something. Norwood leaned closer. "Speak up!"

"I said," spoke Jamie slowly, gasping for breath, "we were sent."

"Indeed? By whom?"

"The Army," mumbled Jamie, staring at the floor.

Norwood was very interested now. "What for?"

"We—we were ordered to take someone."

Norwood backed up a little. "Take someone? From Norwood House? Who? Who were you supposed to take?"

"Not you." I put in my twopence.

"Who?"

"Sean Culhane," said Jamie.

Norwood's eyes narrowed. "Culhane . . . He was to be here for dinner, yes." He nodded thoughtfully. "Why did they want him?"

Jamie pretended to roll his eyes around as if they hurt him because of the blow. He saw Margaret just inside the doorway, hesitating. Margaret, I thought in agony, go on, get out, get out!

"For informing," muttered Jamie. Sydney pursed his lips.

"I see. Assassins. But there was something more to it, I think. Yes, Culhane was only part of it. You came to kill my brother and me, didn't you?" Suddenly he grinned down at Charlie's body.

"You see, I've done your job for you. And Culhane? His daughter told us he was dead drunk at home and couldn't be got up, didn't you, Margaret?" He turned and, when he saw her heading into the great center hallway, he leaped, agile as a deer, after her, calling the men ahead of him.

"Get her! Hold her!" he screamed, his voice breaking at the top. Although she was running, they caught her and brought her back to the dining room.

"Oh, God!" groaned Jamie under his breath.

"All right, now," Sydney cried, rushing about in great agitation. "Get those two tied up here. I want to know a lot more than they're telling us. And you, you bitch, you knew all about this, didn't you?" He ran over to her and began slapping her back and forth on the face, so that her head was knocked sharply in all directions. Jamie pulled away from the men who held him and raced over to Margaret, but he was felled by a blow on the head and pulled back to where I was being tied up to one of the chairs. I kept staring at poor Margaret. Her lips were bleeding; her face was swollen and tearful, where the tears were washing away the blood. She looked as if she must fall; she wavered there; all color faded from her face, but in an instant she righted herself and stood erect, her eyes fixed on Jamie, a look of complete hauteur and insolence not even Sydney could match.

"I think you'll stay here now, Margaret," sneered Sydney. "But you do have a choice, darling. You can sit here with me now, while I want you, or—" he looked around at the Tans, avidly hanging on his words, and he laughed —"or I'll turn you over to the boys here, as a bonus for tomorrow morning's work."

The men laughed and hooted, and several called out obscenely. One of them shouted, "We can wait, Your Lordship. Just save a bit for the rest of us, eh?"

Margaret looked at them dully, and then back to Sydney. She said nothing, but moved as if in a trance toward the dining table where Culhane's place was still set. Sydney smiled, then swung back to see what they were doing with us. Jamie had been pulled up into a chair and tied there, like myself. He was only half conscious, his head hanging far over, and there was blood oozing from the back where he'd been struck.

Sydney nodded approvingly. "I want to question these two," he said curtly to the men standing by us. "But later. Now there is something else I must attend to." He turned again to Margaret. I had seen what she was doing. Her hand had been resting lightly on the dinner table. Softly she slid it along the edge to where the utensils lay. She seized the knife, clasped her fingers about the hilt and brought the hand slowly and carefully down to her side again, so that the length of the knife was lost in the red folds of her gown.

"Well, my lady, have you made up your mind?" taunted Sydney. "Which shall it be, me or the boys?"

There was a mock groan of disappointment from the

Tans as Margaret straightened up, raised her head with a reckless smile and slowly walked forward the few steps it took to reach Norwood. She put her left hand on his shoulder and held her face up to him. Sydney laughed cynically, eyeing his men who were cheering him on, and took her in his arms. Now her right hand, holding the knife, raised as if to embrace him in return. But just as she had the knife poised to thrust into his back, the men shouted in alarm. Sydney twisted around, knocking her away. The knife fell to the floor between them. Margaret uttered a terrible sob, staring down at it. And Sydney, now hysterical with fear and fury, shrieked, "She's all yours! Go on, take her!" And he flung her bodily across the room, into a cluster of Tans, who reached out and grabbed her and began pulling her from one to the other, kissing her, tearing at her clothing, whilst she screamed and struggled desperately.

By now Jamie had recovered consciousness. He saw what was happening to Margaret and shouted unintelligible words, pulling and straining at the ropes which held him. But they were done up by professionals and seemed to me impossible to loosen.

"Upstairs with her!" someone yelled, and they picked Margaret up and marched, laughing and singing, a few of them pretending to beat on drums as they went, out into the center hall and the main staircase, as she screamed and screamed without end. I thought I must die if she did not stop screaming. I thought they would soon gag her into silence. If I had had a knife I would have cut my hand off if it would have gotten me loose and at her side. I saw the sweat stand out on Jamie's head and face, and his muscles jerked convulsively as he still tugged and yanked in vain at the taut ropes about him.

We could see quite clearly into the hall and the whole of the staircase up to the second floor. At the top of the steps, Margaret managed to break free of them and ran down the hall, with them after her like a pack of bloodhounds running a stag to bay.

Sydney, meanwhile, stalked out into the hall and stood looking up, laughing hysterically. "Won't you come to me now, darling?" he called. One of the Tans, lumbering drunkenly after her, threw her down on the floor, then lifted her up on high in his two arms, laughing and calling down to Norwood, "Come on along, guv; there's enough for all!"

The others thought this a great joke. They crowded in, throwing her from one to the other of them up and down the hall, pawing at her and clawing at her body, kissing her, tossing her to the next fellow. And all the while Sydney stood below, watching and smiling, his two hands straight down at his sides, fists opening and closing spasmodically. Then, in another moment, he followed out toward the staircase, shouting up, "That's all now. Let her go."

But they didn't seem to understand him. They peered over the railing, leering down, winking, guffawing, snickering and shaking their heads. Sydney repeated his words, this time more sharply.

" 'Ey, what's that? You want her back, is that it, Your Lordship?" called down the man who had hold of her just then. He was a thick-bellied devil with a week's growth of black beard on his face and a red scar cutting across his left eyebrow and up into his scalp. He was holding her as if she were a marionette, his arms about her waist as she flopped over, only half conscious, her long black hair hanging down before her face like a soft, merciful veil.

"Well, you 'eard wot the gen'lman says," shouted another, poking his comrade playfully. " 'E wants 'is girly back!"

"At once!" demanded Sydney, his voice ever on the rise, his hands still trembling into fists. He even started one or two steps up toward them. But they were too far gone to comply. They had watched her and felt of her and smelled her and their blood was up as it had never been before; the night itself was strange beyond understanding: their master lay dead in the dining room and at dawn the battle would be fought. Murder had been done, in a most intimate way. They had witnessed it; they were a part of it, and it was over this very woman they had lusted after for months, and they would not stand it.

"Norwood, for God's sake, get her away from them!" shouted Jamie in anguish.

Sydney stopped climbing and looked straight up at the pack, shaking from head to foot with anger. Never before had they disobeyed him, his trusty pack of running hounds they were, and he could not understand them now.

"Norwood!" cried Jamie again, pulling so hard on his bonds that his chair fell over sideways. And yet once more, "Norwood!" he pleaded.

"Shut up!" said Norwood, not even turning back. Then, to the Tans, he called once more, "I order you to release that woman now, at once, do you hear me?"

They looked sullenly at one another. The snickering died away. The smiles were all gone, the camaraderie lost, and they shifted from foot to foot in silence. Jamie and I watched barely breathing, praying for once that Norwood's control over them would win out.

Then suddenly, breaking the strained silence abruptly, the man holding her shouted down, "All right, then, Norwood, take her back!" He lifted her slender body high above his head, so that the red silk stuff of her dress hung down like a sheet of blood; then, with an oath, he threw her down, over the railing, down the great sweeping staircase, at Sydney.

"Jamie!" she called, and the name ended in a breathless scream of terror, joined by the scream that tore itself from Jamie's own mouth and did not die from his throat but stayed moaning itself into a wraith as we saw her body smashed against the white marble stairs, tumbling over and over, till at last she lay quite still at the bottom, blood gushing from her dead, open mouth.

I stopped trying to work myself loose then, for I no longer cared if I was free or not. Margaret, Margaret *ashthore,* was that really to be the end of it, there, in such a way, in such a place? Why, girl, you hadn't lived at all; now you were dead, and our hearts along with you!

Jamie lay very still, his eyes closed. For a wild half

second, I thought he was dead, too. Until I saw his chest drawing out a long, ragged breath, and I looked away very fast, for it is very hard to watch a man lose his heart.

Sydney had moved aside to avoid being knocked down. He clung now to the bannister, shaking and trembling, laughing his hysterical, unstrung giggle, as the Tans leaned down from the second-floor landing and stared in dim consternation at Margaret's body.

"I never meant no 'arm!" wheezed the man who'd done it. "I never meant it, I swear!"

"Shut your mouth!" cried another, starting down the stairs. He called to the others, "Well, come on, pick her up. Whatcher lookin' at?"

But they would not move. He walked slowly past Norwood, stopped, looked at him, and, in a sudden fit of rage, the fellow barked, "Will you keep quiet? Will you!"

But Sydney only shook his head and pushed the man away from him.

At that moment, there was a great explosion outside. Jamie and I looked at each other, dazed. We'd forgotten about the attack!

"What's that?" shouted the Tans, now tumbling downstairs, running about distractedly. More explosions, closer to the house, shouting outside seeming to come from all directions at once, rifle fire, a grenade and submachine-gun barrage as the action began. Our men were outside, on three sides, leaving open only the front doors, in a box barrage Riordan had drilled us in for weeks. Our main attack was to come through the front entrance.

"Jesus, it's the IRA!" they cried. "They've moved up the attack!"

Sydney snapped out of his hysteria and began shouting orders at his men. A spray of bullets crashed through the hall windows, sending all of them flat on their bellies on the floor.

Sydney scurried across the room to a telephone, picked up the receiver and frantically banged on it to get the operator. When he realized the phone was dead, he hurled it from him.

"Get to the radio!" he shouted. "Tell them to send anything they've got! Quick!"

A man went running toward the back, the barracks way, but the Army was waiting outside; he never made it through, but came reeling back in, grasping his stomach and vomiting blood.

"Jerry, roll over here!" yelled Jamie, dragging himself and his chair upright, so that he sat with his back to me.

I inched across toward him, pushing the chair I was tied to along with my feet, until at last we were sitting back to back and trying to untie the knots of the rope around each other's wrists and hands. But it was no use.

Then Jamie had a thought. "Where's the old knife?"

"What knife?"

"That bloody old thing you used on the telephone line. You still got it?"

I'd forgotten the thing, and it in my back pocket all the time! Twisting his fingers till the rope cut into them, Jamie was just able to get it out of my pocket. "God, it'll take a month with this thing!" he moaned, but set to work anyway.

No one was paying the slightest heed to the two of us. One of the Tans crawled on his hands and knees to the telephone, picked it up and called into it, "Operator, operator, emergency, military priority, operator!"

"The lines are cut, you fool!" shouted Sydney.

Outside we heard several more violent explosions. The walls shook; several of the windows cracked, sending showers of glass through the air.

"That'll be Farrell over at the barracks," I muttered. "Hurry, can't you?"

But Jamie only swore at me and kept on steadily sawing away with the knife. The Tans set themselves up about the windows, firing at will. I could hear quick footsteps on the stone terrace outside, much shouting, and continuous firing of machine guns. They seemed to be moving in closer to the house.

"There, now, give a pull," Jamie said. I gave a great wrench and my hands were free at last. Quickly I undid the ropes that bound him, and in a moment we had loosened those around our feet as well.

We were free, but unarmed. I couldn't seem to find our two guns. We looked about us carefully before making a move. There was a large bay window with a window seat about seven feet from us. Three of the Tans were there, shooting out the broken window. As we watched, one of them was hit. He gave a soft cry and crumpled up on the floor. With a nod to Jamie, I began working my way carefully along the wall. Jamie took a length of the rope they'd used to tie us with, slipped up behind one of the Tans and yanked it around his neck, slowly strangling the man till he fell at last, upheld only by the rope. Jamie seized his rifle and let him fall out of the way. Then he turned, pointed the rifle at the other two by the bay window, fired, and shot them both dead. Quickly I got hold of their weapons, and the two of us walked backward toward each other, the rifles trained on the rest of them.

When they finally saw us and called out in alarm, Sydney screeched, "Get them! Get them!" Out of the corner of my eye I saw one of them heading toward us, but I shot him down before he'd got very far.

"Jerry, open the doors,' said Jamie, never taking his eyes off of Sydney.

I ran to open the latch on the great front doors of Norwood House, being careful to keep out of our own line of fire. As they were opened, I peered outside into the night air and saw it lit up with the burning barracks, and much fierce fighting going on outside on the lawns and along the driveways.

But we were in a very bad spot. The Tans outside were falling back toward the house. We were caught between two groups of them, those inside and those outside. I called out as loudly as I could for Riordan and the rest, and I couldn't tell if they heard me or not, for a grenade landed right in the open doorway and I had to hop like a hare to get out of the way of it. I kicked it back outside to where the Tans were clumped together about a machine gun, and a second later it blew them off of Irish soil forever.

I heard O'Rourke's voice, "In here, come ahead!" And Jamie calling back to him, "Come on, come on!" Then everything around me burst into action: Norwood dived away to one side as the Tans came at us suddenly, all together, those just coming in the doorway turning about in surprise and firing blindly. I threw myself down on top of one of them and we both grappled for his gun. I saw Sydney heading for the stairs, as O'Rourke broke in, a tommy gun in his hand. He stood in the doorway, moving the gun in a wide arc from left to right, shooting everything in sight, whilst the lads behind crowded in around him and the two forces joined battle there in the hall.

Norwood was halfway up the stairs when Jamie overtook him, turning him about so that he spun like a top. Norwood screamed as he saw the look on Jamie's face. He put his two hands over his own face, cowering backward and crying, "No, no, no!" over and over again. Jamie seemed to be considering him very carefully, taking all the time in the world, although perhaps a hundred men were at that moment fighting for their lives inside the huge rooms and the hallway downstairs. But it seemed then as if there were only those two in all the universe. Jamie's back was to me. I saw that he towered over Sydney Norwood, holding him by hand on his shoulder, gripping the elegant dinner jacket till it ripped from the seam. And then Jamie's other hand began to speak. He punched Norwood in the face, back and forth, as Norwood had done to Margaret earlier, and Norwood screamed like the squeal of the rabbit as the fox breaks its neck. But, despite his pain and terror, he still found strength somewhere to reach a hand into his breast pocket. I could see him do it. I tried to call out to warn Jamie, but then my own hands were full, what with kicking one fellow I'd thought was down for good and slugging it away with his mate opposite me.

"Jamie, he's got a gun!" I shouted across the great expanse of hallway. Jamie's hand darted out; the gun in Sydney's hand went flying and clattering down the stairs. Norwood stared at Jamie, a ghastly nervous smile trembling on his colorless lips. Then Jamie raised his hand sideways and cracked him across the windpipe. Sydney's head snapped back. He did not utter another sound, but fell limp across the bannister and hung there, for a moment, backward. I did not see where he fell. I got a glimpse of Conn Aherne running in through the doorway, shouting something, and some of the men ran out again with him. I remembering wondering where Jamie had got to, for I did not see him on the stairs again, and then I caught sight of him. He threaded his way between men fighting and men dying, until he reached Margaret's body, which still lay where it had fallen.

Jamie picked her up in his arms and looked about him; then he carried her to a long leather sofa in the hallway by the stairs. He put her down, but he did not look at her at all. His movements were very deliberate and scrupulously neat. He got up from his knees, looked about, rubbed his hand over his eyes and pushed his hair back from his forehead.

And then I saw him leap back into the dining room, where the fighting continued unabated. Like a berserk animal Jamie flung himself into the midst of it, without uttering a sound, although there were cries and shouts aplenty then, of pain and death and defeat and triumph too. I tried to work my way over to him, but someone came up behind me and hit me so that I was stunned for a moment. I came to myself a bit later to find myself on the floor, with Conn Aherne, who had come back in, treading on my back, fighting like a tiger with the lout who'd thrown Margaret down the stairs. I could not find what had become of the rifle I'd taken, and, for want of anything better, I grabbed up an elegant carving knife from the table, threw my arm about the man's thick neck and cut his throat like you would that of a pig.

I remember the blood spurting out wildly, going all over poor Conn, and he was mighty angry, backing off, trying to clean himself and growling at me. But I didn't care. If it is wicked to confess that killing a man has given you satisfaction, then wicked I was then and am now still, for nothing I have ever done since has pleased me as much as the sight of that wretch dead at my feet.

Chapter XXVII

Now you know why it was that Jamie Daley left Ireland, although he was a lad who loved his country more than any other thing in the world. Margaret was all part of it, part of his love for Ireland: she was created of the Irish earth and sun and sea and rains and mists, and when she died I don't think Jamie could see Ireland very well anymore. I think it must have been like suddenly going blind and knowing by the heat of it that there's a sun shining down on you and hearing everyone around you speak of it and you not seeing it and suddenly hating them that could and, my God, I suppose even hating the sun itself! Sure what good is the damned thing anyway if you can't see it? What good is it to love someone who can't know it? Ah, whisht, now, there's so much damn waste to his life! . . .

The dying man felt his heart racing as if to give the lie into the teeth of the mortal shock that had rent it and was even now preparing one more mighty tear, and that the last. Now Jerry had come to it, and this part of the story could no longer be dammed up into the backwaters of his mind as he had forced it for fifty years. He had known that he must keep away from it, that he could not even allow himself to feel around the edges of it, for the slightest touch would bring the big pains, the ones that could not be borne, the ones there was no escaping once they got started.

He was surprised now that the pain did not come all at once, or even for a very long time. He wondered why that was, for he too could see once more Margaret's body flashing through the air of Norwood House, red gown, white skin, black hair all whirling and streaking together, white marble step, red blood—but just as he prepared for the pain to come, even willed it to come, gave himself up to it, it did not happen. He felt, instead, a rushing behind his ears, thunder pounding like Farrell's explosives, and a wild exultation seized him, a hot feeling ran through his body like electric current through a wire.

He saw himself carefully putting a body out of the way of battle, neatly and carefully, the feet arranged just so, the hands folded so, on a couch somewhere in the corner. Whose body was it? He couldn't seem to remember. Then he had turned around and seen men everywhere fighting, killing, shooting, ripping, slashing, and he had thrown himself into the middle of it, instinctively reaching out to the combat going on about him as to a lifeline.

He had grabbed one man, scarcely noticing whether it was a Tan or one of his own, and had said to him very politely, "Will you go home now, do you think? Will you do that?" And when the man had stared at him, retching in terror, he had not waited for an answer, but had laughed a bit and then broken the man's neck, flinging him aside at once, for, as soon as he had seen the look of death upon the man's ashen face, a strange pang had struck his heart and something had told him, quick, look away. It reminded him of something, some other face, he couldn't remember, but it troubled him. He looked about, saw another man and killed him, and again the fear struck him. He ran about grabbing and asking his crazy question and seeing the looks of terror on the faces. The faces always looked the same to him. They were all the same, all, and after each was dead the fear grabbed hold again. After a while he began dimly to wonder about it, what it was and where it came from, but he never slowed down what he was doing nor ceased asking them all if they would go home at last. Yet a part of his mind, somewhere separate and quite far off, looked in on him and wondered nonetheless.

You could hear him all over the hall and into the other rooms as he chased them and threw them down and slew them one by one. Around him the battle had raged, but in him the battle was seething and would not take its teeth away, although all the flesh was seared and scorching and there was a pain through him that his mother might have understood, or like the death of a black tomcat he'd had once as a child.

He was four or five and the cat had died in his lap, lying very still, very sick and listless and then, suddenly, horribly springing to life, seizing life, grasping for it, fighting for it, its agony mute in its rolling eyes as it had stared up at him and seemed to beg for help in his struggle. He had tried to help it, tears spilling from his own eyes, holding the suffering creature, patting it, trying to talk to it. He thought as long as he kept talking to it and it kept on listening to him, then surely it could not be dead. It had to listen when someone was talking to it, didn't it? And he had known all along, he could see it and could not fight it and could not stop it, that life was being dragged out of the cat and it died bit by bit in his hands, its back legs and hindquarters, its very tail stiff and dead, while the heart still beat and the tongue still lolled feverishly from the tiny tender white-fanged mouth, and the eyes still looked at him in steady agony and the fringe-tipped ears still tried so faithfully to listen to him, still believing as he did, that death was not even then moving through it, taking life out with it. And then, with a hideous cry that terrified the boy, life had been wrung out through the mouth, the nostrils; the eyes leaped once, then glassed over; the front paws sprang, but not far, and the cat was still and very, very dead and he was still talking to it and stroking it, and he learned then, as he watched the cat grow hard and felt the first coldness death leaves behind under his young hands, and he knew he had seen death in action and that it tore the soul from the living body as relentlessly and as painfully as life itself tore the babe from the mother's living body, and nothing can be done to stop either the one or the other.

He did not stop killing that night until the pain inside him grew so exquisite that he thought he was mortally wounded somewhere and must lie down soon and give

over. By that time, Jerry and the others had gone outside,
for someone had thought they'd spotted a patrol car on
the road, and it had stopped, then turned around and
sped back in the same direction from which it had been
coming. Men had been sent out to catch up with it, if
possible, in one of Norwood's fancy cars, or to shoot it
off the road before the regular army could be fetched in.
Here and there on the grounds, in the smashed greenhouses, through the gardens and ruined flower beds, came
sporadic bursts of gunfire. There were men talking, the
strange saurian sound of fire burning its sliver-tongued
way along.

But inside Norwood House everything was very quiet
now. Jamie had stood in the middle of the upstairs hall,
whence he had raced after two Tans, caught them trying
to sneak to the third-floor servants' quarters and shot them
down. He stood there, quite alone, in the great house,
looking down from the second floor, where the dead and
the dying lay together and the door swung open, half off
its hinges so that, had he cared to, he might have looked
outside and seen that IRA troops had the situation in
hand. Riordan was out there with a couple of the boys,
talking quietly, pointing down the road.

But he did not care to look outside. He let the gun fall
out of his hand and he sank down on the top step, very
weary indeed. He sat there to one side of the staircase,
leaning his head a bit against the railing, staring down toward the bottom. And there it was, of course. The pain
gripped him unabated then, and fifty years from then. He
had been too tired to fight it. Besides, there was no one
else to kill to keep it from his heart, so he had given in
to it, let himself be swallowed up in it. It swept over him
and dragged him undertowed along with it, then in and
back again and out again, and it was Margaret he was
looking at, and now he remembered that she was dead
and all of it had been for nothing.

So he just sat there, his hand that had held the gun
lying limp and forgotten in his lap. There was no one left
to kill and the pain came washing in, in beats, like a
heartbeat. He sat there and looked down at Margaret's

body, but he did not really see it. He saw her still alive,
or, rather, at the moment she had been flung into the air,
and it seemed to him that she had never come down at
all, but had disappeared somewhere, and it troubled him.
His eyes searched the air. He could not see her anywhere.
He looked down again, but he saw only the bright waxed
wooden floors of Norwood's fine house. He sat there with
the dead silent all about him and with her broken body
under his eyes; the minutes ticked by; occasional distant
shouts disturbed him not at all. He did not hear the voices,
nor the lorries pulling out, nor a stray shot that rang out
now and again. He heard nothing, he saw nothing. He sat
there up on the top step of that enormous marble staircase, his long, heavily muscled arms weak and useless, his
eyes thoughtful, searching, trying to piece through the
odd, glimmering curtain that hung in the air all around
him and would not let him see what he was searching
for.

Footsteps ran up the front steps. A man shouted, "I'll
see whether anyone's still——" And the voice had stopped.
The fellow had walked in, shuddered as he saw the bodies
piled about, then murmured "God help us!" and crossed
himself when he caught sight of Margaret and of Jamie
sitting high above her, staring about anxiously at nothing
whatever. Without another word or a glance to the left or
to the right, he had hastily backed off, bumping into the
door, bringing it crashing down from its last weakened
hinge. He had cried out in fear and shock, then he turned
and ran, yelling, out and down the front steps. And it was
silent in the hall again.

As Jamie sat there and the time went on and it grew so
very quiet on the grounds again and far off he could hear,
if he were listening, if he were hearing anything, the
wheezing drone of sirens from Dungarvan—after a long
while, thoughts began to form again inside his head. At
first it was only a change of the fixed pictures going back
through the night and the day before it and then going
forward again. Already he was coming to life again. He
felt about him for the gun, picked it up from where it
had fallen, and automatically his finger tightened about

the trigger. His face began to feel again; his eyes focused again. And he saw her. With a scream that raped the already bloody night and echoed starkly through the quiet house and over the dewy grounds, a scream he could not stop and did not think he would ever stop, he saw Margaret's body. He stood up, grasped the bannister, and stared down at her. For his mind was now up to date; she had finally hurtled through the air and come down on the stairs, and he could push it away from him no longer.

He felt the gun, raised his hand and looked at it, cried out, "No!" and threw it from him in loathing. Again he cried out "No, no, no, no!" as he stumbled down the stairs to her. He threw himself down by her side, picked up her head, leaned over and kissed her face, pushing the hair away, rocking her against him, holding her in his arms against the world. And, it was true, the world could not hurt her anymore. With a shaking hand he gently wiped the drying blood from her soft mouth and kissed her lips and cried and sat there with her, and talked to her. . . .

I'd looked all over the damned place for him. I thought he was dead. I didn't know what to think! Riordan was elated but nervous. We had to get out, but still he let us look about for Jamie. I didn't remember if he had been with us when we'd run outside to regroup on the lawn, but that had been an hour before and I had not seen him since, nor had any of the men with me. Then one of the new fellows, his face sick and gray, came stumbling out from the front door, pointing behind him and shouting something about a fellow sitting up on the stairs staring at a girl's body. And I knew where I would find Jamie.

I walked in slowly and stood in the shadows by the door. It was ghastly seeing him there with her in his arms, and he crooning to her and patting her and urging her to come away with him right then and there. I walked to him quietly and, God, my heart went out to him, and then I heard Riordan right behind me.

"Jerry, for the love of God, will you— Ah, no!" He stopped speaking and stayed behind me with some of the others who had followed me in, whilst I went over to Jamie.

I stood by him stiffly, I was so filled up with horror and pity and grief, and I leaned over close to him.

"Jamie," I said quietly. "Jamie, come away. It's over, Jamie."

He looked up at me and smiled a bit.

"Jamie, I'll help you. Come on, lad," I urged him, seeing him start to get to his feet. But he shook his head.

Riordan called out, "Help him, then, Jerry!"

But I could not. He wouldn't let me touch her. He struggled up somehow, lifting her in his arms.

"We'll bury her, up in the hills, if you like, Jamie. Only come on now, they'll be on us soon."

But it was no use. He turned away from me and cradled her head against his chest. Then, still not speaking, he started to walk toward the door, and the men quietly moved aside to make a way for him, and we all turned and watched him carry Margaret out into the early gray light of another dawn, with a mist rising up from the seas.

"Go after him, Jerry," said Riordan. I needed no orders.

I ran outside, but at first I could not see him. The sirens were getting closer. Then I did see him, walking slowly along, apparently not hearing anything. He had turned away from the road and walked through the fields, with the tinders from the burning barracks snapping and falling and crashing black around him, all smoking and charred, but he saw nothing. I knew where he was going then, and I merely followed behind.

We were soon away from Norwood House, hidden by the rising hills and the mists. Riordan, in a lorry, pulled up alongside me, and I got in. "Shouldn't you stay with him?" he asked anxiously.

I shook my head. "No. I know where he's taking her. He'll be safe enough in that direction. Let's go."

We were all pretty busy when we got back to camp. Riordan was on the radio reporting the success of the attack to Dublin. We'd lost twenty-two men, and, as far as we could tell, there wasn't a Tan left in Dunknealy that day. Most of our boys had a scratch or two and we spent a bit of time getting everyone bandaged and a bite of breakfast into them.

When it was all over, I went to him. He had carried her body in his arms all the way up to the top of our Running Hill, as I knew he would, and there I found him, sitting beside her with the sunlight of morning emptying itself like a liquid buttercup on their faces. He looked up as I came, and I wondered, with dread, if he would still be so far off from the world. But he gave me a little, absent-minded smile which died aborning, as his eyes fell once again on her pale, cold, upturned face.

"It's over," I said, not sure he yet realized it. And I was right; he wasn't too sure about anything.

"Norwood?" he asked without real interest.

"Dead. You killed him on the stairs," I told him.

He nodded, then the two of us sat over her without talking for a while, as we had when his father had been killed, as we had when my own father was buried. There was no one left to kill now, no one we needed to find out and destroy. The destruction was over. And Margaret was dead forever.

Later I said softly, "We'll have to bury her, Jamie."

He raised his head as if it weighed unbearably heavy on his neck. "I know," he said pathetically, as a child would, "but not yet."

"No," I sighed, and I could no longer bear the sight of them, the one so cold and dead, and the other so desperate to be the same. I turned away, looking past them, up into the mountains and into the white clouds that hung so calmly over us.

It seemed so quiet. I wondered why. What sound did I call for in the presence of death, I wondered? What was it, so still there? There seemed to be a lack of something. But what *was* it? And then I knew.

"You wept when Johnny O'Donnell died," I said suddenly, for it was the sound of weeping that I missed.

His mouth twisted in pain. "I wept with her in my arms a month ago," he said. "A fool! A fool who wept when everything he wanted lay in his arms alive! Men are all fools, Jerry. All poor, damn fools!"

Without looking at me, he lifted her slim shoulders and her head off the soft green and held her nestled against him. I watched him, and my breath caught at the sight of the two of them. If I had not known she was dead, they might have been two lovers cradled close and loving in the grass. He bent his face and rubbed his cheek in her tossed black hair and kissed her small ear tenderly.

"Jamie—" I began, and stopped. What use to speak now?

"Lovers," he said with that awful, twisted little smile. "Culhane called us that. Lovers. How much time we wasted, didn't we? And there was only the one time that it was true. I thought it must go on forever, but she knew. She left me standing on the shore and rode away from me, and she took my life away with her."

The memories were too much for him. He picked up Margaret's poor crushed body and held her now on his lap, covering her cold face with wild kisses, taking her cheeks between his two hands, as if he would command her to respond to his feverish caresses.

"Jamie!" I cried in despair. "Don't, don't. She's gone, Jamie. Jamie."

"No, Jerry," he insisted. "You won't understand. I was home and it was peace, all the dead were buried back in England and my father was plowing the west field with the team. It was peace, Jerry, can't you see it? She held me. She loved me. She was comfort and peace and she was everything! Margaret, Margaret—"

He shouted it across the valley and it came back an empty echo. I knew there was no taking her from him then. I'd have to wait until he'd rested from his grief.

"I'll leave you for a bit," I whispered, thinking to go a bit away and wait by myself. He didn't even hear me. I started to get up, but my eyes fell on Margaret once again, Margaret who knew now, at last, that there had been two of us who had loved her. God bless and keep her safe in heaven! I lifted her frail white arm and thought Jamie would never notice at all. Quickly, like the lost fool

I was, along with him, I pressed my lips against her little hand, but Jamie's eyes met mine in the instant and I knew that he had known all along how I had loved her, how I had always loved her.

He smiled so sweetly then and kept nodding his head whilst the tears poured down at last, and his smile was terrible. He reached out his other arm and pulled me to him, as he held her, now he crushed my head against his chest, so that my face was almost touching hers, and I sobbed there, holding her dead hand, the three of us clasped for the last time in this life in each other's arms, and I would have defied God himself to separate us at that moment.

He would not see her buried. Instead, he rode down to Norwood's stables like a madman, into the midst of them all, and stole Byron out and rode him wildly through all the miles of countryside we had traveled together, and stayed away from camp for a week whilst Riordan tore his hair and raved and threatened to have him shot and such nonsense. I did not go to look for him. If it was meant that he would live through it, then he would come back.

We buried Margaret as I had promised, up in the hills. It was not till years later that her grave was moved, and her remains placed in the cemetery at Holy Rosary churchyard. Aunt Ellen and my mother and other women came and wept over her and did the thousand little things that women try to do for the dead they loved, little touches that say the words they know would be useless to say aloud but must be said by the heart somehow. Women do that with their hands. I have known women with angry voices and angry eyes and good reasons for both, yet their hands spoke gentle truths.

And, at length, Jamie did come back to us, silent and exhausted, on foot, and none living ever saw old Byron again. He did not ask to see her grave, or even where it was. There was news that day. The whole countryside was full of joy and hope at last. The church bells rang from dawn to sunset and then on through the night.

Peace had come at last, peace and freedom for the

south at least. Jamie took the news with odd disinterest. I told him how our efforts that night had helped turn the tide in Ireland's favor, and I tried to find out what was in his mind about the future. It was then he told me he was going to America as soon as it could be arranged. And, though I was sick and shorn with both of them to be gone, I never tried to talk him out of it. Ah, I could no more have held Jamie Daley from leaving Ireland than I could have brought Margaret back from her grave, gay and laughing and wild and willful again, racing Black Byron across the green fields of home.

And now we've come full circle, Jamie and I, back to the beginning and on to the end. It's Easter Sunday again, another Easter Sunday. The sun is coming up grand. The night is over; the story is well-nigh done. I wish Jamie could have seen this one last Easter. It seems Easter was the start of it all, doesn't it? And now, oh, Jamie boy . . .

The man on the bed could not hear the steady, tired drone of Jerry's voice any longer. His mind, for a moment, was filled with the memory of death, all those deaths so long ago, and he was sick with that memory. Once, after listening to some stories told by an old friend about the days of the fighting in Ireland, his daughter had asked him if *he* had ever had to kill anyone. He'd turned pale, trembled, and she'd known then. But it was a question asked in wartime. America had been at war, and other girls' fathers were fighting and killing somewhere. She had been a child and he was troubled that she'd felt proud and told others of it. He was not proud to have killed. Couldn't someone find a better way?

Suddenly a great hideous bolt of pain blacked out his thoughts for a second. I'm dying! He allowed the idea to linger in terrible dread. Shouldn't somebody be here, talk to me, do something . . . He did not hear Jerry still speaking to him, calling his name. He did not see Jerry leaning over him as if he would close out the touch of death's hand with the solidity of his own body.

Again it came, worse, and then once more, and then he thought he saw Margaret's laughing face just before him! He felt the pain rip at him again, and the image of her grew stronger and clearer. He reached out to touch her. She slipped into his arms and he laughed with her. It had all been a dream, all of it, just a dream. Margaret. He kissed her and his arms held her and he knew, even as he felt the pain dying away, that he would never have to let go of her again.

"Margaret," he said quite distinctly. "Margaret."

He's gone. It's all over now and he's with her at last. Ah, sure it would always be Margaret, at the end. You see, Jamie didn't so much go away from Ireland as he tried to thrust Ireland away from him. I guess it was the only way he could go on living. I stayed here, maybe because I never had Margaret's love as he had. It was easier for me to bear, because it was all dreams and wishes. A man who's never had his dream come true can, as the years pass by, half-dream himself into believing it was real, and that eases some of the emptiness and loneliness. But when a man's known fullness and contentment and all his dreams have nestled within his hand's span, why, then, when it has gone from him, he cannot know peace again. He cannot lull himself or fool himself as to what *might* have been, for he has known what *was*. Nothing can ever fill that empty place. No new dream can make him forget. That's what drove him on. That kept him seeking and that brought him back, at the end, for he knew it was here, in this land that bred them both, that he must find the dream again, and lie down with her forever.

What of the girl he married in America, that pretty gray-eyed little Mary with the sweet voice? Didn't he love her at all? Yes, of course he did, with all his heart, all the heart he brought with him from home. I don't think there's any lack of room or of love among all who once shared each other's lives. And it is to that end I face my own life's drawing out, for there will be a welcome for gray-eyed Mary and for me, among the lovers and the loved.

'Tis the dream I dream at evening fire, when the sun is setting. One evening, I pray, I will fall asleep and join them out there. And that night, when the sea roars dark and full-throated and white foam beats on the shores, when the black night sky glows moonly gold and shadows slip away across the fields, we'll all be together on the hillside and we'll watch Ireland proudly open her hot arms to all her lovers from the sea.